THE SECRET GARDEN OF ZOMBIES

By E. A. Pyne and Frances Hodgson Burnett

THE SECRET GARDEN OF ZOMBIES @ 2014 by E. A. Pyne

Published by Rowan Tree Books

Rowan Tree Creative LLC

Orlando, Fl 32821

Cover design by Robert Torres

Illustrations @ 2014 by Robert Torres

ISBN-13: 978-0615987309 (Rowan Tree Books)

ISBN-10: 0615987303

I am writing in the garden (of zombies). To write as one should of a garden (of zombies) one must write not outside it or merely somewhere near it, but in the garden... (of zombies).

Frances Hodgson Burnett

THE SECRET GARDEN OF ZOMBIES

Table of Contents:

Chapter 1: There is No One Left 7
Chapter 2: Bloody Mary Quite Contrary 18
Chapter 3: Across the Moor 31
Chapter 4: Martha 38
Chapter 5: The Cry in the Corridor 61
Chapter 6: Of Accursed Mice and Men 71
Chapter 7: The Key to the Garden 82
Chapter 8: The Robin Who Showed the Way 92
Chapter 9: The Strangest House Anyone Ever Lived In 103
Chapter 10: Dickon 117
Chapter 11: The Nest of the Missel Thrush 134
Chapter 12: Might I Have a Bit of Earth? 145
Chapter 13: The Undead Boy and the Ghost 157
Chapter 14: A Young Cannibalistic Rajah 177
Chapter 15: Nest Building 194
Chapter 16: The Angel and the King of the Accursed 213
Chapter 17: A Tantrum 224
Chapter 18: The Demons Inside 235
Chapter 19: It Has Come! 247
Chapter 20: I Shall NOT Live Forever-And Ever! 264
Chapter 21: Ben Weatherstaff 279
Chapter 22: When the Sun Went Down 296
Chapter 23: Dark Magic/ White Magic 305
Chapter 24: Let Them Rot 325
Chapter 25: The Curtain and Hidden Door 344
Chapter 26: It's Mother! 357
Chapter 27: In the Garden 393

Chapter 1: There Is No One Left

When Mary Lennox was sent to Misselthwaite Manor after surviving the deadly Scourge contamination of India everybody said she was the most disagreeable-looking child ever seen. It was true, too. She had a little thin face and a little thin body, thin light hair and a sour expression. Those that bothered to comment said they might have taken her for an Accursed One if her grey eyes had not shone with such bitterness. Her hair was yellow, and her face was yellow because she had been born in India, had always been ill in one way or another, and had been malnourished during her time in the Indian refugee camps after The Fall. Her father had held a position under the English Government and had always been busy and ill himself, and her mother had been a great beauty who cared only to go to parties and amuse herself with gay people. She had not wanted a little girl at all, and when Mary was born she handed her over to the care of an Ayah, who was made to understand that if she wished to please the Mem Sahib she must keep the child out of sight as much as possible.

So when she was a sickly, fretful, ugly little baby she was kept out of the way, and when she became a sickly, fretful, toddling thing she was kept out of the way also. She never remembered seeing familiarly anything but the dark faces of her Ayah and the other native servants, and as they always obeyed her and gave her her own way in everything, because the Mem Sahib would be angry if she was disturbed by her crying, by the time she was six years old she was as tyrannical and selfish a little demon as ever lived. She often demanded the native servants to tell her stories, and because the servants disliked Mary they would attempt to scare her with dark tales of the Aghori, Hindu cannibals that worshiped the God Shiva. The Aghori would hold dark rituals in cemeteries to steal the spirits of the dead so they would rise again in the bodies of those who consumed them. They would eat the raw human flesh believing they would gain the power of the spirit within.

Mary never showed any fear, however, even as the dark skinned servants told of men, women and even children, wearing nothing but the shrouds of corpses and covered in cremation ground ashes, used dead bodies as alters for their spells. The young English governess who came to teach Mary to read and write disliked her so much that she gave up her place in three months, and when other governesses came to try to fill it they always went away in a shorter time than the first one, perhaps because of Mary's strange fascination with the Aghori and other dark tales of murder and man-eating Bhutas. So if Mary had not chosen to really want to know how to read books she would never have learned her letters at all.

One frightfully hot morning, when she was about nine years old, she awakened feeling very cross, and she became crosser still when she saw that the servant who stood by her bedside was not her Ayah.

"Why did you come?" she said to the strange woman. "I will not let you stay. Send my Ayah to me."

The woman's once dark skin was pallid and her mouth gaped streaming a thick black liquid onto the bed. Realizing the Ayah could not come, Mary threw herself into a passion and beat and kicked the woman who clawed at her until finally several other servants pulled the snarling woman away saying it was not possible for the Ayah to come to Missie Sahib.

There was something mysterious in the air that morning. Nothing was done in its regular order and several of the native servants seemed missing, while those whom Mary saw had deep, bloody wounds or hurried about with ashy and scared faces. But no one would tell her anything and her Ayah did not come. She was actually left alone as the morning went on, and at last she wandered out into the garden and began to play by herself under a tree near the veranda. She pretended that she was making a flower-bed, and she stuck big scarlet hibiscus blossoms into little heaps of earth, all the time growing more and more angry and muttering to herself the things she would say and the names she would call her Ayah when she returned.

"Gaandu! Pig! Daughter of Pigs!" she said, because to call a native a pig is the worst insult of all.

She was grinding her teeth and saying this over and over again when she heard her mother come out on the veranda with someone. She was with a sickly young man and they stood talking together in low strange voices. Mary knew the sweating young man who looked like a boy, though he seemed much altered. She had heard that he was a very young officer who had just come from England. The child stared at him, his eyes seemed sunken and his hands shook, but she stared most at her mother. She always did this when she had a chance to see her, because the Mem Sahib—Mary used to call her that oftener than anything else—was such a tall, slim, pretty person and wore such lovely clothes. Her hair was like curly silk and she had a delicate little nose which seemed to be disdaining things, and she had large laughing eyes. All her clothes were thin and floating, and Mary said they were "almost ghostly." They floated more ghostly than ever this morning, but her eyes were not laughing at all. They were large and scared and lifted imploringly to the boy officer's face.

"Is it so very bad? Oh, is it?" Mary heard her say.

"Awfully," the young man answered in a trembling voice. "Awfully, Mrs. Lennox. We have been safe here all these years but now... Hundreds have transformed and the ghouls are violently devouring people who then rise up half- eaten. They will attack anyone still living. It is worse than death they say. And none of us may escape it. You ought to have gone to the hills two weeks ago."

The Mem Sahib wrung her hands.

"Oh, I know I ought!" she cried. "I only stayed to go to that silly dinner party. What a fool I was!"

At that very moment such a loud sound of wailing broke out from the servants' quarters that she clutched the young man's arm, and Mary stood shivering from head to foot. The wailing grew wilder and wilder. "What is it? What is it?" Mrs. Lennox gasped. "It is the Accursed," answered the boy officer. "You did not say it had broken out among your servants."

"I did not know!" the Mem Sahib cried. "Come with me! Come with me!" and she turned and ran into the house.

The boy officer suddenly jolted violently. He coughed and heaved, disgorging black fluid from his mouth. His head turned towards Mary so fast she was surprised his neck did not break. He stared at her breathing in and out deeply, and Mary sat quietly as his eyes yellowed and within a black fluid seemed to flow like a dark river over a dimming sun. He took a jarring step towards Mary when the voice of her mother pierced the air screaming for God to forgive his servants.

The boy officer turned towards the mother's screaming and ran into the house. The sound of her unholy wail filled the air and then suddenly ceased. After that, appalling things happened, and the mysteriousness of the morning was explained to Mary by a servant who paused only for a moment and then ran away cradling her arm wrapped in bloody bandages.

The Scourge, a horrific infection, had broken out in the city causing those that once felt and thought and lived to suddenly feel nothing, think nothing, and live no more. They became the Forsaken, the Accursed, the Tormented Ones. They sought to eat the flesh of others and nothing could abate their insane hunger. If not killed, the infected would die within a day, and then rise again with yellowed eyes filled with black blood.

The Ayah had been taken ill in the night, and it was because she had just died that the servants had wailed in the huts as she tore them apart. Before the next day three other servants were dead and others had run away in terror. There was panic on every side, and wounded and dying people in all the bungalows.

During the confusion and bewilderment of the second day Mary hid herself in the nursery and was forgotten by everyone. Nobody thought of her, nobody wanted her, and strange things happened of which she knew nothing.

She did not know that before she was even born a contagion had been contracted when a man consumed a rotting corpse during an unholy Aghori ritual ceremony. She did not know that small villages throughout India and the unknown East had been decimated by this plague and that because the infected have nearly twenty-four hours before they die and reanimate as monstrous demons, the Scourge had spread farther and faster than letters could spread the news of it. She did not know that she had been living in a protected zone her entire life nor had she heard that much of the known world had been overrun in the years known as The Fall. She had rarely ever left the house and had seen nothing of the world. She *did* know that no one ever told her anything.

Mary alternately cried and slept through the hours. She only knew that people were ill and that she heard mysterious crunching and tightening sounds. Once she crept into the dining-room and found it empty, though a partly finished meal was on the table and chairs and plates looked as if they had been hastily pushed back when the diners rose suddenly for some reason. Lumps of meat that Mary could not understand lay upon the floor in pools of dried blood. The child ate some fruit and biscuits, and being thirsty she drank a glass of wine which stood nearly filled. It was sweet, and she did not know how strong it was. Very soon it made her intensely drowsy, and after grabbing one of the large dinner knives, she went back to her nursery and shut herself in again, frightened by cries she heard in the huts and by the hurrying sound of feet followed by slow dragging sounds. The wine made her so sleepy that she could scarcely keep her eyes open and she lay down on her bed and knew nothing more for a long time.

Many things happened during the hours in which she slept so heavily, she was not disturbed by the wails, screaming and the popping sound of gun fire.

When she awakened she lay and stared at the wall. The house was perfectly still. She had never known it to be so silent before. She heard neither voices nor footsteps, and wondered if everybody had got well of the strange disease and all the trouble was over. She wondered also who would take care of her now her Ayah was dead. There would be a new Ayah, and perhaps she would know some new stories. Mary had been rather tired of the old ones. She did not cry because her nurse had died. She was not an affectionate child and had never cared much for any one. The noise and hurrying about and wailing as the dead rose craving live flesh had frightened her, and she had been angry because no one seemed to remember that she was alive. Everyone was too panic-stricken to think of a little girl no one was fond of. When people were being chased by the Tormented Ones it seemed that they remembered nothing but themselves. But if everyone had got well again, surely someone would remember and come to look for her.

But no one came, and as she lay waiting the house seemed to grow more and more silent. She heard something rustling on the matting and when she looked down she saw a little snake gliding along and watching her with eyes like black jewels. The snake had a deep wound as if it had been bitten. Mary was not frightened, even though the snake behaved strangely and came right for her with its mouth gaping and oozing thick black fluid. Mary wondered if it might be the very snake of Shiva himself and she took her knife and stabbed the snake through the head. It died quickly and Mary felt satisfied that she had gotten revenge against the corpse eating, Shiva worshipping, monsters that now freely roamed.

"How queer and quiet it is," she said. "It sounds as if there were no one in the bungalow but me and the demon snake."

She decided to keep the snake prisoner and would not let Shiva have it back until he sent someone for her.

Almost the next minute she heard footsteps in the compound, and then on the veranda. They were men's footsteps, and Mary thought for a moment they might be the Accursed coming to find her. The men entered the bungalow and talked in low voices. No one went to meet or speak to them and they seemed to open doors and look into rooms. "What desolation!" she heard one voice say. "That pretty, pretty woman! I suppose the child, too. I heard there was a child, though no one ever saw her."

Mary was standing in the middle of the nursery when they opened the door a few minutes later. She looked an ugly, cross little thing, holding a large knife in one hand and a dead snake in the other, and was frowning because she was beginning to be hungry and feel disgracefully neglected. The first man who came in was a large officer she had once seen talking to her father. He looked tired and troubled, but when he saw her he was so startled that he jumped back thinking she was afflicted.

"Barney!" he cried out. "There is one of the Accursed here! Help!"

A man appeared with a large machete and raised it waiting for the child to attack.

"I am Mary Lennox," the little girl said, drawing herself up stiffly. "I fell asleep when everyone had the illness and I have only just wakened up. Why does nobody come?"

"A child alone! In a place like this! Mercy on us, who is she?!" cried the man with the machete.

Mary thought the man was very rude to call her father's bungalow 'A place like this!'

"It is the child no one ever saw!" exclaimed the man, turning to his companion. "She has actually been forgotten!"

"Why was I forgotten?" Mary said, stamping her foot. "Why does nobody come?"

The young man whose name was Barney looked at her very sadly. Mary even thought she saw him wink his eyes as if to wink tears away.

"Poor little kid!" he said. "There is nobody left to come."

It was in that strange and sudden way that Mary found out that she had neither father nor mother left; that they had died and become the undead and fed upon the flesh of the living, and that the few native servants who had not transformed or been eaten also had left the house as quickly as they could get out of it, none of them even remembering that there was a Missie Sahib. That was why the place was so quiet. It was true that there was no one in the bungalow but herself and the little Accursed snake.

Chapter 2: Bloody Mary Quite Contrary

Mary had liked to look at her mother from a distance and she had thought her very pretty, but as she knew very little of her she could scarcely have been expected to love her or to miss her very much now that she had become a mindless cannibal. She did not miss her at all, in fact, and as she was a self-absorbed child she gave her entire thought to herself, as she had always done. If she had been older she would no doubt have been very anxious at the idea of demon blood infecting everyone she knew turning them into blood-thirsty, gore consuming, savages, but she was very young, and as she had always been taken care of, she supposed she always would be. What she thought was that she would like to know if she was going to uninfected people, who would be polite to her and give her her own way as her Ayah and the other native servants had done.

She knew that she was not going to stay long at the heavily guarded Refugee Camp for the Untainted outside Mumbai where she was taken at first. To get into the camp she had to stay in a separated area for an entire day with others who came. After twenty-four hours anyone who had not transformed and been shot was allowed inside the compound and declared "clean". She did not want to stay. Everyone in the refugee camp was poor and hundreds of orphaned children wore shabby clothes and were always quarreling and snatching small bits of food from each other. Mary hated their untidy bungalow and was so disagreeable to everyone that after the first day or two nobody would play with her or bring her food. The children entertained each other with stories but the only stories Mary knew were of the twisted Aghori rituals and the monsters of Indian lore. By the second day the children had given her a nickname which made her furious.

It was Basil who thought of it first. Basil was a little boy whose father had eaten his mother and his sisters, and Mary hated him. She was playing by herself under a tree, just as she had been playing the day the Accursed infection broke out in her home. She was making heaps of earth and paths for a garden and Basil came and stood near to watch her. Presently he got rather interested and suddenly asked a question.

"Why have you put those small stones there? Are you pretending it is one the Aghori graveyards from your stories?" he said. "There in the middle," and he leaned over her to point.

"Go away!" cried Mary. "I don't want boys. Go away!"

For a moment Basil looked angry, and then he began to tease. He was always teasing his sisters before their brains had been devoured in front of him. He danced round and round her and made faces and sang and laughed.

"Bloody Mary, quite contrary,

How does your garden grow?

With Hellebore and Asphodel,

And gravestones all in a row."

He sang it until the other children heard and laughed, too; and the crosser Mary got, the more they sang "Bloody Mary, quite contrary"; and after that as long as she stayed with them they called her "Bloody Mary Quite Contrary" when they spoke of her to each other, and often when they spoke to her.

"You are going to be sent home," Basil said to her, "at the end of the week. And we're glad of it."

"I am glad of it, too," answered Mary. "Where is home?"

"She doesn't know where home is!" said Basil, with seven-year-old scorn. "It's England, of course. My grandmama lives there and my only surviving sister Mabel was sent to her last year. You are not going to your grandmama. You have none. You are going to your uncle. His name is Mr. Archibald Craven."

"I don't know anything about him," snapped Mary.

"I know you don't," Basil answered. "You don't know anything. Girls never do. I heard some of the British Sikh soldiers talking about him. He is a mad doctor and he lives in a great, big, desolate old house in the country and no one goes near him. He's so cross he won't let them, and they wouldn't come if he would let them. He's a hunchback, and he's horrid. He does ghastly experiments on the Rotters."

"I don't believe you," said Mary; and she turned her back and stuck her fingers in her ears, because she would not listen any more.

But she thought over it a great deal afterward; and when the British army men told her that night that she was going to sail away to England in a few days and go to her uncle, Mr. Archibald Craven, who lived at Misselthwaite Manor, she looked so stony and stubbornly uninterested that they did not know what to think about her. They tried to be kind to her, but she spit when her new caretaker, Mrs. Crawford, attempted to kiss her, and she screamed as if she was having her entrails pulled out when a soldier patted her shoulder.

"She is such a plain child," Mrs. Crawford said pityingly, afterward. "And her mother was such a pretty creature. She had a very pretty manner, too, and Mary has the most unattractive ways I ever saw in a child. The children call her 'Bloody Mary Quite Contrary,' and though it's naughty of them, one can't help understanding it."

"Perhaps if her mother had carried her pretty face and her pretty manners oftener into the nursery Mary might have learned some pretty ways too. It is very sad, now the poor beautiful thing has become a wretched murdering hag, to remember that many people never even knew that she had a child at all."

"I believe she scarcely ever looked at her," sighed Mrs. Crawford. "When her Ayah was dead there was no one to give a thought to the little thing. Think of the servants running away and leaving her all alone surrounded on all sides by the Accursed. Colonel McGrew said he nearly jumped out of his skin when he opened the door and found her standing by herself in the middle of the room. He nearly killed her thinking she was one of them. And with where she is now going, perhaps it would have been better for her if he had."

Mary made the long voyage to England under the care of an officer's wife, who was taking her children away from the terrible Scourge. She was very much absorbed in her own little boy and girl, and did not notice the young servant who lay in the fetal position in a corner of the low deck shaking and sweating. Mary noticed him and thought he looked like the boy officer whose eyes had filled with dead blood. Mary had not eaten in many hours and her empty stomach put her in a sour mood. She left the officer's wife and her children and moved to a higher deck so she would no longer have to look at the disgusting young man who had begun to twitch violently. She later learned that the infection had broken out on the lower deck and over a hundred people were devoured or infected before the British naval officers opened fire and threw all the bodies, dead or infected out to sea. Mary could not later find the officer's wife or her two children and the officer who took her in his charge was rather glad to hand the child over to the woman Mr. Archibald Craven sent to meet her, in London.

The woman was his housekeeper and head of security at Misselthwaite Manor, and her name was Mrs. Medlock. She was a stout woman, with very red cheeks and sharp black eyes. She wore a very purple dress, a black silk mantle with jet fringe on it and a black bonnet with purple velvet flowers which stuck up and trembled when she moved her head. Around her waist she wore a black leather belt holding two large knives in black leather sheaths. Mary did not like her at all, but as she very seldom liked people there was nothing remarkable in that; besides which it was very evident Mrs. Medlock did not think much of her. "My word! She's a plain little piece of goods! She looks as if she might be infected!" she said. "And we'd heard that her mother was a beauty. She hasn't handed much of it down, has she?"

"Perhaps she will improve as she grows older," the officer said good-naturedly. "If she were not so sallow and had a nicer expression, her features are rather good. Children alter so much."

"She'll have to alter a good deal," answered Mrs. Medlock. "And, there's nothing likely to improve children at Misselthwaite— if you ask me! At least it is so far from the cities that The Forsaken are rare and easily dispatched." They thought Mary was not listening because she was standing a little apart from them at the security compound near the boat docks. She was watching the passing boats and people, but she heard quite well and was made very curious about Misselthwaite and how the Scourge came to England nearly ten years earlier. Listening she discovered the infection was brought by sailors many years ago who would not speak of what had befallen them in India. What sort of a place was Misselthwaite Manor, and what would her uncle be like? What was a hunchback? She had never seen one. Perhaps there were none in India.

Since she had been living in the refugee camps and on the boat and had had no Ayah, she had begun to feel lonely and to think queer thoughts which were new to her. She had begun to wonder why she had never seemed to belong to anyone even when her father and mother had been alive. Other children seemed to belong to their fathers and mothers, but she had never seemed to really be anyone's little girl. She had had servants, and food and clothes, but no one had taken any notice of her. No one wanted to save her when the Accursed Ones came to the house. Her mother did not even notice her in the garden when she tried to escape the ravenous servants. She did not know that this was because she was a disagreeable child; but then, of course, she did not know she was disagreeable. She often thought that other people were, but she did not know that she was so herself.

She thought Mrs. Medlock the most disagreeable person she had ever seen, with her common, highly colored face and her common fine bonnet. The only thing interesting at all about her were the sheathed knives that hung from her waist. As she walked behind Mrs. Medlock, Mary stared at the black handles that shined like obsidian. When the next day they set out on their journey to Yorkshire, she walked through the station to the railway carriage with her head up and trying to keep as far away from her as she could, because she did not want to seem to belong to her. It would have made her angry to think people imagined she was her little girl.

But Mrs. Medlock was not in the least disturbed by her and her thoughts. She was the kind of woman who would "stand no nonsense from young ones and would show the Accursed no mercy." At least, that is what she would have said if she had been asked. She had not wanted to go to London just when the remains of her sister Maria's daughter were going to be buried. Only two days prior a small band of The Forsaken had crashed into their home and tore the girl apart, eating her even as the girl continued to scream.

But she had a comfortable, well paid place as housekeeper and Defense Commander at Misselthwaite Manor and the only way in which she could keep it was to do at once what Mr. Archibald Craven told her to do. She never dared even to ask a question.

"Captain Lennox and his wife died of the Scourge," Mr. Craven had said in his short, cold way. "Captain Lennox was my wife's brother and I am their daughter's guardian. The child is to be brought here. You must risk the journey to London and bring her yourself."

So she packed her small trunk and made the treacherous journey only encountering a few dozen of the Accursed near the train entrance to London. As the walls were moved for the train, Purifiers, or soldiers that battle the Accursed, opened fire on the rotting corpses, cutting down any that made it through.

Mary sat in her corner of the railway carriage and looked plain and fretful. She had nothing to read or to look at, and she had folded her thin little black-gloved hands in her lap. Her black dress made her look yellower than ever, and her limp light hair straggled from under her black crepe hat.

"A more marred-looking young one I never saw in my life," Mrs. Medlock thought. (Marred is a Yorkshire word and means spoiled and pettish.) She had never seen a child who sat so still without doing anything; it was hard to believe this child was not Accursed and at last she got tired of watching her and began to talk in a brisk, hard voice.

"I suppose I may as well tell you something about where you are going to," she said. "Do you know anything about your uncle?"

"No," said Mary.

"Never heard your father and mother talk about him?"

"No," said Mary frowning. She frowned because she remembered that her father and mother had never talked to her about anything in particular. Certainly they had never told her things.

"Humph," muttered Mrs. Medlock, staring at her queer, unresponsive little face. She did not say any more for a few moments and then she began again.

"I suppose you might as well be told something—to prepare you. You are going to a queer place."

Mary said nothing at all, and Mrs. Medlock looked rather discomfited by her apparent indifference, but, after taking a breath, she went on.

"Not but that it's a grand big place in a gloomy way, and Mr. Craven's proud of it in his way—and that's gloomy enough, too. The house is six hundred years old and it's on the edge of the moor, where even the Forsaken dare not go. And there's near a hundred rooms in it, though most of them's shut up and locked. And there's pictures and fine old furniture and things that's been there for ages, and there's a big park round it and gardens and trees with branches trailing to the ground—some of them. The outer walls are spiked, the windows are barred and the doors fortified with iron locks to keep out the Forsaken." She paused and took another breath. "But there's nothing else," she ended suddenly.

Mary had begun to listen in spite of herself. It all sounded so unlike India, and anything new and morbid rather attracted her.

But she did not intend to look as if she were interested. That was one of her unhappy, disagreeable ways. So she sat still.

"Well," said Mrs. Medlock. "What do you think of it?"

"Nothing," she answered. "I know nothing about such places."

That made Mrs. Medlock laugh a short sort of laugh.

"Eh!" she said, "but you are like a dying old woman. Don't you care?"

"It doesn't matter" said Mary, "whether I care or not."

"You are right enough there," said Mrs. Medlock. "It doesn't. What you're to be kept at Misselthwaite Manor for I don't know, unless because it's the safest way. We know more about the Forsaken than most, and the Manor is impenetrable. He's not going to trouble himself about you, that's sure and certain. He never troubles himself about no one."

She stopped herself as if she had just remembered something in time.

"He's got a crooked back," she said. "That set him wrong. He was a sour young man and got no good of all his money and big place till he was married."

Mary's eyes turned toward her in spite of her intention not to seem to care. She had never thought of the hunchback's being married and she was a trifle surprised. Mrs. Medlock saw this, and as she was a talkative woman she continued with more interest. This was one way of passing some of the time, at any rate.

"She was a sweet, pretty thing and he'd have walked the world over to get her a blade o' grass she wanted. Nobody thought she'd marry him, but she did, and people said she married him for his money. But she didn't—she didn't." She trailed off for a moment and her eyes darkened. Clearly, she was remembering something very unpleasant. "When she died—"

Mary gave a little involuntary jump.

"Oh! Did she die?" she exclaimed, quite without meaning to. She had just remembered a French fairy story she had once read called "Riquet a la Houppe." It had been about a poor hunchback and a beautiful princess and it had made her suddenly sorry for and perversely interested in Archibald Craven.

"Yes, she died... terribly," Mrs. Medlock answered. "And it made him queerer than ever. He cares about nobody. He won't see people. He takes out his resentment and wrath on the Accursed wraiths of this land. He is obsessed with killing them. Most of the time he goes away to hunt and study the Accursed, even as a Hunchback, and when he is at Misselthwaite he shuts himself up in the West Wing and won't let anyone but Pitcher see him. Pitcher's an old fellow, but he took care of him when he was a child and he knows his ways."

It sounded like something in a book and it did not make Mary feel cheerful. A house with a hundred rooms, nearly all shut up and with their doors barred with iron locks—a house on the edge of a moor—whatsoever a moor was—sounded dreary. The thought that the Accursed could be just outside the doors waiting to crunch on her bones with no Indian Army to protect her. A man who studied the Accursed with a crooked back who shut himself up also! So it was true, Lord Craven experimented on those that would not die. She stared out of the window with her lips pinched together, and it seemed quite natural that the rain should have begun to pour down in gray slanting lines and splash and stream down the window-panes. If the pretty wife had been alive she might have made things cheerful by being something like her own mother and by running in and out and going to parties as she had done in frocks "light as a ghost." But she was not there anymore.

"You needn't expect to see him, because ten to one you won't," said Mrs. Medlock. "And you mustn't expect that there will be people to talk to you. You'll have to play about and look after yourself. You'll be told what rooms you can go into and what rooms you're to keep out of. There's gardens enough, but stick to the path, getting lost won't save you if the Accursed ever come back. But when you're in the house don't go wandering and poking about. Master Craven won't have it."

"I shall not want to go poking about," said sour little Mary and just as suddenly as she had begun to be rather sorry for Mr. Archibald Craven she began to cease to be sorry and to think he was unpleasant enough to deserve all that had happened to him.

And she turned her face toward the streaming panes of the window of the railway carriage and gazed out at the gray rainstorm which looked as if it would go on forever and ever. She could see gray shapes of people wandering the hills and fields, people who dragged their feet and groped out in front of them as if they hoped they might grasp one more bite of sweet flesh that their whole being ached for. She watched it so long and steadily that the grayness grew heavier and heavier before her eyes and she fell asleep.

Chapter 3: Across the Moor

She slept a long time, and when she awakened Mrs. Medlock had bought a lunch basket at one of the security stations and they had some chicken and cold beef and bread and butter and some hot tea. The rain seemed to be streaming down more heavily than ever and everybody in the station wore wet and glistening waterproofs and carried guns, axes and long machetes. The guard lighted the lamps in the carriage, and Mrs. Medlock cheered up very much over her tea and chicken and beef. She ate a great deal and afterward fell asleep herself, and Mary sat and stared at her and watched her fine bonnet slip on one side until she herself fell asleep once more in the corner of the carriage, lulled by the splashing of the rain against the windows. It was quite dark when she awakened again. The train had stopped at a station and Mrs. Medlock was shaking her.

"You have had a sleep!" she said. "It's time to open your eyes! We're at Thwaite Station and we've got a long dangerous drive before us."

Mary stood up and tried to keep her eyes open while Mrs. Medlock collected her parcels. The little girl did not offer to help her, because in India native servants always picked up or carried things and it seemed quite proper that other people should wait on one.

The security station was a small one and nobody but themselves seemed to be getting out of the train. The station-master spoke to Mrs. Medlock in a rough, good-natured way, pronouncing his words in a queer broad fashion which Mary found out afterward was Yorkshire.

"I see tha's made it back'n one piece," he said. "An' tha's browt th' young 'un with thee."

"Aye, that's her," answered Mrs. Medlock, speaking with a Yorkshire accent herself and jerking her head over her shoulder toward Mary. "How's thy Missus?"

"Died. I got'en to her tho' before she turn'. It were wha she woulda asked fo'. Th' carriage is waitin' outside for thee."

A brougham stood on the road before the little outside platform. Mary saw that it was a smart carriage fortified with iron bars across the windows, and that it was a smart footman who helped her in. His long waterproof coat and the waterproof covering of his hat and the sickle sword on his belt were shining and dripping with rain as everything was, the burly heavily armed station-master included.

When he shut the door, mounted the box with the coachman, and drove through the opening iron gates, the little girl found herself seated in a comfortably cushioned corner, but she was not inclined to go to sleep again as the footman and coachman cleaved the heads off several Accursed who had waited just outside the gate. She sat and looked out of the window, curious to see if any of the Tormented Ones would appear out of the dark on the road over which she was being driven to the queer place Mrs. Medlock had spoken of. She was not at all a timid child and she was not exactly frightened, but she felt that there was no knowing what might happen in a house with a hundred rooms nearly all shut up, a house so far from any protection from mindless putrefying cannibals, a house standing on the edge of a moor.

"What is a moor?" she said suddenly to Mrs. Medlock.

"Look out of the window in about ten minutes and you'll see," the woman answered. "We've got to drive five miles across Missel Moor before we get to the Manor. You won't see much because it's a dark night, but you can see something."

Mary asked no more questions but waited in the darkness of her corner, keeping her eyes on the window. The carriage lamps cast rays of light a little distance ahead of them and she caught glimpses of the things they passed. After they had left the station they had driven through a tiny village where decomposing and decapitated bodies lay outside the whitewashed cottages and the remains of a burned down public house. Then they had passed an abandoned church and a dark vicarage that appeared to be boarded up from the inside. Mary wondered if the Accursed had gotten in or if there were still people hiding in there, praying for help to come. Then they were on the highroad and she saw hedges and trees. After that there seemed nothing different for a long time—or at least it seemed a long time to her.

At last the horses began to go more slowly, as if they were climbing up-hill, and presently there seemed to be no more hedges and no more trees. She could see nothing, in fact, but a dense darkness on either side. She leaned forward and pressed her face against the window just as the carriage gave a big jolt.

"Eh! A body right in the middle of the road! Ghastly! We're on the moor now sure enough," said Mrs. Medlock.

The carriage lamps shed a yellow light on a rough-looking road which seemed to be cut through bushes and low-growing things which ended in the great expanse of dark apparently spread out before and around them. A wind was rising and making a singular, wild, low, rushing sound.

"It's—it's not the sea, is it?" said Mary, looking round at her companion.

"No, not it," answered Mrs. Medlock. "Nor it isn't fields nor mountains, it's just miles and miles and miles of wild land that nothing grows on but heather and gorse and broom, and nothing lives on but wild ponies and sheep."

"I feel as if it might be the sea, if there were water on it," said Mary. "It sounds like the sea just now."

"That's the wind blowing through the bushes," Mrs. Medlock said. "It's a wild, dreary enough place to my mind, though there's plenty that likes it—particularly when the heather's in bloom, and the Accursed don' like to cross it. Maybe it is the howlin' wind, or the wide expanse with nothin' to tempt their sinister cravings, but it is a rare day when the Forsaken cross the Moor to Misselthwaite. Though that they took th' parish over that last week is disturbing."

On and on they drove through the darkness, and though the rain stopped, the wind rushed by and whistled and made strange sounds. Mary thought she could hear low moaning in the wind but Mrs. Medlock did not seem concerned. The road went up and down, and several times the carriage passed over a little bridge beneath which water rushed very fast with a great deal of noise.

Mary felt as if the drive would never come to an end and that the wide, bleak moor was a wide expanse of black ocean through which she was passing on a strip of dry land.

"I don't like it," she said to herself. "I don't like it," and she pinched her thin lips more tightly together.

The horses were climbing up a hilly piece of road when she first caught sight of a light. Mrs. Medlock saw it as soon as she did and drew a long sigh of relief though she looked irritated.

"Eh, I am glad to see that bit o' light twinkling, though we have strict guidelines about lights on in the windows." she exclaimed. "It's the light that attracts the Forsaken. We shall get a good cup of tea after a bit, at all events."

It was "after a bit," as she said, for when the carriage passed through the high, spiked park gates there was still two miles of avenue to drive through and the trees (which nearly met overhead) made it seem as if they were driving through a long dark vault.

They drove out of the vault into a clear space and stopped before an immensely long but low-built house which seemed to ramble round a stone court. At first Mary thought that there were no lights at all in the windows, but as she got out of the carriage she saw that one room in a corner upstairs showed a dull glow. Mrs. Medlock kept her hand on one of the knife handles as they walked from the carriage to the front door.

The entrance door was a huge one made of massive, curiously shaped panels of oak studded with big iron nails and bound with great iron bars. It opened into an enormous hall, which was so dimly lighted that the faces in the portraits on the walls and the figures in the suits of armor made Mary feel that she did not want to look at them. Knives and swords hung from wooden plaques and some of them were low enough that Mary could have touched one if she dared. As she stood on the stone floor she looked a very small, odd little black figure, and she felt as small and lost and odd as she looked.

A neat, thin old man stood near the manservant who opened the door for them. He had an old musket slung around his back.

"You are to take her to her room," he said in a husky voice. "He doesn't want to see her. He's going to London in the morning."

"Very well, Mr. Pitcher," Mrs. Medlock answered. "So long as I know what's expected of me, I can manage."

"What's expected of you, Mrs. Medlock," Mr. Pitcher said, "is that you make sure that he's not disturbed and that he doesn't see what he doesn't want to see."

And then Mary Lennox was led up a broad staircase and down a long corridor and up a short flight of steps and through another corridor and another, until a door opened in a wall and she found herself in a room with a fire in it and a supper on a table.

Mrs. Medlock said unceremoniously, "Well, here you are! This room and the next are where you'll live—and you must keep to them. At night keep the heavy curtains drawn and allow no light to escape the room. Their eyes may be filled with blackness but they can see the live blood pumping in our veins. Don't you forget that!"

It was in this way Bloody Mary arrived at Misselthwaite Manor and she had perhaps never felt quite so contrary in all her life.

Chapter 4: Martha

When she opened her eyes in the morning it was because a young housemaid had come into her room to light the fire and was kneeling on the hearth-rug raking out the cinders noisily. Mary lay and watched her for a few moments and then began to look about the room. She had never seen a room at all like it and thought it curious and gloomy. The fireplace was very large and had an iron shield within the hearth.The walls were covered with tapestry with a forest scene embroidered on it. There were fantastically dressed people under the trees and in the distance there was a glimpse of the turrets of a castle. There were hunters and horses and dogs and ladies. Mary felt as if she were in the forest with them. Out of a deep window she could see a great climbing stretch of land which seemed to have no trees on it, and to look rather like an endless, dull, purplish sea.

"What is that?" she said, pointing out of the window.

Martha, the young housemaid, who had just risen to her feet, looked and pointed also. "That there?" she said.

"Yes."

"That's th' moor," with a good-natured grin. "Does tha' like it?"

"No," answered Mary. "I hate it."

"That's because tha'rt not used to it," Martha said, going back to her hearth. "Tha' thinks it's too big an' bare now. But tha' will like it."

"Do you?" inquired Mary.

"Aye, that I do," answered Martha, cheerfully polishing away at the grate. "I just love it. It's none bare. It's covered wi' growin' things as smells sweet. It's fair lovely in spring an' summer when th' gorse an' broom an' heather's in flower. It smells o' honey an' there's such a lot o' fresh air—an' th' sky looks so high an' th' bees an' skylarks makes such a nice noise hummin' an' singin'. And th' Accurse' don' come near it! And if tha' do, they gets lost and wander forever until th' wind sweeps them away. Eh! I wouldn't live away from th' moor for anythin'."

Mary listened to her with a grave, puzzled expression. The native servants she had been used to in India were not in the least like this. They were obsequious and servile and did not presume to talk to their masters as if they were their equals. They made salaams and called them "protector of the poor" and names of that sort. Indian servants were commanded to do things, not asked. It was not the custom to say "please" and "thank you" and Mary had always slapped her Ayah in the face when she was angry. She wondered a little what this girl would do if one slapped her in the face. She was a round, rosy, good-natured-looking creature, but she had a sturdy way which made Mistress Mary wonder if she might not even slap back—if the person who slapped her was only a little girl.

"You are a strange servant," she said from her pillows, rather haughtily.

Martha sat up on her heels, with her blacking brush in her hand, and laughed, without seeming the least out of temper.

"Eh! I know that," she said. "If there was a grand Missus at Misselthwaite I should never have been even one of th' under house-maids. I might have been let to be scullery maid but I'd never have been let upstairs. I'm too common an' I talk too much Yorkshire. An' I always carry protection 'gainst th' Accurse', no matter what th' house rules ar'." Martha patted a small pouch on her hip and Mary wondered what might be inside. "But this is a funny house for all it's so grand. Seems like there's neither Master nor Mistress except Mr. Pitcher an' Mrs. Medlock. Lord Craven, he won't be troubled about anythin' when he's here, an' he's nearly always away. Mrs. Medlock gave me th' place out o' kindness and 'cause I help' slay two o' th' Tormented Ones a couple o' years ago tha' got into th' gardens. She told me she could never have done it if Misselthwaite had been like other big houses."

"Are you going to be my servant and bodyguard?" Mary asked, still in her imperious little Indian way.

Martha began to rub her grate again.

"I'm Mrs. Medlock's servant," she said stoutly. "An' she's Master Craven's—but I'm to do the housemaid's work up here an' wait on you a bit. But you won't need much waitin' on. An' I don' do no bodyguardin', if you please, Miss. But I'll help if'n I'm needed."

"Who is going to dress me?" demanded Mary.

Martha sat up on her heels again and stared. She spoke in broad Yorkshire in her amazement.

"Canna' tha' dress thysen!" she said.

"What do you mean? I don't understand your language," said Mary.

"Eh! I forgot," Martha said. "Mrs. Medlock told me I'd have to be careful or you wouldn't know what I was sayin'. I mean can't you put on your own clothes?"

"No," answered Mary, quite indignantly. "I never did in my life. My Ayah dressed me, of course."

"Well," said Martha, evidently not in the least aware that she was impudent, "it's time tha' should learn. Tha' cannot begin younger. It'll do thee good to wait on thysen a bit. Why, how can you defen' yourself again' the Scourge if ya can' even dress tha'self. My mother always said she couldn't see why grand people's children didn't all turn out food for demons—what with nurses an' bein' washed an' dressed an' took out to walk as if they was puppies!"

"It is different in India," said Mistress Mary disdainfully. She could scarcely stand this.

But Martha was not at all crushed.

"Eh! I can see it's different," she answered almost sympathetically. "I dare say it's because there's such a lot o' heathen cannibals there instead o' respectable people. When I heard you was comin' from India I thought you was a native too."

Mary sat up in bed furious.

"What!" she said. "What! You thought I was a... You—you Aghori lover, whore of demons!" It was the worst insult Mary could think of though she did not understand it.

Martha stared and looked hot.

"Who are you callin' names?" she said. "You needn't be so vexed. That's not th' way for a young lady to talk. I've nothin' against th' natives. When you read about 'em in tracts they're always very religious. You always read as a black's a man an' a brother. I've never seen a black an' I was fair pleased to think I was goin' to see one close. When I come in to light your fire this mornin' I crep' up to your bed an' pulled th' cover back careful to look at you. An' there you was," disappointedly, "no more black than me—for all you're so yeller."

Mary did not even try to control her rage and humiliation. "You thought I was a native! You dared! You don't know anything about natives! They are not people—they're servants who must salaam to you. You know nothing about India. You know nothing about anything!"

She was in such a rage and felt so helpless before the girl's simple stare, and somehow she suddenly felt so horribly lonely and far away from everything she understood and which understood her, and so angry that she had not in fact escaped the Scourge as it was here too in this dreadful country, that she threw herself face downward on the pillows and burst into passionate sobbing. She sobbed so unrestrainedly that good-natured Yorkshire Martha was a little frightened and quite sorry for her. She went to the bed and bent over her.

"Eh! you mustn't cry like that there!" she begged. "You mustn't for sure. I didn't know you'd be vexed. I don't know anythin' about anythin'—just like you said. I beg your pardon, Miss. Do stop cryin'."

There was something comforting and really friendly in her queer Yorkshire speech and sturdy way which had a good effect on Mary. She gradually ceased crying and became quiet. Martha looked relieved.

"It's time for thee to get up now," she said. "Mrs. Medlock said I was to carry tha' breakfast an' tea an' dinner into th' room next to this. It's been made into a nursery for thee. I'll help thee on with thy clothes if tha'll get out o' bed. If th' buttons are at th' back tha' cannot button them up tha'self."

When Mary at last decided to get up, the clothes Martha took from the wardrobe were not the ones she had worn when she arrived the night before with Mrs. Medlock.

"Those are not mine," she said. "Mine are black."

She looked the thick white wool coat and dress over, and added with cool approval:

"Those are nicer than mine."

"These are th' ones tha' must put on," Martha answered. "Mr. Craven ordered Mrs. Medlock to get 'em in London. He said 'I won't have a child dressed in black wanderin' about like a soulless ghoul,' he said. 'Plus it provides nice camouflage in the mist from the Accursed. It'd make the place sadder than it is if she is eaten. Put concealments on her.' Mother she said she knew what he meant. Mother always knows what a body means. She doesn't hold with black hersel'."

"I hate black things," said Mary thinking about the black emulsion that spewed from the mouths of the undead.

The dressing process was one which taught them both something. Martha had "buttoned up" her little sisters and brothers but she had never seen a child who stood still and waited for another person to do things for her as if she had neither hands nor feet of her own.

"Why doesn't tha' put on tha' own shoes?" she said when Mary quietly held out her foot. "Tha' can't run from the ravenous cannibals if tha' can' put on tha' own shoes."

"My Ayah did it," answered Mary, staring. "It was the custom."

She said that very often—"It was the custom." The native servants were always saying it. If one told them to do a thing their ancestors had not done for a thousand years they gazed at one mildly and said, "It is not the custom" and one knew that was the end of the matter. Apparently eating a rotting corpse on charnal ground during an eclipse while engaging in a secret tantric ritual is "not the custom", but so it was done and the Scourge began.

It had not been the custom that Mistress Mary should do anything but stand and allow herself to be dressed like a doll, but before she was ready for breakfast she began to suspect that her life at Misselthwaite Manor would end by teaching her a number of things quite new to her—things such as putting on her own shoes and stockings, and picking up things she let fall. If Martha had been a well-trained fine young lady's maid she would have been more subservient and respectful and would have known that it was her business to brush hair, and button boots, and pick things up and lay them away. She was, however, only an untrained Yorkshire rustic who had been brought up in a moorland cottage with a swarm of little brothers and sisters who had never dreamed of doing anything but waiting on themselves and on the younger ones who were either babies in arms or just learning to totter about and tumble over things.

If Mary Lennox had been a child who was ready to be amused she would perhaps have laughed at Martha's readiness to talk, but Mary only listened to her coldly and wondered at her freedom of manner. At first she was not at all interested, but gradually, as the girl rattled on in her good-tempered, homely way, Mary began to notice what she was saying.

"Eh! you should see 'em all," she said. "There's twelve of us an' my father only gets sixteen shilling a week. I can tell you my mother's put to it to get porridge for 'em all. They tumble about on th' moor an' play there all day an' mother says th' air of th' moor fattens 'em. She says she believes they eat th' grass same as th' wild ponies do. But you mus' watch out fo' some of the animals, they can carry the demon spirits if they get bit by the Accursed. Our Dickon, he's twelve years old and he found a young pony that was one o' the Accursed."

"Where did he find it?" asked Mary remembering her little snake of Shiva.

"He found it on th' moor over its dead mother. The pony's head was covere' in blood as it ate out the entrails of the mare. Dickon remembered him. When the pony was a little one, he began to make friends with it an' give it bits o' bread an' pluck young grass for it. And it had got to like him so it followed him about, but none o' that mattered anymore. Once the demons have taken hold all that was you dies, your mind and your body. But you keep going, killin', spreading the demon seed through blood.

Dickon's a kind lad an' animals likes him, but 'e had to slay th' pony, and it broke his heart to do it."

Mary had never possessed an animal pet of her own, except her dead snake which she she kept hidden in a small box with her clothes, and had always thought she should like one. So she began to feel a slight interest in Dickon, and as she had never before been interested in anyone but herself, it was the dawning of a healthy sentiment. When she went into the room which had been made into a nursery for her, she found that it was rather like the one she had slept in. It was not a child's room, but a grown-up person's room, with gloomy old pictures on the walls and heavy old oak chairs. A table in the center was set with a good substantial breakfast. But she had always had a very small appetite, and she looked with something more than indifference at the first plate Martha set before her.

"I don't want it," she said.

"Tha' doesn't want thy porridge!" Martha exclaimed incredulously.

"No."

"Tha' doesn't know how good it is. Put a bit o' treacle on it or a bit o' sugar."

"I don't want it," repeated Mary.

"Eh!" said Martha. "I can't abide to see good victuals go to waste. If our children was at this table they'd clean it bare in five minutes."

"Why?" said Mary coldly.

"Why!" echoed Martha. "Because they scarce ever had their stomachs full in their lives. They're as hungry as young hawks an' foxes."

"I always had plenty of food at home," said Mary shutting out memories of the Refugee Camps with the indifference of ignorance. She was so sour that she didn't realize hunger was the reason for the pain in her side and the weakness of her body. She did not understand that it was hunger had made her angry and tired.

Martha looked indignant.

"Well, it would do thee good to try it. I can see that plain enough," she said outspokenly. "I've no patience with folk as sits an' just stares at good bread an' meat. My word! Don't I wish Dickon and Phil an' Jane an' th' rest of 'em had what's here under their pinafores."

"Why don't you take it to them?" suggested Mary.

"It's not mine," answered Martha stoutly. "An' this isn't my day out. I get my day out once a month same as th' rest. Then I go home an' clean up for mother an' give her a day's rest."

Mary drank some tea and ate a little toast and some marmalade.

"You wrap up warm an' run out an' play you," said Martha. "It'll do you good and give you some stomach for your meat."

Mary went to the window. There were gardens and paths and big trees, but everything looked dull and wintry.

"Out? Why should I go out on a day like this? What if there are Forsaken out there?"

"Th' moor and the walls keeps 'um away. Well, if tha' doesn't go out tha'lt have to stay in, an' what has tha' got to do?"

Mary glanced about her. There was nothing to do. When Mrs. Medlock had prepared the nursery she had not thought of amusement. Perhaps it would be better to go and see what the gardens were like.

"Who will go with me?" she inquired.

Martha stared.

"You'll go by yourself," she answered. "You'll have to learn to play like other children does when they haven't got sisters and brothers. And you'll have ta learn to be vigilant and keep your ears awake for footsteps that seem unnatural. Our Dickon goes off on th' moor by himself an' plays for hours. That's how he made friends with th' pony. He's got sheep on th' moor that knows him, an' birds as comes an' eats out of his hand. However little there is to eat, he always saves a bit o' his bread to coax his pets."

It was really this mention of Dickon which made Mary decide to go out, though she was not aware of it. There would be birds outside though there would not be ponies or sheep. They would be different from the birds in India and it might amuse her to look at them. She felt it would be safe, for surely Martha would not let her go out if the Accursed might be near.

Martha found her coat and hat for her and a pair of stout little boots and she showed her the way downstairs.

"If tha' goes round that way tha'll come to th' gardens," she said, pointing to a gate in a wall of shrubbery. "There's lots o' flowers in summer-time, but there's nothin' bloomin' now." She seemed to hesitate a second before she added, "One of th' gardens is locked up. No one has been in it for ten years."

"Why?" asked Mary in spite of herself. Here was another locked door added to the hundred in the strange house.

"Master Craven had it shut when his wife died so sudden. He won't let no one go inside. It was her garden. He locked th' door an' dug a hole and buried th' key. There's Mrs. Medlock's bell ringing—I must run. Be watchful now."

After she was gone Mary turned down the walk which led to the door in the shrubbery. She could not help thinking about the garden which no one had been into for ten years. She wondered what it would look like and whether there were any flowers still alive in it. When she had passed through the shrubbery gate she found herself in great gardens, with wide lawns and winding walks with clipped borders. There were trees, and flower-beds, and evergreens clipped into strange shapes, and a large pool with an old gray fountain in its midst. But the flower-beds were bare and wintry and the fountain was not playing. This was not the garden which was shut up. How could a garden be shut up? You could always walk into a garden.

She was just thinking this when she saw that, at the end of the path she was following, there seemed to be a long wall, with ivy growing over it. She was not familiar enough with England to know that she was coming upon the kitchen-gardens where the vegetables and fruit were growing. She went toward the wall and found that there was a green door in the ivy, and that it stood open. This was not the closed garden, evidently, and she could go into it.

She went through the door and found that it was a garden with walls all round it and that it was only one of several walled gardens which seemed to open into one another. She saw another open green door, revealing bushes and pathways between beds containing winter vegetables. Fruit-trees were trained flat against the wall, and over some of the beds there were glass frames. The place was bare and ugly enough, Mary thought, as she stood and stared about her. It might be nicer in summer when things were green, but there was nothing pretty about it now.

Mary heard footsteps on the other side of the wall. Dragging footsteps. She froze staring at the open door of the garden. Her mind was blank and fear filled her eyes. She couldn't move, though she yelled at herself to run. She could only stand waiting for whatever it was to appear in the door.

Presently an old man with a spade over his shoulder walked through the door leading from the second garden. He looked startled when he saw Mary, pulling a long blade from his belt faster than Mary would have thought of an old man, and then realizing who she was he touched his cap. Mary was relieved and angry all at once. What would she have done had it actually been one of the Accursed? The man had a surly old face, and did not seem at all pleased to see her—but then she was displeased with his dead, creepy garden and wore her "quite contrary" expression, and certainly did not seem at all pleased to see him.

"What is this place?" she asked.

"One o' th' kitchen-gardens," he answered.

"What is that?" said Mary, pointing through the other green door.

"Another of 'em," he said shortly. "There's another on t'other side o' th' wall an' there's th' orchard t'other side o' that."

"Can I go in them?" asked Mary.

"If tha' likes. But there's nowt to see. An' ya shouldn' be wanderin' free round here. Walls ar' high and gates ar' locked, but one never knows..."

Mary made no response. She went down the path and through the second green door. She pretended that the old gardener was a Tormented One, and ran down the path looking behind her as if she was being chased. She found more walls and winter vegetables and glass frames, but in the second wall there was another green door and it was not open. Perhaps it led into the garden which no one had seen for ten years. As she was not at all a timid child and always did what she wanted to do, Mary went to the green door and turned the handle. She hoped the door would not open because she wanted to be sure she had found the mysterious garden—but it did open quite easily and she walked through it and found herself in an orchard. There were walls all round it also and trees trained against them, and there were bare fruit-trees growing in the winter-browned grass—but there was no green door to be seen anywhere. Mary looked for it, noting that this would not be a safe place to run if she had actually been chased by the rotting undead, and yet when she had entered the upper end of the garden she had noticed that the wall did not seem to end with the orchard but to extend beyond it as if it enclosed a place at the other side. She could see the tops of trees above the wall, and when she stood still she saw a little bird with a bright red breast sitting on the topmost branch of one of them, and suddenly he burst into his high and sweet winter song—almost as if he had caught sight of her and was calling to her.

"Hush bird, or you'll call the Accursed!" She cried, surprised by own voice in the dead-end orchard. She stopped and listened to him and somehow his excited chirping gave her a pleased feeling— even a disagreeable little girl may be lonely, and the big closed house and big bare moor and big bare gardens had made this one feel as if there was no one left in the world but herself. If she had been an affectionate child, who had been used to being loved, it would have broken her heart, but even though she was "Bloody Mary Quite Contrary" she was desolate, and the little Robin with the red breast brought a look into her sour little face which was almost a smile. She listened to him until he flew away. He was not like an Indian bird and she liked him and wondered if she should ever see him again. Perhaps he lived in the mysterious garden and knew all about it.

Perhaps it was because she had nothing whatever to do that she thought so much of the deserted garden. She was curious about it and wanted to see what it was like. Why had Mr. Archibald Craven buried the key? If he had liked his wife so much why did he hate her garden? She wondered if she should ever see him, but she knew that if she did she should not like him, and he would not like her, and that she should only stand and stare at him and say nothing, though she should be wanting dreadfully to ask him why he had done such a queer thing.

"People never like me and I never like people," she thought. "And I never could talk as the Crawford children used to before they were eaten. They were always talking and laughing and making noises."

She thought of the red-breasted bird and of the way he seemed to sing his song at her, and as she remembered the tree-top he perched on she stopped rather suddenly on the path.

"I believe that tree was in the secret garden—I feel sure it was," she said. "There was a wall round the place and there was no door."

She walked back into the first kitchen-garden she had entered and found the old man digging there. She went and stood beside him and watched him a few moments in her cold little way. He took no notice of her and so at last she spoke to him.

"I have been into the other gardens," she said.

"There was nothin' to prevent thee," he answered crustily.

"I went into the orchard."

"There was no Accursed at th' door to bite thee," he answered.

"There was no door there into the other garden," said Mary.

"What garden?" he said in a rough voice, stopping his digging for a moment.

"The one on the other side of the wall," answered Mistress Mary. "There are trees there—I saw the tops of them. A bird with a red breast was sitting on one of them and he sang."

To her surprise the surly old weather-beaten face actually changed its expression. A creepy smile spread over it and the gardener looked quite different. It made her think that it was curious how much scarier a person looked when he smiled with his mouth and not his eyes. She had not thought of it before.

He turned about to the orchard side of his garden and began to whistle—a low soft whistle. She could not understand how such a chilling man could make such a coaxing sound. Almost the next moment Mary was startled when she heard a soft little rushing flight through the air—and it was the bird with the red breast flying to them, and he actually alighted on the big clod of earth quite near to the gardener's foot. It held something in its mouth that Mary thought was a worm.

"Here he is," snarled the old man, and then he spoke to the bird as if he were speaking to a delinquent child.

"Where has tha' been, tha' cheeky little beggar? Still scavenging off the dead?" he said.The bird flew up onto a tree branch over head and Mary gasped as she realized the worm was in fact a long piece of sinew attached to an eyeball. It was swinging back and forth until the bird threw its head back and swallowed the entire thing.

"I've not seen thee before today. Has tha' begun tha' searchin' this early in th' season? Tha'rt too forrad. They shouldn' be coming round til the wet season."

The bird put his tiny head on one side and looked up at him with his soft bright eye which was like a dewdrop. He seemed quite familiar and not the least afraid. He hopped about and pecked the earth briskly, looking for seeds and insects. It actually gave Mary a queer feeling in her heart, because he was so intent and aware and seemed so like a person. He had a plump body and a large beak, and slender scaly legs.

"Will he always come when you call him?" she asked almost in a whisper.

"Aye, that he will. I've knowed him ever since he was a fledgling. He come out of th' nest in th' other garden an' when first he flew over th' wall he was too weak to fly back for a few days an' we got friendly. When he went over th' wall again th' rest of th' brood was gone an' he was lonely an' he come back to me. He knows things, he warns me."

"Warns you about what?"

"Wha'do you think?" The old man's eyes narrowed and a shiver ran up Mary's spine.

"What kind of a bird is he?" Mary asked.

"Doesn't tha' know? He's a robin an' they're usually th' most helpful curiousest birds alive. They're almost as smart as dogs—if you know how to get on with 'em. Watch him peckin' about there an' lookin' round at us now an' again. He knows we're talkin' about him. He's a been peckin' a' th' dead. Doesn't turn Accurse' though, this 'un. It's as if red breasted robins has some holy protection."

It was the queerest thing in the world to see the old fellow. He looked at the little bird as if he were both proud and scared of him.

"He's a conceited one," he chuckled. "He likes to hear folk talk about him. An' curious—bless me, there never was his like for curiosity an' meddlin'. He's always keepin' a watch out for the Forsaken. He knows all th' things Mester Craven never troubles hissel' to find out. He's th' head gardener, he is."

The robin hopped about busily pecking the soil and now and then stopped and looked at them a little. Mary thought his dark dewdrop eyes gazed at her with great curiosity. It really seemed as if he were finding out all about her. The queer feeling in her heart increased. "Where did the rest of the brood fly to?" she asked.

"There's no knowin'. The old ones turn 'em out o' their nest an' make 'em fly an' they're scattered before you know it. This one was a knowin' one an, he knew he was abandoned and lonely and he knew 'bout the dangers, he stayed to help."

Mistress Mary went a step nearer to the robin and looked at him very hard.

"I'm lonely," she said.

She had not known before that this was one of the things which made her feel sour and cross. She seemed to find it out when the robin looked at her and she looked at the robin.

The old gardener pushed his cap back on his bald head and stared at her a minute.

"Art tha' th' little wench from India?" he asked.

Mary nodded.

"Then no wonder tha'rt lonely. Tha'lt be lonlier before tha's done," he said.

"What do you mean? Will people be leaving?" Mary asked.

He began to dig again, driving his spade deep into the rich black garden soil while the robin hopped about very busily employed also seeming to avoid the question.

"What is your name?" Mary inquired.

He stood up to answer her.

"Ben Weatherstaff," he answered, and then he added with a surly chuckle, "I'm lonely mysel' except when he's with me," and he jerked his thumb toward the robin. "He's th' only friend I've got."

"I have no friends at all," said Mary. "I never had. My Ayah didn't like me and I never played with anyone."

It is a Yorkshire habit to say what you think with blunt frankness, and old Ben Weatherstaff was a Yorkshire moor man.

"Tha' an' me are a good bit alike," he said. "We was wove out of th' same cloth. We're neither of us good lookin' an' we're both of us as sour as we look. We've got the same nasty tempers, both of us, I'll warrant. An' we both 'ave seen dark things a body ought not e'suppose to see less'n in the depths of Hell."

This was plain speaking, and Mary Lennox had never heard the truth about herself in her life. Native servants always salaamed and submitted to you, whatever you did. She had never thought much about her looks, but she wondered if she was as unattractive as Ben Weatherstaff and she also wondered if she looked as sour as he had looked before the robin came. She actually began to wonder also if she was "nasty tempered." She felt uncomfortable.

Suddenly a clear rippling little sound broke out near her and she turned round. She was standing a few feet from a young apple-tree and the robin had flown on to one of its branches and had burst out into a scrap of short sharp chirps. Ben Weatherstaff gripped his shovel and looked about him.

"What did he do that for?" asked Mary.

"Nothin'... It's nothin'," Ben Weatherstaff moved to the green garden door and slowly closed it. "He's made up his mind to help protect thee," replied Ben. "Dang me if he hasn't took a fancy to thee?"

She spoke to the robin just as if she was speaking to a person. "Would you?" And she did not say it either in her hard little voice or in her imperious Indian voice, but in a tone so soft and eager and coaxing that Ben Weatherstaff was as surprised as she had been when she heard him whistle.

"Why," he cried out, "tha' said that as nice an' human as if tha' was a real child instead of a sharp old woman. Tha' said it almost like Dickon talks to his wild things on th' moor."

"Do you know Dickon?" Mary asked, turning round rather in a hurry.

"Everybody knows him. Dickon's wanderin' about everywhere. Th' very blackberries an' heather-bells knows him. I warrant th' foxes shows him where their cubs lies an' th' skylarks doesn't hide their nests from him. He helps th' animals tha' been Accursed, and puts them out of the' misery."

Mary would have liked to ask some more questions. She was almost as curious about Dickon as she was about the deserted garden. But just that moment the robin, who had stopped his warning call, gave a little shake of his wings, spread them and flew away. He had tried to warn them of danger but had other things to do.

"He has flown over the wall!" Mary cried out, watching him. "He has flown into the orchard—he has flown across the other wall—into the garden where there is no door!"

"He lives there," said old Ben. "He came out o' th' egg there. If he's courtin', he's makin' up to some young madam of a robin that lives among th' old rose-trees there."

"Rose-trees," said Mary. "Are there rose-trees?"

Ben Weatherstaff took up his spade again and began to dig.

"There was ten year' ago," he mumbled.

"I should like to see them," said Mary. "Where is the green door? There must be a door somewhere."

Ben drove his spade deep and looked as uncompanionable as he had looked when she first saw him.

"There was ten year' ago, but there isn't now," he said.

"No door!" cried Mary. "There must be."

"None as anyone can find, an' none as is anyone's business. Don't you be a meddlesome wench an' poke your nose where it's no cause to go. Here, I must go on with my work. Get you gone an' play you. I've no more time."

And he actually stopped digging, threw his spade over his shoulder and walked off dragging his feet, without even glancing at her or saying good-by.

Chapter 5: The Cry in the Corridor

At first each day which passed by for Mary Lennox was exactly like the others. Every morning she awoke in her tapestried room and found Martha kneeling upon the hearth building her fire; every morning she ate her breakfast in the nursery which had nothing amusing in it; and after each breakfast she gazed out of the window across to the huge moor which seemed to spread out on all sides and climb up to the sky, and after she had stared for a while searching for any movement in the mist, she realized that if she did not go out she would have to stay in and do nothing—and so she went out. She did not know that this was the best thing she could have done, despite potential danger, and she did not know that, when she began to walk quickly or even run along the paths and down the avenue pretending an Accursed pony was after her, she was stirring her slow blood and making herself stronger by fighting with the wind which swept down from the moor. She ran as if all Hell's spawn was behind her, and she hated the wind which rushed at her face and roared and held her back as if it were some giant she could not see. But the big breaths of rough fresh air blown over the heather filled her lungs with something which was good for her whole thin body and whipped some red color into her cheeks and brightened her dull eyes when she did not know anything about it.

But after a few days spent almost entirely out of doors she wakened one morning knowing what it was to be hungry, and when she sat down to her breakfast she did not glance disdainfully at her porridge and push it away, but took up her spoon and began to eat it and went on eating it until her bowl was empty.

"Tha' got on well enough with that this mornin', didn't tha'?" said Martha.

"It tastes nice today," said Mary, feeling a little surprised herself.

"It's th' air of th' moor that's givin' thee stomach for tha' victuals," answered Martha. "It's lucky for thee that tha's got victuals as well as appetite. There's been twelve in our cottage as had th' stomach an' nothin' to put in it. You go on playin' you out o' doors every day an' you'll get some flesh on your bones an' you won't be so yeller."

"I don't play," said Mary. "I have nothing to play with."

"Nothin' to play with!" exclaimed Martha. "Our children plays with sticks and stones. They just runs about an' shouts an' looks at things. They whittle sticks to sharp points and practices slicing into the skulls o'th' Forsaken." Mary did not shout, but she looked at things. There was nothing else to do. She walked round and round the gardens and wandered about the paths in the park. Sometimes she thought she heard strange noises coming from outside the gardens, but when she went to look, she couldn't find anything. She often looked for Ben Weatherstaff, but though several times she saw him at work he was too busy to look at her or was too surly. Once when she was walking toward him he picked up his spade and turned away as if he did it on purpose.

One place she went to oftener than to any other. It was the long walk outside the gardens with the walls round them. There were bare flower-beds on either side of it and against the walls ivy grew thickly. There was one part of the wall where the creeping dark green leaves were more bushy than elsewhere. It seemed as if for a long time that part had been neglected. The rest of it had been clipped and made to look neat, but at this lower end of the walk it had not been trimmed at all.

A few days after she had seen Ben Weatherstaff, Mary decided she would avoid him as if he were a Tormented One. Her game allowed her to creep around corners and look for him before she entered a garden. And when she saw him she would run the other way and hide. She listened for his dragging footsteps. Running through the orchard she suddenly paused and was looking up at a long spray of ivy swinging in the wind when she saw a gleam of shiny red feathers and heard a brilliant chirp, and there, on the top of the wall, perched Ben Weatherstaff's robin watcher, tilting forward to look at her with his head on one side.

"Oh!" she cried out, "is it you—is it you?" And it did not seem at all queer to her that she spoke to him as if she were sure that he would understand and answer her.

He did answer. He twittered and chirped and hopped along the wall as if he were telling her all sorts of things. It seemed to Mistress Mary as if she understood him, too, though he was not speaking in words. It was as if he was joining in on her game and he said: "Stop running around attracting attention to yourself! Be still! Be quiet as a mouse! Follow me!"

Mary began to follow him, and as he hopped and took little flights along the wall she moved quickly, her feet light upon the ground. Poor little thin, sallow, ugly Mary—she actually looked almost strong for a moment.

"Is danger near? Are the Forsaken about?" she whispered playfully, pattering down the walk; and she chirped sharply and tried to whistle, which she did not know how to do in the least. But the robin seemed to be quite satisfied and chirped and whistled back at her. At last he spread his wings and made a darting flight to the top of a tree, where he perched and sang loudly. That reminded Mary of the first time she had seen him. He had been swinging on a tree-top then and she had been standing in the orchard. Now she was on the other side of the orchard and standing in the path outside a wall—much lower down—and there was the same tree inside.

"It's in the garden no one can go into," she said to herself. "It's the garden without a door. He lives in there. How I wish I could see what it is like!"

She ran up the walk to the green door she had entered the first morning. Then she ran down the path through the other door and then into the dead-end orchard, and when she stood and looked up there was the tree on the other side of the wall, and there was the robin just finishing his song and beginning to preen his feathers with his beak.

"It is the garden," she said. "I am sure it is."

She walked round and looked closely at that side of the orchard wall, but she only found what she had found before—that there was no door in it. Then she ran through the kitchen-gardens again and out into the walk outside the long ivy-covered wall, and she walked to the end of it and looked at it, but there was no door; and then she walked to the other end, looking again, but there was no door.

"It's very queer," she said. "Ben Weatherstaff said there was no door and there is no door. But there must have been one ten years ago, because Mr. Craven buried the key."

This gave her so much to think of that she began to be quite interested and feel that she was not sorry that she had come to Misselthwaite Manor. In India she had always felt hot and too languid to care much about anything. The fact was that the fresh wind from the moor had begun to blow the cobwebs out of her young brain and the thought of being attacked at any moment by the violent undead began to waken her up a little.

She stayed out of doors nearly all day, and when she sat down to her supper at night she felt hungry and drowsy and comfortable. She did not feel cross when Martha chattered away. She felt as if she rather liked to hear her, and at last she thought she would ask her a question. She asked it after she had finished her supper and had sat down on the hearth-rug before the fire.

"Why did Mr. Craven hate the garden?" she said.

She had made Martha stay with her and Martha had not objected at all. She was very young, and used to a crowded cottage full of brothers and sisters, and she found it dull in the great servants' hall downstairs where the footman and upper-housemaids made fun of her Yorkshire speech and looked upon her as a common little thing, and sat and whispered among themselves. Martha liked to talk, and the strange child who had lived in India, and had her entire family viciously devoured or left to become Accursed was novelty enough to attract her.

She sat down on the hearth herself without waiting to be asked.

"Art tha' thinkin' about that garden yet?" she said. "I knew tha' would. That was just the way with me when I first heard about it."

"Why did he hate it?" Mary persisted.

Martha tucked her feet under her and made herself quite comfortable.

"Listen to th' wind wutherin' round the house," she said. "You could bare stand up on the moor if you was out on it tonight."

Mary did not know what "wutherin'" meant until she listened, and then she understood. It must mean that hollow shuddering sort of roar which rushed round and round the house as if a thousand Forsaken no one could see were moaning and beating at the walls and windows to try to break in. But one knew they could not get in, and somehow it made one feel very safe and warm inside a room with a red coal fire.

"But why did he hate it so?" she asked, after she had listened. She intended to know if Martha did.

Then Martha gave up her store of knowledge.

"Mind," she said, "Mrs. Medlock said it's not to be talked about. There's lots o' things in this place that's not to be talked over. That's Mr. Craven's orders. His troubles are none servants' business, he says. But for th' garden he wouldn't be like he is. It was Mrs. Craven's garden that she had made when first they were married an' she just loved it, an' they used to 'tend the flowers themselves. An' none o' th' gardeners was ever let to go in. Him an' her used to go in an' shut th' door an' stay there hours an' hours, readin' and talkin'. There was an old tree with a branch bent like a seat on it. An' she made roses grow over it an' she used to sit there. But one day when she was sittin' there th' Scourge came without any warnin'. They must 'ave come through the unlocked door hearing them inside. Two of the Accursed came in and wen' straight for her. She was jus' a bit of a girl an' the murderous cannibals ripped her flesh right ta th' bone. Mr. Craven had not a weapon with him and he kill'd it wit' his cane! She was still alive an' he carried 'er back to th' house."

Martha paused then and thought as if she wasn't sure how to continue the story then she said, "After about a day she did die. But she weren' dead, Miss, she turned into the demon's slave. He couldn't bring himself to kill her though, so he took her to the garden all chained up and left her there moaning all hours in her hunger and torment. Finally, after he couldn' take seeing her like it no more, he opened the door, wen' in hiself an' killed her. After that, he locked the door to the garden and hid the key. Th' doctors thought he'd go out o' his mind an' die, too. That's why he hates it. No one's never gone in since, an' he won't let anyone talk about it."

Mary did not ask any more questions. She looked at the red fire and listened to the wind "wutherin'." It seemed to be "wutherin'" louder than ever. At that moment a very good thing was happening to her. Four good things had happened to her, in fact, since she came to Misselthwaite Manor. She had felt as if she had understood a robin and that he had understood her; she had run in the wind until her blood had grown warm; she had been healthily hungry for the first time in her life; and she had found out what it was to be sorry for someone. She was beginning to transform from being near like a Forsaken One into a strong girl.

But as she was listening to the wind she began to listen to something else. She did not know what it was, because at first she could scarcely distinguish it from the wind itself. It was a curious sound—it seemed almost as if a child were crying somewhere. Sometimes the wind sounded rather like a child crying, but presently Mistress Mary felt quite sure this sound was inside the house, not outside it. It was far away, but it was inside. She turned round and looked at Martha.

"Do you hear any one crying?" she said.

Martha suddenly looked confused.

"No," she answered. "It's th' wind. Sometimes it sounds like as if someone was lost on th' moor an' wailin'. It's got all sorts o' sounds."

"But listen," said Mary. "It's in the house—down one of those long corridors."

And at that very moment a door must have been opened somewhere downstairs; for a great rushing draft blew along the passage and the door of the room they sat in was blown open with a crash, and as they both jumped to their feet the light was blown out and the moaning sound was swept down the far corridor so that it was to be heard more plainly than ever.

"There!" said Mary. "I told you so! It is some one crying—it sounds like the Accursed!"

Martha ran and shut the door and turned the key, but before she did it they both heard the sound of a door in some far passage shutting with a bang, and then everything was quiet, for even the wind ceased "wutherin'" for a few moments.

Mary stared up at Martha who stood in front of the door holding a knife in her hand. She looked frightened but her hands did not shake.

"Is there something out there?" Mary asked as she slowly stood up.

"It was th' wind," said Martha stubbornly putting away her knife in the folds of her apron. "An' if it wasn't, it was little Betty Butterworth, th' scullery-maid. She's had th' toothache all day."

But something troubled and awkward in her manner made Mistress Mary stare very hard at her. She did not believe she was speaking the truth.

Chapter 6: Of Accursed Mice and Men

The next day the rain poured down in torrents again, and when Mary looked out of her window the moor was almost hidden by gray mist and cloud. There could be no going out today.

"What do you do in your cottage when it rains like this?" she asked Martha.

"Try to keep from under each other's feet mostly," Martha answered. "Eh! there does seem a lot of us then. Mother's a good-tempered woman but she gets fair moithered. The biggest ones goes out in th' cow-shed and practices slayin' the'soulless Forsaken there. Dickon he doesn't mind th' wet. He goes out just th' same as if th' sun was shinin'. He says the Accursed come out more in the rain and they need to be watched. The rain softens the ground and those that was buried infected might find it easier to claw their way up out of the hard cold ground and he says he sees things on rainy days as doesn't show when it's fair weather. He once found a little fox cub half dead in its hole and he brought it home in th' bosom of his shirt to keep it warm. Its mother had been killed nearby clearly by a desperate Accursed, an' th' rest o' th' litter was dead. He's got it at home now. He found a half-drowned young crow another time an' he brought it home, too, an' tamed it. It's named Soot because it's so black, an' it hops an' flies about with him everywhere. That dark bird seems to be a herald of death. It always knows if the Accursed are near an' even if a person is infected with it a'fore they turn."

The time had come when Mary had forgotten to resent Martha's familiar talk. She had even begun to find it interesting and to be sorry when she stopped or went away. The stories she had been told by her Ayah when she lived in India had been quite unlike those Martha had to tell about the moorland cottage which held fourteen people who lived in four little rooms, trained to fight the Tormented Ones, and never had quite enough to eat. The children seemed to battle and amuse themselves like a pack of rough ravenous wolves. Mary sometimes wished she was strong and could fight, but she couldn't and no one would teach her. Mary was most attracted by the mother and Dickon. When Martha told stories of what "mother" said or did they always sounded comfortable and brave.

"If I had a raven or a fox cub I could play with it, or a weapon to learn to fight with," said Mary. "But I have nothing."

Martha looked perplexed.

"Has tha' never learned to fight or use weapons in India?"

"No," answered Mary.

"Can tha' knit or sew?" she asked.

"No."

"Can tha' read?"

"Yes."

"Then why doesn't tha' read somethin' about battle? Tha'st old enough to be learnin' about defendin' yerself a good bit now. Once you've got in yer head about fightin' the cold soulless ones, perhaps you can begin practicin'."

"I haven't any books like that," said Mary. "And those I had were left in India."

"That's a pity," said Martha. "If Mrs. Medlock'd let thee go into th' library, there's thousands o' books there."

Mary did not ask where the library was, because she was suddenly inspired by a new idea. She made up her mind to learn to fight and find some weapons. She thought that somewhere in the hundred closed rooms there must be a knife or a staff that no one would miss. She was not troubled about Mrs. Medlock. Mrs. Medlock seemed always to be in her comfortable housekeeper's sitting-room downstairs. In this queer place one scarcely ever saw any one at all. In fact, there was no one to see but the servants, and when their master was away they lived a luxurious life below stairs, where there was a huge kitchen hung about with shining brass and pewter, and a large servants' hall where there were four or five abundant meals eaten every day, and where a great deal of lively romping and practice fighting went on when Mrs. Medlock was out of the way.

Mary's meals were served regularly, and Martha waited on her, but no one troubled themselves about her in the least. Mrs. Medlock came and looked at her every day or two, but no one inquired what she did or told her what to do. She supposed that perhaps this was the English way of treating children. In India she had always been attended by her Ayah, who had followed her about and waited on her, hand and foot. She had often been tired of her company. Now she was followed by nobody and was learning to dress herself because Martha looked as though she thought she was silly and stupid when she wanted to have things handed to her and put on.

"Hasn't tha' got good sense?" she said once, when Mary had stood waiting for her to put on her gloves for her. "Our Susan Ann is twice as sharp as thee an' she's only four year' old. Sometimes tha' looks fair soft in th' head."

Mary had worn her contrary scowl for an hour after that, but it made her think several entirely new things.

She stood at the window for about ten minutes this morning after Martha had swept up the hearth for the last time and gone downstairs. She was thinking over the new idea which had come to her when she heard of the library. She did not care very much about the library itself, because she had read very few books; but to hear of it brought back to her mind the hundred rooms with closed doors. She wondered if they were all really locked and what she would find if she could get into any of them. Were there a hundred really? Did they hide anything interesting? Why shouldn't she go and see how many doors she could count? It would be something to do on this morning when she could not go out. She had never been taught to ask permission to do things, and she knew nothing at all about authority, so she would not have thought it necessary to ask Mrs. Medlock if she might walk about the house, even if she had seen her.

She opened the door of the room and went into the corridor, and then she began her wanderings. It was a long corridor and it branched into other corridors and it led her up short flights of steps which mounted to others again. There were doors and doors, and there were pictures on the walls. Sometimes they were pictures of dark, curious landscapes, but oftenest they were portraits of men and women in queer, grand costumes made of satin and velvet. She found herself in one long gallery whose walls were covered with these portraits. She had never thought there could be so many in any house. She walked slowly down this place and stared at the faces which also seemed to stare at her. She felt as if they were wondering what a little girl from India was doing in their house. Some were pictures of children—little girls in thick satin frocks which reached to their feet and stood out about them, and boys with puffed sleeves and lace collars and long hair, or with big ruffs around their necks. She always stopped to look at the children, and wonder what their names were, and where they had gone, and why they wore such odd clothes. One particular portrait drew Mary's attention because it had a long tear across it, as if someone had taken a knife to it. There was a stiff, plain little girl rather like herself. She wore a green brocade dress and held a green parrot on her finger. Her eyes had a sharp, curious look.

"Where do you live now?" said Mary aloud to herself. "I wish you were here."

Surely no other little girl ever spent such a queer morning. It seemed as if there was no one in all the huge rambling house but her own small self, wandering about upstairs and down, through narrow passages and wide ones, where it seemed to her that no one but herself had ever walked. Since so many rooms had been built, people must have lived in them, but it all seemed so empty that she could not quite believe it true. What might have happened to all the people here?

It was not until she climbed to the second floor that she thought of turning the handle of a door. All the doors were shut, as Mrs. Medlock had said they were, but at last she put her hand on the handle of one of them and turned it. She was almost frightened for a moment when she felt that it turned without difficulty and that when she pushed upon the door itself it slowly and heavily opened. It was a massive door and opened into a big bedroom. There were embroidered hangings on the wall, and inlaid furniture such as she had seen in India stood about the room. A broad window with leaded panes looked out upon the moor; and over the mantel was another portrait of the stiff, plain little girl who seemed to stare at her more curiously than ever. Even more curious was that this portrait too was damaged, as if someone had taken a hammer to the frame.

"Perhaps she slept here once," said Mary. "She stares at me so that she makes me feel queer."

After that she opened more and more doors. She saw so many rooms that she became quite tired and began to think that there must be a hundred, though she had not counted them. Many of the rooms seemed to have been left untouched for years. Several rooms had over turned furniture and unmade beds. In all of them there were old pictures or old tapestries with strange scenes worked on them. There were curious pieces of furniture and curious ornaments in nearly all of them. But no rooms for children and nothing she could play with.

In one room, which looked like a lady's sitting-room, the hangings were all embroidered velvet, and in a cabinet were about a hundred little elephants made of ivory. They were of different sizes, and some had their mahouts or palanquins on their backs. Some were much bigger than the others and some were so tiny that they seemed only babies. Mary had seen carved ivory in India and she knew all about elephants. She opened the door of the cabinet and stood on a footstool and played with these for quite a long time. When she got tired she set the elephants in order except for one she planned to take back to her room and hide under her pillow.

In all her wanderings through the long corridors and the empty rooms, she had seen nothing alive; but in this room she saw something. Just after she had closed the cabinet door she heard a tiny rustling sound. It made her jump and look around at the sofa by the fireplace, from which it seemed to come. In the corner of the sofa there was a cushion, and in the velvet which covered it there was a hole, and out of the hole peeped a tiny head with a pair of tightened black eyes in it.

Mary crept softly across the room to look. The dark eyes belonged to a little gray mouse, and the mouse had eaten a hole into the cushion and made a comfortable nest there. Six dead baby mice were half eaten near her. They had all had their brains devoured leaving tiny cavities behind.

"I wonder how long this little mouse has been Accursed!" said Mary. "It can't have been for very long because mice do not live more than a few years! How did the mouse become infected and did it find these babies unwatched?" Mary wondered if in fact it was the mother consuming her own children than dismissed the thought.

That would mean that the mouse became Accursed here in the manor and not very long ago. She peered at the mouse a moment longer and as she turned to leave the little thing leapt from the velvet cushion and opened its jaws wide towards Mary's ankle. Mary moved out of the way just in time and threw the ivory elephant at the little mouse, hitting it hard in the face causing black globs to stain the carpet.

The mouse lay still and Mary slowly approached to see if she had killed it. Leaning in close, Mary wondered if the Accursed mouse only ate their own kind or would they feast on anything living?

The mouse awoke and without so much as a twitch moved for Mary's foot so fast that Mary jerked in surprise and stomped down on the mouse leaving a black stain of gray fur beneath her shoe. Mary wiped her shoe the best she could on the carpet and covered the crushed mouse with the velvet cushion. Mary carefully closed the door behind her hoping no one would go in and discover the mess she had made.

She had wandered about long enough to feel too tired to wander any farther, and she turned back. Two or three times she lost her way by turning down the wrong corridor and was obliged to ramble up and down until she found the right one; but at last she reached her own floor again, though she was some distance from her own room and did not know exactly where she was.

"I believe I have taken a wrong turning again," she said, standing still at what seemed the end of a short passage with a tapestry on the wall. "I don't know which way to go. How still everything is!"

It was while she was standing here and just after she had said this that the stillness was broken by a sound. It was another cry, but not quite like the one she had heard last night; it was only a short one, a fretful childish whine muffled by passing through walls.

"It's nearer than it was," said Mary, her heart beating rather faster. "And it is crying."

She put her hand accidentally upon the tapestry near her, and then sprang back, feeling quite startled. The tapestry was the covering of a door which fell open and showed her that there was another part of the corridor behind it, and a man was stumbling down the hall clawing at a chain that was around its neck. Mary fell backwards in terror. It was one of the undead, a Tormented One inside the manor! It saw her and a gurgling moan came up from its throat. Its wrists were locked together in an iron bar weighing down its hands as it reached out for Mary. A servant Mary had never seen was coming up from behind the creature holding it away with a long bar attached to its neck iron. Mrs. Medlock was right behind him with her bunch of keys in her hand and a very cross look on her face. She grew very angry at the sight of Mary and motioned for the man to take the Accursed creature back.

"What are you doing here?" she said, and she took Mary fiercely by the arm and pulled her away. "What did I tell you?"

"I turned round the wrong corner," explained Mary. "I didn't know which way to go and I heard someone crying. There was an Accursed in the corridor!" She quite hated Mrs. Medlock at the moment, but she hated her more the next.

"You didn't hear or see anything of the sort," said the housekeeper. "You come along back to your own nursery or I'll box your ears."

And she took her by the arm and half pushed, half pulled her up one passage and down another until she pushed her in at the door of her own room.

"Now," she said, "you stay where you're told to stay or you'll find yourself locked up. The master had better get you a governess, same as he said he would. You're one that needs someone to look sharp after you. I've got enough to do."

She went out of the room and slammed the door after her, and Mary went and sat on the hearth-rug, pale with rage. She did not cry, but ground her teeth.

"There was some one crying and there *was* an Accursed in the corridor—there was—there was!" she said to herself.

She had heard it twice now, and sometime she would find out. She had found out a great deal this morning. She felt as if she had been on a long journey, and at any rate she had had something to amuse her all the time, and she had played with the ivory elephants and had slain the Accursed gray mouse who had devoured its babies in their nest in the velvet cushion. She had still more to discover. She wondered why Medlock would keep an Accursed on a chain and who could be making the crying sounds down that hidden corridor. She wondered if she would ever leave this cold and horrid manor.

Chapter 7: The Key to the Garden

Two days after this, when Mary opened her eyes she sat upright in bed immediately, and called to Martha.

"Look at the moor! Look at the moor!"

The rainstorm had ended and the gray mist and clouds had been swept away in the night by the wind. The wind itself had ceased and a brilliant, deep blue sky arched high over the moorland. Never, never had Mary dreamed of a sky so blue. In India skies were hot and blazing; this was of a deep cool blue which almost seemed to sparkle like the waters of some lovely bottomless lake, and here and there, high, high in the arched blueness floated small clouds of snow-white fleece. She imagined becoming a bird and soaring far from Misselthwaite, over the far-reaching world of the moor that itself looked softly blue instead of gloomy purple-black or awful dreary gray. Mary gasped as she looked down from the sky over the bare expanse of the land.

"Aye," said Martha with a cheerful grin. "Th' storm's over for a bit. It does like this at this time o' th' year. It goes off in a night like it was pretendin' it had never been here an' never meant to come again. That's because th' springtime's on its way. It's a long way off yet, but it's comin'."

"I don't care about that!" Mary exclaimed. "Look, there's someone out there!"

"Eh! no!" said Martha, sitting up on her heels among her black lead brushes. "Nowt o' th' soart!"

"What does that mean?" asked Mary seriously. In India the natives spoke different dialects which only a few people understood, so she was not surprised when Martha used words she did not know.

Martha laughed as she had done the first morning. "There now," she said. "I've talked broad Yorkshire again like Mrs. Medlock said I mustn't. 'Nowt o' th' soart' means 'nothin'-of-the-sort,' but it takes so long to say it. I mean' t' say, there's no one ever out there this close to the Manor."

Mary looked out the window again. In the far distance, she could see someone, a man, walking slowly. He appeared to stumble and disappeared for a moment but was back up and continued walking. Then another man came into view, arms swinging limply by his sides.

Mary said, "I'm telling you someone is out there! The sky is so clear now and I can see a far ways off!"

"Yorkshire's th' sunniest place on earth when it is sunny. I told thee tha'd like th' moor after a bit. Just you wait till you see th' gold-colored gorse blossoms an' th' blossoms o' th' broom, an' th' heather flowerin', all purple bells, an' hundreds o' butterflies flutterin' an' bees hummin' an' skylarks soarin' up an' singin'. You'll want to get out on it as sunrise an' live out on it all day like Dickon does."

Mary couldn't believe Martha was completely ignoring what she was saying. Just like when Mary heard the boy crying, she pretended it wasn't there.

"Is it safe out there? If your brother feels safe out on the moor, could I ever get out there?" asked Mary, thinking about how she might ever leave. The men were beyond her sight now and the moor was so big, like a vast sea, she felt caged on an island of stone.

"I don't know," answered Martha. "Th' wall is very high surroundin' Misselthwaite and it can be dangerous out there if'n yer not used to escapin' the Forsaken. Tha's never used tha' legs since tha' was born, it seems to me. Tha' couldn't walk five mile. It's five mile to our cottage."

"I should like to see your cottage. I think I could get there."

Martha stared at her a moment curiously before she took up her polishing brush and began to rub the grate again. She was thinking that the small plain face did not look quite as inept at this moment as it had done the first morning she saw it. After all, this little thing had survived the Scourge invasion of the West Indian Safe Zone.

"I'll ask my mother about it," she said. "She's one o' them that nearly always sees a way to do things. It's my day out today an' I'm goin' home. Eh! I am glad. Mrs. Medlock thinks a lot o' mother. Perhaps she could talk to her."

"I like your mother," said Mary.

"I should think tha' did," agreed Martha, polishing away.

"I've never seen her," said Mary.

"No, tha' hasn't," replied Martha. She sat up on her heels again and rubbed the end of her nose with the back of her hand as if puzzled for a moment, but she ended quite positively.

"Well, she's that sensible an' hard workin' an' goodnatured an' can take down the Rotters like no other so that no one could help likin' her whether they'd seen her or not. She trained up all us children to defen' ourselves an' Dickon is the best of us. When I'm goin' home to her on my day out I just jump for joy when I'm crossin' the moor."

"I like Dickon," added Mary. "And I've never seen him."

"Well," said Martha stoutly, "I've told thee that th' very birds likes him an' th' rabbits an' wild sheep an' ponies, an' th' foxes themselves. I wonder," staring at her reflectively, "what Dickon would think of thee?"

"He wouldn't like me," said Mary in her stiff, cold little way. "No one does."

Martha looked reflective again. "How does tha' like thysel'?" she inquired, really quite as if she were curious to know.

Mary hesitated a moment and thought it over. "Not at all—really," she answered. "But I never thought of that before."

Martha grinned a little as if at some homely recollection.

"Mother said that to me once," she said. "I was in a bad temper an' talkin' ill of folk who just stood still in terror and did nothin' when the Accursed was upon them, an' she turns round on me an' says: 'Tha' young vixen, tha'! There tha' stands sayin' tha' doesn't like this one an' tha' doesn't like that one. How does tha' like thysel'?' It made me laugh an' it brought me to my senses in a minute."

She went away in high spirits as soon as she had given Mary her breakfast. She was going to walk five miles alone across the moor to the cottage, and she was going to help her mother with the washing and do the week's baking and enjoy herself thoroughly.

Mary felt lonelier than ever when she knew Martha was no longer in the house. She went out into the garden as quickly as possible, and the first thing she did was to run round and round the fountain flower garden ten times. She pretended she was being chased over the moor by the undead as she ran to reach Martha's cottage and when she had finished she felt in better spirits. The sunshine made the whole place look different. The high, deep, blue sky arched over Misselthwaite as well as over the moor, and she kept lifting her face and looking up into it, trying to imagine what it would be like to lie down on one of the little snow-white clouds and float about. She went into the first kitchen-garden and found Ben Weatherstaff working there with two other gardeners. The change in the weather seemed to have done him good. He spoke to her of his own accord. "Springtime's comin,'" he said. "You know what that means?"

Mary shook her head.

It means the soil is warming and softening, it means the moor is clearing, it means the winds are flowing sending scents farther across the land. But it also means the Accursed can start crossing the moor.

"I thought they couldn't cross the moor. Everyone said they don't like it, that we were safe." Mary's expression changed to look very contrary.

"That were when the cold biting wind and frozen ground and deep mist kept 'um away. It was in the Spring that they came ten year ago, it was in the Spring that..." Ben Weatherstaff suddenly stopped seeing the look on Mary's face. "But don' you worry 'bout any of tha'. Here in Misselthwaite you are perfectly safe. The Spring brings th' good rich earth," he answered, digging away. "It's in a good humor makin' ready to grow things. It's glad when plantin' time comes. It's dull in th' winter when it's got nowt to do. In th' gardens out there things will be stirrin' down below in th' dark... flowers I mean o'course. Th' sun's warmin' 'em. You'll see bits o' green spikes stickin' out o' th' black earth after a bit."

"What will they be?" asked Mary trying to not think about hoards of undead marching across the moor towards them.

"Crocuses an' snowdrops an' daffydowndillys. Has tha' never seen them?"

"No. Everything is hot, and wet, and green after the rains in India," said Mary. "And I think things grow up in a night."

"These won't grow up in a night," said Weatherstaff. "Tha'll have to wait for 'em. They'll poke up a bit higher here, an' push out a spike more there, an' uncurl a leaf this day an' another that. You watch 'em."

"I am going to," answered Mary. And she thought she would also watch for signs of the Forsaken. After all, she has seen them up close and she knows what someone looks like before they turn.

Very soon she heard the soft rustling flight of wings and she knew at once that the robin had come again. He was very pert and lively, and hopped about so close to her feet, and put his head on one side and looked at her so slyly that she asked Ben Weatherstaff a question.

"Do you think he remembers me?" she said.

"Remembers thee!" said Weatherstaff indignantly. "He knows every cabbage stump in th' gardens, let alone th' people. He's never seen a little wench here before, an' he's bent on findin' out all about thee. Tha's no need to try to hide anything from him."

"Are things stirring down below in the dark in that garden where he lives?" Mary inquired.

"What? Nothings buried there...What garden?" grunted Weatherstaff, becoming surly again.

"The one where the old rose-trees are." She could not help asking, because she wanted so much to know. "Are all the flowers dead, or do some of them come again in the summer? And what's buried?"

"Ask him," said Ben Weatherstaff, hunching his shoulders toward the robin. "He's the only one as knows. No one else has seen inside it for ten year'."

Ten years was a long time, Mary thought. She had been born ten years ago. She walked away, slowly thinking. She had begun to like the garden just as she had begun to like the robin and Dickon and Martha's mother. She liked the idea of a place that no one could get into. A place she could hide and lock up and be safe all the time. It was many things to like when one wasn't used to liking things at all. She went to her walk outside the long, ivy-covered wall over which she could see the tree-tops; and the second time she walked up and down the most dangerous and exciting thing happened to her, and it was all through Ben Weatherstaff's robin.

She heard a chirp and a twitter, and when she looked at the bare flower-bed at her left side there he was hopping about and pecking at the ground looking extremely agitated. Mary moved closer to see what could be causing the little bird so much stress. Just then a large mouse ran out from a hole in the flower-bed to Mary's foot and bit down into her shoe! Mary jumped and stomped and kicked until the mouse flung across the garden and into a wall. Mary did not make the same mistake twice. She picked up a shovel that the gardener had left behind and ran over to vile creature that vomited black blood onto the soil and smashed it until nothing was left of the mouse but a gruesome mixture of gooey black fur. She buried it quickly and trembled a little.

"You tried to warn me!" she cried to the robin. "You knew the mouse was Accursed and tried to tell me! You are prettier than anything else in the world!"

She chirped, and talked, and coaxed and he hopped, and flirted his tail and clipped his beak. It was as if he were talking. Mary brought the shovel to where the bird circled and dug out the hole where the mouse had come from. She unearthed several dead half eaten mice and she wondered how this little mouse became Accursed. The robin watched and his feathers were like satin and he puffed his tiny red breast out and was so fine and so grand and so pretty that it was really as if he were showing her how important and like a human person a robin could be. Bloody Mary forgot that she had ever been contrary in her life when he allowed her to draw closer and closer to him, and bend down and talk and try to make something like robin sounds.

Wherever the robin hopped Mary would dig it up. She unearthed several dens of dead mice and finally came across another undead one. She smashed it and chopped it up with the shovel and the robin screeched in excitement.

He flew onto the handle of the shovel as Mary held it. Oh! To think that he should actually let her come as near to him as that! He knew nothing in the world would make her put out her hand toward him or startle him in the least tiniest way. He must have been very happy she killed that murderous mouse and dug up its dens.

Mary inspected the dug up soil for more mice and as she looked she saw something almost buried in the newly-turned soil. It was something like a ring of rusty iron or brass and when the robin flew up into a tree nearby she put out her hand and picked the ring up. It was more than a ring, however; it was an old key which looked as if it had been buried a long time.

Mary stood up and looked at it with an almost frightened face as it hung from her finger.

"Perhaps it has been buried for ten years," she said in a whisper. "Perhaps it is the key to the garden!"

Chapter 8: The Robin Who Showed the Way

She looked at the key quite a long time. She turned it over and over, and thought about it. She was not a child who had been trained to ask permission or consult her elders about things. All she thought about the key was that if it was the key to the closed garden, and she could find out where the door was, she could perhaps open it and see what was inside the walls, and what had happened to the old rose-trees. It was because it had been shut up so long that she wanted to see it. It seemed as if it must be different from other places and that something strange must have happened to it during ten years. Besides that, if she liked it she could go into it every day and shut the door behind her, and play all that she wanted because nobody would ever know where she was, but would think the door was still locked and the key buried in the earth. She could also hide there if ever the Scourge came again and the thought of that pleased her very much.

Living as it were, all by herself in a house with a hundred mysteriously closed rooms and having nothing whatever to do to amuse herself, had set her inactive brain to working and was actually awakening her imagination. There is no doubt that the fresh, strong, pure air from the moor had a great deal to do with it. Just as it had given her an appetite, and killing the undead mice had stirred her blood, so the same things had stirred her mind. In India she had always been too hot and languid and weak to care much about anything, but in this place she was beginning to care and to want to do new things. Already she felt less "contrary," though she did not know why.

She put the key in her pocket and walked up and down her walk. No one but herself ever seemed to come there, so she could walk slowly and look at the wall, or, rather, at the ivy growing on it. The ivy was the baffling thing. Howsoever carefully she looked she could see nothing but thickly growing, glossy, dark green leaves. She was very much disappointed. Something of her contrariness came back to her as she paced the walk and looked over it at the tree-tops inside. It seemed so silly, she said to herself, to be near it and not be able to get in. She placed the key in her pocket when she went back to the house, and she made up her mind that she would always carry it with her when she went out, so that if she ever should find the hidden door she would be ready.

Mrs. Medlock had allowed Martha to sleep all night at the cottage, but she was back at her work in the morning with cheeks redder than ever and in the best of spirits.

"I got up at four o'clock," she said. "Eh! It was pretty on th' moor with th' birds gettin' up an' th' rabbits scamperin' about an' th' sun risin'."

"And no dangers?" Mary asked. "You didn't see... anything on your walk?"

"I didn't walk all th' way. A man gave me a ride in his cart an' I did enjoy myself."

She was full of stories of the delights of her day out. Her mother had been glad to see her and they had got the baking and washing all out of the way. She had even made each of the children a doughcake with a bit of brown sugar in it.

"I had 'em all pipin' hot when they came in from playin' on th' moor. An' th' cottage all smelt o' nice, clean hot bakin' an' there was a good fire, an' they just shouted for joy. Our Dickon he said our cottage was good enough for a king."

In the evening they had all sat round the fire, and Martha and her mother had sewed patches on torn clothes and mended stockings and Martha had told them about the little girl who had come from India and who had been waited on all her life by what Martha called "blacks" until she didn't know how to put on her own stockings.

"Eh! They did like to hear about you," said Martha. "They wanted to know all about th' Untainted Camps an' about th' ship you came in. I couldn't tell 'em enough."

Mary reflected a little.

"I'll tell you a great deal more before your next day out," she said, "so that you will have more to talk about. I dare say they would like to hear about riding on elephants and camels, and about the officers going to hunt the Aghori."

"My word!" cried delighted Martha. "It would set 'em clean off their heads. Would tha' really do that, Miss? It would be same as a wild beast show like we heard they had in York once."

"India is quite different from Yorkshire," Mary said slowly, as she thought the matter over. "I never thought of that. Did Dickon and your mother like to hear you talk about me?"

"Why, our Dickon's eyes nearly started out o' his head, they got that round," answered Martha. "But mother, she was put out about your seemin' to be all by yourself like. She said, 'Hasn't Mr. Craven got no governess for her, nor no nurse?' and I said, 'No, he hasn't, though Mrs. Medlock says he will when he thinks of it, but she says he mayn't think of it for two or three years.'"

"I don't want a governess," said Mary sharply.

"But mother says you ought to be learnin' your book by this time an' you ought to have a woman to look after you, an' she says: 'Now, Martha, you just think how you'd feel yourself, in a big place like that, wanderin' about all alone, an' no mother. You do your best to cheer her up,' she says, an' I said I would."

Mary gave her a long, steady look. "You do cheer me up," she said. "I like to hear you talk."

Presently Martha went out of the room and came back with something held in her hands under her apron.

"What does tha' think," she said, with a cheerful grin. "I've brought thee a present."

"A present!" exclaimed Mistress Mary. How could a cottage full of fourteen hungry people give anyone a present!

"A man was drivin' across the moor peddlin'," Martha explained. "An' he stopped his cart at our door. He had pots an' pans an' odds an' ends, but mother had no money to buy anythin'. Just as he was goin' away our 'Lizabeth Ellen called out, 'Mother, he's got crooked knives with real oak handles and leather sheaths!' An' mother she calls out quite sudden, 'Here, stop, mister! How much are they?' An' he says 'Tuppence', an' mother she began fumblin' in her pocket an' she says to me, 'Martha, tha's brought me thy wages like a good lass, an' I've got four places to put every penny, but I'm just goin' to take tuppence out of it to buy that child some'in', an' she bought one an' here it is."

She brought it out from under her apron and exhibited it quite proudly. It was a small sickled blade no longer than the key Mary found with an oak handle and a strong slender rope attached to it, but Mary Lennox had never seen a knife like this before. She gazed at it with a mystified expression.

"What is it for?" she asked curiously.

"For!" cried out Martha. "Does tha' mean that they've not got throwing blades in India, for all they've got elephants and tigers and camels! No wonder most of the country's Accursed. This is what it's for; just watch me."

And she ran into the middle of the room and, taking the rope in her left hand, began to twirl the rope, first on one side, then the other, then over her head. And she began to walk around the room while the blade swung round and round in the air while Mary turned in her chair to stare at her, and the queer faces in the old portraits seemed to stare at her, too, and wonder what on earth this common little cottager had the impudence to be doing under their very noses. But Martha did not even see them. The interest and curiosity in Mistress Mary's face delighted her, and she went on spinning the blade until she spotted a dark patch on the curtains. She swung the blade forward releasing the rope slack and the blade hooked into the dark patch on the curtain with perfect accuracy.

"I could hit a target smaller than that," she said when she stopped. "I've hooked targets as far as twenty feet when I was twelve, but I wasn't as fat then as I am now, an' I was in practice."

Mary got up from her chair beginning to feel excited herself.

"It looks useful," she said. "Your mother is a kind woman. Do you think I could ever hook things like that?"

"You just try it," urged Martha, handing her the knife. "You can't hook anythin' at first, but if you practice you'll 'come more accurate. That's what mother said. She says, 'Nothin' will do her more good than learnin' a weapon. It's th' sensiblest thing a child can have. Let her play out in th' fresh air runnin' and spinnin' the blade an' it'll stretch her legs an' arms an' give her some strength in 'em.'"

It was plain that there was not a great deal of strength in Mistress Mary's arms and legs when she first began to spin the blade. She was not very clever at it, but she liked it so much that she did not want to stop.

"Put on tha' things and run an' try it o' doors," said Martha. "Mother said I must tell you to keep out o' doors as much as you could, even when it rains a bit, so as tha' wrap up warm. Once you get the hookin' right, I'll show ya how it can be used agains' the damned Forsaken."

Mary put on her coat and hat and took her rope and blade over her arm. She opened the door to go out, and then suddenly thought of something and turned back rather slowly.

"Martha," she said, "they were your wages. It was your two-pence really. Thank you." She said it stiffly because she was not used to thanking people or noticing that they did things for her. "Thank you," she said, and held out her hand because she did not know what else to do.

Martha gave her hand a clumsy little shake, as if she was not accustomed to this sort of thing either. Then she laughed.

"Eh! th' art a queer, old-womanish thing," she said. "If tha'd been our 'Lizabeth Ellen tha'd have given me a kiss."

Mary looked stiffer than ever.

"Do you want me to kiss you?"

Martha laughed again. "Nay, not me," she answered. "If tha' was different, p'raps tha'd want to thysel'. But tha' isn't. Run off outside an' play with thy knife."

Mistress Mary felt a little awkward as she went out of the room. Yorkshire people seemed strange, and Martha was always rather a puzzle to her. At first she had disliked her very much, but now she did not. The spinning blade was a wonderful thing. She spun and ran, and aimed and threw, until her cheeks were quite red, and she was more interested than she had ever been since she was born. The sun was shining and a little wind was blowing—not a rough wind, but one which came in delightful little gusts and brought a fresh scent of newly turned earth with it. She chucked the blade at the garden fountain hitting the cherub statue in face, knocking off its little nose.

Up one walk and down another she whipped the blade round and tried to hit certain things that caught her eye. She ran at last into the kitchen-garden and saw Ben Weatherstaff digging and talking to his robin, which was hopping about him. She came down the walk toward him and he lifted his head and looked at her with a curious expression. She had wondered if he would notice her. She wanted him to see her practice with her blade.

"Well!" he exclaimed. "Upon my word. P'raps tha' art a fighter, after all, an' p'raps tha's got warrior's blood in thy veins instead of sour buttermilk. Tha's run red into thy cheeks as sure as my name's Ben Weatherstaff. I wouldn't have believed tha' could do it."

"I never had a weapon before," Mary said. "I'm just beginning."

"Tha' keep on," said Ben. "Tha' shapes well enough at it for a young 'un that's lived with heathen. Just see how he's watchin' thee," jerking his head toward the robin. "He followed after thee yesterday. He'll be at it again today. He'll be bound to find out what th' throwing-blade is. He's never seen one. Eh!" shaking his head at the bird, "tha' curiosity will be th' death of thee sometime if tha' doesn't look sharp."

Mary practiced hooking things round all the gardens and round the orchard, resting every few minutes. At length she went to her own special walk and made up her mind to try if she could hook some of leaves of the ivy. She began slowly, but before long she had hooked and pulled many winding vines. She whipped the blade around with all her strength and was about to release it when there, lo and behold, was the robin in front of her swaying on a long branch of ivy. He had followed her and he greeted her with a chirp. As Mary approached him she felt something heavy in her pocket strike against her, and when she saw the robin she laughed.

"You showed me where the key was yesterday," she said. "You ought to show me the door today; but I don't believe you know!"

The robin flew from his swinging spray of ivy on to the top of the wall and he opened his beak and sang a loud, lovely trill, merely to show off. Nothing in the world is quite as adorably lovely as a robin when he shows off—and they are nearly always doing it.

Mary Lennox had heard a great deal about Magic in her Ayah's stories, white magic and black magic, and she always said that what happened almost at that moment was White Magic.

One of the nice little gusts of wind rushed down the walk, and it was a stronger one than the rest. It was strong enough to wave the branches of the trees, and it was more than strong enough to sway the trailing sprays of untrimmed ivy hanging from the wall. Mary had stepped close to the robin, and suddenly the gust of wind swung aside some loose ivy trails, and more suddenly still she jumped toward it and caught it in her hand. This she did because she had seen something under it—a round knob which had been covered by the leaves hanging over it. It was the knob of a door.

She put her hands under the leaves and began to pull and push them aside. Thick as the ivy hung, it nearly all was a loose and swinging curtain, though some had crept over wood and iron. Mary's heart began to thump and her hands to shake a little in her delight and excitement. The robin kept singing and twittering away and tilting his head on one side, as if he were as excited as she was. What was this under her hands which was square and made of iron and which her fingers found a hole in?

It was the lock of the door which had been closed ten years and she put her hand in her pocket, drew out the key and found it fitted the keyhole. She put the key in and turned it. It took two hands to do it, but it did turn.

And then she took a long breath and looked behind her up the long walk to see if any one was coming. No one was coming. No one ever did come, it seemed, and she took another long breath, because she could not help it, and she held back the swinging curtain of ivy and pushed back the door which opened slowly— slowly.

Then she slipped through it, and shut it behind her, and stood with her back against it, looking about her and breathing quite fast with excitement, and wonder, and delight.

She was standing inside the secret garden.

Chapter 9: The Strangest House
Anyone Ever Lived In

It was the sweetest, most mysterious-looking place any one could imagine. The high walls which shut it in were covered with the leafless stems of climbing roses which were so thick that they were matted together. Mary Lennox knew they were roses because she had seen a great many roses in India. All the ground was covered with grass of a wintry brown and out of it grew clumps of bushes which were surely rosebushes if they were alive. There were numbers of standard roses which had so spread their branches that they were like little trees. There were other trees in the garden, and one of the things which made the place look strangest and loveliest was that climbing roses had run all over them and swung down long tendrils which made light swaying curtains, and here and there they had caught at each other or at a far-reaching branch and had crept from one tree to another and made lovely bridges of themselves.

There were neither leaves nor roses on them now and Mary did not know whether they were dead or alive, but their thin gray or brown branches and sprays looked like a sort of hazy mantle spreading over everything, walls, and trees, and even brown grass, where they had fallen from their fastenings and run along the ground. It was this hazy tangle from tree to tree which made it all look so mysterious. Mary had thought it must be different from other gardens which had not been left all by themselves so long; and indeed it was different from any other place she had ever seen in her life.

"How still it is!" she whispered. "How still!"

Then she waited a moment and listened at the stillness. The robin, who had flown to his treetop, was still as all the rest. He did not even flutter his wings; he sat without stirring, and looked at Mary.

"No wonder it is still," she whispered again. "I am the first person who has spoken in here for ten years."

She moved away from the door, stepping as softly as if she were afraid of awakening someone. She was glad that there was grass under her feet and that her steps made no sounds. She walked under one of the fairy-like gray arches between the trees and looked up at the sprays and tendrils which formed them. "I wonder if they are all quite dead," she said. "Is it all a quite dead garden? I wish it wasn't."

If she had been Ben Weatherstaff she could have told whether the wood was alive by looking at it, but she could only see that there were only gray or brown sprays and branches and none showed any signs of even a tiny leaf-bud anywhere.

But she was inside the wonderful garden and she could come through the door under the ivy any time and she felt as if she had found a world all her own.

The sun was shining inside the four walls and the high arch of blue sky over this particular piece of Misselthwaite seemed even more brilliant and soft than it was over the moor. The robin flew down from his tree-top and hopped about or flew after her from one bush to another. He chirped a good deal and had a very busy air, as if he were showing her things. Everything was strange and silent and she seemed to be hundreds of miles away from anyone, but somehow she did not feel lonely at all. All that troubled her was her wish that she knew whether all the roses were dead, or if perhaps some of them had lived and might put out leaves and buds as the weather got warmer. She did not want it to be a quite dead garden. If it were a quite alive garden, how wonderful it would be, and what thousands of roses would grow on every side!

Her throwing blade had hung over her arm when she came in and after she had walked about for a while she thought she would practice hooking things round the whole garden, stopping when she wanted to look at things. There seemed to have been grass paths here and there, and in one or two corners there were alcoves of evergreen with stone seats or tall moss-covered flower urns in them.

As she came near the second of these alcoves she stopped spinning the blade and looked. There had once been a flowerbed in it, and she thought she saw something sticking out of the black earth- -some sharp little pale green points. She remembered what Ben Weatherstaff had said and she knelt down to look at them.

"Yes, they are tiny growing things and they might be crocuses or snowdrops or daffodils," she whispered.

She bent very close to them and sniffed the fresh scent of the damp earth. She liked it very much.

"Perhaps there are some other ones coming up in other places," she said. "I will go all over the garden and look."

She walked slowly and kept her eyes on the ground. She looked in the old border beds and among the grass, and after she had gone round, trying to miss nothing, she had found ever so many more sharp, pale green points, and she had become quite excited again.

"It isn't a quite dead garden," she cried out softly to herself. "Even if the roses are dead, there are other things alive."

She did not know anything about gardening, but the grass seemed so thick in some of the places where the green points were pushing their way through that she thought they did not seem to have room enough to grow. She searched about until she found a rather sharp piece of wood and knelt down and dug and weeded out the weeds and grass until she made nice little clear places around them.

"Now they look as if they could breathe," she said, after she had finished with the first ones. "I am going to do ever so many more. I'll do all I can see. If I haven't time today I can come tomorrow."

She went from place to place, and dug and weeded, and enjoyed herself so immensely that she was led on from bed to bed and into the grass under the trees. The exercise made her so warm that she first threw her coat off, and then her hat, and without knowing it she was smiling down on to the grass and the pale green points all the time.

The robin was tremendously busy. He was very much pleased to see gardening begun on his own estate. He had often wondered at Ben Weatherstaff. Where gardening is done all sorts of delightful things to eat are turned up with the soil. Now here was this new kind of creature who was not half Ben's size and yet had had the sense to come into his garden and begin at once.

Mistress Mary worked in her garden until it was time to go to her midday dinner. In fact, she was rather late in remembering, and when she put on her coat and hat, and picked up her blade, she could not believe that she had been working two or three hours. She had been actually happy all the time; and dozens and dozens of the tiny, pale green points were to be seen in cleared places, looking twice as cheerful as they had looked before when the grass and weeds had been smothering them.

"I shall come back this afternoon," she said, looking all round at her new kingdom, and speaking to the trees and the rose-bushes as if they heard her. She breathed in the stillness and quiet of the garden walking through it one more time. Then she noticed that towards the back there was a large dead tree covered in the flowerless rose vines. It seemed to twist and curl down with the weight of them. At the base of the tree was a large decaying tree branch surrounded by little red mushrooms. Mary approached slowly and thought she could hear something in the quiet. A low scratching sound, perhaps there was an animal behind the fallen branch. But it did not seem to be coming from there. Mary took a step forward and listened again, but the sound had stopped. Then she heard her own stomach rumble.

She ran lightly across the grass, pushed open the slow old door and slipped through it under the ivy. She had such red cheeks and such bright eyes and ate such a dinner that Martha was delighted.

"Two pieces o' meat an' two helps o' rice puddin'!" she said. "Eh! Mother will be pleased when I tell her what th' throwin' blade done for thee."

In the course of her digging with her pointed stick Mistress Mary had found herself digging up a sort of white root rather like an onion. She had put it back in its place and patted the earth carefully down on it and just now she wondered if Martha could tell her what it was.

"Martha," she said, "what are those white roots that look like onions?"

"They're bulbs," answered Martha. "Lots o' spring flowers grow from 'em. Th' very little ones are snowdrops an' crocuses an' th' big ones are narcissuses an' jonquils and daffydowndillys. Th' biggest of all is lilies an' purple flags. Eh! they are nice. Dickon's got a whole lot of 'em planted in our bit o' garden."

"Does Dickon know all about them?" asked Mary, a new idea taking possession of her.

"Our Dickon can make a flower grow out of a brick walk. Mother says he just whispers things out o' th' ground."

"Do bulbs live a long time? Would they live years and years if no one helped them?" inquired Mary anxiously.

"They're things as helps themselves," said Martha. "That's why poor folk can afford to have 'em. If you don't trouble 'em, most of 'em'll work away underground for a lifetime an' spread out an' have little 'uns. There's a place in th' park woods here where there's snowdrops by thousands. They're the prettiest sight in Yorkshire when th' spring comes. No one knows when they was first planted."

"I wish the spring was here now," said Mary. "I want to see all the things that grow in England."

She had finished her dinner and gone to her favorite seat on the hearth-rug.

"I wish—I wish I had a little spade," she said.

"Whatever does tha' want a spade for?" asked Martha, laughing. "Art tha' goin' to take to diggin'? I must tell mother that, too."

Mary looked at the fire and pondered a little. She must be careful if she meant to keep her secret kingdom. She wasn't doing any harm, but if Mr. Craven found out about the open door he would be fearfully angry and get a new key and lock it up forevermore. She really could not bear that.

"This is such a big lonely place," she said slowly, as if she were turning matters over in her mind. "The house is lonely, and the park is lonely, and the gardens are lonely. So many places seem shut up. I never did many things in India, but there were more people to look at—natives and soldiers marching by—and sometimes bands playing, and my Ayah told me stories. There is no one to talk to here except you and Ben Weatherstaff. And you have to do your work and Ben Weatherstaff won't speak to me often. I thought if I had a little spade I could dig somewhere as he does, and I might make a little garden if he would give me some seeds."

Martha's face quite lighted up. "There now!" she exclaimed, "if that wasn't one of th' things mother said. She says, 'There's such a lot o' room in that big place, why don't they give her a bit for herself, even if she doesn't plant nothin' but parsley an' radishes? She'd dig an' rake away an' be right down happy over it.' Them was the very words she said."

"Were they?" said Mary. "How many things she knows, doesn't she?"

"Eh!" said Martha. "It's like she says: 'A woman as brings up twelve children learns something besides her A B C. Children's as good as 'rithmetic to set you findin' out things.'"

"How much would a spade cost—a little one?" Mary asked.

"Well," was Martha's reflective answer, "at Thwaite village there's a shop or so an' I saw little garden sets with a spade an' a rake an' a fork all tied together for two shillings. An' they was stout enough to work with, too."

"I've got more than that in my purse," said Mary. "Mrs. Morrison gave me five shillings and Mrs. Medlock gave me some money from Mr. Craven."

"Did he remember thee that much?" exclaimed Martha.

"Mrs. Medlock said I was to have a shilling a week to spend. She gives me one every Saturday. I didn't know what to spend it on."

"My word! that's riches," said Martha. "Tha' can buy anything in th' world tha' wants. Th' rent of our cottage is only one an' threepence an' it's like pullin' eye-teeth to get it. Now I've just thought of somethin'," putting her hands on her hips.

"What?" said Mary eagerly.

"In the shop at Thwaite they sell packages o' flower-seeds for a penny each, and our Dickon he knows which is th' prettiest ones an, how to make 'em grow. He walks over to Thwaite many a day just for th' fun of it. Does tha' know how to print letters?" suddenly.

"I know how to write," Mary answered.

Martha shook her head.

"Our Dickon can only read printin'. If tha' could print we could write a letter to him an' ask him to go an' buy th' garden tools an' th' seeds at th' same time."

"Oh! you're a good girl!" Mary cried. "You are, really! I didn't know you were so nice. I know I can print letters if I try. Let's ask Mrs. Medlock for a pen and ink and some paper."

"I've got some of my own," said Martha. "I bought 'em so I could print a bit of a letter to Mother on a Sunday. I'll go and get it." She ran out of the room, and Mary stood by the fire and twisted her thin little hands together with sheer pleasure.

"If I have a spade," she whispered, "I can make the earth nice and soft and dig up weeds. If I have seeds and can make flowers grow the garden won't be dead at all—it will come alive. And perhaps I could have another throwing blade, and practice with one in each hand!"

She did not go out again that afternoon because when Martha returned with her pen and ink and paper she was obliged to clear the table and carry the plates and dishes downstairs and when she got into the kitchen Mrs. Medlock was there and told her to do something, so Mary waited for what seemed to her a long time before she came back. Then it was a serious piece of work to write to Dickon. Mary had been taught very little because her governesses had disliked her too much to stay with her. She could not spell particularly well but she found that she could print letters when she tried. This was the letter Martha dictated to her:

"My Dear Dickon:

This comes hoping to find you well as it leaves me at present. Miss Mary has plenty of money and will you go to Thwaite and buy her some flower seeds and a set of garden tools to make a flower-bed. Pick the prettiest ones and easy to grow because she has never done it before and lived in India which is different. Also find her another throwing blade just as the one she has. Give my love to mother and every one of you. Miss Mary is going to tell me a lot more so that on my next day out you can hear about elephants and camels and gentlemen going hunting the Aghori heathens.

"Your loving sister, Martha Phoebe Sowerby."

"We'll put the money in th' envelope an' I'll get th' butcher boy to take it in his cart. He's a great friend o' Dickon's," said Martha.

"How shall I get the things when Dickon buys them?"

"He'll bring 'em to you himself. He'll like to walk over this way."

"Oh!" exclaimed Mary, "then I shall see him! I never thought I should see Dickon."

"Does tha' want to see him?" asked Martha suddenly, for Mary had looked so pleased.

"Yes, I do. I never saw a boy foxes and crows loved. I want to see him very much."

Martha gave a little start, as if she remembered something. "Now to think," she broke out, "to think o' me forgettin' that there; an' I thought I was goin' to tell you first thing this mornin'. I asked mother—and she said she'd ask Mrs. Medlock her own self."

"Do you mean—" Mary began.

"What I said Tuesday. Ask her if you might be driven over to our cottage some day and have a bit o' mother's hot oat cake, an' butter, an' a glass o' milk."

It seemed as if all the interesting things were happening in one day. To think of going over the moor in the daylight and when the sky was blue! To think of going into the cottage which held twelve children!

"Does she think Mrs. Medlock would let me go?" she asked, quite anxiously.

"Aye, she thinks she would. She knows what a fightin' woman mother is and how safe she keeps the cottage."

"If I went I should see your mother as well as Dickon," said Mary, thinking it over and liking the idea very much. "She doesn't seem to be like the mothers in India."

Her work in the garden and the excitement of the afternoon ended by making her feel quiet and thoughtful. Martha stayed with her until tea-time, but they sat in comfortable quiet and talked very little. But just before Martha went downstairs for the tea-tray, Mary asked a question.

"Martha," she said, "has the scullery-maid had the toothache again today?"

Martha certainly started slightly.

"What makes thee ask that?" she said.

"Because when I waited so long for you to come back I opened the door and walked down the corridor to see if you were coming. And I heard that far-off crying again, just as we heard it the other night. There isn't a wind today, so you see it couldn't have been the wind."

"Eh!" said Martha restlessly. "Tha' mustn't go walkin' about in corridors an' listenin'. Mr. Craven would be that there angry an' there's no knowin' what he'd do."

"I wasn't listening," said Mary. "I was just waiting for you—and I heard it. That's three times."

"My word! There's Mrs. Medlock's bell," said Martha, and she almost ran out of the room.

"It's the strangest house any one ever lived in," said Mary drowsily, as she dropped her head on the cushioned seat of the armchair near her. Fresh air, and digging, and practicing her throwing blade had made her feel so comfortably tired that she fell asleep.

Chapter 10: Dickon

The sun shone down for nearly a week on the secret garden. The secret garden was what Mary called it when she was thinking of it. She liked the name, and she liked still more the feeling that when its beautiful old walls shut her in no one knew where she was. It seemed almost like being shut out of the world in some fairy place. The few books she had read and liked had been fairy-story books, and she had read of secret gardens in some of the stories. Sometimes people went to sleep in them for a hundred years, which she had thought must be rather stupid. She had no intention of going to sleep, and, in fact, she was becoming wider awake every day which passed at Misselthwaite. She was beginning to like to be out of doors; she no longer hated the wind, but enjoyed it. She could run faster, and longer, and she could hit a petal on a flower with her curved blade. She used her blade to help pull weeds throughout the garden. The bulbs in the secret garden must have been much astonished. Such nice clear places were made round them that they had all the breathing space they wanted, and really, if Mistress Mary had known it, they began to cheer up under the dark earth and work tremendously. The sun could get at them and warm them, and when the rain came down it could reach them at once, so they began to feel very much alive.

Mary was an odd, determined little person, and now she had something interesting to be determined about, she was very much absorbed, indeed. She worked and dug and pulled up weeds steadily, only becoming more pleased with her work every hour instead of tiring of it. It seemed to her like a fascinating sort of play. She found many more of the sprouting pale green points than she had ever hoped to find. They seemed to be starting up everywhere and each day she was sure she found tiny new ones, some so tiny that they barely peeped above the earth. There were so many that she remembered what Martha had said about the "snowdrops by the thousands," and about bulbs spreading and making new ones. These had been left to themselves for ten years and perhaps they had spread, like the snowdrops, into thousands. She wondered how long it would be before they showed that they were flowers. Sometimes she stopped digging to look at the garden and try to imagine what it would be like when it was covered with thousands of lovely things in bloom.

During that week of sunshine, she became more intimate with Ben Weatherstaff. She surprised him several times by seeming to start up beside him as if she sprang out of the earth. The truth was that she was afraid that he would pick up his tools and go away if he saw her coming, so she always walked toward him as silently as possible. But, in fact, he did not object to her as strongly as he had at first. Perhaps he was secretly rather flattered by her evident desire for his elderly company. Then, also, she was more civil than she had been. He did not know that when she first saw him she spoke to him as she would have spoken to a native, and had not known that a cross, sturdy old Yorkshire man was not accustomed to salaam to his masters, and be merely commanded by them to do things.

"Tha'rt like th' robin," he said to her one morning when he lifted his head and saw her standing by him. "I never knows when I shall see thee or which side tha'll come from."

"He's friends with me now," said Mary.

"That's like him," snapped Ben Weatherstaff. "Makin' up to th' women folk just for vanity an' flightiness. There's nothin' he wouldn't do for th' sake o' showin' off an' flirtin' his tail-feathers. He's as full o' pride as an egg's full o' meat."

He very seldom talked much and sometimes did not even answer Mary's questions except by a grunt, but this morning he said more than usual. He stood up and rested one hobnailed boot on the top of his spade while he looked her over.

"How long has tha' been here?" he jerked out.

"I think it's about a month," she answered.

"Tha's beginnin' to do Misselthwaite credit," he said. "Tha's a bit fatter than tha' was an' tha's not quite so yeller. Tha' looked like a young plucked crow, or a starvin' Accursed when tha' first came into this garden. Thinks I to myself I never set eyes on an uglier, sourer faced young 'un."

Mary was not vain and as she had never thought much of her looks she was not greatly disturbed.

"I know I'm fatter," she said. "My stockings are getting tighter. They used to make wrinkles. There's the robin, Ben Weatherstaff."

There, indeed, was the robin, and she thought he looked nicer than ever. His coat was as glossy as satin and he flitted his wings and tail and tilted his head and hopped about with all sorts of lively graces. He seemed determined to make Ben Weatherstaff admire him. But Ben was sarcastic.

"Aye, there tha' art!" he said. "Tha' can put up with me for a bit sometimes when tha's got no one better. Tha's been polishin' thy feathers this two weeks. I know what tha's up to. Tha's courtin' some bold young madam somewhere tellin' thy lies to her about bein' th' finest cock robin on Missel Moor an' ready to fight all th' rest of 'em."

"Oh! look at him!" exclaimed Mary.

The robin was evidently in a fascinating, bold mood. He hopped closer and closer and looked at Ben Weatherstaff more and more engagingly. He flew on to the nearest currant bush and tilted his head and sang a little song right at him.

"Tha' thinks tha'll get over me by doin' that," said Ben, wrinkling his face up in such a way that Mary felt sure he was trying not to look pleased. "Tha' thinks no one can stand out against thee—that's what tha' thinks."

The robin spread his wings—Mary could scarcely believe her eyes. He flew right up to the handle of Ben Weatherstaff's spade and alighted on the top of it. Then the old man's face wrinkled itself slowly into a new expression. He stood still as if he were afraid to breathe—as if he would not have stirred for the world, lest his robin should start away. He spoke quite in a whisper.

"Well, I'm danged!" he said as softly as if he were saying something quite different. "Tha' does know how to get at a chap—tha' does! Tha's fair unearthly, tha's so knowin'."

And he stood without stirring—almost without drawing his breath—until the robin gave another flirt to his wings and flew away. Then he stood looking at the handle of the spade as if there might be Magic in it, and then he began to dig again and said nothing for several minutes.

But because he kept breaking into a slow grin now and then, Mary was not afraid to talk to him.

"Have you a garden of your own?" she asked.

"No. I'm bachelor an' lodge with Martin at th' gate."

"If you had one," said Mary, "what would you plant?"

"Cabbages an' 'taters an' onions."

"But if you wanted to make a flower garden," persisted Mary, "what would you plant?"

"Bulbs an' sweet-smellin' things—but mostly roses."

Mary's face lighted up.

"Do you like roses?" she said.

Ben Weatherstaff rooted up a weed and threw it aside before he answered.

"Well, yes, I do. I was learned that by a young lady I was gardener to. She had a lot in a place she was fond of, an' she loved 'em like they was children—or robins. I've seen her bend over an' kiss 'em." He dragged out another weed and scowled at it. "That were as much as ten year' ago."

"Where is she now?" asked Mary, much interested.

"Heaven," he answered, and drove his spade deep into the soil, "'cording to what parson says. But she wen' through Hell to get there!"

"What happened to her?" Mary asked. Ben was silent and his fist tightened around the handle of his spade.

"What happened to the roses?" Mary asked again, more interested than ever.

"They was left to themselves."

Mary was becoming quite excited. "Did they quite die? Do roses quite die when they are left to themselves?" she ventured.

"Well, I'd got to like 'em—an' I liked her—an' she liked 'em," Ben Weatherstaff admitted reluctantly. "Once or twice a year I'd go an' work at 'em a bit—prune 'em an' dig about th' roots. They run wild, but they was in rich soil, so some of 'em lived."

"When they have no leaves and look gray and brown and dry, how can you tell whether they are dead or alive?" inquired Mary.

"Wait till th' spring gets at 'em—wait till th' sun shines on th' rain and th' rain falls on th' sunshine an' then tha'll find out."

"How—how?" cried Mary, forgetting to be careful.

"Look along th' twigs an' branches an' if tha' see a bit of a brown lump swelling here an' there, watch it after th' warm rain an' see what happens." He stopped suddenly and looked curiously at her eager face. "Why does tha' care so much about roses an' such, all of a sudden?" he demanded.

Mistress Mary felt her face grow red. She was almost afraid to answer.

"I—I want to play that—that I have a garden of my own," she stammered. "I—there is nothing for me to do. I have nothing—and no one."

"Well," said Ben Weatherstaff slowly, as he watched her, "that's true. Tha' hasn't."

He said it in such an odd way that Mary wondered if he was actually a little sorry for her. She had never felt sorry for herself;

she had only felt tired and cross, because she disliked people and things so much. But now the world seemed to be changing and getting nicer. If no one found out about the secret garden, she should enjoy herself always.

She stayed with him for ten or fifteen minutes longer and asked him as many questions as she dared. He answered every one of them in his queer grunting way and he did not seem really cross and did not pick up his spade and leave her. He said something about roses just as she was going away and it reminded her of the ones he had said he had been fond of.

"Do you go and see those other roses now?" she asked.

"Not been this year. My rheumatics has made me too stiff in th' joints."

He said it in his grumbling voice, and then quite suddenly he seemed to get angry with her, though she did not see why he should.

"Now look here!" he said sharply. "Don't tha' ask so many questions. Tha'rt th' worst wench for askin' questions I've ever come across. Get thee gone an' play thee. I've done talkin' for today."

And he said it so crossly that she knew there was not the least use in staying another minute. She went slowly down the outside walk, thinking him over and saying to herself that, queer as it was, here was another person whom she liked in spite of his crossness. She liked old Ben Weatherstaff. Yes, she did like him. She always wanted to try to make him talk to her. Also she began to believe that he knew everything in the world about flowers.

There was a laurel-hedged walk which curved round the secret garden and ended at a large iron gate which opened into a wood, in the park. She knew she should not leave the protected area of the gardens, but she thought she would slip round this walk and just look into the wood and see if there were any rabbits or mice she could practice targeting with her throwing blade. She enjoyed hooking flowers very much, but she hoped to try a moving target. When she reached the iron gate she lifted the large metal bar with great difficulty to unlock it and pushed the heavy gate open. She walked a little ways into the wood and paused because she heard a low, peculiar groaning sound.

She hid behind a tree and watched. It was a very strange thing indeed. She quite caught her breath as she stopped to look at it. It was a man. He wore tattered clothes and seemed very thin. He walked funny, as if he had hurt his foot and had to stumble. His cheeks were sunken in, his hair thin, and finger nails stained and his eyes... Mary gasped, his eyes were black with dead blood.

At the slight sound of her gasp, the creature turned around, his black eyes widening. Mary fumbled to ready her throwing knife but the creature moved much faster than she thought possible. He was upon her and his nails dug into the puffed sleeves of her dress. Mary fell to the ground and the man was on top of her snarling and opening his black dripping mouth. Mary could not think, she could only feel the intensely strong hands on her shoulders and the weight of the man pressing down on her. She saw the rotting flesh hanging from his black teeth and smelled the putrid odor of death as he breathed on her. Mary closed her eyes.

Then the weight was lifted from her. The horrible breath and sound of gurgling disappeared. Mary opened her eyes and watched as a young boy, whose cheeks were as red as poppies, held the Accursed creature from behind swinging him violently into a tree. The affected man quickly recovered and the boy pulled a long fat blade from a leather sheath on his back. The Accursed lunged for the boy and as Mary watched in astonishment, the funny looking boy about twelve stepped quickly to the side and leapt upon the creatures back! It turned to Mary and reached out to her snarling in a desperate lunge. Mary screamed and the boy plunged his knife directly into the side of the man's head. Black fluid streamed from the mouth and eyes of the Accursed and as the boy pulled his blade from the head, black blood spurted from the opened wound. The boy quickly kicked the creature down and it lay still in the grass.

Mary collapsed and watched as he sat down at the base of a tree and cleaned his blade on the soft clovers. She continued to sit still in the grass and stare at him. Never had Mary seen such round and such blue eyes in any boy's face. And on the trunk of the tree he leaned against, a brown squirrel was clinging and watching him, and from behind a bush nearby a cock pheasant was delicately stretching his neck to peep out, and quite near him were two rabbits sitting up and sniffing with tremulous noses—and actually it appeared as if they were all drawing near to him now that it was safe to come out.

Mary moved to stand up and he held up his hand and spoke to her in a low voice "Don't tha' move," he said. "Fers, tha' mus check tha'self." He stared at her intensely with round blue eyes.

"What do you mean?" Mary asked. "Check for what?"

"Fer a bite or a scratch. Did it break your skin?"

Mary checked her arms and legs and felt her head and neck. She pulled down the shoulders of her dress to look where the Accursed had grabbed her.

"I don't think so. I can't feel or see any wounds."

"I'll check for tha'." Mary remained motionless as the boy put down his knife. He moved so slowly that it scarcely seemed as though he were moving at all, but at last he stood on his feet and then the squirrel scampered back up into the branches of his tree, the pheasant withdrew his head and the rabbits dropped on all fours and began to hop away, though not at all as if they were frightened.

He came and checked her shoulders slowly pulling back the sleeves of her dress. He lifted her hair to go over her neck and back. He seemed satisfied.

"I'm Dickon," the boy said. "I know tha'rt Miss Mary."

Then Mary realized that somehow she had known at first that he was Dickon. Who else could have killed that dreadful creature so effortlessly or been charming rabbits and pheasants as the natives charm snakes in India? He had a wide, red, curving mouth and his smile spread all over his face.

"You saved me." Mary said plainly. She did not know how to thank people for things.

"I did." Dickon said. "You should learn to move when the Forsaken are near. They move faster than you'd think. 'specially if'n they're hungry. He looks as if he hasn't had anything in months! If tha' makes a quick move it attracts 'em. A body 'as to move gentle an' speak low when Accursed things is about."

He did not speak to her as if they had never seen each other before but as if he knew her quite well. Mary knew nothing about boys and she spoke to him a little stiffly because she felt rather shy.

"Did you get Martha's letter?" she asked.

He nodded his curly, rust-colored head. "That's why I come."

He stooped to pick up his knife and something which had been lying on the ground beside it.

"I've got th' garden tools. There's a little spade an' rake an' a fork an' hoe. Eh! they are good 'uns. There's a trowel, too. An' th' woman in th' shop threw in a packet o' white poppy an' one o' blue larkspur when I bought th' other seeds."

"Will you show the seeds to me?" Mary said.

She wished she could talk as he did. His speech was so quick and easy. It sounded as if he liked her and was not the least afraid she would not like him, though he was only a common moor boy, in patched clothes and with a funny face and a rough, rusty-red head. As she came closer to him she noticed that there was a clean fresh scent of heather and grass and leaves about him, almost as if he were made of them. She liked it very much and when she looked into his funny face with the red cheeks and round blue eyes she forgot that she had felt shy.

"Let us sit down on this log and look at them," she said.

They sat down and he took a clumsy little brown paper package out of his coat pocket. He untied the string and inside there were ever so many neater and smaller packages with a picture of a flower on each one.

"There's a lot o' mignonette an' poppies," he said. "Mignonette's th' sweetest smellin' thing as grows, an' it'll grow wherever you cast it, same as poppies will. Them as'll come up an' bloom if you just whistle to 'em, them's th' nicest of all." He stopped and turned his head quickly, his poppy-cheeked face looking suddenly alert.

"Where's that robin as is callin' us?" he said.

The chirp came from a thick holly bush, bright with scarlet berries, and Mary thought she knew whose it was.

"Is it really calling us?" she asked.

"Aye," said Dickon, as if it was the most natural thing in the world, "he's callin' some one he's friends with, to warn 'um. That's same as sayin' 'Beware, friend! There's something unnatural coming near and you're in danger!' There he is in the bush. Whose is he?"

"He's Ben Weatherstaff's, but I think he knows me a little," answered Mary.

"Aye, he knows thee," said Dickon in his low voice again. "He's took thee on. Thinks you need watchin'. He'll tell me all about thee in a minute."

He moved quite close to the bush with the slow movement Mary had noticed before, and then he made a sound almost like the robin's own twitter. The robin listened a few seconds, intently, and then answered quite as if he were replying to a question.

"Aye, he's a friend o' yours, he thinks he's your protector, and there'ar more of the Forsaken Ones headed this way." Dickon looked around quickly and moved towards the iron gate.

"Is he my protector?" cried Mary eagerly. She did so want to know. "Do you think he really wants to watch out for me?"

"He wouldn't come near thee if he didn't," answered Dickon. "Birds is rare choosers an' a robin can flout a body worse than a man. See, he's tryin' to warn thee now. 'Cannot tha' see the danger comin'?' he's sayin'."

And it really seemed as if it must be true. He so sidled and twittered and tilted as he hopped on his bush. Dickon quickly picked up the gardening tools and held his large knife tight in his hand.

"Come now, through the gate into the gardens. It's no longer safe out here," Dickon shuffled Mary and his small following of animals through before closing and locking the iron gate. "Nor is it safe on the moor," he muttered.

"Do you understand everything birds say?" said Mary.

Dickon's grin spread until he seemed all wide, red, curving mouth, and he rubbed his rough head.

"I think I do, and they think I do," he said. "I've lived on th' moor with 'em so long. I've watched 'em break shell an' come out an' fledge an' learn to fly an' begin to sing, till I think I'm one of 'em. Sometimes I think p'raps I'm a bird, or a fox, or a rabbit, or a squirrel, or even a beetle, an' I don't know it."

He laughed and began to talk about the flower seeds again. He told her what they looked like when they were flowers; he told her how to plant them, and watch them, and feed and water them.

"See here," he said suddenly, turning round to look at her. "I'll plant them for thee myself. Where is tha' garden?"

Mary's thin hands clutched each other as they lay on her lap. She did not know what to say, so for a whole minute she said nothing. She had never thought of this. She felt miserable. And she felt as if she went red and then pale.

"Tha's got a bit o' garden, hasn't tha'?" Dickon said.

It was true that she had turned red and then pale. Dickon saw her do it, and as she still said nothing, he began to be puzzled.

"Wouldn't they give thee a bit?" he asked. "Hasn't tha' got any yet?"

She held her hands tighter and turned her eyes toward him.

"I don't know anything about boys," she said slowly. "Could you keep a secret, if I told you one? It's a great secret. I don't know what I should do if any one found it out. I believe I should die!" She said the last sentence quite fiercely.

Dickon looked more puzzled than ever and even rubbed his hand over his rough head again, but he answered quite good-humoredly. "I'm keepin' secrets all th' time," he said. "If I couldn't keep secrets from th' other lads, secrets about foxes' cubs, an' birds' nests, an' wild things' holes, there'd be naught safe on th' moor. Aye, I can keep secrets."

Mistress Mary did not mean to put out her hand and clutch his sleeve but she did it.

"I've stolen a garden," she said very fast. "It isn't mine. It isn't anybody's. Nobody wants it, nobody cares for it, nobody ever goes into it. Perhaps everything is dead in it already. I don't know."

She began to feel hot and as contrary as she had ever felt in her life.

"I don't care, I don't care! Nobody has any right to take it from me when I care about it and they don't. They're letting it die, all shut in by itself," she ended passionately, and she threw her arms over her face and burst out crying-poor little Mistress Mary.

Dickon's curious blue eyes grew rounder and rounder. "Eh-h-h!" he said, drawing his exclamation out slowly, and the way he did it meant both wonder and sympathy.

"I've nothing to do," said Mary. "Nothing belongs to me. I found it myself and I got into it myself. I was only just like the robin, and they wouldn't take it from the robin."

"Where is it?" asked Dickon in a dropped voice.

"Come with me and I'll show you," she said. Mistress Mary walked away from the iron gate at once. She knew she felt contrary again, and obstinate, and she did not care at all. She was imperious and Indian, and at the same time hot and sorrowful.

Mary did not see, but several of the Accursed had walked into view and were inspecting the body Dickon had left under the tree. Dickon's animals fled under cover of bushes and down the path. Dickon double checked the heavy iron lock and quickly followed Mary hoping the undead cannibals had not seen them.

She led him round the laurel path and to the walk where the ivy grew so thickly. Dickon followed her with a queer, almost pitying, look on his face. He felt as if he were being led to look at some strange bird's nest and must move softly. When she stepped to the wall and lifted the hanging ivy he started. There was a door and Mary pushed it slowly open and they passed in together, and then Mary stood and waved her hand round defiantly.

"It's this," she said. "It's a secret garden, and I'm the only one in the world who wants it to be alive."

Dickon looked round and round about it, and round and round again.

"Eh!" he almost whispered, "it is a queer, pretty place! A place far from the world that's endin'. It's like as if a body was in a dream and the whole world was reborn."

Chapter 11: The Nest of the Missel Thrush

For two or three minutes he stood looking round him, while Mary watched him, and then he began to walk about softly, even more lightly than Mary had walked the first time she had found herself inside the four walls. His eyes seemed to be taking in everything—the gray trees with the gray creepers climbing over them and hanging from their branches, the tangle on the walls and among the grass, the evergreen alcoves with the stone seats and tall flower urns standing in them.

"I never thought I'd see this place," he said at last, in a whisper.

"Did you know about it?" asked Mary.

She had spoken aloud and he made a sign to her.

"We must talk low," he said, "or some one'll hear us an' wonder what's to do in here. No sense attractin' attention neither from the livin' nor the dead. "

"Oh! I forgot!" said Mary, feeling frightened and putting her hand quickly against her mouth. "Did you know about the garden?" she asked again when she had recovered herself. Dickon nodded.

"Martha told me there was one as no one ever went inside," he answered. "Us used to wonder what it was like."

He stopped and looked round at the lovely gray tangle about him, and his round eyes looked queerly happy.

"Eh! the nests as'll be here come springtime," he said. "It'd be th' safest nestin' place in England. No one never comin' near an' tangles o' trees an' roses to build in. The Accursed could never get in! I wonder all th' birds on th' moor don't build here."

Mistress Mary put her hand on his arm again without knowing it.

"Will there be roses?" she whispered. "Can you tell? I thought perhaps they were all dead."

"Eh! No! Not them—not all of 'em!" he answered. "Look here!"

He stepped over to the nearest tree—an old, old one with gray lichen all over its bark, but upholding a curtain of tangled sprays and branches. He took his thick knife out of its sheath and held the sharp blade against a branch.

"There's lots o' dead wood as ought to be cut out," he said. "An' there's a lot o' old wood, but it made some new last year. This here's a new bit," and he touched a shoot which looked brownish green instead of hard, dry gray. Mary touched it herself in an eager, reverent way.

"That one?" she said. "Is that one quite alive?"

Dickon curved his wide smiling mouth.

"It's as wick as you or me," he said; and Mary remembered that Martha had told her that "wick" meant "alive" or "lively."

"I'm glad it's wick!" she cried out in her whisper. "I want them all to be wick. Let us go round the garden and count how many wick ones there are."

She quite panted with eagerness, and Dickon was as eager as she was. They went from tree to tree and from bush to bush. Dickon carried his knife in his hand and showed her things which she thought wonderful.

"They've run wild," he said, "but th' strongest ones has fair thrived on it. The delicatest ones has died out, but th' others has growed an' growed, an' spread an' spread, till they's a wonder. See here!" and he pulled down a thick gray, dry-looking branch. "A body might think this was dead wood, but I don't believe it is— down to th' root. I'll cut it low down an' see."

He knelt and with his knife cut the lifeless-looking branch through, not far above the earth.

"There!" he said exultantly. "I told thee so. There's green in that wood yet. Look at it."

Mary was down on her knees before he spoke, gazing with all her might.

"When it looks a bit greenish an' juicy like that, it's wick," he explained. "When th' inside is dry an' breaks easy, like this here piece I've cut off, it's done for. There's a big root here as all this live wood sprung out of, an' if th' old wood's cut off an' it's dug round, and took care of there'll be—" he stopped and lifted his face to look up at the climbing and hanging sprays above him— "there'll be a fountain o' roses here this summer."

They went from bush to bush and from tree to tree. He was very strong and clever with his knife and knew how to cut the dry and dead wood away, and could tell when an unpromising bough or twig had still green life in it. In the course of half an hour Mary thought she could tell too, and when he cut through a lifeless-looking branch she would cry out joyfully under her breath when she caught sight of the least shade of moist green. The spade, and hoe, and fork were very useful. He showed her how to use the fork while he dug about roots with the spade and stirred the earth and let the air in.

They were working industriously round one of the biggest standard roses when he caught sight of something which made him utter an exclamation of surprise.

"Why!" he cried, pointing to the grass a few feet away. "Who did that there?"

It was one of Mary's own little clearings round the pale green points.

"I did it," said Mary.

"Why, I thought tha' didn't know nothin' about gardenin'," he exclaimed.

"I don't," she answered, "but they were so little, and the grass was so thick and strong, and they looked as if they had no room to breathe. So I made a place for them. I don't even know what they are."

Dickon went and knelt down by them, smiling his wide smile.

"Tha' was right," he said. "A gardener couldn't have told thee better. They'll grow now like Jack's bean-stalk. They're crocuses an' snowdrops, an' these here is narcissuses," turning to another patch, "an here's daffydowndillys. Eh! they will be a sight."

He ran from one clearing to another.

"Tha' has done a lot o' work for such a little wench," he said, looking her over.

"I'm growing fatter," said Mary, "and I'm growing stronger. I used always to be tired. When I dig I'm not tired at all. I like to smell the earth when it's turned up."

"It's rare good for thee," he said, nodding his head wisely. "There's naught as nice as th' smell o' good clean earth, except th' smell o' fresh growin' things when th' rain falls on 'em. I get out on th' moor many a day when it's rainin' an' I lie under a bush an' listen to th' soft swish o' drops on th' heather an, I just sniff an, sniff. My nose end fair quivers like a rabbit's, mother says."

"Do you never catch cold?" inquired Mary, gazing at him wonderingly. She had never seen such a funny boy, or such a nice one.

"Not me," he said, grinning. "I never ketched cold since I was born. I wasn't brought up nesh enough. I've chased about th' moor in all weathers same as th' rabbits does. Mother says I've sniffed up too much fresh air for twelve year' to ever get to sniffin' with cold. I'm as tough as a white-thorn knobstick."

He was working all the time he was talking and Mary was following him and helping him with her fork or the trowel.

"There's a lot of work to do here!" he said once, looking about quite exultantly.

"Will you come again and help me to do it?" Mary begged. "I'm sure I can help, too. I can dig and pull up weeds, and do whatever you tell me. Oh! do come, Dickon!"

"I'll come every day if tha' wants me, rain or shine, Forsaken or none." he answered stoutly. "It's the best fun I ever had in my life—shut in here an' wakenin' up a garden."

"If you will come," said Mary, "if you will help me to make it alive I'll—I don't know what I'll do," she ended helplessly. What could you do for a boy like that?

"I'll tell thee what tha'll do," said Dickon, with his happy grin. "Tha'll get fat an' tha'll get as hungry as a young fox an' tha'll learn how to talk to th' robin same as I do. You'll learn how to fight and protect yourself from the Fallen Ones. I'll show you the softes' parts of their heads to slay 'um. Oh! Tha' reminds me. I also got you a second throwin' blade, to match the firs'." He pulled from his pocket a blade identical to the other and Mary clasped her hands together in excitement.

"Now I shall practice spinning two blades at once!" She remembered to whisper just in time.

"Aye, an' I'll show thee how hook 'um right in the eye and take 'um down quick. Eh! we'll have a lot o' fun." He began to walk about, looking up in the trees and at the walls and bushes with a thoughtful expression as Mary fumbled with the two ropes of the blades.

"I wouldn't want to make it look like a gardener's garden, all clipped an' spick an' span, would you?" he said. "It's nicer like this with things runnin' wild, an' swingin' an' catchin' hold of each other."

"Don't let us make it tidy," said Mary anxiously. "It wouldn't seem like a secret garden if it was tidy."

Dickon stood rubbing his rusty-red head with a rather puzzled look. "It's a secret garden sure enough," he said, "but seems like someone besides th' robin must have been in it since it was shut up ten year' ago."

"But the door was locked and the key was buried," said Mary. "No one could get in."

"That's true," he answered. "It's a queer place. Seems to me as if there'd been a bit o' prunin' done here an' there, later than ten year' ago."

"But how could it have been done?" said Mary.

He was examining a branch of a standard rose and he shook his head.

"Aye! how could it!" he murmured. "With th' door locked an' th' key buried."

Mistress Mary always felt that however many years she lived she should never forget that first morning when her garden began to grow. Of course, it did seem to begin to grow for her that morning. When Dickon began to clear places to plant seeds, she remembered what Basil had sung at her when he wanted to tease her.

"Are there any flowers called Hellebore?" she inquired.

"Aye, they can be purple or pinkish, but they can be deadly poisonous if tha' eat um," he answered, digging away with the trowel.

"What about Asphodel, and Death Caps, and Night Shade?" Mary asked.

"Aye..." Dickon said slowly.

"Let's plant some," said Mary.

"There's Death Cap mushrooms here already; I saw 'em. They'll have growed too close in a spot an' we'll have to separate 'em, but there's plenty. I can get Hellebore seeds in the market. There's Asphodel planted in the cemetery behind the church. I can bring you some bits o' plants. Not sure about the Atropa Night Shade, hard to get. Why does tha' want 'em?"

Then Mary told him about Basil and his friends in India and of how she had hated them and of their calling her "Bloody Mary Quite Contrary."

"They used to dance round and sing at me. They sang—

'Bloody Mary, quite contrary,

How does your garden grow?

With Death Caps and Night Shade,

And corpses all in a row.'

"I just remembered it and it made me wonder if there were really something called Night Shade."

She frowned a little and gave her trowel a rather spiteful dig into the earth.

"I wasn't as contrary as they were."

But Dickon laughed.

"Eh!" he said, and as he crumbled the rich black soil she saw he was sniffing up the scent of it. "There doesn't seem to be no need for no one to be contrary when there's flowers an' such like, an' such lots o' friendly wild things runnin' about makin' homes for themselves, or buildin' nests an' singin' an' whistlin', does there?"

Mary, kneeling by him holding the seeds, looked at him and stopped frowning.

"Dickon," she said, "you are as nice as Martha said you were. I like you, and you make the fifth person. I never thought I should like five people."

Dickon sat up on his heels as Martha did when she was polishing the grate. He did look funny and delightful, Mary thought, with his round blue eyes and red cheeks and happy looking turned-up nose.

"Only five folk as tha' likes?" he said. "Who is th' other four?"

"Your mother and Martha," Mary checked them off on her fingers, "and the robin and Ben Weatherstaff."

Dickon laughed so that he was obliged to stifle the sound by putting his arm over his mouth.

"I know tha' thinks I'm a queer lad," he said, "but I think tha' art th' queerest little lass I ever saw."

Then Mary did a strange thing. She leaned forward so that she was very close to Dickon and he went still as a statue. She asked him a question she had never dreamed of asking any one before. And she tried to ask it in Yorkshire because that was his speech, and in India a native was always pleased if you knew his speech.

"Does tha' like me?" she said.

"Eh!" he whispered heartily, "that I does. I likes thee wonderful, Bloody Mary." Dickon quickly added, "an' so does th' robin, I do believe!"

"That's two, then," said Mary leaning back. "That's two for me."

And then they began to work harder than ever and more joyfully. Mary was startled and sorry when she heard the big clock in the courtyard strike the hour of her midday dinner.

"I shall have to go," she said mournfully. "And you will have to go too, won't you?"

Dickon grinned.

"My dinner's easy to carry about with me," he said. "Mother always lets me put a bit o' somethin' in my pocket."

He picked up his coat from the grass and brought out of a pocket a lumpy little bundle tied up in a quite clean, coarse, blue and white handkerchief. It held two thick pieces of bread with a slice of something laid between them.

"It's oftenest naught but bread," he said, "but I've got a fine slice o' fat bacon with it today."

Mary thought it looked a queer dinner, but he seemed ready to enjoy it.

"Run on an' get thy victuals," he said. "I'll be done with mine first. I'll get some more work done before I start back home. Mind you watch all around thee walkin' alone. And if'n you see Forsaken, keep thee quiet, move softly, and quickly hide."

He sat down with his back against a tree.

"I'll call th' robin up to watch thee," he said, "when he comes back to let me know you're safe I'll give him th' rind o' th' bacon to peck at. They likes a bit o' fat wonderful."

Mary could scarcely bear to leave him. Suddenly it seemed as if he might be a sort of wood fairy who might be gone when she came into the garden again. He seemed too good to be true. She went slowly half-way to the door in the wall and then she stopped and went back.

"Whatever happens, you—you never would tell?" she said.

His poppy-colored cheeks were distended with his first big bite of bread and bacon, but he managed to smile encouragingly.

"If tha' was a missel thrush an' showed me where thy nest was, does tha' think I'd tell anyone? Not me," he said. "Tha' art as safe as a missel thrush."

And she was quite sure she was.

Chapter 12: Might I Have a Bit of Earth?

Mary ran so fast that she was rather out of breath when she reached her room. Her hair was ruffled on her forehead and her cheeks were bright pink. Her dinner was waiting on the table, and Martha was waiting near it.

"Tha's a bit late," she said. "Where has tha' been?"

"I've seen Dickon!" said Mary. "I've seen Dickon!"

"I knew he'd come," said Martha exultantly. "How does tha' like him?"

"I think—I think he's beautiful!" said Mary in a determined voice.

Martha looked rather taken aback but she looked pleased, too.

"Well," she said, "he's th' best lad as ever was born, but us never thought he was handsome. His nose turns up too much."

"I like it turned up," said Mary.

"An' his eyes is so round," said Martha, a trifle doubtful. "Though they're a nice color."

"I like them round," said Mary. "And they are exactly the color of the sky over the moor."

Martha beamed with satisfaction.

"Mother says he made 'em that color with always lookin' up at th' birds an' th' clouds. But he has got a big mouth, hasn't he, now?"

"I love his big mouth," said Mary obstinately. "I wish mine were just like it."

Martha chuckled delightedly.

"It'd look rare an' funny in thy bit of a face," she said. "But I knowed it would be that way when tha' saw him. How did tha' like th' seeds an' th' garden tools? Have you been practicin' with your double blades?"

"How did you know he brought them?" asked Mary.

"Eh! I never thought of him not bringin' 'em. He'd be sure to bring 'em if they was in Yorkshire. He's such a trusty lad."

Mary was afraid that she might begin to ask difficult questions, but she did not. She was very much interested in the seeds and gardening tools, and there was only one moment when Mary was frightened. This was when she began to ask where the flowers were to be planted.

"Who did tha' ask about it?" she inquired.

"I haven't asked anybody yet," said Mary, hesitating.

"Well, I wouldn't ask th' head gardener. He's too grand, Mr. Roach is."

"I've never seen him," said Mary. "I've only seen undergardeners and Ben Weatherstaff."

"If I was you, I'd ask Ben Weatherstaff," advised Martha. "He's not half as bad as he looks, for all he's so crabbed. Mr. Craven lets him do what he likes because he was here when Mrs. Craven was alive, an' he used to make her laugh. She liked him. Perhaps he'd find you a corner somewhere out o' the way."

"If it was out of the way and no one wanted it, no one could mind my having it, could they?" Mary said anxiously.

"There wouldn't be no reason," answered Martha. "You wouldn't do no harm."

Mary ate her dinner as quickly as she could and when she rose from the table she was going to run to her room to put on her hat again, but Martha stopped her.

"I've got somethin' to tell you," she said. "I thought I'd let you eat your dinner first. Mr. Craven came back this mornin' and I think he wants to see you."

Mary turned quite pale.

"Oh!" she said. "Why! Why! He didn't want to see me when I came. I heard Pitcher say he didn't."

"Well," explained Martha, "Mrs. Medlock says it's because o' mother. She was walkin' to Thwaite village an' she found him on the road, his carriage overturned. It seems the Moor has been so clear the Accursed are managing to cross it and they spooked the horses. The fiends ravaged the driver and the footman, they were half eaten when mother came across them. Mr. Craven was trapped inside the overturned carriage and could only watch as the Forsaken disemboweled the servants! Well, Mother made short work of them with her axe and pulled Mr. Craven out and stood him on his feet. She'd never spoke to him before, but Mrs. Craven had been to our cottage two or three times. I don't know what she said to him about you but she said somethin' as put him in th' mind to see you before he goes away again, tomorrow."

"Oh!" cried Mary, "is he going away tomorrow? I am so glad!"

"He's goin' for a long time. He mayn't come back till autumn or winter. He's goin' to travel in foreign places. He's always doin' it. Somethin' to do with studyin' the Accursed and meetin' up with other great men about it." Martha muttered under her breath, "I wish he'd give up the whole business and give us peace round 'ere."

"Oh! I'm so glad he will be gone—so glad!" said Mary thankfully.

If he did not come back until winter, or even autumn, there would be time to watch the secret garden come alive. Even if he found out then and took it away from her she would have had that much at least.

"When do you think he will want to see—"

She did not finish the sentence, because the door opened, and Mrs. Medlock walked in. She had on her best black dress and cap, and her collar was fastened with a large brooch with a picture of a man's face on it. It was a colored photograph of Mr. Medlock who had died at the hands of the Accursed years ago in London working the train gates, and she always wore it when she was dressed up. She looked nervous and excited.

"Your hair's rough," she said quickly. "Go and brush it. Martha, help her to slip on her best dress. Mr. Craven sent me to bring her to him in his study."

All the pink left Mary's cheeks. Her heart began to thump and she felt herself changing into a stiff, plain, silent child again. She did not even answer Mrs. Medlock, but turned and walked into her bedroom, followed by Martha. She said nothing while her dress was changed, and her hair brushed, and after she was quite tidy she followed Mrs. Medlock down the corridors, in silence. What was there for her to say? She was obliged to go and see Mr. Craven and he would not like her, and she would not like him. She knew what he would think of her.

She was taken to a part of the house she had not been into before. At last Mrs. Medlock knocked at a door, and when someone said, "Come in," they entered the room together. A man was sitting in an armchair before the fire, and Mrs. Medlock spoke to him.

"This is Miss Mary, sir," she said.

"You can go and leave her here. I will ring for you when I want you to take her away," said Mr. Craven.

When she went out and closed the door, Mary could only stand waiting, a plain little thing, twisting her thin hands together. She could see that the man in the chair was not so much a hunchback as a man with high, rather crooked shoulders, and he had black hair streaked with white. He turned his head over his high shoulders and spoke to her.

"Come here!" he said.

Mary went to him.

He was not ugly. His face would have been handsome if it had not been so miserable. He looked as if the sight of her worried and fretted him and as if he did not know what in the world to do with her.

"Are you well?" he asked.

"Yes," answered Mary.

"Do they take good care of you?"

"Yes."

He rubbed his forehead fretfully as he looked her over.

"You are very thin," he said.

"I am getting fatter," Mary answered in what she knew was her stiffest way.

What an unhappy face he had! His black eyes seemed as if they scarcely saw her, as if they were seeing something else, and he could hardly keep his thoughts upon her.

"I forgot you," he said. "How could I remember you? I intended to send you a governess or a nurse, or someone of that sort, but I forgot."

"Please," began Mary. "Please—" and then the lump in her throat choked her.

"What do you want to say?" he inquired.

"I am—I am too big for a nurse," said Mary. "And please—please don't make me have a governess yet."

He rubbed his forehead again and stared at her.

"That was what the Sowerby woman said," he muttered absentmindedly.

Then Mary gathered a scrap of courage.

"Is she—is she Martha's mother?" she stammered.

"Yes, I think so," he replied.

"She knows about children," said Mary. "She has twelve. She knows."

He seemed to rouse himself. "What do you want to do?"

"I want to play out of doors," Mary answered, hoping that her voice did not tremble. "I never liked it in India. It makes me hungry here, and I am getting fatter."

He was watching her. "Mrs. Sowerby said it would do you good. Perhaps it will," he said. "She thought you had better get stronger before you had a governess."

"It makes me feel strong when I play and the wind comes over the moor," argued Mary.

"Where do you play?" he asked next.

"Everywhere," gasped Mary. "I explore and run—and I look about to see if things are beginning to stick up out of the earth. I don't do any harm."

"Don't look so frightened," he said in a worried voice. "You could not do any harm, a child like you! You may do what you like."

Mary put her hand up to her throat because she was afraid he might see the excited lump which she felt jump into it. She came a step nearer to him.

"May I?" she said tremulously.

Her anxious little face seemed to worry him more than ever.

"Don't look so frightened," he exclaimed. "Of course you may. I am your guardian, though I am a poor one for any child. I cannot give you time or attention. I am too ill, and wretched and distracted; but I wish you to be happy and comfortable. I don't know anything about children, but Mrs. Medlock is to see that you have all you need. I sent for you today because Mrs. Sowerby said I ought to see you. Her daughter had talked about you. She thought you needed fresh air and freedom and running about."

"She knows all about children," Mary said again in spite of herself.

"She ought to," said Mr. Craven. "I thought her rather courageous to save me on the moor today, and she said—Mrs. Craven had been kind to her." It seemed hard for him to speak his dead wife's name. "She is a respectable woman. Now I have seen you I think she said sensible things. Play out of doors as much as you like. It's a big place and you may go where you like and amuse yourself as you like. Is there anything you want?" as if a sudden thought had struck him. "Do you want toys, books, dolls?"

"Might I," quavered Mary, "might I have a bit of earth?"

In her eagerness she did not realize how queer the words would sound and that they were not the ones she had meant to say. Mr. Craven looked quite startled.

"Earth!" he repeated. "What do you mean?"

"To plant seeds in—to make things grow—to see them come alive," Mary faltered.

He gazed at her a moment and then passed his hand quickly over his eyes.

"Do you—care about gardens so much," he said slowly.

"I didn't know about them in India," said Mary. "I was always ill and tired and it was too hot. I sometimes made little beds in the sand and stuck flowers in them. But here it is different."

Mr. Craven got up and began to walk slowly across the room.

"A bit of earth," he said to himself, and Mary thought that somehow she must have reminded him of something. When he stopped and spoke to her his dark eyes looked almost soft and kind.

"You can have as much earth as you want," he said. "You remind me of someone else who loved the earth and things that grow. When you see a bit of earth you want," he said with something like a smile, "take it, child, and make it come alive."

"May I take it from anywhere—if it's not wanted?"

"Anywhere," he answered. "There! You must go now, I am tired." He touched the bell to call Mrs. Medlock. "Good-bye. I shall be away all summer."

Mrs. Medlock came so quickly that Mary thought she must have been waiting in the corridor.

"Mrs. Medlock," Mr. Craven said to her, "now I have seen the child I understand what Mrs. Sowerby meant. She must be less delicate before she begins lessons. Give her simple, healthy food. Let her run wild in the garden. Don't look after her too much. She needs liberty and fresh air and romping about. Mrs. Sowerby is to come and see her now and then and she may sometimes go to the cottage."

Mrs. Medlock looked pleased. She was relieved to hear that she need not "look after" Mary too much. She had felt her a tiresome charge and had indeed seen as little of her as she dared. In addition to this she was fond of Martha's mother.

"Thank you, sir," she said. "Susan Sowerby and me went to school together and she's as sensible and good-hearted a woman as you'd find in a day's walk. I never had any children myself and she's had twelve, and there never was healthier or better ones. Miss Mary can get no harm from them. I'd always take Susan Sowerby's advice about children myself. She's what you might call healthy-minded—if you understand me."

"I understand," Mr. Craven answered. "Take Miss Mary away now and send Pitcher to me."

When Mrs. Medlock left her at the end of her own corridor Mary flew back to her room. She found Martha waiting there. Martha had, in fact, hurried back after she had removed the dinner service.

"I can have my garden!" cried Mary. "I may have it where I like! I am not going to have a governess for a long time! Your mother is coming to see me and I may go to your cottage! He says a little girl like me could not do any harm and I may do what I like—anywhere!"

"Eh!" said Martha delightedly, "that was nice of him wasn't it?"

"Martha," said Mary solemnly, "he is really a nice man, only his face is so miserable and his forehead is all drawn together."

She ran as quickly as she could to the garden. She had been away so much longer than she had thought she should and she knew Dickon would have to set out early on his five-mile walk. When she slipped through the door under the ivy, she saw he was not working where she had left him. The gardening tools were laid together under a tree. She ran to them, looking all round the place, but there was no Dickon to be seen. He had gone away and the secret garden was empty—except for the robin who had just flown across the wall and sat on a standard rose-bush watching her. "He's gone," she said woefully. "Oh! was he—was he—was he only a wood fairy?"

Something white fastened to the standard rose-bush caught her eye. It was a piece of paper, in fact, it was a piece of the letter she had printed for Martha to send to Dickon. It was fastened on the bush with a long thorn, and in a minute she knew Dickon had left it there. There were some roughly printed letters on it and a sort of picture. At first she could not tell what it was. Then she saw it was meant for a nest with a bird sitting on it. Underneath were the printed letters and they said:

"I will cum bak."

Chapter 13: The Undead Boy and the Ghost

Mary took the picture back to the house when she went to her supper and she showed it to Martha.

"Eh!" said Martha with great pride. "I never knew our Dickon was as clever as that. That there's a picture of a missel thrush on her nest, as large as life an' twice as natural."

Then Mary knew Dickon had meant the picture to be a message. He had meant that she might be sure he would keep her secret. Her garden was her nest and she was like a missel thrush. Oh, how she did like that queer, common boy!

She hoped he would come back the very next day and she fell asleep looking forward to the morning.

But you never know what the weather will do in Yorkshire, particularly in the springtime. She was awakened in the night by the sound of rain beating with heavy drops against her window. It was pouring down in torrents and the wind was "wuthering" round the corners and in the chimneys of the huge old house. Mary sat up in bed and felt miserable and angry.

"The rain is as contrary as I ever was," she said. "It came because it knew I did not want it."

Mary remembered what Martha had said about the rain softening the ground and those that were infected and buried might find it easier to claw there way up out of the hard cold ground. She imagined hundreds of the Accursed coming across the Moor towards Misselthwaite Manor.

She threw herself back on her pillow and buried her face. She did not cry, but she lay and hated the sound of the heavily beating rain, she hated the wind and its "wuthering." She could not go to sleep again. The mournful sound kept her awake because she felt mournful herself. If she had felt happy it would probably have lulled her to sleep. How it "wuthered" and how the big raindrops poured down and beat against the pane!

"It sounds just like a person lost on the moor and wandering on and on crying," she said.

She had been lying awake turning from side to side for about an hour, when suddenly something made her sit up in bed and turn her head toward the door listening. She listened and she listened.

"It isn't the wind now," she said in a loud whisper. "That isn't the wind. It is different. It is that crying I heard before."

The door of her room was closed and the sound seemed to come down the corridor and through the wall by the fireplace, a far-off faint sound of fretful moaning. She listened for a few minutes and each minute she became more and more sure. She felt as if she must find out what it was. It seemed even stranger than the secret garden and the buried key. Perhaps the fact that she was in a rebellious mood made her bold. She put her foot out of bed and stood on the floor.

"I am going to find out what it is," she said. "Everybody is in bed and I don't care about Mrs. Medlock—I don't care!"

There was a candle by her bedside and she took it up along with her throwing blades and went to the door of her room. It was locked. Mary had never tried to open the door at night and wondered if it had been locked every night. She listened closely to the moaning and walked along the wall by the fireplace. The moaning was coming from inside the fireplace! The fire was out and Mary leaned in close with her candle. She could feel a soft draft of cool air from behind the blackened iron shield in-laid in the hearth. Stepping into the firebox, Mary pulled at the large iron shield and revealed a space behind it! The bricks had been removed and a small tunnel lay hidden. The cries echoed from inside. Mary held her candle before her and walked softly through the fireplace. The end of the tunnel was blocked, but Mary pushed on the iron barrier and found herself in another fireplace. She brushed the soot off her feet the best she could and found herself in an unused bedroom. She moved to the door and found it unlocked. She was in a familiar corridor just around the corner from her own room. The corridor looked very long and dark, but she was too excited to mind that. She thought she remembered the corners she must turn to find the short corridor with the door covered with tapestry—the one the Accursed and Mrs. Medlock had come through the day she lost herself. The sound had come up that passage. So she went on with her dim light, almost feeling her way, her heart beating so loud that she fancied she could hear it. The far-off faint moaning went on and led her. Sometimes it stopped for a moment or so and then began again. Could it be an

Accursed had gotten into the house? Had someone been hurt? Was this the right corner to turn? She stopped and thought. Yes it was. Down this passage and then to the left, and then up two broad steps, and then to the right again. Yes, there was the tapestry door.

She pushed it open very gently and closed it behind her, and she stood in the corridor and could hear the moaning quite plainly, though it was not loud. It was on the other side of the wall at her left and a few yards farther on there was a door. She could see a glimmer of light coming from beneath it. The Someone was moaning in that room, and it was quite a young Someone.

So she walked to the door and pushed it open, and there she was standing in the room!

It was a big room with ancient, handsome furniture in it. There was a low fire glowing faintly on the hearth and a night light burning by the side of a carved four-posted bed hung with brocade. Heavy chains crisscrossed over the bed and were bolted to the wall above the headboard. Mary's eyes followed the chains down and on the bed was a boy, chained down by his wrists and ankles, crying and moaning fretfully.

Mary wondered if she was in a real place or if she had fallen asleep again and was dreaming without knowing it.

The boy had a sharp, delicate face the color of ivory and he seemed to have dark eyes too big for it. He had also a tangle of hair which tumbled over his forehead in heavy locks and made his thin face seem smaller.

The shackles around his wrists and ankles left deep scars where they had sliced deep into his skin then healed and were cut open again. He looked like a boy who had been ill, or possibly infected and was moaning in fever and pain.

Mary stood near the door with her candle in her hand, holding her breath. Then she crept across the room, and, as she drew nearer, the light attracted the boy's attention and he turned his head on his pillow and stared at her, his gray eyes opening so wide that they seemed immense. Mary thought surely this was an Accursed chained up, but why she could not fathom.

"Who are you?" he said at last in a half-frightened whisper. "Are you a ghost?"

"No, I am not," Mary answered, her own whisper sounding half frightened. "Are a Forsaken One?"

He stared and stared and stared. Mary could not help noticing what strange eyes he had. They were agate gray and they looked too big for his face because they had black lashes all round them. Mary had never thought that the Accursed could speak so she tried to understand why this boy was confined to the bed.

"No, not yet" he replied after waiting a moment or so. "I am Colin."

"Who is Colin?" she faltered.

"I am Colin Craven. Who are you?"

"I am Mary Lennox. Mr. Craven is my uncle."

"He is my father," said the boy.

"Your father!" gasped Mary. "No one ever told me he had a boy! Why didn't they?"

"Come here," he said, still keeping his strange eyes fixed on her with an anxious expression.

She came close to the bed and he put out his hand and touched her.

"You are real, aren't you?" he said. "I have such real dreams very often. You might be one of them."

Mary had slipped on a woolen wrap before she left her room and she put a piece of it between his fingers.

"Rub that and see how thick and warm it is," she said. "I will pinch you a little if you like, to show you how real I am. For a minute I thought you might be a dream too."

"Where did you come from?" he asked.

"From my own room. The wind wuthered so I couldn't go to sleep and I heard some one crying and wanted to find out who it was. What were you crying for?"

"Because I couldn't go to sleep either and my head ached. Tell me your name again."

"Mary Lennox. Did no one ever tell you I had come to live here?"

He was still fingering the fold of her wrap, but he began to look a little more as if he believed in her reality.

"No," he answered. "They daren't."

"Why?" asked Mary.

"Because I should have been afraid you would see me. I won't let people see me and talk me over."

"Why?" Mary asked again, feeling more mystified every moment.

"Because I am like this always, chained and ill. I am a great danger to you. My father won't let people talk me over either. The servants are not allowed to speak about me. If I were to escape I might get hungry and attempt to devour you, I might turn you into one of my kind. I should like to live like other people, but I shan't live. My father hates to think I may be like my mother."

"Oh, what a queer house this is!" Mary said. "What a queer house! Everything is a kind of secret. Rooms are locked up and gardens are locked up—and you! Have you been locked up for a long time?"

"Yes. All my life I have stayed in this room because if am moved out or see too many people I might go insane with cannibalistic cravings. I am always hungry, you see. Trying to escape tires me too much."

"Does your father come and see you?" Mary ventured.

"He doesn't want to see me. I am an abomination. I am God's curse."

"Why do you say that?" Mary could not help asking again.

A sort of angry shadow passed over the boy's face.

"My mother was infected by the Accursed and suffered a great fever when I was born. Then she died. I was born Accursed. The infection is in my blood. It makes him wretched to look at me, but he cannot bring himself to kill me. He needs me to complete his experiments. He thinks I don't know, but I've heard people talking. He hates me."

"He hates the garden too, because that is where she died," said Mary half speaking to herself.

"What garden?" the boy asked.

"Oh! just—just a garden she used to like," Mary stammered. "Have you been here always?"

"Nearly always. When I was very young they would take me out to the seaside and see how I would react to people, but that didn't go well. Sometimes I have been taken to the basement chained by the neck but allowed to run around. They throw raw meat at me and yell but they are always just out of reach. I want to kill them when they yell. Sometimes people just come and stare at me. I hate when people stare at me. So when they come close I try to bite them! I used to wear an iron thing around my head to keep me from biting, but a grand doctor came from London to see me and said it was stupid. He told them to take it off and feed me regular food and let me go outside in the fresh air. I hate fresh air and I don't want to go out. Medlock said if I ever got outside I would kill so many people."

"I didn't like to go outside when first I came here. And I don't think you'd kill people. You don't want to kill me," said Mary. Colin's gray eyes were glassy and unblinking. "Why do you keep looking at me like that?"

"Because of the dreams that are so real," he answered rather fretfully. "Sometimes when I open my eyes I don't believe I'm awake."

"We're both awake," said Mary. She glanced round the room with its high ceiling and shadowy corners and dim fire-light. "It looks quite like a dream, and it's the middle of the night, and everybody in the house is asleep—everybody but us. We are wide awake."

"I don't want it to be a dream," the boy said restlessly. "Everything always seems to be a nightmare."

Mary thought of something all at once.

"If you hate when people look at you," she began, "do you want me to go away?"

He still held the fold of her wrap and he gave it a little pull.

"No," he said. "I should be sure you were a dream if you went. If you are real, sit down on that big footstool and talk. I want to hear about you."

Mary put down her candle on the table near the bed and sat down on the cushioned stool. She did not want to go away at all. She wanted to stay in the mysterious hidden-away room and talk to the mysterious chained boy. He said he was Accursed, but Mary did not think he acted like one. But Mary did not know enough of the Accursed to know if they could talk, but this boy had grey eyes, not black.

"What do you want me to tell you?" she asked.

He wanted to know how long she had been at Misselthwaite; he wanted to know which corridor her room was on; he wanted to know what she had been doing; if she disliked the moor as he disliked it; where she had lived before she came to Yorkshire. She answered all these questions and many more and he lay back on his pillow and listened. He made her tell him a great deal about the Accursed in India, how the infection had spread and about the Untainted refugee camp and her voyage across the ocean. She found out that because he had been chained as a Forsaken he had not learned things as other children had. One of his keepers had read to him to keep him calm when he was quite little and he learned to read by listening and following along. He was always reading and looking at pictures in splendid books.

"Looking at pictures makes me forget how hungry I am all the time. Medlock says that I will be hungry forever and never satisfied. That is my doom. When I do eat too much I usually can't stomach it and I heave it up. The doctor, my uncle Dr. Craven, thinks regular food will always be disgusting to me. He says it is human flesh I need, but of course they won't give that to me."

Though his father rarely saw him, he was given all sorts of wonderful things to amuse himself with. He never seemed to have been amused, however. He was not interested in toys or other things boys liked. They put a rabbit in a cage next to his bed and he would feed it bits of grass. But then no one came to see him for several days and the rabbit died. Colin became so hungry he was forced to eat the rabbit along with pages from his books and anything else he could reach while chained. He had used the wire from the cage to unlock his wrist and ankle chains and he drank the water from the flower vases. When his keeper finally returned his bed was soiled, he was covered in blood and all his books had been torn up. It took four men to wrestle him back into the chains. "They never left me again after that." Colin said. He could have anything he asked for and was never made to do anything he did not like to do. "Everyone is obliged to do what pleases me," he said indifferently. "It makes me ill to be angry. They all want me dead but they must keep me alive, in a manner of speaking. I shall always be an Accursed demon."

He said it as if he was so accustomed to the idea that it had ceased to matter to him at all. He seemed to like the sound of

Mary's voice. As she went on talking he listened in a drowsy, interested way. Once or twice she wondered if he were not gradually falling into a doze. But at last he asked a question which opened up a new subject.

"How old are you?" he asked.

"I am ten," answered Mary, forgetting herself for the moment, "and so are you."

"How do you know that?" he demanded in a surprised voice.

"Because when you were born the garden door was locked and the key was buried. And it has been locked for ten years."

Colin half sat up, turning toward her, leaning on his elbows.

"What garden door was locked? Who did it? Where was the key buried?" he exclaimed as if he were suddenly very much interested.

"It—it was the garden Mr. Craven hates," said Mary nervously. "He locked the door. No one—no one knew where he buried the key."

"What sort of a garden is it?" Colin persisted eagerly.

"No one has been allowed to go into it for ten years," was Mary's careful answer.

But it was too late to be careful. He was too much like herself. He too had had nothing to think about and the idea of a hidden garden attracted him as it had attracted her. He asked question after question. Where was it? Had she never looked for the door? Had she never asked the gardeners?

"They won't talk about it," said Mary. "I think they have been told not to answer questions."

"I would make them," said Colin.

"Could you?" Mary faltered, beginning to feel frightened. If he could make people answer questions, who knew what might happen!

"Everyone is obliged to please me. I told you that," he said. "If they don't I become very ill. I feel like the Forsaken part of me takes over and I feel like killing them all, and they are scared of me. My father won't let them kill me. I may live forever, and this place would sometime belong to me. They all know that. I would make them tell me."

Mary had not known that she herself had been spoiled, but she could see quite plainly that this mysterious boy had been. He thought that the whole world belonged to him and that he could kill anyone who disobeyed him. How peculiar he was and how coolly he spoke of not living.

"Do you think you aren't alive?" she asked, partly because she was curious and partly in hope of making him forget the garden.

"I don't suppose I am," he answered as indifferently as he had spoken before. "Ever since I remember anything I have heard people say I am an Accused, a dead foul ghoul who only wants to eat human flesh. I've never had any so I wouldn't know. At first they thought I was too little to understand and now they think I don't hear. But I do. My doctor is my father's cousin. He is quite poor and if I become an insane wretch or I am finally killed he will have all Misselthwaite when my father is dead. I should think he wouldn't want me to live."

"Do you want to live?" inquired Mary.

"No," he answered, in a cross, tired fashion. "But I don't want to die. When I feel ill I lie here and think about losing my mind to the devil's hunger or being beheaded until I cry and cry."

"I have heard you crying three times," Mary said, "but I did not know who it was. Were you crying about that?" She did so want him to forget the garden.

"I dare say," he answered. "Let us talk about something else. Talk about that garden. Don't you want to see it?"

"Yes," answered Mary, in quite a low voice.

"I do," he went on persistently. "I don't think I ever really wanted to see anything before, but I want to see that garden. I want the key dug up. I want the door unlocked. I would have them take me there in my chair. I am going to make them open the door." Mary looked over at a hideous metal chair with iron locks for the ankles, wrists and neck.

Colin had become quite excited and his strange eyes began to shine like stars and looked more immense than ever.

"They have to please me," he said. "Or one day I will kill them all! I will spit in their eyes and make them Accursed. I will make them take me there and I will let you go, too."

Mary's hands clutched each other. Everything would be spoiled—everything! Dickon would never come back. She would never again feel like a missel thrush with a safe-hidden nest.

"Oh, don't—don't—don't—don't do that!" she cried out.

He stared as if he thought she had gone crazy!

"Why?" he exclaimed. "You said you wanted to see it."

"I do," she answered almost with a sob in her throat, "but if you make them open the door and take you in like that it will never be a secret again."

He leaned still farther forward.

"A secret," he said. "What do you mean? Tell me."

Mary's words almost tumbled over one another.

"You see—you see," she panted, "if no one knows but ourselves—if there was a door, hidden somewhere under the ivy—if there was—and we could find it; and if we could slip through it together and shut it behind us, and no one knew anyone was inside and we called it our garden and pretended that—that we were missel thrushes and it was our nest, and if we played there almost every day and dug and planted seeds and made it all come alive—"

"Is it dead?" he interrupted her.

"It soon will be if no one cares for it," she went on. "The bulbs will live but the roses—"

He stopped her again as excited as she was herself.

"What are bulbs?" he put in quickly.

"They are daffodils and lilies and snowdrops. They are working in the earth now—pushing up pale green points because the spring is coming."

"Is the spring coming?" he said. "What is it like? You don't see it in rooms if you are chained up like an animal."

"It is the sun shining on the rain and the rain falling on the sunshine, and things pushing up and working under the earth," said Mary. "If the garden was a secret and we could get into it we could watch the things grow bigger every day, and see how many roses are alive. Don't you see? Oh, don't you see how much nicer it would be if it was a secret?"

He dropped back on his pillow and lay there with an odd expression on his face.

"I never had a secret," he said, "except that one about everyone wanting me dead and using me in their experiments. They don't know I know that, so it is a sort of secret. But I like this kind better."

"If you won't make them take you to the garden," pleaded Mary, "perhaps—I feel almost sure I can find out how to get in sometime. I could help you escape from here and then—if someone puts you in your chair, and if you can scare everyone away, perhaps—perhaps we might find some boy who would push you, and we could go alone and it would always be a secret garden."

"I should—like—that," he said very slowly, his eyes looking dreamy. "I should like that. I should not mind fresh air in a secret garden."

Mary began to recover her breath and feel safer because the idea of escaping and keeping the secret seemed to please him. She felt almost sure that if she kept on talking and could make him see the garden in his mind as she had seen it he would like it so much that he could not bear to think that everybody might tramp in to it when they chose.

"I'll tell you what I think it would be like, if we could go into it," she said. "It has been shut up so long things have grown into a tangle perhaps."

He lay quite still and listened while she went on talking about the roses which might have clambered from tree to tree and hung down—about the many birds which might have built their nests there because it was so safe from the Accursed. And then she told him about the robin and Ben Weatherstaff, and there was so much to tell about the robin and it was so easy and safe to talk about it that she ceased to be afraid. The robin pleased him so much that he smiled until he looked almost beautiful, and at first Mary had thought that he was even plainer than herself, with his big sunken eyes, pale skin, and heavy tangled locks of hair.

"I did not know birds could be like that," he said. "But if you are bound in a room you never see things. What a lot of things you know. I feel as if you had been inside that garden."

She did not know what to say, so she did not say anything. He evidently did not expect an answer and the next moment he gave her a surprise.

"I am going to let you look at something," he said. "Do you see that rose-colored silk curtain hanging on the wall over the mantel-piece?"

Mary had not noticed it before, but she looked up and saw it. It was a curtain of soft silk hanging over what seemed to be some picture.

"Yes," she answered.

"There is a cord hanging from it," said Colin. "Go and pull it."

Mary got up, much mystified, and found the cord. When she pulled it the silk curtain ran back on rings and when it ran back it uncovered a picture. It was the picture of a girl with a laughing face. She had bright hair tied up with a blue ribbon and her gay, lovely eyes were exactly like Colin's unhappy ones, agate gray and looking twice as big as they really were because of the black lashes all round them.

"She is my mother," said Colin complainingly. "I don't see why she died. Sometimes I hate her for doing it."

"How queer!" said Mary.

"If she had lived I believe I should not have been Accursed," he grumbled. "I dare say I should have lived, too. And my father would not have hated to look at me. I dare say I should have had not been chained my whole life and kept alive with being force fed raw meat and porridges. Draw the curtain again."

Mary did as she was told and returned to her footstool.

"She is much prettier than you," she said, "but her eyes are just like yours—at least they are the same shape and color. Why is the curtain drawn over her?"

He moved uncomfortably.

"I made them do it," he said. "Sometimes I don't like to see her looking at me. She smiles too much when I am ill and miserable. Besides, she is mine and I don't want everyone to see her." There were a few moments of silence and then Mary spoke.

"What would Mrs. Medlock do if she found out that I had been here?" she inquired.

"She would do as I told her to do," he answered. "And I should tell her that I wanted you to come here and talk to me every day. I am glad you came."

"So am I," said Mary. "I will come as often as I can, but"—she hesitated—"I shall have to look every day for the garden door."

"Yes, you must," said Colin, "and you can tell me about it afterward."

He lay thinking a few minutes, as he had done before, and then he spoke again.

"I think you shall be a secret, too," he said. "I will not tell them until they find out. I can always send the nurse out of the room and say that I want to be by myself. Do you know Martha?"

"Yes, I know her very well," said Mary. "She waits on me."

He nodded his head toward the outer corridor.

"She is the one who is asleep in the other room. The nurse went away yesterday to stay all night with her sister and she always makes Martha attend to me when she wants to go out. Martha shall tell you when to come here."

Then Mary understood Martha's troubled look when she had asked questions about the crying.

"Martha knew about you all the time?" she said.

"Yes; she often attends to me. The nurse likes to get away from me and then Martha comes."

"I have been here a long time," said Mary. "Shall I go away now? Your eyes look sleepy."

"I wish I could go to sleep before you leave me," he said rather shyly.

"Shut your eyes," said Mary, drawing her footstool closer, "and I will do what my Ayah used to do in India. I will pat your hand and stroke it and sing something quite low."

"I should like that perhaps," he said drowsily.

Somehow she was sorry for him and did not want him to lie awake, so she leaned against the bed and began to stroke and pat his hand and sing a very low little chanting song in Hindustani.

"That is nice," he said more drowsily still, and she went on chanting and stroking, but when she looked at him again his black lashes were lying close against his cheeks, for his eyes were shut and he was fast asleep. So she got up softly, took her candle and crept away without making a sound. Going back her room, she pulled the iron shields into place and wiped away traces of her footprints in the ashes.

Chapter 14: A Young Cannibalistic Rajah

The moor was hidden in mist when the morning came, and the rain had not stopped pouring down. There could be no going out of doors. Martha was so busy that Mary had no opportunity of talking to her, but in the afternoon she asked her to come and sit with her in the nursery. She came bringing the stocking she was always knitting when she was doing nothing else.

"What's the matter with thee?" she asked as soon as they sat down. "Tha' looks as if tha'd somethin' to say."

"I have. I have found out what the crying was," said Mary.

Martha let her knitting drop on her knee and gazed at her with startled eyes.

"Tha' hasn't!" she exclaimed. "Never!"

"I heard it in the night," Mary went on. "And I got up and went to see where it came from. It was Colin. I found him."

Martha's face became red with fright.

"Eh! Miss Mary!" she said half crying. "Tha' shouldn't have done it—tha' shouldn't! You could've been bitten! Tha'll get me in trouble. I never told thee nothin' about him—but tha'll get me in trouble. I shall lose my place and what'll Mother do!"

"You won't lose your place," said Mary. "He was glad I came. And he didn't try and bite me, we talked and talked and he said he was glad I came."

"Was he?" cried Martha. "Art tha' sure? Tha' doesn't know what he's like when anything vexes him. He's a big lad to cry and moan so, but when he's in a passion he'll fair scream just to frighten us. He knows us daren't call our souls our own."

"He wasn't vexed," said Mary. "I asked him if I should go away and he made me stay. He asked me questions and I sat on a big footstool and talked to him about India and about the robin and gardens. He wouldn't let me go. He let me see his mother's picture. Before I left him I sang him to sleep. If he hadn't told me, I wouldn't have thought anything about him being Accursed. The Accursed do not sleep."

Martha fairly gasped with amazement.

"I can scarcely believe thee!" she protested. "It's as if tha'd walked straight into a lion's den. If he'd been like he is most times he'd have throwed himself into one of his ravin' tantrums and roused th' house. He won't let strangers look at him."

"He let me look at him. I looked at him all the time and he looked at me. We stared!" said Mary.

"I don't know what to do!" cried agitated Martha. "If Mrs. Medlock finds out, she'll think I broke orders and told thee and I shall be packed back to Mother."

"He is not going to tell Mrs. Medlock anything about it yet. It's to be a sort of secret just at first," said Mary firmly. "And he says everybody is obliged to do as he pleases."

"Aye, that's true enough— He must be kept alive at any cost, an' we do everythin' to calm his tempers, th' evil creature!" sighed Martha, wiping her forehead with her apron.

"He says Mrs. Medlock must. And he wants me to come and talk to him every day. And you are to tell me when he wants me."

"Me!" said Martha; "I shall lose my place—I shall for sure!"

"You can't if you are doing what he wants you to do and everybody is ordered to obey him," Mary argued.

"Does tha' mean to say," cried Martha with wide open eyes, "that he was nice to thee! He didn't try to attack thee?"

"I think he almost liked me," Mary answered. "He didn't seem hungry at all."

"Then tha' must have bewitched him!" decided Martha, drawing a long breath.

"Do you mean Magic?" inquired Mary. "I've heard about Magic in India, but I can't make it. I just went into his room and I was so surprised to see him I stood and stared. And then he turned round and stared at me. And he thought I was a ghost or a dream and I thought perhaps he was. And it was so queer being there alone together in the middle of the night and not knowing about each other. And we began to ask each other questions. And when I asked him if I must go away he said I must not."

"Th' world's comin' to an end!" gasped Martha.

"Why is he always chained to the bed? And what is the matter with him?" asked Mary.

"Nobody knows for sure and certain," said Martha. "Master Craven went off his head like when he was born. Th' doctors thought he'd have to be killed. It was because of the way Mrs.

Craven died like I told you. She was infected, but Mr. Craven brought her home and tha' night gave birth to th' baby, and Master Craven had to... well after she'd turned...kill her. He wouldn't set eyes on th' baby. He just raved and said it'd be another Accursed like his mother and it'd better die.

"Is Colin truly Accursed?" Mary asked. "He doesn't have the eyes of one."

"He is an' he isn't," said Martha. "Dr. Craven, the Master's cousin, realized that Colin was different and he took the infant's blood. Accordin' to his scopes Colin carries the infection but still retained his mind. This got the Doctor thinkin' he might be able to create a cure. But he began all wrong.

Mother said that there was enough trouble and raging in th' house to set any child wrong. They was afraid he could infect others and no one wanted to touch him. He would cry with hunger but no nurse would let him suckle. He was given goat's milk and his face an' hands had to be covered whenever he was changed. They were always takin' his blood and 'e would wail and wail! When he was able to move around his'self he had to be caged then chained keepin' him lyin' down and not lettin' him walk. Once they made him wear a brace over his mouth but he fretted so till he was downright insane."

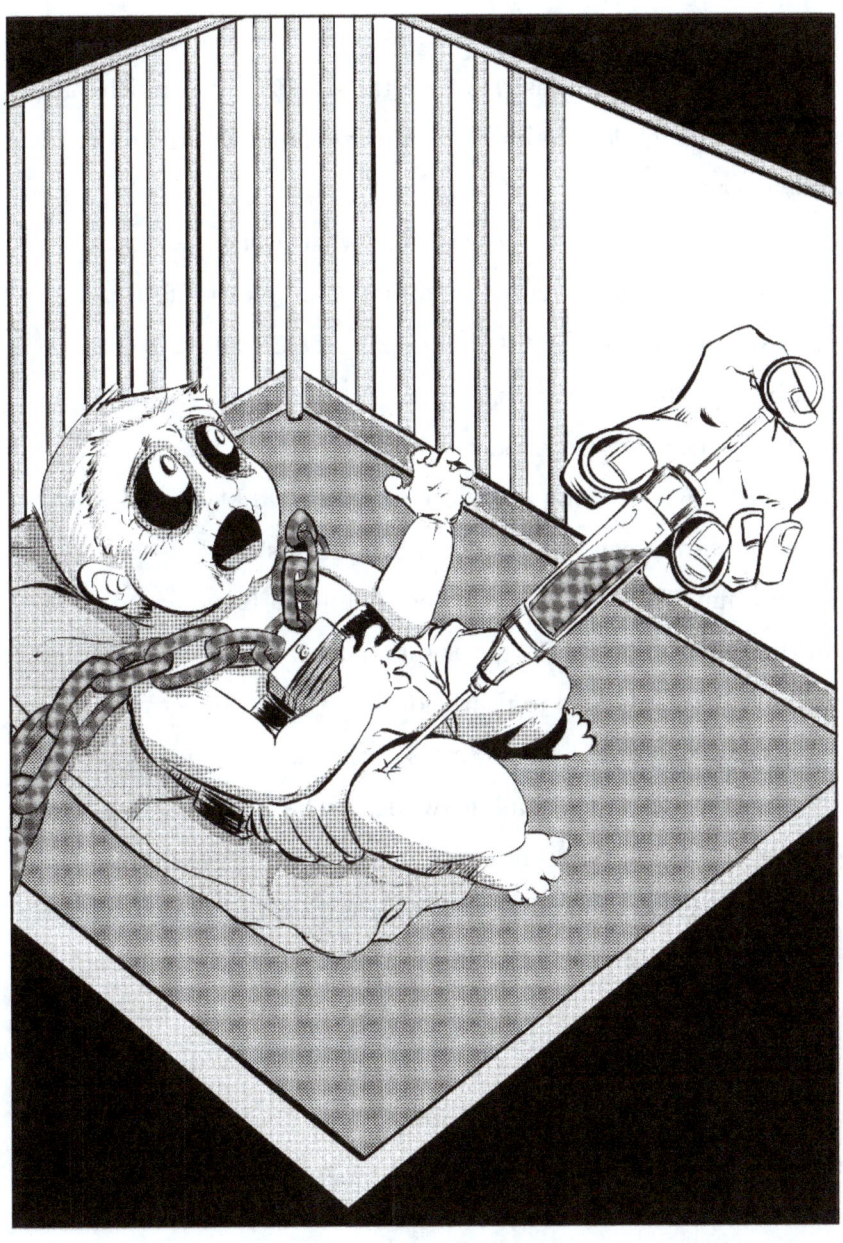

"Then a big London doctor came to see him an' made them take it off. He talked to Dr. Craven quite rough—in a polite way. But he didn't understand the Accursed at the time. He didn't know how dangerous Colin was. He said there'd been too much raw foods, not enough letting him free, and too much lettin' him have his own way.

Everyone is scared not to give him what ever he wants. If he goes into a fit he starts spitting and that could mean infection if it got in you. Plus, his blood is unique, Master Craven says, and he must be kept alive at all costs."

"I think he's a very spoiled boy," said Mary.

"He's th' worst young nowt as ever was!" said Martha. "I won't say as he hasn't been ill a good bit. He's been sick with the foods given to him. The doctor says he needs human blood and organs and that anything else will never satisfy him. He's had infections and fevers that's seemed to nearly kill him two or three times. But we all know that only a trama to his brain will ever truly kill him. Once he had not eaten for a long while and he was chewin' off his own fingertips. Anything they made him eat he heaved right out. He became near a skeleton. Eh! Mrs. Medlock did get a fright then. He'd been out of his head an' she was talkin' to th' nurse, thinkin' he didn't know nothin', an' she said, 'He'll die this time sure enough, an' best thing for him an' for everybody.' An' she looked at him an' there he was with his big eyes open, starin' at her as sensible as she was herself. She didn't know wha'd happen but he just stared at her an' says, 'You give me some water an' stop talkin'.'"

"Do you think he can die?" asked Mary.

"Mother says there's no reason why any child should live that is half cursed, gets no fresh air an' doesn't do nothin' but lie on his back chained to a bed all day. He's weak and hates being locked in his chair and th' trouble o' bein' taken out o' doors, an' he gets cold so easy he says it makes him ill."

Mary sat and looked at the fire. "I wonder," she said slowly, "if it would not do him good to go out into a garden and watch things growing. It did me good."

"One of th' worst fits he ever had," said Martha, "was one time they took him out where the roses is by the fountain. He'd been readin' in a paper about people goin' around outside killing the Accursed by shooting them or stabbing them in the head and said that people must be coming to cut off *his* head. An' then a new gardener as didn't know th' rules passed by an' looked at him curious then yelled and ran off. Master Colin threw himself into a passion an' he said he'd looked at him knowin' he was Accursed and wanted to kill him. He snapped at everyone and moaned himself into a fever an' was ill all night."

"If he ever gets angry at me, I'll never go and see him again," said Mary.

"He'll have thee if he wants thee," said Martha. "Tha' may as well know that at th' start."

Very soon afterward a bell rang and she rolled up her knitting.

"I dare say th' nurse wants me to stay with him a bit," she said. "I hope he's in a good temper."

She was out of the room about ten minutes and then she came back with a puzzled expression.

"Well, tha' has bewitched him," she said. "He's sitting up still and asked for his chains to be loosened. Anytime he goes wild we have to pull them tight again. He's told the nurse to stay away until six o'clock. I'm to wait in the next room. Th' minute she was gone he called me to him an' says, 'I want Mary Lennox to come and talk to me, and remember you're not to tell anyone.' You'd better go as quick as you can."

Mary was quite willing to go quickly. She did not want to see Colin as much as she wanted to see Dickon; but she wanted to see him very much.

There was a bright fire on the hearth when she entered his room, but with the windows completely blocked no one would know it was daylight outside. She saw it could have been a very beautiful room indeed if not for the large rusted chains that ran long the walls on a pulley system and the dark wooden table stained with blood augmented with bolted manacles for the ankles, wrists and neck. There were rich colors in the rugs and hangings and pictures and books on the walls, but also a cage in the corner in the shape of a person where one would be unable to move inside. The falling rain beat down on the covered windows. Colin looked cheerful; as cheerful as one could look with sunken grey eyes, pallid skin and a bone thin body wrapped in an old, faded velvet dressing-gown. He sat up against a big brocaded cushion with fresh cuts to his wrists and a red mark on each cheek.

"Come in," he said. "I've been thinking about you all morning."

"I've been thinking about you, too," answered Mary. "You don't know how frightened Martha is. She says Mrs. Medlock will think she told me about you and then she will be sent away."

He frowned.

"Go and tell her to come here," he said. "She is in the next room."

Mary went and brought her back. Poor Martha was shaking in her shoes. Colin was still frowning.

"Have you to do what I please or have you not?" he demanded.

"I have to do what you please, sir," Martha faltered, turning quite red.

"Because if you do not, what will I do?" Colin demanded.

"You'll wail and spit and tear at your chains. You give us all a fright, sir." Martha's knees nearly buckled.

"That's right! Has Medlock to do what I please?"

"Everybody has, sir," said Martha. "You are still Master, even if..." Martha diminished and looked as if she wanted to run.

"Well, then, if I order you to bring Miss Mary to me, how can Medlock send you away if she finds it out?"

"Please don't let her, sir," pleaded Martha.

"I'll send her away if she dares to say a word about such a thing," said Master Craven grandly. "She wouldn't like that, I can tell you."

"Thank you, sir," bobbing a curtsy, "I want to do my duty, sir."

"What I want is your duty" said Colin more grandly still. "I am still Master, as you said. I'll take care of you. Now go away."

When the door closed behind Martha, Colin found Mistress Mary gazing at him as if he had set her wondering.

"Why do you look at me like that?" he asked her. "What are you thinking about?"

"I am thinking about two things."

"What are they? Sit down and tell me."

"This is the first one," said Mary, seating herself on the big stool. "Once in India I saw a boy who was a Rajah. He had rubies and emeralds and diamonds stuck all over him. He spoke to his people just as you spoke to Martha. Everybody had to do everything he told them—in a minute. I think they would have been killed if they hadn't."

"I shall make you tell me about Rajahs presently," he said, "but first tell me what the second thing was."

"I was thinking," said Mary, "how different you are from Dickon."

"Who is Dickon?" he said. "What a queer name!"

She might as well tell him, she thought she could talk about Dickon without mentioning the secret garden. She had liked to hear Martha talk about him. Besides, she longed to talk about him. It would seem to bring him nearer.

"He is Martha's brother. He is twelve years old," she explained. "He is not like anyone else in the world. He can charm foxes and squirrels and birds just as the natives in India charm snakes. He saves them from the Accurs..." Mary stopped herself from telling Colin that Dickon could slay the Accursed better than she had ever seen anyone else.

"Is he magic to charm animals to like him? I've only ever seen a few live animals and they hated me. They were caged like me and scared out of their minds. I hated seeing them that way. I put the horrid rabbit out of his misery, plus I was so hungry."

"He doesn't call it Magic." Mary explained. "He says it's because he lives on the moor so much and he knows their ways.

He says he feels sometimes as if he was a bird or a rabbit himself, he likes them so. I think he asked the robin questions. It seemed as if they talked to each other in soft chirps."

Colin lay back on his cushion and his eyes grew larger and larger and the spots on his cheeks burned.

"Tell me some more about him," he said.

"He knows all about eggs and nests," Mary went on. "And he knows where foxes and badgers and otters live. He keeps them secret so that other boys won't find their holes and frighten them. He knows about everything that grows or lives on the moor."

"Does he like the moor?" said Colin. "How can he when it's such a great, bare, dreary place? I was told the Forsaken do not like to cross it and if I ever tried to escape I would get lost out on the Moor forever."

"It's the most beautiful place," protested Mary. "Thousands of lovely things grow on it and there are thousands of little creatures all busy building nests and making holes and burrows and chippering or singing or squeaking to each other. They are so busy and having such fun under the earth or in the trees or heather. It's their world."

"How do you know all that?" said Colin, turning on his elbow to look at her.

"I have never been there once, really," said Mary suddenly remembering. "I only drove over it in the dark. I thought it was hideous. Martha told me about it first and then Dickon. When Dickon talks about it you feel as if you saw things and heard them and as if you were standing in the heather with the sun shining and the gorse smelling like honey—and all full of bees and butterflies."

"You never see anything if you are chained up," said Colin restlessly. He looked like a person listening to a new sound in the distance and wondering what it was.

"You can't if you stay in a room," said Mary.

"I couldn't go on the moor," he said in a resentful tone.

Mary was silent for a minute and then she said something bold.

"You might—sometime."

He moved as if he were startled.

"Go on the moor! How could I? I am half dead and I would hate it. If I got loose and hungry I might go insane and become a mindless cannibal. I might even try to eat you!"

"How do you know?" said Mary unsympathetically. She didn't like the way he had of talking about being dead and killing people. She did not feel very sympathetic. She felt rather as if he almost boasted about it.

"Oh, I've heard it ever since I remember," he answered crossly. "They are always whispering about it and thinking I don't notice. They wish I would just die, too. I know they all want to kill me."

Mistress Mary felt quite contrary. She pinched her lips together.

"If they wished I would die," she said, "I wouldn't do it. Who wishes you would?"

"The servants, they hate trying to dress me and bathe me and feed me thinking they could be infected by me—and of course my uncle, Dr. Craven, because he would get Misselthwaite and be rich instead of poor. He daren't say so, but he always looks cheerful when I am worse. When I nearly starved his face got quite fat. I think my father wishes it, too, despite his research."

"I don't believe he does, he had ordered everyone to keep you alive!" said Mary quite obstinately. "What research does he do?"

"He has them take my blood into many viles when he is here. He goes away for a long time trying to get help finding a cure for the Accursed. He thinks because I can still think and speak there is something special about my infected blood. That's all he cares about, though. And no one else believes him. There is no cure for the Devil's work. God hates me."

Mary stared at him and then he lay back on his cushion and was still, as if he were thinking. And there was quite a long silence. Perhaps they were both of them thinking strange things children do not usually think.

Mary said, "I like the grand doctor from London, because he made them take the iron thing off your head," said Mary at last. "Did he say you should be killed?"

"No."

"What did he say?"

"He didn't whisper," Colin answered. "Perhaps he knew I hated whispering. I heard him say one thing quite aloud. He said, 'The lad might live if he would make up his mind to it. He is between living and dead and needs be put in the humor.' It sounded as if he was in a temper."

"I'll tell you who would put you in the humor, perhaps," said Mary reflecting. She felt as if she would like this thing to be settled one way or the other. "I believe Dickon would. He's always talking about live things. He never talks about dead things or things that are ill. He's always looking up in the sky to watch birds flying—or looking down at the earth to see something growing. He has such round blue eyes and they are so wide open with looking about. And he laughs such a big laugh with his wide mouth—and his cheeks are as red—as red as cherries." She pulled her stool nearer to the bed and her expression quite changed at the remembrance of the wide curving mouth and wide open eyes.

"See here," she said. "Don't let us talk about dying or killing; I don't like it. Let us talk about living. Let us talk and talk about Dickon. And then we will look at your pictures."

It was the best thing she could have said. To talk about Dickon meant to talk about the moor and about the cottage and the fourteen people who lived in it on sixteen shillings a week—and the children who got fat on the moor grass like the wild ponies. And about Dickon's mother and the moor with the sun on it—and about pale green points sticking up out of the black sod. And it was all so alive that Mary talked more than she had ever talked before—and Colin both talked and listened as he had never done either before. He had only known thoughts of death and the stench of raw meat and the pain of shackles and hunger. Now they both began to laugh over nothings as children will when they are happy together. And they laughed so that in the end they were making as much noise as if they had been two ordinary healthy natural ten-year-old creatures—instead of a hard, little, unloving girl and a tortured boy who believed that he was dead and would one day become an immortal cannibal.

They enjoyed themselves so much that they forgot the pictures and they forgot about the time. They had been laughing quite loudly over Ben Weatherstaff and his robin, and Colin was actually sitting up as if he had forgotten about his ankle and wrist chains, when he suddenly remembered something. "Do you know there is one thing we have never once thought of," he said. "We are cousins."

It seemed so queer that they had talked so much and never remembered this simple thing that they laughed more than ever, because they had got into the humor to laugh at anything. And in the midst of the fun the door opened and in walked the uncle, Dr. Craven, and Mrs. Medlock.

Dr. Craven started in actual alarm and Mrs. Medlock almost fell back because he had accidentally bumped against her.

"Good Lord!" exclaimed poor Mrs. Medlock with her eyes almost starting out of her head. "Good Lord!"

"What is this?" said Dr. Craven, coming forward. "Get away from him, stupid girl, he's dangerous!"

Then Mary was reminded of the boy Rajah again. Colin answered as if neither the doctor's alarm nor Mrs. Medlock's terror were of the slightest consequence. He was as little disturbed or frightened as if an elderly cat and dog had walked into the room.

"This is my cousin, Mary Lennox," he said. "I asked her to come and talk to me. I like her. She must come and talk to me whenever I send for her."

Dr. Craven turned reproachfully to Mrs. Medlock. "Oh, sir" she panted. "I don't know how it's happened. There's not a servant on the place tha'd dare to talk—they all have their orders."

"Nobody told her anything," said Colin. "She heard me moaning and found me herself. I am glad she came. Don't be silly, Medlock."

Mary saw that Dr. Craven did not look pleased, but it was quite plain that he dare not oppose his patient. He looked at the fresh cuts on Colin's wrists from his moving around too much.

"I am afraid there has been too much excitement. Excitement is not good for you, it can make you hungry. You could have an ...episode." he said.

"I should be excited if she kept away," answered Colin, his eyes beginning to look dangerously sparkling. "I feel less tired, less hungry. But I shall eat if Mary wishes to. Have the nurse bring our meals together, Medlock.

Mrs. Medlock and Dr. Craven looked at each other in a troubled way, but there was evidently nothing to be done.

"He does look rather more alive, sir," ventured Mrs. Medlock. "But"—thinking the matter over— "he looked that way this morning before she came into the room."

"She came into the room last night. She stayed with me a long time. So you can see that I did not try to kill her. If I wanted to kill her I'd have done it," said Colin. Mary started but did not move from her seat by the bed.

Dr. Craven did not stay very long. He talked to the nurse for a few minutes when she came into the room and said a few words of warning to Colin. He must not talk too much; he must not forget that he was infected and dangerous; he must not forget that he was very easily tired. Mary thought that there seemed to be a number of uncomfortable things he was not to forget.

Colin looked fretful and kept his strange black-lashed eyes fixed on Dr. Craven's face.

"I want to forget it," he said at last. "She makes me forget it. That is why I want her."

Dr. Craven did not look happy when he left the room. He gave a puzzled glance at the little girl sitting on the large stool. She had become a stiff, silent child again as soon as he entered and he could not see what the attraction was. The boy actually did look brighter, however—and he sighed rather heavily as he went down the corridor.

"They are always wanting me to eat things when I don't want to," said Colin, as the nurse brought in a tray of tea and muffins for Mary and a covered tray for Colin and put it on the table by the bed. "Now, if you'll eat I will." Mary stared as Colin lifted the tray lid to reveal a fresh raw plucked hen and some raw vegetables dripping in a red sauce that could only be blood. Colin put the tray on his lap and frowning, bit into the raw hen, pink blood dripping down his chin. He gulped it down and drank the some water. After wiping his mouth he said, "Now tell me about Rajahs."

Chapter 15: Nest Building

After another week of rain the high arch of blue sky appeared again and the sun which poured down was quite hot. Though there had been no chance to see either the secret garden or Dickon, Mistress Mary had enjoyed herself very much. The week had not seemed long. She had spent hours of every day with Colin in his room, talking about Rajahs or gardens or Dickon and the cottage on the moor. They had looked at the splendid books and pictures and sometimes Mary had read things to Colin, and sometimes he had read a little to her. When he was amused and interested she thought he scarcely looked like an Accursed at all, except that his face was so colorless, he was so thin, and he was always chained to the bed.

"You are a sly young one to listen and get out of your bed to go following things up like you did that night," Mrs. Medlock said once. "You could have been bitten and then what would I have done with you? But there's no saying it's not been a sort of blessing to the lot of us. He's not had an insane fit since you made friends. The nurse was just going to give up the case because she was so scared of him, but she says she doesn't mind staying now you've gone on duty with her," Medlock laughed nervously.

In her talks with Colin, Mary had tried to be very cautious about the secret garden. There were certain things she wanted to find out from him, but she felt that she must find them out without asking him direct questions. In the first place, as she began to like to be with him, she wanted to discover whether he was the kind of boy you could tell a secret to. He was not in the least like Dickon, but he was evidently so pleased with the idea of a garden no one knew anything about that she thought perhaps he could be trusted. But she had not known him long enough to be sure. The second thing she wanted to find out was this: If he could be trusted—if he really could—would it be possible to unlock the chains and take him to the garden without having any one find it out? The grand doctor had said that he must have fresh air and Colin had said that he would not mind fresh air in a secret garden. Perhaps if he had a great deal of fresh air and knew Dickon and the robin and saw things growing he might not think so much about being dead himself. Mary had seen herself in the glass sometimes lately when she had realized that she looked quite a different creature from the child she had seen when she arrived from India. This child looked nicer. Even Martha had seen a change in her.

"Th' air from th' moor has done thee good already," she had said. "Tha'rt not nigh so yeller and scrawny. Even tha' hair doesn't slamp down on tha' head so flat. It's got some life in it so as it sticks out a bit."

"It's like me," said Mary. "It's growing stronger and fatter. I'm sure there's more of it."

"It looks it, for sure," said Martha, ruffling it up a little round her face. "Tha'rt not half so ugly when it's that way an' there's a bit o' red in tha' cheeks."

If gardens and fresh air had been good for her perhaps they would be good for Colin. But then, if he hated people to look at him, perhaps he would not like to see Dickon.

"Why does it make you angry when you are looked at?" she inquired one day.

"I always hated it," he answered, "even when I was very little. When they took me to the seaside and I used to lie chained down in my carriage everybody used to stare and ladies would stop and talk to my nurse and then they would begin to whisper and I knew then they were saying I shouldn't be kept alive. It was unnatural and dangerous to keep the Forsaken. Then sometimes the ladies would look closely and say 'Poor child! Poor Tormented One!' They thought because I was chained down I couldn't hurt them. Once when a lady put her hand too close to pat my head I screamed out loud and bit her hand. She was so frightened she ran away. Know one knew what became of her."

"She probably thought she'd die and become a cannibal," said Mary, not at all admiringly.

"I don't care what she became," said Colin, frowning.

"I wonder why you didn't scream and bite me when I came into your room?" said Mary. Then she began to smile slowly.

"I thought you were a ghost or a dream," he said. "You can't bite a ghost or a dream, and if you scream they don't care."

"Would you hate it if—if a boy looked at you?" Mary asked uncertainly.

He lay back on his cushion and paused thoughtfully.

"There's one boy," he said quite slowly, as if he were thinking over every word, "there's one boy I believe I shouldn't mind. It's that boy who knows where the foxes live—Dickon."

"I'm sure you wouldn't mind him," said Mary glad she had never told about Dickon stabbing the Accursed man in the head.

"The birds don't and other animals," he said, still thinking it over, "perhaps that's why I shouldn't. He's a sort of animal charmer and I am a boy animal."

Then he laughed and she laughed too; in fact it ended in their both laughing a great deal and finding the idea of a boy animal chained in a cage very funny indeed.

What Mary felt afterward was that she need not fear about Dickon. Mary realized that she was quite alone with Colin and no servants or nurses or Medlocks were anywhere nearby. She wondered what would happen if she just let Colin loose.

She looked closely at Colin's chains around his wrists. "How do they remove these?" Mary asked gingerly touching the metal cuffs.

"First they put a mask over my face so that I can't bite. Then they tie my hands behind my back. There is a sort of key, like a metal rod they use to unlock the shackles. Then they unlock my ankles last. I cannot move my legs so they are not afraid of me kicking."

Where is the metal rod?"

"Don't know. Medlock has one on her ring of keys and the nurse has one but I don't know where she keeps it."

Mary walked into the room where the nurse normally slept and found there was a little desk there. Looking through all the drawers she did not find a key anywhere and just as she was giving up, Mary spotted a small box on a shelf above the little cot. She was up on the cot in an instant and opening the box she found two keys. One that looked like the small rod shape Colin had told her about, and the other was thick and heavy.

Colin looked at both of them and recognized the wrist cuff key instantly. "I have never seen this key before," He said looking at the thick iron key. "I wonder what it opens?"

"Nevermind this key anyway," Mary said, "What if we unshackle you? Wouldn't that give them all a surprise. You could show them that you aren't a threat." She put the little rod shaped key into the hole in the iron cuffs around Colin's wrists.

"What?" Colin pulled away. "No! They would surely never trust leaving us alone together again. And you don't know what they do, Mary, when they think I am in a rage and might fully turn on them. They try ever so many drugs on me and drain my blood and stuff handkerchiefs into my mouth and other horrid things. And what if I actually did try to hurt you once I was unchained?

"What are you talking about? You've never tried to hurt me, though I sat right next to you on the bed." Mary moved closer and took his hand. "Come on, no one will know. Just be free for a little while."

Colin stared at Mary as she put the key in the lock and turned it. The iron cuffs fell to the blanket. Then Mary crawled to the foot of the bed and unlocked his ankle cuffs. Colin rubbed his wrists and lay on the bed not moving and but smiling.

"Well, are you going to get up?" Mary asked.

"I can't get up. My legs are broken."

"They aren't broken! They are just skinny. You need to try." Mary took his feet and pulled them to the bed's edge. Colin sat looking down at the floor.

"If I became Accursed and got free, I suppose I would have to drag myself around trying to kill people. I would never catch anyone.

"I bet I could drag myself faster than you." Mary jumped off the bed and lay on the floor looking up at Colin.

He grinned and slowly lowered himself down having to finally let go and land on his shoulder. "I will be the fastest leg-less Accursed you have ever seen!"

Colin used his arms to pull himself across the floor towards Mary. She moaned like the undead and pulled herself along.

"Is that what they sound like?" Colin asked.

"Yes, they moan because they no longer know how to speak. But they seem to do it when they are just wandering. They hiss too, like a cat's hiss, when they are about to attack.

Colin moaned and dragged himself towards Mary and he grabbed her ankle. He pulled her towards him and opened his mouth wide. She turned back and hissed at him and they both began giggling.

"Can you imagine if Medlock walked in here now?" Mary said trying to stifle her giggling.

"I think she would behead us both. I should probably get back into bed."

"Colin." Mary suddenly looked concerned staring at him. "Colin, what are you doing?"

"What do you mean?" He asked.

"Let go!"

Colin suddenly realized he held Mary's ankle still in a tight grasp. He quickly released his hold and Mary rubbed her red skin. "For someone who claims to be so weak, you have a firm grip."

Colin sat up embarrassed. "Sorry, Mary. I wasn't aware. I should have been paying attention. Will you help me back into bed?"

Mary stood and walked behind him. For an instant she imagined him to be Accursed and thought about him turning suddenly and biting her in the neck or shoulder. She took a breath and put her arms underneath his and lifted him as high as she could. Getting him back on the bed was difficult and required Mary to lean him against the bed and then pull up his legs as he held on to the sheets. Colin was able to turn himself around but breathed heavily from exertion as Mary locked the iron cuffs around his ankles and wrists. After returning the keys, she turned to leave but Colin called after her.

"Thank you, Mary, for a few moments of freedom. I didn't hurt you, did I?"

"Of course not," she said, the skin was not broken though her ankle did feel a bit sore.

"And I will see you tomorrow?" he asked hopefully.

"I promise."

On that first morning when the sky was blue again Mary wakened very early. The sun was pouring in slanting rays through the blinds and there was something so joyous in the sight of it that she jumped out of bed and ran to the window. She drew up the blinds and opened the window itself and a great waft of fresh, scented air blew in upon her. The moor was blue and the whole world looked as if something Magic had happened to it. There was not a sign of the Accursed anywhere and there were tender little fluting sounds here and there and everywhere, as if scores of birds were beginning to tune up for a concert. Mary put her hand out of the window and held it in the sun.

"It's warm—warm!" she said. "It will make the green points push up and up and up, and it will make the bulbs and roots work and struggle with all their might under the earth."

She kneeled down and leaned out of the window as far as she could, breathing big breaths and sniffing the air until she laughed because she remembered what Dickon's mother had said about the end of his nose quivering like a rabbit's. "It must be very early," she said. "The little clouds are all pink and I've never seen the sky look like this. No one is up. I don't even hear the stable boys."

A sudden thought made her scramble to her feet.

"I can't wait! I am going to see the garden!"

She had learned to dress herself by this time and she put on her clothes in five minutes. Pocketing her throwing blades, she flew downstairs in her stocking feet and put on her shoes in the hall. She knew a small side door by the kitchens which she could unbolt herself and she unchained and unbolted and unlocked and when the door was finally open she sprang across the step with one bound, and there she was standing on the grass, which seemed to have turned green overnight, and with the sun pouring down on her and warm sweet wafts about her and the fluting and twittering and singing coming from every bush and tree. She clasped her hands for pure joy and looked up in the sky and it was so blue and pink and pearly and white and flooded with springtime light that she felt as if she must flute and sing aloud herself and knew that thrushes and robins and skylarks could not possibly help it. She ran around the shrubs and paths towards the secret garden.

"It is all different already," she said. "The grass is greener and things are sticking up and things are uncurling and green buds of leaves are showing. This afternoon I am sure Dickon will come."

The long warm rain had done strange things to the herbaceous beds which bordered the walk by the lower wall. There were things sprouting and pushing out from the roots of clumps of plants and there were actually here and there glimpses of royal purple and yellow unfurling among the stems of crocuses. Six months before Mistress Mary would not have seen how the world was waking up, but now she missed nothing.

When she had reached the place where the door hid itself under the ivy, she was startled by a curious loud sound. It was the caw—caw of a crow and it came from the top of the wall, and when she looked up, there sat a big glossy-plumaged blue-black bird, looking down at her very wisely indeed. She had never seen a crow so close before and he made her a little nervous, she always thought of crows as omens of death, but the next moment he spread his wings and flapped away across the garden. She hoped he was not going to stay inside and she pushed the door open wondering if he would. When she got fairly into the garden she saw that he probably did intend to stay because he had alighted on a dwarf apple-tree and under the apple-tree was lying a little reddish animal with a bushy tail, and both of them were watching the stooping body and rust-red head of Dickon, who was kneeling on the grass working hard.

Mary flew across the grass to him.

"Oh, Dickon! Dickon!" she cried out. "How could you get here so early! How could you! The sun has only just got up!"

He got up himself, laughing and glowing, and tousled; his eyes like a bit of the sky.

"Eh!" he said. "I was up long before him. How could I have stayed abed! Th' world's all fair begun again this mornin', it has. An' it's workin' an' hummin' an' scratchin' an' pipin' an' nest-buildin' an' breathin' out scents, till you've got to be out on it 'stead o' lyin' on your back. When th' sun did jump up, th' moor went mad for joy, an' I was in the midst of th' heather, an' then what came up spoilin' the whole bliss o' the world? A pair o' Accursed, an' nowt the slow rotting type neither, they was newly afflicted, fast as can be and furious with hunger. I run like mad, shoutin' fer help. No help come so I finally 'ad to turn and face 'em."

"What happened?" Mary was worried though Dickon stood before her safe and sound.

"I had to run at *them*! Might've shocked 'em if'n they could be shocked. I had my knife out and stabbed the male one in the head and kept runnin'. Had to leave me knife though cause I didn' have time to pull it out and the other Accursed was comin' fast. Fumin' at me'self for not bringing my pocket knife or slingshot and decided there was nothin' for it. As she caught up with me I threw meself down and rolled toward her. She tripped right over me and fell. I jump'd up quick and made it back to my knife just as she caught back up with me and she threw herself down upon me!"

Mary gasped as though she did not know the outcome.

"But my trusty knife went right into her eye and I left the the nasty couple heaped on eachotha'. Then Soot started makin' a fuss and I knowed more were comin', an' I come runnin' straight here. The safest place in the world."

Mary put her hands on her chest, panting, as if she had been running herself.

"Oh, Dickon! Dickon!" she said. "I'm so happy you are safe I can scarcely breathe!"

"Ain't nothin' gonna stop me from comin'. I couldn't have stayed away. Why, th' garden was lyin' here waitin'!"

Seeing him talking to a stranger, the little bushy-tailed animal rose from its place under the tree and came to him, and the rook, cawing once, flew down from its branch and settled quietly on his shoulder.

"This is th' little fox cub," he said, rubbing the little reddish animal's head. "It's named Captain. An' this here's Soot. He can smell the Accursed from a distance and always warns me. Soot he flew across th' moor with me an' Captain he run same as if th' hounds had been after him."

Neither of the creatures looked as if he were the least afraid of Mary. When Dickon began to walk about, Soot stayed on his shoulder and Captain trotted quietly close to his side.

"See here!" said Dickon. "See how these has pushed up, an' these an' these! An' Eh! Look at these here!"

He threw himself upon his knees and Mary went down beside him. They had come upon a whole clump of crocuses burst into purple and orange and gold. Mary bent her face down and kissed and kissed them.

"You never kiss a person in that way," she said when she lifted her head. "Flowers are so different."

He looked puzzled but smiled.

"Eh!" he said, "I've kissed mother many a time that way when I come in from th' moor after a day's roamin' an' she stood there at th' door in th' sun, lookin' so glad an' comfortable."

They ran from one part of the garden to another and found so many wonders that they were obliged to remind themselves that they must whisper or speak low. He showed her swelling leafbuds on rose branches which had seemed dead. He showed her ten thousand new green points pushing through the mould. They put their eager young noses close to the earth and sniffed its warmed springtime breathing; they dug and pulled and laughed low with rapture until Mistress Mary's hair was as tumbled as Dickon's and her cheeks were almost as poppy red as his.

There was every joy on earth in the secret garden that morning, and in the midst of them came a delight more delightful than all, because it was more wonderful. Swiftly something flew across the wall and darted through the trees to a close grown corner, a little flare of red-breasted bird with something hanging from its beak. Dickon stood quite still and put his hand on Mary almost as if they had suddenly found themselves laughing in a church.

"We munnot stir," he whispered in broad Yorkshire. "We munnot scarce breathe. I knowed he was mate-huntin' when I seed him last. It's Ben Weatherstaff's robin. He's buildin' his nest. He'll stay here if us don't fight him." They settled down softly upon the grass and sat there without moving.

"Us mustn't seem as if us was watchin' him too close," said Dickon. "He'd be out with us for good if he got th' notion us was interferin' now. He'll be a good bit different till all this is over. He's settin' up housekeepin'. He'll be shyer an' readier to take things ill. He's got no time for visitin' an' gossipin'. Us must keep still a bit an' try to look as if us was grass an' trees an' bushes. Then when he's got used to seein' us I'll chirp a bit an' he'll know us'll not be in his way."

Mistress Mary was not at all sure that she knew, as Dickon seemed to, how to try to look like grass and trees and bushes. But he had said the queer thing as if it were the simplest and most natural thing in the world, and she felt it must be quite easy to him, and indeed she watched him for a few minutes carefully, wondering if it was possible for him to quietly turn green and put out branches and leaves. But he only sat wonderfully still, and when he spoke he dropped his voice to such a softness that it was curious that she could hear him, but she could.

"It's part o' th' springtime, this nest-buildin' is," he said. "I warrant it's been goin' on in th' same way every year since th' world was begun. They've got their way o' thinkin' and doin' things an' a body had better not meddle. You can lose a friend in springtime easier than any other season if you're too curious."

"If we talk about him I can't help looking at him," Mary said as softly as possible. "We must talk of something else. There is something I want to tell you."

"He'll like it better if us talks o' somethin' else," said Dickon. "What is it tha's got to tell me?"

"Well—do you know about Colin?" she whispered.

He turned his head to look at her.

"What does tha' know about him?" he asked.

"I've seen him. I have been to talk to him every day this week. He wants me to come. He says I'm making him forget about being Accursed," answered Mary.

Dickon looked actually relieved as soon as the surprise died away from his round face.

"I am glad o' that," he exclaimed. "I'm right down glad. It makes me easier. I knowed I must say nothin' about him an' I don't like havin' to hide things."

"Don't you like hiding the garden?" said Mary.

"I'll never tell about it," he answered. "But I says to mother, 'Mother,' I says, 'I got a secret to keep. It's not a bad 'un, tha' knows that. It's no worse than hidin' where a bird's nest is. Tha' doesn't mind it, does tha'?'"

Mary always wanted to hear about mother.

"What did she say?" she asked, not at all afraid to hear.

Dickon grinned sweet-temperedly.

"It was just like her, what she said," he answered. "She give my head a bit of a rub an' laughed an' she says, 'Eh, lad, tha' can have all th' secrets tha' likes. I've knowed thee twelve year'.'"

"How did you know about Colin?" asked Mary.

"Everybody as knowed about Mester Craven knowed there was a little lad as was like to die being born the way he was, infected and all. An' they knowed Mester Craven didn't like him to be talked about. Folks is sorry for Mester Craven because Mrs. Craven was such a pretty young lady an' they was so fond of each other. Terrible how she was attacked and with no warnin'. They tore her up good before she later turned into one o' them." Dickon paused a moment as if he had given away too much. "Mrs. Medlock stops in our cottage whenever she goes to Thwaite an' she doesn't mind talkin' to mother before us children, because she knows us has been brought up to be trusty. How did tha' find out about him? Martha was in fine trouble th' last time she came home. She said tha'd heard him frettin' an' tha' was askin' questions an' she didn't know what to say."

Mary told him her story about the midnight wuthering of the wind which had wakened her and about the faint far-off sounds of the complaining voice which had led her down the dark corridors with her candle and had ended with her opening of the door of the dimly lighted room with the carven four-posted bed in the corner. When she described the small ivory-white face and the strange black-rimmed eyes Dickon shook his head.

"Them's just like his mother's eyes, only hers was always laughin', they say," he said. "They say as Mr. Craven can't bear to see him when he's awake an' it's because his eyes is so like his mother's an' yet looks so different in his miserable bit of a face."

"Do you think he wants to die?" whispered Mary.

"No, but he wishes he'd never been born. Mother says that's th' worst thing on earth for a child. Them as is not wanted scarce ever thrives. Mester Craven he'd buy anythin' as money could buy for th' poor lad, but when one is chained and experimented on, there's not much one would want, eh? Aside from the blood vials he comes to collect I think Mester Craven 'ed like to forget as he's on earth. For one thing, he's afraid he'll look at him some day and find he's gone black eyed and insane, craving flesh like the others. Then he'd have to kill him... like his wife."

"Colin's so afraid of it himself that he won't even try to escape his chains," said Mary. "He says he's always thinking that if he should see decay on his skin or feel the insanity and inhuman hunger coming he should be so scared he'd scream until his death."

"Eh! he oughtn't to lie there thinkin' things like that," said Dickon. "No lad could get well as thought them sort o' things."

The fox was lying on the grass close by him, looking up to ask for a pat now and then, and Dickon bent down and rubbed his neck softly and thought a few minutes in silence. Presently he lifted his head and looked round the garden.

"When first we got in here," he said, "it seemed like everything was gray. Look round now and tell me if tha' doesn't see a difference."

Mary looked and caught her breath a little.

"Why!" she cried, "the gray wall is changing. It is as if a green mist were creeping over it. It's almost like a green gauze veil."

"Aye," said Dickon. "An' it'll be greener and greener till th' gray's all gone. Can tha' guess what I was thinkin'?"

"I know it was something nice," said Mary eagerly. "I believe it was something about Colin."

"I was thinkin' that if he was out here he wouldn't be thinkin' bout cannibalism or decayin' or about his father killin' his mother; he'd be watchin' for buds to break on th' rose-bushes, an' he'd likely be healthier," explained Dickon. "I was wonderin' if us could ever get him in th' humor to come out here an' lie under th' trees in his push chair."

"I've been wondering that myself. I've thought of it almost every time I've talked to him," said Mary. "I've wondered if he could keep a secret and I've wondered if we could bring him here without any one seeing us. I thought perhaps you could push his chair. He'd still be chained, but I know he wouldn't try to hurt you. The doctor said he must have fresh air and if he wants to be left alone no one would dare disobey him. We could sneak him out at night and bring him back at dawn. If Medlock leaves, we could even bring him out during the day. He could order the nurse to keep away so she wouldn't find out."

Dickon was thinking very hard as he scratched Captain's back.

"It'd be good for him, I'll warrant," he said. "Us'd not be thinkin' he'd better never been born. Us'd be just two children watchin' a garden grow, an' he'd be another. Two lads an' a little lass just lookin' on at th' springtime. I warrant it'd be better than doctor's stuff."

"He's been chained in his room so long and he's always been so afraid of turning into one of the Forsaken that it has made him queer," said Mary. "He knows a good many things out of picture books but he doesn't know anything else. He says he has been too ill to notice things and he hates going out of doors and hates people looking at him. But he likes to hear about this garden because it is a secret. I daren't tell him much but he said he wanted to see it."

"Us'll have him out here sometime for sure," said Dickon. "I could push his chair well enough. Has tha' noticed how th' robin an' his mate has been workin' while we've been sittin' here? Look at him perched on that branch wonderin' where it'd be best to put that twig he's got in his beak."

He made one of his low whistling calls and the robin turned his head and looked at him inquiringly, still holding his twig. Dickon spoke to him as Ben Weatherstaff did, but Dickon's tone was one of friendly advice.

"Wheres'ever tha' puts it," he said, "it'll be all right. Tha' knew how to build tha' nest before tha' came out o' th' egg. Get on with thee, lad. Tha'st got no time to lose."

"Oh, I do like to hear you talk to him!" Mary said, laughing delightedly. "Ben Weatherstaff scolds him and makes fun of him, and he hops about and looks as if he understood every word, and I know he likes it. Ben Weatherstaff says he is so conceited he would rather have stones thrown at him than not be noticed."

Dickon laughed too and went on talking.

"Tha' knows us won't trouble thee," he said to the robin. "Us is near bein' wild things ourselves. Us is nest-buildin' too, bless thee. Look out tha' doesn't tell on us."

And though the robin did not answer, because his beak was occupied, Mary knew that when he flew away with his twig to his own corner of the garden the darkness of his dew-bright eye meant that he would not tell their secret for the world.

Chapter 16: The Angel and the King of the Accursed

They found a great deal to do that morning and Mary was late in returning to the house and was also in such a hurry to get back to her work that she quite forgot Colin until the last moment.

"Tell Colin that I can't come and see him yet," she said to Martha. "I'm very busy in the garden."

Martha looked rather frightened.

"Eh! Miss Mary," she said, "it may put him all out of humor when I tell him that."

But Mary was not as afraid of him as other people were and she was not a self-sacrificing person.

"I can't stay," she answered. "Dickon's waiting for me," and she ran away.

The afternoon was even lovelier and busier than the morning had been. Already nearly all the weeds were cleared out of the garden and most of the roses and trees had been pruned or dug about. Dickon had brought a spade of his own and he had taught Mary to use all her tools, so that by this time it was plain that though the lovely wild place was not likely to become a "gardener's garden" it would be a wilderness of growing things before the springtime was over.

"There'll be apple blossoms an' cherry blossoms overhead," Dickon said, working away with all his might. "An' there'll be peach an' plum trees in bloom against th' walls, an' th' grass'll be a carpet o' flowers."

Mary practiced throwing her blades as hard as she could as Dickon showed her how to aim for the soft spots in the skulls of the Accursed. The little fox was as happy and busy as they were, and the robin and his mate flew backward and forward like tiny streaks of lightning. Sometimes the rook flapped his black wings and soared away over the tree-tops in the park as if he was keeping watch. He flew around the garden slowly seeming to look for something. Each time he came back and perched near Dickon and cawed several times as if he were relating his unsuccessful search, and Dickon talked to him just as he had talked to the robin. Once when Dickon was so busy that he did not answer him at first, Soot flew on to his shoulders and gently tweaked his ear with his large beak.

"Alright! Soot cawed again in frustration and flew to the garden wall. When Mary wanted to rest a little Dickon sat down with her under a tree and once he took his pipe out of his pocket and played the soft strange little notes and two squirrels appeared on the wall and looked and listened.

I KNOW YOU THINK THAT SOMETHING FOUL
MIGHT BE NEAR BUT WE ARE SAFE IN HERE!

"Tha's a good bit stronger than tha' was," Dickon said, looking at her as she was digging. "Tha's beginning to look different, for sure."

Mary was glowing with exercise and good spirits.

"I'm getting fatter and fatter every day," she said quite exultantly. "Mrs. Medlock will have to get me some bigger dresses. Martha says my hair is growing thicker. It isn't so flat and stringy."

The sun was beginning to set and sending deep gold-colored rays slanting under the trees when they parted.

"It'll be fine tomorrow," said Dickon. "I'll be at work by sunrise."

"So will I," said Mary.

She ran back to the house as quickly as her feet would carry her. She wanted to tell Colin about Dickon's fox cub and the rook and about what the springtime had been doing. She felt sure he would like to hear. So it was not very pleasant when she opened the door of her room, to see Martha standing waiting for her with a shaken, timorous face.

"What is the matter?" she asked. "What did Colin say when you told him I couldn't come?"

"Eh!" said Martha, "I wish tha'd gone. He was nigh goin' into one o' his raging fits. There's been a nice to do all afternoon to keep him quiet. He went on and on' bout infecting everyone and wanting everyone dead. He had to be stretched down and a rag stuffed in his mouth so he wouldn't scratch or bite himself. He would watch the clock all th' time for your return and I fear he may do thee harm."

Mary's lips pinched themselves together. She was no more used to considering other people than Colin was and she saw no reason why an ill-tempered boy should interfere with the thing she liked best. She knew nothing about the pitifulness of people who had been infected and nervous and who did not know that they could control their tempers and need not make other people fearful and nervous, too. When she had had a headache in India she had done her best to see that everybody else also had a headache or something quite as bad. And she felt she was quite right; but of course now she felt that Colin was quite wrong. Just because he was infected and lonely and starving doesn't mean he should want to murder others or keep her from having a good time.

He was not stretched down by the chains when she went into his room. He was lying flat on his back in bed and he did not turn his head toward her as she came in. This was a bad beginning and Mary marched up to him with her stiff manner.

"Why didn't you get up?" she said.

"I did get up this morning when I thought you were coming," he answered, without looking at her. "I even had them chain me in the chair but I made them put me back in bed this afternoon. My back ached and my head ached and I was tired. Why didn't you come?"

"I was working in the garden with Dickon," said Mary.

Colin frowned and condescended to look at her.

"I won't let that boy come here if you go and stay with him instead of coming to talk to me," he said.

Mary flew into a fine passion. She could fly into a passion without making a noise. She just grew sour and obstinate and did not care what happened.

"If you send Dickon away, I'll never come into this room again!" she retorted.

"You'll have to if I want you," said Colin.

"I won't!" said Mary.

"I'll make you," said Colin. "They shall drag you in. I'll have them chain you down too!"

"Shall they, Mr. Rajah! King of the Accursed!" said Mary fiercely. "They may drag me in and chain me down but they can't make me talk when they get me here. I'll sit and clench my teeth and never tell you one thing. I won't even look at you. I'll stare at the floor!"

They were a nice agreeable pair as they glared at each other. If they had been two little street boys they would have sprung at each other and had a rough-and-tumble fight. As it was, they did the next thing to it.

"You are a selfish thing!" cried Colin.

"What are you?" said Mary. "Selfish people always say that. Anyone is selfish who doesn't do what they want. You're more selfish than I am. You're the most selfish boy I ever saw."

"I'm not!" snapped Colin. "I'm not as selfish as your fine Dickon is! He keeps you playing in the dirt when he knows I am suffering all by myself. He's selfish, if you like!"

Mary's eyes flashed fire.

"He's nicer than any other boy that ever lived!" she said. "He's—he's like an angel!" It might sound rather silly to say that but she did not care.

"A nice angel!" Colin sneered ferociously. "He's a common cottage boy off the moor!"

"He's better than a common Rajah!" retorted Mary. "He's a thousand times better!"

Because she was the stronger of the two she was beginning to get the better of him. The truth was that he had never had a fight with any one like himself in his life and, upon the whole, it was rather good for him, though neither he nor Mary knew anything about that. He turned his head on his pillow and shut his eyes and a big tear was squeezed out and ran down his cheek. He was beginning to feel pathetic and sorry for himself—not for anyone else.

"I'm not as selfish as you, because I'm always ill, and I'm sure my skin is beginning to decay and my hair is falling out and my bones are becoming brittle," he said. "And I am going to die besides, then when I rise again my father will want to kill me."

"You're not going to die!" contradicted Mary unsympathetically.

He opened his eyes quite wide with indignation. He had never heard such a thing said before. He was at once furious and slightly pleased, if a person could be both at one time.

"I'm not?" he cried. "I am! You know I am! Everybody says so."

"I don't believe it!" said Mary sourly. "You just say that to make people afraid of you. I believe you're proud of it. I don't believe it! I don't believe you will ever turn. If you were a nice boy it might be true—but you're too nasty!"

In spite of his weak body Colin sat up in bed in quite a healthy rage rattling the chains around the bed and walls.

"Get out of the room!" he shouted and he caught hold of his pillow and threw it at her. He was not strong enough to throw it far and it only fell at her feet, but Mary's face looked as pinched as a nutcracker.

"I'm going," she said. "And I won't come back!" She walked to the door and when she reached it she turned round and spoke again.

"I was going to tell you all sorts of nice things," she said. "Dickon brought his fox and his rook and I was going to tell you all about them. Now I won't tell you a single thing!"

She marched out of the door and closed it behind her, and there to her great astonishment she found the trained nurse standing as if she had been listening and, more amazing still—she was laughing. She was a big handsome young woman who ought not to have been a trained nurse at all, as she could not bear the afflicted and she was always making excuses to leave Colin to Martha or any one else who would take her place. Mary had never liked her, and she simply stood and gazed up at her as she stood giggling into her handkerchief.

"What are you laughing at?" she asked her.

"At you two young ones," said the nurse. "It's the best thing that could happen to the disgusting pampered thing to have someone to stand up to him that's as spoiled as himself," and she laughed into her handkerchief again. "If he'd had a young vixen of a sister to fight with it would have been the saving of him."

"Is he going to die?"

"I don't know and I don't care as long as he stays chained up," said the nurse. "Hysterics and temper are half what ails him."

"What are hysterics?" asked Mary.

"You'll find out if you work him into a tantrum after this—but at any rate you've given him something to have hysterics about, and I'm glad of it."

Mary went back to her room not feeling at all as she had felt when she had come in from the garden. She was cross and disappointed but not at all sorry for Colin. She had looked forward to telling him a great many things and she had meant to try to make up her mind whether it would be safe to trust him with the great secret. She had been beginning to think it would be, but now she had changed her mind entirely. She would never tell him and he could stay in his room and never get any fresh air and die if he liked! It would serve him right to be a Forsaken! She felt so sour and unrelenting that for a few minutes she almost forgot about Dickon and the green veil creeping over the world and the soft wind blowing down from the moor.

Martha was waiting for her and the trouble in her face had been temporarily replaced by interest and curiosity. There was a wooden box on the table and its cover had been removed and revealed that it was full of neat packages.

"Mr. Craven sent it to you," said Martha. "It looks as if it had picture-books in it."

Mary remembered what he had asked her the day she had gone to his room. "Do you want anything—dolls—toys—books?" She opened the package wondering if he had sent a doll, and also wondering what she should do with it if he had. But he had not sent one. There were several beautiful books such as Colin had, and two of them were about gardens and were full of pictures. There were two or three games and there was a beautiful little writing-case with a gold monogram on it and a gold pen and inkstand.

Everything was so nice that her pleasure began to crowd her anger out of her mind. She had not expected him to remember her at all and her hard little heart grew quite warm.

"I can write better than I can print," she said, "and the first thing I shall write with that pen will be a letter to tell him I am much obliged."

If she had been friends with Colin she would have run to show him her presents at once, and they would have looked at the pictures and read some of the gardening books and perhaps tried playing the games, and he would have enjoyed himself so much he would never once have thought he was going to die or have looked in the mirror at his sunken face with the purple bags looking to see if his eyes had changed from gray to black. He had a way of doing that which she could not bear. It gave her an uncomfortable frightened feeling because he always looked so frightened himself. He said that if he saw any blackness in his eyes he'd know if he was turning and he was sure his father would have to shoot him in the head. Something he had heard Mrs. Medlock whispering to the nurse had given him the idea and he had thought over it in secret until it was quite firmly fixed in his mind. Mrs. Medlock had said that once his mother became Accursed his father had taken his mother outside alone and shot her in the head then buried her himself in an unmarked grave. He had never told anyone but Mary that most of his "tantrums" as they called them grew out of his hysterical hidden fear that his father would shoot him and no one would ever know where his body lay. Mary had been sorry for him when he had told her.

"He always began to think about it when he was cross or tired," she said to herself. "And he has been cross today. Perhaps—perhaps he has been thinking about it all afternoon."

She stood still, looking down at the carpet and thinking.

"I said I would never go back again—" she hesitated, knitting her brows—"but perhaps, just perhaps, I will go and see—if he wants me—in the morning. Perhaps he'll try to throw his pillow at me again, but—I think—I'll go."

Chapter 17: A Tantrum

She had got up very early in the morning and had worked hard in the garden and practiced throwing her knives hard at targets and she was tired and sleepy, so as soon as Martha had brought her supper and she had eaten it, she was glad to go to bed. As she laid her head on the pillow she murmured to herself:

"I'll go out before breakfast and work with Dickon and then afterward—I believe—I'll go to see him."

She thought it was the middle of the night when she was awakened by such dreadful sounds that she jumped out of bed in an instant. What was it—what was it? It sounded as though the Accursed were eviscerating on old woman. The next minute she felt quite sure she knew. Doors were opened and shut and there were hurrying feet in the corridors and someone was crying and screaming at the same time, screaming and crying in a horrible way.

"It's Colin," she said. "He's having one of those tantrums the nurse called hysterics. How awful it sounds."

As she listened to the sobbing screams she did not wonder that people were so frightened that they gave him his own way in everything rather than hear them. She put her hands over her ears and felt sick and shivering.

"I don't know what to do. I don't know what to do," she kept saying. "I can't bear it."

Once she wondered if he would stop if she dared go to him and then she remembered how he had driven her out of the room and thought that perhaps the sight of her might make him worse. Even when she pressed her hands more tightly over her ears she could not keep the awful sounds out. She hated them so and was so terrified by them that suddenly they began to make her angry and she felt as if she should like to fly into a tantrum herself and frighten him as he was frightening her. She was not used to anyone's tempers but her own. She took her hands from her ears and sprang up and stamped her foot.

"He ought to be stopped! Somebody ought to make him stop! Somebody ought to beat him!" she cried out.

Just then she heard feet almost running down the corridor and her door was unlocked and the nurse came in. She was not laughing now by any means. She even looked rather pale.

"He's worked himself into hysterics," she said in a great hurry. "He'll do himself harm. One of his chains has come loose and no one can get near him or risk infection! No one can do anything with him. You come and try, like a good child. He likes you."

"He turned me out of the room this afternoon," said Mary, stamping her foot with excitement.

The stamp rather pleased the nurse. The truth was that she had been afraid she might find Mary crying and hiding her head under the bed-clothes.

"That's right," she said. "You're in the right humor. You go and scold him. Give him something new to think of. Do go, child, as quick as ever you can."

It was not until afterward that Mary realized that the thing had been funny as well as dreadful—that it was funny that all the grown-up people were so frightened that they came to a little girl just because they guessed she was almost as bad as Colin himself, and they knowingly risked her life rather than their own.

She flew along the corridor and the nearer she got to the screams the higher her temper mounted. She felt quite wicked by the time she reached the door. She slapped it open with her hand and ran across the room to the four-poster bed. She was so angry she didn't stop to remember that his chain was loose or that she was within spitting distance.

"You stop!" she almost shouted. "You stop! I hate you! Everybody hates you! I wish everybody would run out of the house and let you scream yourself to death! You will scream yourself to death in a minute, and I wish you would! Then you would turn into the hideous demon you are!" A nice sympathetic child could neither have thought nor said such things, but it just happened that the shock of hearing them was the best possible thing for this hysterical boy whom no one had ever dared to contradict.

The chains holding his right wrist had broken off the wall bolts allowing Colin to flail and turn. He had knocked his mirror onto the floor in a rage and it shattered leaving small pieces of glass scattered on the floor. He had been lying on his face beating his pillow with his hands and he actually almost jumped around, he turned so quickly at the sound of the furious little voice. His face looked dreadful, white and red and swollen, and he was gasping and choking; but savage little Mary did not care an atom.

"If you scream another scream," she said, "I'll scream too—and I can scream louder than you can and I'll frighten you, I'll frighten **you**!"

He actually had stopped screaming because she had startled him so. The scream which had been coming almost choked him. The tears were streaming down his face and he shook all over.

"I can't stop!" he gasped and sobbed. "I can't—I can't!"

"You can!" shouted Mary. "Half that ails you is hysterics and temper—just hysterics—hysterics—hysterics!" and she stamped each time she said it.

"I saw the blackness, the black blood—I saw it," choked out Colin. "I knew I should. My eyes shall fill with blood and then I shall become Accursed," and he began to writhe again and turned on his face and sobbed and wailed but he didn't scream.

"You didn't see any blackness or black blood!" contradicted Mary fiercely. "If you did it was only a hysterical blackout. Hysterics causes blackouts! There's nothing the matter with your eyes—nothing but hysterics! Sit still and let me look at them!"

She liked the word "hysterics" and felt somehow it had an effect on him. He was probably like herself and had never heard it before.

"Nurse," she commanded, "come here and re-chain him this minute!"

The nurse, Mrs. Medlock and Martha had been standing huddled together near the door staring at her, their mouths half open. All three had gasped with fright more than once. The nurse came forward as if she were deathly afraid. Colin was heaving with great breathless sobs.

"Perhaps he—he won't let me," she hesitated in a low voice.

Colin heard her, however, and he gasped out between two sobs:

"J...Just do it! She-she'll see then!"

The nurse slowly came forward and Colin was still as she re-threaded his chains. Mary crawled onto the bed and came very close to Colin. Closer then anyone else dared. It was a poor thin face to look at. The sunken eyes and jutting cheekbones made Colin almost appear half dead, though Mistress Mary did not blink as she leaned in close and examined him with a solemn savage little face. She looked so sour and old-fashioned that the nurse turned her head aside to hide the twitching of her mouth. There was just a minute's silence, for even Colin tried to hold his breath while Mary looked closely into his eyes, and then she felt his thin arms, soft hands and brittle nails, next examining his thin legs and bony back as intently as if she had been the great doctor from London.

"There's no black blood! And no dying flesh or blue nails!" she said at last. "There's nothing on you that's dead or decaying! Except that you're thin and pale and weak. I was same myself, and they thought I was Accursed when they first found me, until I began to get fatter, and I am not yet fat enough. There's no rotting and no one is going to kill you! If you ever say so again, I shall laugh!"

No one but Colin himself knew what effect those crossly spoken childish words had on him. If he had ever had anyone to talk to about his secret terrors—if he had ever dared to let himself ask questions—if he had had childish companions and had not been chained on his back in the huge closed house, fed raw meat and treated like a rabid animal, breathing an atmosphere heavy with the fears of people who were most of them ignorant and scared of him, he would have found out that most of his fright and illness was created by himself. But he had lain and thought of himself and his aches and weariness for hours and days and months and years. And now that an angry unsympathetic little girl insisted obstinately that he was not slowly decaying or becoming the undead as he thought he was he actually felt as if she might be speaking the truth.

"I didn't know," ventured the nurse, "that he thought he was transforming and people wanted to kill him. He is chained because he could spread infection. I could have told him he hasn't shown any sign of turning." Colin gulped and turned his face a little to look at her.

"C-could you?" he said pathetically.

"Yes, sir."

"There!" said Mary, and she gulped too.

Colin turned on his face again and but for his long-drawn broken breaths, which were the dying down of his storm of sobbing, he lay still for a minute, though great tears streamed down his face and wet the pillow. Actually the tears meant that a curious great relief had come to him. Presently he turned and looked at the nurse again and strangely enough he was not like a Rajah at all as he spoke to her.

"Do you think—I could—live to grow up?" he said.

The nurse was neither clever nor soft-hearted but she could repeat some of the London doctor's words.

"You probably will if you will do what you are told to do and not give way to your temper, and not attack or bite at those caring for you! If you could be trusted not to spread infection you might get some fresh air."

Colin's tantrum had passed and he was weak and worn out with crying and this perhaps made him feel gentle. He put out his hand a little toward Mary, and her own tantrum having passed, she was softened too and met him half-way with her hand, so that it was a sort of making up.

"I'll—I'll go out with you, Mary," he said. "I shan't hate fresh air if we can find—" He remembered just in time to stop himself from saying "if we can find the secret garden" and he ended, "I shall like to go out with you if Dickon will come and push my chair. I do so want to see Dickon and the fox and the crow. I promise... I promise I won't harm any of them and I shan't be hungry for them at all."

The nurse remade the tumbled bed and fixed the ropes on the pulleys attached to the iron wrist and ankle shackles. Then she made Colin a cup of raw beef tea and gave a cup of cooked beef to Mary, who really was very glad to get it after her excitement. Mrs. Medlock and Martha gladly slipped away, and after everything was neat and calm and in order the nurse looked as if she would very gladly slip away also. She was a healthy young woman who resented being robbed of her sleep and she yawned quite openly as she looked at Mary, who had pushed her big footstool close to the four-posted bed and was holding Colin's hand.

"You must go back and get your sleep out," the nurse said. "He'll drop off after a while—if he's not too upset. Then I'll lie down myself in the next room."

"Would you like to try some of my cooked beef instead of eating that raw stuff?" Mary whispered quietly to Colin.

His hand pulled hers gently and he turned his tired eyes on her appealingly.

"Oh, yes!" he answered. "I should like to try that, if you like it. Then I shall go to sleep in a minute."

"I will put him to sleep," Mary said to the yawning nurse. "You can go if you like."

"Well," said the nurse, with an attempt at reluctance. "If he doesn't go to sleep in half an hour you must call me."

"Very well," answered Mary.

The nurse was out of the room in a minute and as soon as she was gone Mary took away the bowl of raw meat in warm broth and handed Colin her soup. Colin gingerly picked out a piece of cooked beef with his fingers and put it in his mouth. He chewed and made a face.

"It is hard to eat and not very juicy. It tastes bland, doesn't have the bitterness."

"Bitterness of blood, you mean. Do you like it?" Mary asked. She was sure the only reason he ate the raw meat was because that was all he was ever given.

"Yes, but..." Colin swallowed hard. "It is harder to get down."

"Maybe just one more bite. We don't want your stomach upset."

Colin ate one more piece and then pulled Mary's hand again.

"I almost told," he said, "but I stopped myself in time. I won't talk and I'll go to sleep, but you said you had a whole lot of nice things to tell me. Have you—do you think you have found out anything at all about the way into the secret garden?"

Mary looked at his poor little tired face and swollen eyes and her heart relented.

"Ye-es," she answered, "I think I have. And if you will go to sleep I will tell you tomorrow." His hand quite trembled.

"Oh, Mary!" he said. "Oh, Mary! If I could get into it I think I should live to grow up! Do you suppose that you could just tell me softly as you did that first day what you imagine it looks like inside? I am sure it will make me go to sleep."

"Yes," answered Mary. "Shut your eyes."

He closed his eyes and lay quite still and she held his hand and began to speak very slowly and in a very low voice.

"I think it has been left alone so long—that it has grown all into a lovely tangle. I think the roses have climbed and climbed and climbed until they hang from the branches and walls and creep over the ground—almost like a strange gray mist. Some of them have died but many are alive and when the summer comes there will be curtains and fountains of roses. I think the ground is full of daffodils and snowdrops and lilies and iris. Things that were dead are coming alive again working their way out of the dark. Now the spring has begun—perhaps—perhaps—"

The soft drone of her voice was making him stiller and stiller and she saw it and went on.

"Perhaps they are coming up through the grass—perhaps there are clusters of purple crocuses and gold ones—even now. Perhaps the leaves are beginning to break out and uncurl—and perhaps— the gray is changing and a green gauze veil is creeping—and creeping over—everything. And the birds are coming to look at it—because it is—so safe and still. And perhaps—perhaps— perhaps—" very softly and slowly indeed, "the robin has found a mate—and is building a nest. It is the safest place in the world where nothing could harm us."

And Colin was asleep.

Chapter 18: The Demons Inside

Of course Mary did not waken early the next morning. She slept late because she was tired, and when Martha brought her breakfast she told her that though Colin was quite quiet he was ill and feverish as he always was after he had worn himself out with a fit of crying. Mary ate her breakfast slowly as she listened.

"He says he wishes tha' would please go and see him as soon as tha' can," Martha said. "It's queer what a fancy he's took to thee. Tha' did give it him last night for sure—didn't tha? To get so close while his shackles were undone! Nobody else would have dared to do it. Eh! poor lad! He's been both tortured and spoiled till salt won't save him. Mother says as th' two worst things as can happen to a child is never to have his own way—or always to have it. She doesn't know which is th' worst. Tha' was in a fine temper tha'self, too. But he says to me when I went into his room, 'Please ask Miss Mary if she'll please come an' talk to me?' Think o' him saying please! Will you go, Miss?"

"I'll run and see Dickon first," said Mary. "No, I'll go and see Colin first and tell him—I know what I'll tell him," with a sudden inspiration.

She had her hat on when she appeared in Colin's room and for a second he looked disappointed. He was in bed. His face was pitifully white and there were dark circles round his eyes.

"I'm glad you came," he said. "My head aches and I ache all over because I'm so tired. Are you going somewhere?"

Mary went and leaned against his bed.

"I won't be long," she said. "I'm going to Dickon, but I'll come back. Colin, it's—it's something about the garden."

His whole face brightened and a little color came into it.

"Oh! is it?" he cried out. "I dreamed about it all night I heard you say something about gray changing into green, and I dreamed I was standing in a place all filled with trembling little green leaves—and there were birds on nests everywhere and they looked so soft and still. I'll lie and think about it until you come back."

In five minutes Mary was with Dickon in their garden. The fox and the crow were with him again and this time he had brought two tame squirrels. "I came over on the pony this mornin'," he said. "Eh! he is a good little chap—Jump is! I brought these two in my pockets. This here one he's called Nut an' this here other one's called Shell."

When he said "Nut" one squirrel leaped on to his right shoulder and when he said "Shell" the other one leaped on to his left shoulder.

When they sat down on the grass with Captain curled at their feet, Soot solemnly listening on a tree and Nut and Shell nosing about close to them, it seemed to Mary that it would be scarcely bearable to leave such delightfulness, but when she began to tell her story somehow the look in Dickon's funny face gradually changed her mind. She could see he felt sorrier for Colin than she did. He looked up at the sky and all about him.

"Just listen to them birds—th' world seems full of 'em—all whistlin' an' pipin'," he said. "Look at 'em dartin' about, an' hearken at 'em callin' to each other. Come springtime seems like as if all th' world's callin'. The leaves is uncurlin' so you can see 'em— an', my word, th' nice smells there is about!" sniffing with his happy turned-up nose. "An' that poor lad lyin' shut up an' seein' so little that he gets to thinkin' o' things as sets him screamin'. Eh! My, we mun get him out here—we mun get him watchin' an listenin' an' sniffin' up th' air an' get him just soaked through wi' sunshine. We'll be careful 'bout it, 'case he really is Accursed. If he is lookin' like he might attack us, Soot won' be quiet about it. An' we munnot lose no time about it."

When he was very much interested he often spoke quite broad Yorkshire though at other times he tried to modify his dialect so that Mary could better understand. But she loved his broad Yorkshire and had in fact been trying to learn to speak it herself. So she spoke a little now.

"Aye, that we mun," she said (which meant "Yes, indeed, we must"). "I'll tell thee what us'll do first," she proceeded, and Dickon grinned, because when the little wench tried to twist her tongue into speaking Yorkshire it amused him very much. "He's took a graidely fancy to thee. He wants to see thee and he wants to see Soot an' Captain. Soot will tell thee if'n he's safe or not. When I go back to the house to talk to him I'll ax him if tha' canna' come an' see him tomorrow mornin'—an' bring tha' creatures wi' thee—an' then—in a bit, when the sun is hid by clouds, an' we can be sure no other people are about, we'll get him to come out an' tha' shall push him in his chair he'll be shackled into, an' we'll bring him here an' show him everything."

When she stopped she was quite proud of herself. She had never made a long speech in Yorkshire before and she had remembered very well.

"Tha' mun talk a bit o' Yorkshire like that to Mester Colin," Dickon chuckled. "Tha'll make him laugh an' there's nowt as good for ill folk as laughin' is. Mother says she believes as half a hour's good laugh every mornin' 'ud cure a chap as was making ready to turn into the undead."

"I'm going to talk Yorkshire to him this very day," said Mary, chuckling to herself trying to imagine a person laughing as they suffered the tormented sickness.

The garden had reached the time when every day and every night it seemed as if Magicians were passing through it drawing loveliness out of the earth and the boughs with wands. It was hard to go away and leave it all, particularly as Nut had actually crept on to her dress and Shell had scrambled down the trunk of the apple-tree they sat under and stayed there looking at her with inquiring eyes. But she went back to the house and when she sat down close to Colin's bed he began to sniff as Dickon did though not in such an experienced way.

"You smell like flowers and—and fresh things," he cried out quite joyously. "What is it you smell of? It's cool and warm and sweet all at the same time."

"It's th' wind from th' moor," said Mary. "It comes o' sittin' on th' grass under a tree wi' Dickon an' wi' Captain an' Soot an' Nut an' Shell. It's th' springtime an' out o' doors an' sunshine as smells so graidely."

She said it as broadly as she could, and you do not know how broadly Yorkshire sounds until you have heard some one speak it. Colin began to laugh.

"What are you doing?" he said. "I never heard you talk like that before. How funny it sounds."

"I'm givin' thee a bit o' Yorkshire," answered Mary triumphantly. 'I canna' talk as graidely as Dickon an' Martha can but tha' sees I can shape a bit. Doesn't tha' understand a bit o' Yorkshire when tha' hears it? An' tha' a Yorkshire lad thysel' bred an' born! Eh! I wonder tha'rt not ashamed o' thy face."

And then she began to laugh too and they both laughed until they could not stop themselves and they laughed until the room echoed and Mrs. Medlock opening the door to come in drew back into the corridor and stood listening amazed.

"Well, upon my word!" she said, speaking rather broad Yorkshire herself because there was no one to hear her and she was so astonished. "Whoever heard th' like! Whoever on earth would ha' thought it! Laughin' comin' from the Fallen. Course I suppose he's only half cursed, and today the human side is winnin'."

There was so much to talk about. It seemed as if Colin could never hear enough of Dickon and Captain and Soot and Nut and Shell and the pony whose name was Jump. Mary had run round into the wood with Dickon to see Jump. He was a tiny little shaggy moor pony with thick locks hanging over his eyes and with a pretty face and a nuzzling velvet nose. He was rather thin with living on moor grass but he was as tough and wiry as if the muscle in his little legs had been made of steel springs. He had lifted his head and whinnied softly the moment he saw Dickon and he had trotted up to him and put his head across his shoulder and then Dickon had talked into his ear and Jump had talked back in odd little whinnies and puffs and snorts. Dickon had made him give Mary his small front hoof and kiss her on her cheek with his velvet muzzle.

"Does he really understand everything Dickon says?" Colin asked.

Mary moved a little closer to talk, sitting on the edge of the bed. "It seems as if he does," she answered. "Dickon says anything will understand if you're friends with it for sure, but you have to be friends for sure."

Colin lay quiet a little while and his strange gray eyes seemed to be staring at the wall, but Mary saw he was thinking.

"I wish I was friends with things," he said at last, "but I'm not. I never had anything to be friends with, and I can't bear people."

"Can't you bear me?" asked Mary.

"Yes, I can," he answered. "It's funny but I even like you."

"Ben Weatherstaff said I was like him," said Mary. "He said he'd warrant we'd both got the same nasty tempers. I think you are like him too. We are all three alike—you and I and Ben Weatherstaff. He said we were neither of us much to look at and we were as sour as we looked. But I don't feel as sour as I used to before I knew the robin and Dickon."

He asked, "Did you feel as if you hated people?"

"Yes," answered Mary without any affectation. "I should have detested you if I had seen you before I saw the robin and Dickon."

Colin put out his thin hand and touched her wrist.

"Mary," he said, "I wish I hadn't said what I did about sending Dickon away. I hated you when you said he was like an angel and I laughed at you but—but perhaps he is."

"Well, it was rather funny to say it," she admitted frankly, "because his nose does turn up and he has a big mouth and his clothes have patches all over them and he talks broad Yorkshire, but—but if an angel did come to Yorkshire and live on the moor— if there was a Yorkshire angel—I believe he'd understand the green things and know how to make them grow and he would know how to talk to the wild creatures as Dickon does and they'd know he was friends for sure."

"I shouldn't mind Dickon looking at me," said Colin. "I want to see him."

"I'm glad you said that," answered Mary, "because—because—"

Quite suddenly it came into her mind that this was the minute to tell him. Colin knew something new was coming.

"Because what?" he cried eagerly.

Mary was so anxious that she brought her legs up onto the bed to fully turn to him and caught hold of both his hands.

"Can I trust you? I trusted Dickon because birds trusted him. Can I trust you—for sure—for sure?" she implored.

Her face was so solemn that he almost whispered his answer.

"Yes—yes!"

"Well, Dickon will come to see you tomorrow morning, and he'll bring his creatures with him."

"Oh! Oh!" Colin cried out in delight.

"But that's not all," Mary went on, almost pale with solemn excitement. "The rest is better. There is a door into the garden. I found it. It is under the ivy on the wall."

If he had been a strong healthy boy Colin would probably have shouted "Hooray! Hooray! Hooray!" but he was weak and rather hysterical; his eyes grew bigger and bigger and he gasped for breath.

"Oh! Mary!" he cried out with a half sob. "Shall I see it? Shall I get into it? Shall I live to get into it?" and he clutched her hands and dragged her toward him.

"Of course you'll see it!" snapped Mary indignantly. "Of course you'll live to get into it! Don't be silly!"

Colin suddenly became aware that he and Mary were very close. Closer than he had ever been to a person unchained. He could smell not just the soil and flowers on her but the bitter sweet smell of her perspiration and even her blood pumping below the skin. He felt an intense desire like he had never known and he grabbed her arms with a strength he did not know he possessed. He held her tightly, her neck up to his gaping mouth. Mary held perfectly still, hardly daring to breathe, her heart pounding and she remembered what she was told about the Forsaken being able to see the blood in your veins. She closed her eyes and waited. Colin slowly breathed in, smelling her skin. He licked his lips as if tasting. She remembered when he had grabbed her ankle, as if he didn't know what he was doing. Mary opened her eyes and softly said, "Colin. Colin, it's Mary."

Colin's grip loosened and Mary slid off to the side. He looked at her terrified. He grabbed his own chains and pulled himself over. Mary touched her neck where she could still feel warmth from his lips.

"I... I'm sorry, Mary. I didn't mean... I haven't felt that in... You were just so close and I could feel your heart beating and..." Colin turned and shoved his face into the pillow. "I can feel the demons come in, Mary. They want to do bad things, terrible things. Sometimes when I'm lying here alone all I think about is killing everyone in this house. They say that if they let me loose I would eventually kill someone. And maybe they are right. For a second Mary, I wanted to... If I had..."

Colin looked up at her with tears in eyes. Mary was nearly in tears too.

"I wish I had an angel to fight these demons away. Maybe Dickon really is an angel sent to help me. I want to see him as soon as I can. But from now on I must be chained around you. We've become too relaxed around each other. NURSE!!"

Colin screamed so loud and so suddenly that Mary jumped off the bed in fright. The nurse came running in.

"Tighten my chains up immediately. You have been neglecting your duties and I am very upset by it!"

The surprised and confused nurse ran to pull the ropes on the walls and Colin's arms were stretched down.

"You may go now," he said as he made certain he could not lift his arms. Mary turned to leave after the nurse.

"Not you. Please stay. I'm safe now. It won't happen again, I promise."

Mary sat on the stool and remaining silent. She wasn't sure what she felt about Colin's sudden outburst. She realized he truly did carry the infection, and maybe he was affected by it, a little. She knew that she had been closer to death than ever before but she wasn't afraid or angry. She was confused by her own feelings. She had been excited! She felt exhilarated and felt the desire to rush out onto the moor in search of more danger. She had never before thought that she would ever want real danger, but then before the secret garden most of her games were pretending to run from the Accursed. She realized now that she had enjoyed wandering alone through the big empty house and she had felt very lively after killing the Accursed mice. She wanted to feel that electricity again of facing death. She smiled at Colin and she was so un-hysterical and natural that he began to wonder if he had just imaged the whole thing.

"Mary, what are thinking? Are you upset?"

"No Colin, and tomorrow you shall meet your angel and we shall take you out where you will be able to see the birds fly and flowers grow. And you will be yourself in the garden."

Then she began telling him not what she imagined the secret garden to be like but what it really was, and Colin's aches and tiredness were forgotten and he was listening enraptured.

"It is just what you thought it would be," he said at last. "It sounds just as if you had really seen it. You know I said that when you told me first."

Mary hesitated about two minutes and then boldly spoke the truth.

"I had seen it—and I had been in," she said. "I found the key and got in weeks ago. But I daren't tell you—I daren't because I was so afraid I couldn't trust you—for sure!"

Colin swallowed fearing the answer to his next question. "And... do you still trust me? Even though?"

Mary stood and walked to the ropes on the wall. She reached out and untied the knot loosening his chains again. "I trust you-for sure."

Chapter 19: It Has Come!

Of course the Uncle Dr. Craven had been sent for the morning after Colin had had his tantrum. He was always sent for at once when such a thing occurred and he always found, when he arrived, a white shaken boy, chained to his bed with the ropes pulled tight, sulky and still so hysterical that he was ready to break into fresh screaming and moaning at the least word. In fact, Dr. Craven dreaded and detested the difficulties of these visits. On this occasion he was away from Misselthwaite Manor until afternoon.

"How is he?" he asked Mrs. Medlock rather irritably when he arrived. "He will break a blood-vessel in one of those fits some day. I have looked at his blood many times over the years and it remains unchanged. He still carries the infection. He is Accursed, but only half so. He is a carrier but it seems to be dormant due to receiving the infection through the womb. The boy is half insane with hysteria and blood lust."

"Well, sir," answered Mrs. Medlock, "you'll scarcely believe your eyes when you see him. That plain sour-faced child that's almost as bad as himself has just bewitched him. How she's done it there's no telling. The Lord knows she's nothing to look at and you scarcely ever hear her speak, but she did what none of us dare do. She just flew at him like a little cat last night, and stamped her feet and ordered him to stop screaming, and somehow she startled him so that he actually did stop, and this afternoon—well just come up and see, sir. It's past crediting."

The scene which Dr. Craven beheld when he entered his patient's room was indeed rather astonishing to him. As Mrs. Medlock opened the door he heard laughing and chattering. Colin was in his dressing-gown, chains loosed and he was sitting up quite straight looking at a picture in one of the garden books and talking to the plain child who at that moment could scarcely be called plain at all because her face was so glowing with enjoyment. She was sitting on the edge of the bed so close to him the doctor nearly cried out in terror that she was in mortal peril.

"Those long spires of blue ones—we'll have a lot of those," Colin was announcing. "They're called Del-phin-iums."

"Dickon says they're larkspurs made big and grand," cried Mistress Mary. "There are clumps there already."

Then they saw Dr. Craven and stopped. Mary became quite still and Colin looked fretful.

"I am sorry to hear you were ill last night, my boy," Dr. Craven said a trifle nervously. He was rather a nervous man and did not want to upset Colin in the least, not with the girl right next him and his shackles so slack.

"I'm better now, Uncle—much better," Colin answered, rather like a Rajah. "I'm going out in my chair in a day or two if it is fine. I want some fresh air."

Dr. Craven stood two feet away from Colin's bedside and and motioned that he hold out his arm. Colin did and the doctor felt his pulse and looked at him curiously.

"Your heart is beating too strongly," he said, "and you must be very careful not to tire yourself."

"Fresh air won't tire me," said the young Rajah.

As there had been occasions when this same young gentleman had shrieked aloud with rage and had insisted that fresh air would kill him and he would bite anyone who made him go out, it is not to be wondered at that his doctor felt somewhat startled.

"I thought you did not like fresh air," he said.

"I don't when I am by myself," replied the Rajah; "but my cousin is going out with me."

"And the nurse, of course?" suggested Dr. Craven.

"No, I will not have the nurse," so magnificently that Mary could not help remembering how the young native Prince had looked with his diamonds and emeralds and pearls stuck all over him and the great rubies on the small dark hand he had waved to command his servants to approach with salaams and receive his orders.

"My cousin knows how to take care of me. I am always better when she is with me. She made me better last night. A very strong boy I know will push my carriage."

Dr. Craven felt rather alarmed. If this tiresome hysterical boy should chance to not transform into a mindless cannibal, he himself would lose all chance of inheriting Misselthwaite; but he was not a completely unscrupulous man, though he was a weak one who would see Colin dead, he did not intend to risk him harming anyone else.

"You must be strapped into your chair at all times. What if you infected your cousin, or this boy? He must be a strong boy and a steady boy," he said. "And I must know something about him. Who is he? What is his name?"

"It's Dickon," Mary spoke up suddenly. She felt somehow that everybody who knew the moor must know Dickon. And she was right, too. She saw that in a moment Dr. Craven's serious face relaxed into a relieved smile. He knew that Dickon would dispatch of Colin quickly if there was the slightest bit of danger.

"Oh, Dickon," he said. "If it is Dickon you will be safe enough. He's as strong as a moor pony, is Dickon."

"And he's trusty," said Mary. "He's th' trustiest lad i' Yorkshire." She had been talking Yorkshire to Colin and she forgot herself.

"Did Dickon teach you that?" asked Dr. Craven, laughing outright.

"I'm learning it as if it was French," said Mary rather coldly. "It's like a native dialect in India. Very clever people try to learn them. I like it and so does Colin."

"Well, well," he said disliking this positive behavior in Colin. "If it amuses you perhaps it won't do you any harm. Did you take your bromide last night, Colin?"

"No," Colin answered. "I wouldn't take it at first and after Mary made me quiet she talked me to sleep—in a low voice—about the spring creeping into a garden."

"That sounds soothing," said Dr. Craven, more perplexed than ever and glancing sideways at Mistress Mary sitting on her stool and looking down silently at the carpet. The bromide compound sedative kept Colin quiet and Dr. Craven used it often knowing that it might cause him to develop hallucinations, temporary dementia and skin rashes to accelerate the appearance of his transformation. "You are evidently a little better, but you must remember—"

"I don't want to remember," interrupted the Rajah, appearing again. "When I lie by myself and remember that I am born of the dead I begin to have pains everywhere and I think of things that make me begin to scream because I hate them so. I can feel my skin cracking and my eyes blackening and my nails becoming yellow. If there was a doctor anywhere who could make you forget you were ill instead of remembering it I would have him brought here." And he waved a thin hand which ought really to have been covered with royal signet rings made of rubies. "It is because my cousin makes me forget my flesh may soon begin to rot that she makes me better."

Dr. Craven had never made such a short stay after a "tantrum"; usually he was obliged to remain a very long time and do a great many things. This afternoon he did not give any medicine or tie Colin to a post and have the servants toss buckets of freezing water onto his bare flesh to prevent the Fever of the Accursed, and he was spared any disagreeable scenes of Colin spitting and hissing and trying to bite through the leather straps. When he went downstairs he looked very thoughtful and when he talked to Mrs. Medlock in the library she felt that he was a much puzzled man.

"Well, sir," she ventured, "could you have believed it?"

"It is certainly a new state of affairs," said the doctor. "And there's no denying it is better than the old one. He seems not as inclined to fully turn now as he did."

"I believe Susan Sowerby's right—I do that," said Mrs. Medlock. "I stopped in her cottage on my way to Thwaite yesterday and had a bit of talk with her. And she says to me, 'Well, Sarah Ann, she mayn't be a good child, an' she mayn't be a pretty one, but she's a child, an' children needs children. Even the undead needs a bit o' cheer in their lives. She may be the sunshine to turn his black concentration. If she can't you should cut the little monster's head off before he breaks free of the chains.We went to school together, Susan Sowerby and me."

"She's the best Accursed slayer I know," said Dr. Craven. "When I find her in a cottage I know the chances are all the Forsaken have been vanquished and we are safe."

Mrs. Medlock smiled. She was fond of Susan Sowerby.

"She's got a way with her, has Susan," she went on quite volubly. "I've been thinking all morning of one thing she said yesterday. She says, 'Once when I was givin' th' children a bit of a preach after they'd been fightin' off the Forsaken horde from our village, I says to 'em all, "Back when the Accursed first came, I was reading up on how to kill 'um, my 'natomy book told as th' head were as soft as a melon, an' I found out before the first Accursed came near the Moor that th' brain were protected by no more than thin bone that only the lightest amount of pressure could rupture. One o' the Accursed is easily bested with no more than a well thrown river stone. But don't you—none o' you—think as you can best the hordes on your own or you'll find out you're mistaken, an' you won't find it out without hard knocks. You need each other to watch your backs, for the Tormented may have lost all sense of self and life, but they can be quiet as mouses when they wander into your room where you sleep. They are unblinking and never tire. They are insatiable and have ground their teeth sharp on bones.

Though dead their nails still seem to grow and they become sharp as talons for clawing into your skin." 'What children learns from children,' she says, 'is that there's no sense in tryin' to battle the whole world of murderous death alone. If you do you'll likely not save even your own home, and you'll become one of them that we have to slaughter."

"She's a shrewd woman," said Dr. Craven, putting on his coat.

"Well, she's got a way of saying things," ended Mrs. Medlock, much pleased. "Sometimes I've said to her, 'Eh! Susan, if you was a different woman an' didn't talk such broad Yorkshire or slice your arm to mark the number of the Tormented you'd killed, why I've seen the times when I should have said you was clever.'"

That night Colin slept without once awakening in terror from dreams of his mother being devoured and when he opened his eyes in the morning he lay still and smiled without knowing it— smiled and bit his lips remembering the taste... he opened his eyes and pushed away those thoughts. It was actually nice to be awake, for he felt that his chains were not so tight as they normally were, and he turned over and stretched his limbs luxuriously. He felt as if the tight straps which had held him had loosened themselves and let him go. He did not know that Mary had snuck in during the night and cut the straps and given slack to the chains. He wiggled his toes and looked curiously at his long toenails. He had heard once that nails continue to grow even after death. He wondered how long his nails would grow if he died. But then in an instant, he forgot those melancholy thoughts and instead of lying and staring at the wall and wishing he had not awakened, his mind was full of the plans he and Mary had made yesterday, of pictures of the garden and of Dickon and his wild creatures. It was so nice to have things to think about other then ones own demise and decay. And he had not been awake more than ten minutes when he heard feet running along the corridor and Mary was at the door. The next minute she was in the room and had run across to his bed, bringing with her a waft of fresh air full of the scent of the morning.

"You've been out! You've been out! There's that nice smell of leaves!" he cried.

She had been running and her hair was loose and blown and she was bright with the air and pink-cheeked. For a moment Colin thought he could see her blood pumping through her body and hear her rapid heart beating. But he then blinked and the vision was gone.

"It's so beautiful!" she said, a little breathless with her speed. "You never saw anything so beautiful! It has come! I thought it had come that other morning, but it was only coming. It is here now! It has come, the Spring! Dickon says so!"

"Has it?" cried Colin, and though he really knew nothing about it he felt his heart beat. He actually sat up in bed.

"Open the window!" he added, laughing half with joyful excitement and half at his own fancy. "Perhaps we may hear golden trumpets!"

And though he laughed, Mary was at the window in a moment and in a moment more it was opened wide and freshness and softness and scents and birds' songs were pouring through.

"That's fresh air," she said. "Lie on your back and draw in long breaths of it. That's what Dickon does when he's lying on the moor. He says he feels it in his veins and it makes him strong and he feels as if he could live forever and ever. Breathe it and breathe it."

She was only repeating what Dickon had told her, but she caught Colin's fancy.

"'Forever and ever'! Does it make him feel like that?" he said, and he did as she told him, drawing in long deep breaths over and over again. The thought of living forever reminded him of becoming a wretched mindless Accursed, but the thought of *not* living forever and ever, but just a normal life as a healthy boy, free of his affliction made Colin feel that something quite new and delightful was happening to him. Mary was at his bedside again.

"Things are crowding up out of the softening earth," she ran on in a hurry. "And there are flowers uncurling and buds on everything and the green veil has covered nearly all the gray and the birds are in such a hurry about their nests for fear they may be too late that some of them are even fighting for places in the secret garden. And the rose-bushes look as wick as wick can be, and there are primroses in the lanes and woods, and the seeds we planted are up, and Dickon has brought the fox and the crow and the squirrels and a new-born lamb."

And then she paused for breath. The new-born lamb Dickon had found three days before, lying by its eviscerated mother among the gorse bushes on the moor. An Accursed must have come upon her in the night. Dickon had said there would be more Accursed rising as the ground softened and people not properly dispatched and buried or burned would dig their way up. It was not the first motherless lamb he had found and he knew what to do with it. He had taken it to the cottage wrapped in his jacket and he had let it lie near the fire and had fed it with warm milk. It was a soft thing with a darling silly baby face and legs rather long for its body. Dickon had carried it over the moor in his arms and its feeding bottle was in his pocket with a squirrel, and when Mary had sat under a tree with its limp warmness huddled on her lap she had felt as if she were too full of strange joy to speak. A lamb— a lamb! A living lamb who lay on your lap like a baby!

She was describing it with great joy and Colin was listening and drawing in long breaths of air when the nurse entered. She started a little at the sight of the open window. She had sat stifling in the room many a warm day because her patient was sure that someone might see him or that something in the air would make him ill.

"Are you sure you are not chilly, Master Colin?" she inquired.

"No," was the answer. "I am breathing long breaths of fresh air. It makes you strong. I am going to get up to the sofa for breakfast. My cousin will have breakfast with me."

The nurse noticed his bed straps were dangling from the bed onto the floor and went away quickly, praying that Colin would not become too hungry to devour his cousin, and to give the order for two breakfasts. She found the servants' hall a more amusing place than the Cursed One's chamber and just now everybody wanted to hear the news from upstairs. There was a great deal of joking about the unpopular young demon who, as the cook said, "had found his Master, and good for him."

The servants' hall had been very tired of the tantrums, and the constant threat of death or worse, and the butler, who had lost his entire family to a hoard of the Fallen, had more than once expressed his opinion that the Cursed One would be all the better "for a decapitation and burning."

When Colin was on his sofa and re-chained, and the breakfast for two was put upon the table he made an announcement to the nurse in his most Rajah-like manner.

"A boy, and a fox, and a crow, and two squirrels, and a new-born lamb, are coming to see me this morning. I want them brought upstairs as soon as they come," he said. "You are not to begin playing with the animals in the servants' hall and keep them there. I want them here." The nurse gave a slight gasp and tried to conceal it with a cough.

"Yes, sir," she answered. She envisioned the young demon tearing the little lamb to pieces and devouring the squirrels raw.

"I'll tell you what you can do," added Colin, waving his hand. "You can tell Martha to bring them here. The boy is Martha's brother. His name is Dickon and he is an animal charmer."

"I hope the animals will be safe in here, Master Colin," said the nurse nervously. "You bit the last animal we brought in for you."

"Of course they will be safe! I detest eating animals raw. I hate it when you make me! I shall never eat meat again, I declare it!" said Colin austerely. "And I should never bite animals that belong to an animal charmer. They are good animals."

"There are snake-charmers in India," said Mary, "and they can put their snakes' heads in their mouths."

"Goodness!" shuddered the nurse.

They ate their breakfast with the morning air pouring in upon them. Colin's breakfast was a very good one and Mary watched him with serious interest as he pushed away the sausage but ate everything else ravenously.

"You will begin to get fatter just as I did," she said. "I never wanted my breakfast when I was in India and now I always want it."

"I wanted mine this morning," said Colin. "Perhaps it was the fresh air. When do you think Dickon will come?"

He was not long in coming. In about ten minutes Mary held up her hand.

"Listen!" she said. "Did you hear a caw?"

Colin listened and heard it, the oddest sound in the world to hear inside a house, a hoarse "caw-caw."

"Yes," he answered.

"That's Soot," said Mary. "Listen again. Do you hear a bleat—a tiny one?"

"Oh, yes!" cried Colin, quite flushing.

"That's the new-born lamb," said Mary. "He's coming."

Dickon's moorland boots were thick and clumsy and though he tried to walk quietly they made a clumping sound as he walked through the long corridors. Mary and Colin heard him marching— marching, until he passed through the tapestry door on to the soft carpet of Colin's own passage.

"If you please, sir," announced Martha, opening the door, "if you please, sir, here's Dickon an' his creatures."

Dickon came in smiling his nicest wide smile. The lamb was in his arms and the little red fox trotted by his side. Nut sat on his left shoulder and Soot on his right and Shell's head and paws peeped out of his coat pocket.

Colin slowly sat up and stared and stared—as he had stared when he first saw Mary; but this not the blank stare of the undead, this was a stare of wonder and delight. The truth was that in spite of all he had heard he had not in the least understood what this boy would be like. That Dickon's fox and his crow and his squirrels and his lamb were so near to him they seemed almost to be part of himself. Colin had never talked to a boy in his life and he was so overwhelmed by his own pleasure and curiosity that he did not even think of speaking. Everyone before who would find themselves near him would run quickly in the other direction, children would be hastily shuffled away and the bravest of them might spit on him.

But Dickon did not feel the least shy or awkward. He had not felt embarrassed because the crow had not known his language and had only stared and had not spoken to him the first time they met. Creatures were always like that until they found out about you. He could see that Colin could not walk or move much from being chained to the wall so he walked over to Colin's sofa and put the new-born lamb quietly on his lap. Colin and Mary froze, waiting to see how the lamb would react. Immediately the little creature turned to the warm velvet dressing-gown and began to nuzzle and nuzzle into its folds and butt its tight-curled head with soft impatience against his side. The little creature was not afraid of him! This gave Colin great hope that he might not be as close to being Forsaken as he thought. Of course no boy could have helped speaking then.

"It's not afraid of me!" cried Colin. "What does it want?"

"It wants its mother," said Dickon, smiling more and more. "I brought it to thee a bit hungry because I knowed tha'd like to see it feed."

He knelt down by the sofa and took a feeding-bottle from his pocket.

"Come on, little 'un," he said, turning the small woolly white head with a gentle brown hand. "This is what tha's after. Tha'll get more out o' this than tha' will out o' silk velvet coats. There now," and he pushed the rubber tip of the bottle into the nuzzling mouth and the lamb began to suck it with ravenous ecstasy.

After that there was no wondering what to say. By the time the lamb fell asleep questions poured forth and Dickon answered them all. He told them how he had found the lamb just as the sun was rising three mornings ago. He had been standing on the moor watching for the Accursed and listening to a skylark and watching him swing higher and higher into the sky until he was only a speck in the heights of blue.

"I'd almost lost him but for his song an' I was wonderin' how a chap could hear it when it seemed as if he'd get out o' th' world in a minute—an' just then one o' the Forsaken come upon me an' tried to take o' bit o' me neck out. But I flung meself t' th' ground and rolled away quick hav'n me knife ready as it came charg'n toward me. I sliced it 'cross the eyes an' when it stumbled I plunged me knife into its skull; through the temple mind, tis the softest spot. I noticed th' wretched creature had fresh blood o' it's hands and mouth so I started lookin' for who it might 've harmed. Then I heard somethin' far off among th' gorse bushes. It was a weak bleatin' an' I knowed it was a new lamb as was hungry an' I knowed it wouldn't be hungry if it hadn't lost its mother, so I set off searchin'. Eh! I did have a look for it. I went in an' out among th' gorse bushes an' round an' round an' I always seemed to take th' wrong turnin'. But at last I seed a bit o' white by a rock on top o' th' moor an' I climbed up an' found th' little 'un half dead wi' cold an' clemmin'. 'Is mother lay dead spillin' out o' her throat an' stomach where the foul creature ripped her open. " While he talked, Soot flew solemnly in and out of the open window and cawed remarks about the presence (or lack thereof) of undead out on the moor while Nut and Shell made excursions into the big trees outside and ran up and down trunks and explored escape routes from the window. Captain curled up near Dickon, who sat on the hearth-rug from preference.

Colin listened to Dickon, not at all taking offense to the descriptions of killing the Fallen Ones. He knew he was different. He hadn't turned... yet. But if he did turn he would hope that someone would put him down quickly. The thought of aimlessly wandering the moor for eternity eating raw sheep nearly sent him into a panic, but Colin gently stroked the lamb and thought about seeing the Secret Garden.

They looked at the pictures in the gardening books and Dickon knew all the flowers by their country names and knew exactly which ones were already growing in the secret garden.

"I couldna' say that there name," he said, pointing to one under which was written "Aquilegia," "but us calls that a columbine, an' that there one it's a snapdragon and they both grow wild in hedges, but these is garden ones an' they're bigger an' grander. There's some big clumps o' columbine in th' garden. They'll look like a bed o' blue an' white butterflies flutterin' when they're out."

"I'm going to see them," cried Colin. "I am going to see them!"

"Aye, that tha' mun," said Mary quite seriously. "An' tha' munnot lose no time about it."

Chapter 20: I Shall NOT Live Forever—And Ever—And Ever!

They were obliged to wait more than a week because first there came some very windy days and then Colin was threatened with a cold, and then there were reports of Forsaken on the moor approaching one of the villages nearby and no one was to go outside, which three things happening one after the other would no doubt have thrown him into a rage but that there was so much careful and mysterious planning to do and almost every day Dickon came in, if only for a few minutes, to talk about what was happening on the moor and in the lanes and villages. The things he had to tell were about the Accursed rising out of the thawed soil of the church yard two villages over and attacking the church during Sunday mass trapping all the good people inside. Once the newly risen hoard had broken through the boarded windows the people panicked and only the parishioner and a few children escaped by climbing onto the large wooden cross behind the pulpit and jumping through the stained glass windows out the back of the church. Not to mention the roaming undead coming out of the big cities. It were enough to make one almost tremble when one heard all the intimate details from Dickon about how after people abandoned their homes, the Forsaken began to leave the cities in droves searching for the living and one realized with what horrible terror and anxiety the whole wretched world was suffering.

"They're same as us everywhere," said Dickon, "Holdin' up and keepin' watch all the time. It keeps a body so alert as to fair exhaust out a mind."

Colin was very confused, "How are dead rising from the grave? I thought it was caused by infection.

"Sometimes people are jus' buried too early. People are careless an' don' take out the brain o' the infected, they just might knock 'um out or think they're dead. 'Specially in the early years, before anyone knew all Accursed mus' be beheaded or burned, they were buried and would eventually scratch their way out of the caskets and claw their way up through the earth. When the earth is soft it is much easier for them to dig out. No knowin' how many hundreds might be under there now, scratchin' away at the rotting wood and diggin' up through six feet."

Mary was very curious about the security of Misselthwiate Manor and wondered aloud how many of the servants kept watch and what would they do if they saw an Accursed coming close to the Manor. She remembered the huge wall and large iron gates. She also remembered how one had made it to the gates of the garden from the woods.

"Misselthwaite has a good defense." Dickon said to Mary while Colin wasn't listening. "Better than most. It keeps out the living and the dead. But it's gotten too relaxed over the years. I seen lights in windows while I walk up the moor. That will attract 'um as much as any loud noise. I have seen gates left unlocked in the back gardens and some of the iron spikes have begun to rust away and fall off along the walls along the edge of the property. If an Rotter happened upon the weak spots, they would get in."

"And what about animals?" Mary asked Dickon. "Accursed mice can spread infection too can't they?" She wondered how many other little nests of Accursed mice might be at Misselthwaite.

"Aye, they can. But it's different in most animals. It doesn' affect birds or lizards or sea creatures. And with mice, dogs, horses or sheep an' the like they don't seem as crazed and starvin'. Mice n' rats will stay in their holes until something disturbs them.

It was true that Mary was only attacked once she disturbed the nest and dug out the mice. She daren't tell anyone for fear they wouldn't let her outside again.

The most absorbing thing, however, was the preparations to be made before Colin could be transported with sufficient secrecy to the garden. Colin would need to be tied down into his chair-carriage and no one must see him, Dickon or Mary after they turned a certain corner of the shrubbery and entered upon the walk outside the ivy covered wall. As each day passed, Colin had become more and more fixed in his feeling that the mystery surrounding the garden was one of its greatest charms. Nothing must spoil that. No one must ever suspect that they had a secret. People must think that he was simply going out with Mary and Dickon because he liked them, did not object to their looking at him, and had no desire to consume them. They had long and quite delightful talks about their route. They would go up this path and down that one and cross the other and go round among the fountain flower-beds as if they were looking at the "bedding-out plants" the head gardener, Mr. Roach, had been having arranged. That would seem such a rational thing to do that no one would think it at all mysterious. They would turn into the shrubbery walks and lose themselves until they came to the long walls. It was almost as serious and elaborately thought out as the plans of attack made by great generals in taking back London from the Forsaken.

Rumors of the sacrilegious and the curious things which were occurring in the Cursed Boy's apartments had of course filtered through the servants' hall into the stable yards and out among the gardeners, but notwithstanding this, Mr. Roach was startled one day when he received orders from Master Colin's room to the effect that he must report himself in the apartment no outsider had ever seen, as the little demon himself desired to speak to him.

"Well, well," he said to himself as he hurriedly changed his coat, "what's to do now? The Dark Lord that wasn't to be looked at calling up a man he's never set eyes on."

Mr. Roach was not without curiosity. He had never caught even a glimpse of the boy and had heard a dozen exaggerated stories about his blackened eyes, rotting flesh and his insane tempers. The thing he had heard oftenest was that he might turn at any moment and there had been numerous fanciful descriptions of a ravenous appetite for fresh raw meat, teeth like daggers and nails sharp as talons, given by people who had never seen him.

"Things are changing in this house, Mr. Roach," said Mrs. Medlock, as she led him up the back staircase to the corridor on to which opened the hitherto mysterious chamber.

"It is an interesting development from what I heard, Mrs. Medlock," he answered. "They say it appears his symptoms of transformation have slowed due to socialization with his peers. I always assumed he would immediately attempt to devour anyone weaker than himself.

"Don't know about weaker," she continued. "That Miss Mary is quite stronger now since she arrived. All that time outside has been good for her. And her temper can match that of an enraged demon, that I have seen. And Dickon has charmed him like his other animals. Don't you be surprised, Mr. Roach, if you find yourself in the middle of a menagerie and Martha Sowerby's Dickon more at home than you or me could ever be."

There really was a sort of Magic about Dickon, as Mary always privately believed. When Mr. Roach heard his name he smiled quite leniently.

"He'd be at home in Buckingham Palace or in a Forsaken infested pit," he said. "And yet it's not impudence, either. He's just fine, is that lad."

It was perhaps well he had been prepared or he might have been horrified. When the bedroom door was opened a large crow, which seemed quite at home perched on the high back of a carven chair, announced the entrance of a visitor by saying "Caw—Caw" quite loudly. In spite of Mrs. Medlock's warning, Mr. Roach only just escaped being sufficiently undignified to jump backward in fear as Colin was not at all strapped down.

The cursed-born was neither in bed nor on his sofa. He was loosely chained in an armchair and a young lamb was standing by him shaking its tail in feeding-lamb fashion as Dickon knelt giving it milk from its bottle. A squirrel was perched on Dickon's bent back attentively nibbling a nut. The little girl from India was sitting on a big footstool looking on.

"Here is Mr. Roach, Master Colin," said Mrs. Medlock.

The Forsaken boy turned and looked his servitor over as if he was assessing his dinner—at least that was what the head gardener felt happened.

"Oh, you are Roach, are you?" he said. "I sent for you to give you some very important orders."

"Very good, sir," answered Roach, wondering if he was to receive instructions to bring him his young daughters for his evening meal or to transform the gardens into an open arena where he could wander freely and chunks of flesh would be flung to him and piles of bones would be left out for him to chew.

"I am going out in my chair this afternoon," said Colin. "If the fresh air agrees with me I may go out every day. When I go, none of the gardeners are to be anywhere near the Long Walk by the garden walls. No one is to be there. I shall go out about two o'clock and everyone must keep away until I send word that they may go back to their work. Anyone who comes near me puts their life in peril other than Miss Mary and Dickon. Understood?"

"Very good, sir," replied Mr. Roach, much relieved to hear that his daughters would remain safely locked up in his home and his gardens were safe. "Mary," said Colin, turning to her, "what is that thing you say in India when you have finished talking and want people to go?"

"You say, 'Leave or I shall tear your heart out and eat it raw,'" answered Mary stifling a giggle.

The Rajah waved his hand.

"Leave or I shall tear your heart out and eat it raw, Roach," he said. "But, remember, this is very important, everyone must stay away."

"Caw—Caw!" remarked the crow hoarsely but not impolitely.

"Very good, sir. Thank you, sir," said Mr. Roach, and Mrs. Medlock took him out of the room.

Outside in the corridor, being a rather anxious man, he sighed heavily in relief and held his hands to stop them shaking.

"My word!" he said, "he's got a demonic lordly way with him, hasn't he? You'd think he was the Devil himself with the way he threatens the soul."

"Eh!" protested Mrs. Medlock, "we've had to let him torment every one of us ever since he had teeth and he thinks that's what folks was born for."

"Perhaps he'll be cured somehow, if he doesn't turn first," suggested Mr. Roach.

"Well, there's one thing pretty sure," said Mrs. Medlock. "If he does turn and that Indian child stays here I'll warrant she won't lead him around on a chain. As Susan Sowerby says, she'll watch her back and Dickon's too, as stickin together keeps a body alive. She'd do him in if it came to that, I'm sure.

Inside the room Colin was leaning back on his cushions.

"It's all safe now," he said. "And this afternoon I shall see it—this afternoon I shall be in it!"

Dickon went back to the garden with his creatures and Mary stayed with Colin. She did not think he looked tired but he was very quiet before their lunch came and he was quiet while they were eating it. She wondered why and asked him about it.

"What big eyes you've got, Colin," she said. "When you are thinking they get as big as saucers. What are you thinking about now?" Mary hoped it was not due to the absence of raw meat on his plate.

"I can't help thinking about what it will look like," he answered.

"The garden?" asked Mary.

"The springtime," he said. "I was thinking that I've really never seen it before. I scarcely ever went out and when I did go I never looked at it. I didn't even think about it. Everything in my life has been about death and decay. The thought of new things growing and living despite the world's seeming to be ending captivates me."

"I never saw it in India because there wasn't any," said Mary.

Shut in and morbid as his life had been, Colin had more imagination than she had and at least he had spent a good deal of time looking at wonderful books and pictures. But there was one thing he had heard about his entire life and never seen.

"What do they look like, Mary?"

"What?"

"The Accursed Ones. You have seen them haven't you?"

Mary remembered the moment she first saw one up close at her home in India. When she first learned of the Scourge infection and how it had spread. She told Colin about the young soldier who turned right in front of her and how people get infected through a bite or a scratch, and within a day transform into the Shiva worshipping devils, forsaken by God and forced to feed upon the living unable to satisfy their insatiable hunger.

"First, you seem sick, your skin turns pale and yellowish, then your body starts to twitch and you lose control of your body, your stomach turns black and spews out everything inside, then your eyes turn yellow and black blood flows across your eyes. Then you turn and your mind is not your own. You are Forsaken."

Colin sat back in horror. He had no idea Mary knew this much about the Scourge. No one ever wanted to talk to him about it.

He asked, "Who is Shiva?"

"An Indian god my Ayah used to talk about. He caused the Scourge to punish us. Even animals can be infected." Mary told him about the snake she killed in her nursery.

"And how does someone kill one of the Forsaken?" Colin had often wondered if he died would he then rise as a mindless cannibal.

"Only by destroying the brain can you defeat one. They can still live even if they have no arms or legs!"

"Is there a cure?" Colin asked knowing the answer.

"No," Mary shook her head. "If there was a cure, I'm sure Dicken would have known about it. And your uncle, Dr. Craven, would have given it to you."

"I've heard my uncle speak of a cure, but it was strange. He spoke about it as if it would be a bad thing."

Mary crossed her arms. "What do you mean? How could anyone think that?"

Colin thought a moment remembering and said, "It was a long time ago, over a year in fact, but I had frightened one of the kitchen maids when she brought me a supper of raw cow's tongue. I had been so disgusted by it that I ripped it open and threw it at her. She yelled at Dr. Craven that it was a sin to keep me alive living as a horrid monster and that I should be killed. Then he said I must be kept alive and that the damned cure would be the end of him."

Mary thought that was very strange. There was no cure, unless the doctor knew something he was not sharing with the world.

A little later the nurse made Colin ready. She noticed that instead of lying like a log while his clothes were put on he sat up and made some efforts against the chains to help himself, and he talked and laughed with Mary all the time.

"This is one of his good days, sir," the nurse said to Dr. Craven, who dropped in to inspect him. "He's in such good spirits that I fear it makes him stronger. Thought you should know, Doctor, he hasn't been eating very well. Refuses any meat."

"That is a new development. He grows stronger while eating less. I'll call in again later in the afternoon, after he has come in," said Dr. Craven. "I must see how the going out agrees with him. I wish," in a very low voice, "that he would let you go with him."

"I wouldn't go out there with him even if he were chained hand and foot and surrounded by ten Purifiers, sir," answered the nurse with sudden firmness. "All it takes is one little bite or one deep scratch, and don't trust that half demon, sir.

"I hadn't really decided to suggest it," said the doctor, with his slight nervousness. "We'll try the experiment. If Master Colin were to turn on Mistress Mary, Dickon would stop him quick. Dickon's a lad I'd trust with a new-born child."

Colin was indeed chained hand and foot. A collar and face mask muffled his voice and restricted his head movement. Colin did not resist or riot and allowed the strongest footman in the house to carry him down stairs and outside where Dickon was waiting.

Mrs. Medlock, the nurse and many curious servants were there, though Mrs. Medlock had warned them to stay out of sight.

After the manservant had arranged his chains and secured him to the chair, the young demon waved his hand to him and to all the others.

"You have my permission to go. Leave or I shall tear your hearts out and eat them raw," he said, though the words were muffled underneath the face mask that covered his mouth and nose. They all disappeared quickly and sighed with relief when they were safely inside the house, most hoping Colin would never return. Mrs. Medlock had stayed by the window and watched until the children had disappeared into the gardens.

Dickon began to push the wheeled chair slowly and steadily. Mistress Mary walked beside it and Colin leaned back and lifted his face to the sky. The arch of it looked very high and the small snowy clouds seemed like white birds floating on outspread wings below its crystal blueness. Colin could not remember ever seeing such a sky and felt that perhaps he was not so cursed if he could still see towards heaven. The wind swept in soft big breaths down from the moor and was strange with a wild clear scented sweetness.

"Take this horrid mask off me, Mary. I want to breathe in the air." Mary removed the mask and released the chains around his arms. Colin kept lifting his thin chest to draw in the sweet air, and his big eyes looked as if it were they which were listening—listening, instead of his ears.

"There are so many sounds of singing and humming and calling out," he said. "What is that scent the puffs of wind bring?"

"It's gorse on th' moor that's openin' out," answered Dickon. "Eh! th' bees are at it wonderful today."

Not a human creature was to be caught sight of in the paths they took. In fact, every gardener or gardener's lad had been frightened away with the news that the Accursed boy would be in the gardens. But they wound in and out among the shrubbery and out and round the fountain beds, following their carefully planned route for the mere mysterious pleasure of it. But when at last they turned into the Long Walk by the ivy covered walls the excited sense of an approaching thrill made them, for some curious reason they could not have explained, begin to speak in whispers.

"This is it," breathed Mary. "This is where I used to walk up and down and wonder and wonder."

"Is it?" cried Colin, and his eyes began to search the ivy with eager curiousness. "But I can see nothing," he whispered. "There is no door."

"That's what I thought," said Mary.

Then there was a lovely breathless silence and the chair wheeled on.

"That is the garden where Ben Weatherstaff works," said Mary.

"Is it?" said Colin.

A few yards more and Mary whispered again.

"This is where the robin flew over the wall," she said.

"Is it?" cried Colin. "Oh! I wish he'd come again!"

"And that," said Mary with solemn delight, pointing under a big lilac bush, "is where he perched on the little heap of earth and showed me the key."

Then Colin sat up.

"Where? Where? There?" he cried, and his eyes were as big as the Forsaken when they were near to snatching an unaware victim. Dickon stood still and the wheeled chair stopped.

"And this," said Mary, stepping on to the bed close to the ivy, "is where I went to talk to him when he chirped at me from the top of the wall. And this is the ivy the wind blew back," and she took hold of the hanging green curtain.

"Oh! is it—is it!" gasped Colin.

"And here is the handle, and here is the door. Dickon push him in—push him in quickly!"

And Dickon did it with one strong, steady, splendid push.

But Colin had actually dropped back against his cushions, even though he gasped with delight, and he had covered his eyes with his hands and held them there shutting out everything until they were inside and the chair stopped as if by magic and the door was closed. Not till then did he take them away and look round and round and round as Dickon and Mary had done. And over walls and earth and trees and swinging sprays and tendrils the fair green veil of tender little leaves had crept, and in the grass under the trees and the gray urns in the alcoves and here and there everywhere were touches or splashes of gold and purple and white and the trees were showing pink and snow above his head and there were fluttering of wings and faint sweet pipes and humming and scents and scents. And the sun fell warm upon his face like a hand with a lovely touch. And in wonder Mary and Dickon stood and stared at him. He looked so strange and different because a pink glow of color had actually crept all over him—ivory face and neck and hands and all.

"I shall live! I shall get well!" he cried out. "Mary! Dickon! This curse upon me shall be lifted, I feel it! And I shall NOT live forever and ever and ever as horrid wandering thing! But I shall live!"

Chapter 21: Ben Weatherstaff

One of the strange things about living in a cursed world where the dead rise to consume the living is that it is only now and then one believes that the world may yet be healed and that one may not succumb to the eternity of aimless wandering driven by an incessant violent hunger. Getting up at the tender solemn dawn-time and going out and standing alone one prays that the beauty of the world will not be blackened out by the obliteration of the human race. That we may be safe and still witness the pale sky slowly changing and flushing with marvelous unknown things happening until the East almost makes one cry out, only remembering that to make any sound, even of joy, is to beckon the frightful afflicted. One's heart stands still at the strange unchanging majesty of the rising of the sun—which has been happening every morning for thousands and thousands and thousands of years and will continue even if all life on Earth ceases to breathe or grow. But hopes fail and one knows the dark truth when one stands by oneself in a wood at sunset and the mysterious deep gold stillness slanting through and under the branches seems to be saying slowly again and again something one cannot quite hear, only to be horribly interrupted by the hordes of the dead that tear into one's living flesh unable to fight them off however much one tries as they pollute the ground with gore and bile. Then sometimes the immense quiet of the dark blue at night with millions of stars waiting and watching makes one feel safe; and sometimes a sound of far-off gunfire makes it true; and sometimes a look in some one's eyes tells you that not all hope is lost and sometimes new life can make one forget about inexorable death.

And it was like that with Colin when he first saw and heard and felt the Springtime inside the four high walls of a hidden garden. That afternoon the whole world seemed to devote itself to being perfect and radiantly beautiful and kind to one boy. Perhaps out of pure heavenly goodness the spring came and crowded everything it possibly could into that one place. So many good things filled Colin up and pushed out all dark thoughts that made him feel Accursed. More than once Dickon paused in what he was doing and stood still with a sort of growing wonder in his eyes, shaking his head softly.

"Eh! it is graidely," he said. "I'm twelve goin' on thirteen an' there's a lot o' afternoons in thirteen years, but seems to me like I never seed one as graidely as this 'ere."

"Aye, it is a graidely one," said Mary, and she sighed for mere joy. "I'll warrant it's the graidelest one as ever was in this world."

"Does tha' think," said Colin with dreamy carefulness, "as happen it was made loike this 'ere all o' purpose for me?"

"My word!" cried Mary admiringly, "that there is a bit o' good Yorkshire. Tha'rt shapin' first-rate—that tha' art."

For a while Colin forgot that he was infected and delight reigned. They drew the chair under the plum-tree, which was snow-white with blossoms and musical with bees. It was like a king's canopy, a fairy king's. There were flowering cherry-trees near and apple-trees whose buds were pink and white, and here and there one had burst open wide. Between the blossoming branches of the canopy bits of blue sky looked down like wonderful eyes.

Mary and Dickon worked a little here and there and Colin watched them. They brought him things to look at—buds which were opening, buds which were tight closed, bits of twig whose leaves were just showing green, the feather of a woodpecker which had dropped on the grass, the empty shell of some bird early hatched. Dickon pushed the chair slowly round and round the garden, stopping every other moment to let him look at wonders springing out of the earth or trailing down from trees. It was like being taken round the country of a magic king and queen and shown all the mysterious riches it contained.

"I wonder if we shall see the robin?" said Colin.

"Tha'll see him often enow after a bit," answered Dickon. "When th' eggs hatches out th' little chap he'll be kep' so busy it'll make his head swim. Tha'll see him flyin' backward an' for'ard carryin' worms nigh as big as himsel' an' that much noise goin' on in th' nest when he gets there as fair flusters him so as he scarce knows which big mouth to drop th' first piece in. An' gapin' beaks an' squawks on every side. Mother says as when she sees th' work a robin has to keep them gapin' beaks filled, she feels like she was a lady with nothin' to do. She says she's seen th' chaps when it seemed like th' sweat must be droppin' off 'em, though folk can't see it."

This made them giggle so delightedly that they were obliged to cover their mouths with their hands, remembering that they must not be heard by either the living or the dead. Colin had been instructed as to the law of whispers and low voices several days before. He liked the mysteriousness of it and did his best, but in the midst of excited enjoyment it is rather difficult never to laugh above a whisper.

Every moment of the afternoon was full of new things and every hour the sunshine grew more golden. The wheeled chair had been drawn back under the canopy and Dickon had sat down on the grass and had just drawn out his pipe when Colin saw something he had not had time to notice before.

"That's a very old tree over there, isn't it?" he said. Dickon looked across the grass at the tree and Mary looked and there was a brief moment of stillness.

"Yes," answered Dickon, after it, and his low voice had a very gentle sound.

Mary gazed at the tree and thought.

"The branches are quite gray and there's not a single leaf anywhere," Colin went on. "It's quite dead, isn't it?"

"Aye," admitted Dickon. "But them roses as has climbed all over it will near hide every bit o' th' dead wood when they're full o' leaves an' flowers. It won't look dead then. It'll be th' prettiest of all."

Mary still gazed at the tree and thought.

"It looks as if a big branch had been broken off," said Colin. "I wonder how it was done."

"It's been done many a year," answered Dickon. "Eh!" with a sudden relieved start and laying his hand on Colin. "Look at that robin! There he is! He's been foragin' for his mate."

Colin was almost too late but he just caught sight of him, the flash of red with something in his beak. He darted through the greenness and into the close-grown corner and was out of sight. Colin leaned back on his cushion again, laughing a little. "He's taking her tea to her. Perhaps it's five o'clock. I think I'd like some tea myself."

And so they were safe. Colin did not know the particulars of his mother's horrific death and Mary did not want to be the one to tell him.

"It was Magic which sent the robin," said Mary secretly to Dickon afterward. "I know it was Magic." For both she and Dickon had been afraid Colin might ask something about the tree whose branch had broken off ten years ago when the Accursed broke into the secret garden and pulled Mrs. Craven down and had attempted to eat her. They had talked it over together and Dickon had stood and rubbed his head in a troubled way.

"We mun look as if it wasn't no different from th' other trees," he had said. "We couldn't never tell him how it broke, poor lad. If he says anything about it we mun—we mun try to look cheerful."

"Aye, that we mun," had answered Mary.

But she had not felt as if she looked cheerful when she gazed at the tree. Dickon had gone on rubbing his rust-red hair in a puzzled way, but a nice comforted look had begun to grow in his blue eyes.

"Mrs. Craven was a very lovely young lady," he had gone on rather hesitatingly. "An' mother she thinks maybe she's still about Misselthwaite lookin' after Mester Colin, same as all mothers do when they're took out o' th' world. They have to come back, tha' sees. Happen she's been in the garden all the time, an' happen it was her set us to work, an' told us to bring him here."

Mary had thought he meant something about Magic. She was a great believer in Magic. It had been the dark Aghori Magic that began the Scourge and spread it across the world. Secretly she quite believed that Dickon worked Magic, of course good Magic, on everything near him and that was why people liked him so much and wild creatures knew he was their friend. She wondered, indeed, if it were not possible that his gift had brought the robin just at the right moment when Colin asked that dangerous question. She felt that his Magic was working all the afternoon and making Colin look like an entirely different boy. It did not seem possible that he could be the crazy afflicted creature who had screamed and beaten and bitten his pillow. Even his ivory whiteness seemed to change. The faint glow of color which had shown on his face and neck and hands when he first got inside the garden really never quite died away. He looked as if he were made of flesh instead of ivory or wax. It was as if he were a healthy boy and not an infected one.

They saw the robin carry food to his mate two or three times, and it was so suggestive of afternoon tea that Colin felt they must have some.

"Go and make one of the men servants bring some in a basket to the rhododendron walk," he said. "And then you and Dickon can bring it here."

It was an agreeable idea, however, not easily carried out. When they left to fetch a servant they found one near the iron gate to the woods which had been left open. Dickon made sure to re-close the gate and wondered how it had come open when he knew for certain that he had locked it when he had come in that morning. The servant lay dead, his face unrecognizable after the claws of the undead had torn it apart. He had been eviscerated with a trail of blood and entrails leading towards the vegetable gardens. Dickon pulled out his knife and Mary readied her throwing blades. Dickon plunged his knife into the head of the servant, careful to keep his head turned lest the blood get into his eyes or mouth. Following the trail of gore through the gardens, Mary began to hear strange sounds behind the garden walls. A dreadful squishing and shredding noise made Dickon stop in his tracks and motion Mary to be still. They stepped very slowly, Mary concentrating hard to move just as Dickon moved and make no sound. Peering around the garden wall, Mary's heart jumped into her throat stopping her breath. Four of the Forsaken crouched eating one of the kitchen maids. They had torn into her chest and dug out her heart and lungs. Two adults leaned over the body like lions tearing off chucks with their teeth. The younger one, no more than fifteen, was content to knaw on the servant's fingers while the oldest, who may have been a grandfather once, held the half eaten heart in his hands and sucked it as if it was a juicy pomegranate.

Dickon motioned to Mary that he would take the two to the right, leaving Mary with the elder and the teenager. Dickon rushed headlong into the group and thrust his knife into the neck of the closest creature. Mary sprang forward, throwing her knives into the old man's temple. He turned and dropped the heart onto the ground. He stood and stepped towards Mary, squishing the heart under his threadbare shoe. Mary pulled her throwing knives back tearing the flesh from the Accursed man's head. His wound oozed with black putrid blood but he stepped forward again, this time with mouth agape showing Mary the hanging bits of flesh from his last victim. Dickon had successfully decapitated one of the creatures and was preparing to attack the next when he suddenly gasped and stumbled backwards. The female Forsaken crawled towards him snarling.

Mary again threw her knives at the man, this time hitting the eyes. Running around the blinded Accursed, Mary pulled the knives back and then drove them into the spine of the crawling woman. Dickon looked pained and frowned as he stood over the woman struggling to move with the knives in her vertebrate. He took a deep breath and plunged his knife clean through her skull. She instantly fell to the ground and lay still. "Tha' ha' been my favorite teacher." Dickon said. "She always let me bring in the animals."

Mary had no time for sympathy. Realizing more fresh meat was available, the teenage boy stood snarling at her while the blinded old man was clawing towards the sound of Dickon's voice. Mary faced the boy, looking into his blackened bloody eyes and remembered the last time she had seen her mother.

She had been weak then, friendless, stupid and unloved. Her mother had unwittingly saved her with her scream of terror, distracting the young Accursed man. She was no longer weak. She had friends, was wiser now and felt that she was loved at least by a few people. And she loved them. And no one would take that away from her.

She threw her knives at the young man and they imbedded into his neck. She ran behind him and pulled her knives back tearing out his throat. The creature reeled around and faced her, black gore pouring from his neck and mouth. Mary took a breath. Hate filled her. She hated this creature with all its blackness and horribleness and she swung her knives as fast as she could spin them.

She chucked them with all her might at the boy's face and they both landed square between his eyes imbedded in his brain.

The Accursed dropped to the ground and Mary approached slowly. Dickon had been standing by holding his knife ready. But he wanted Mary to have this kill. Mary pulled her knifes from its face. Then with the strength of her hatred and anger she plunged her curved knife into its skull, just to be sure.

Dickon and and Mary stood in silence a moment and then he put his arm around her. "Ye did great, my little lass. A braver Purifier I never knew before. Now let me check you."

"I didn't get touched." Mary said turning to him.

"Aye, but I mus' check for the blood." Dickon looked closely around her lips and wiped some blood spatter off her neck. Then looked at her eyes and Mary looked into his.

She said, "I didn't get any black blood in me. I turned my head as you did."

Dickon replied, "I see tha' is as smart as a misselthrush too."

Mary beamed.

"Come on then!" He said. "We've got to hide all these here bodies quick an' Colin will be waitin' for his tea!"

Mary finally found a servant outside the gardens near the house who rang the bell and a basket was brought out to them at once.

When the white cloth was spread upon the grass, with hot tea and buttered toast and crumpets, a delightfully hungry meal was eaten, and several birds on domestic errands paused to inquire what was going on and were led into investigating crumbs with great activity. Nut and Shell whisked up trees with pieces of cake and Soot took the entire half of a buttered crumpet into a corner and pecked at and examined and turned it over and made hoarse remarks about it until he decided to swallow it all joyfully in one gulp.

Colin enquired about the long wait and Dickon explained that he could not find a lively servant anywhere near, which was expected since they had been ordered to stay away. Mary had to stifle a giggle when Dickon had said a '*lively* servant'.

The afternoon was dragging towards its mellow hour. The sun was deepening the gold of its lances, the bees were going home and the birds were flying past less often. Dickon and Mary were sitting on the grass, the tea-basket was repacked ready to be taken back to the house, and Colin was lying against his cushions with his heavy locks pushed back from his forehead and his face looking quite a natural color.

"I don't want this afternoon to go," he said; "but I shall come back tomorrow, and the day after, and the day after, and the day after."

"You'll get plenty of fresh air, won't you?" said Mary.

"I'm going to get nothing else," he answered. "I've seen the spring now and I'm going to see the summer. I'm going to see everything grow here. I'm going to grow here myself."

"That tha' will," said Dickon. "Us'll have thee walkin' about here an' diggin' same as other folk afore long."

Colin flushed tremendously. "Walk!" he said. "Dig! Shall I?"

Dickon's glance at him was delicately cautious. Neither he nor Mary had ever asked if anything was the matter with his legs.

"For sure tha' will," he said stoutly. "Tha—tha's got legs o' thine own, same as other folks!"

Mary was rather frightened until she heard Colin's answer.

"Nothing really ails them," he said, "but they are so thin and weak from being chained all my years. They shake so that I'm afraid to try to stand on them."

Both Mary and Dickon drew a relieved breath.

"When tha' stops bein' afraid tha'lt stand on 'em," Dickon said with renewed cheer. "An' tha'lt stop bein' afraid in a bit."

"I shall?" said Colin, and he lay still wondering about things. He wondered if he should be able to walk and if he should live and never be Accursed. He wondered if he should grow and become as strong as Dickon. He wondered if his father would want to see him then and not experiment on him.

They were really very quiet for a little while. The sun was dropping lower. It was that hour when everything stills itself, and they really had had a busy and exciting afternoon. Colin looked as if he were resting luxuriously. Even the creatures had ceased moving about and had drawn together and were resting near them. Soot had perched on a low branch and drawn up one leg and dropped the gray film drowsily over his eyes. Mary privately thought he looked as if he might snore in a minute.

In the midst of this stillness it was rather startling when Colin half lifted his head and exclaimed in a loud suddenly alarmed whisper:

"Who is that man?" Dickon and Mary scrambled to their feet.

"Man!" they both cried in low quick voices.

Colin pointed to the high wall. "Look!" he whispered excitedly. "Just look!"

Mary and Dickon wheeled about, their weapons at the ready, and looked. There was Ben Weatherstaff's indignant face glaring at them over the wall from the top of a ladder! He actually shook his fist at Mary.

"If I wasn't a bachelor, an' tha' was a wench o' mine," he cried, "I'd give thee a hidin'!"

"Oh, Ben Weatherstaff!" called out Mary, finding her breath. "I thought you were one of the Rotters climbing the walls and now I hear you I wish you was, so I could dispatch you and have you gone!"

He mounted another step threateningly as if it were his energetic intention to jump down and deal with her; but as she came toward him spinning her throwing blade he evidently thought better of it and stood on the top step of his ladder shaking his fist down at her.

"I never thowt much o' thee!" he harangued. "I couldna' abide thee th' first time I set eyes on thee. A scrawny buttermilk-faced young besom, allus askin' questions an' pokin' tha' nose where it wasna wanted. I never knowed how tha' got so thick wi' me. If it hadna' been for th' robin—Drat him—"

Mary thought about throwing her blade at him but she too thought better of it and called up to him with a sort of gasp. "Ben Weatherstaff, it was the robin who showed me the way!"

Then it did seem as if Ben really would scramble down on her side of the wall, he was so outraged.

"Tha' young bad 'un!" he called down at her. "Layin' tha' badness on a robin—not but what he's impudent enow for anythin'. Him showin' thee th' way! Him! Eh! tha' young nowt"— she could see his next words burst out because he was overpowered by curiosity—"however i' this world did tha' get in?"

"It was the robin who showed me the way," she protested obstinately. "He didn't know he was doing it but he did. And I can't tell you from here while you're shaking your fist at me."

He stopped shaking his fist very suddenly at that very moment and his jaw actually dropped as he stared over her head at something he saw coming over the grass toward him.

At the first sound of his torrent of words Colin had been so surprised that he had only sat up and listened as if he were spellbound. But in the midst of it he had recovered himself and beckoned imperiously to Dickon.

"Wheel me over there!" he commanded. "Wheel me quite close and stop right in front of him!"

And this, if you please, this is what Ben Weatherstaff beheld and which made his jaw drop. A wheeled chair with luxurious cushions and iron chains which came toward him looking rather like some sort of State Coach because a young Rajah leaned back in it with royal command in his great black-rimmed eyes and a thin white hand extended haughtily toward him. And it stopped right under Ben Weatherstaff's nose. It was really no wonder his mouth dropped open.

"Do you know who I am?" demanded the Rajah.

How Ben Weatherstaff stared! His red old eyes fixed themselves on what was before him as if he were seeing a ghost. He gazed and gazed and gulped a lump down his throat and did not say a word. "Do you know who I am?" demanded Colin still more imperiously. "Answer!"

Ben Weatherstaff put his gnarled hand up and passed it over his eyes and over his forehead and then he did answer in a queer shaky voice.

"Who tha' art?" he said. "Aye, that I do—wi' tha' mother's eyes starin' at me out o' tha' face. Lord knows how tha' come here. But tha'rt th' poor crazed Accursed boy what craves raw flesh night and day."

Colin's face flushed scarlet and he sat bolt upright.

"I'm not Accursed!" he cried out furiously. "I'm not!"

"He's not!" cried Mary, almost shouting up the wall in her fierce indignation. "He's not got blackened eyes and he doesn't even eat meat anymore at all!"

Ben Weatherstaff passed his hand over his forehead again and gazed as if he could never gaze enough. His hand shook and his mouth shook and his voice shook. He was an ignorant old man and a tactless old man and he could only remember the things he had heard.

"Tha'—tha' hasn't got teeth ground to points from knawing bones?" he said hoarsely.

"No!" shouted Colin.

"Tha'—tha' hasn't chewed off th'a own left toes makin' thee lopsided?" quavered Ben more hoarsely yet. It was too much. The strength which Colin usually threw into his tantrums rushed through him now in a new way. Never yet had he been accused of chewing off his own toes—even in whispers—and the perfectly simple belief in this which was revealed by Ben Weatherstaff's voice was more than Rajah flesh and blood could endure. His anger and insulted pride made him forget everything but this one moment and filled him with a power he had never known before, an almost unnatural strength.

"Come here!" he shouted to Dickon, and he actually began to tear the coverings off his lower limbs and disentangle himself. "Come here! Come here! This minute!"

Dickon was by his side in a second. Mary caught her breath in a short gasp and felt herself turn pale.

"He can do it! He can do it! He can do it! He can!" she gabbled over to herself under her breath as fast as ever she could.

There was a brief fierce scramble, the rugs were tossed on the ground, Dickon held Colin's arm, the thin legs were out, slippers kicked off and the thin bare feet were on the grass. Colin was standing upright—upright—as straight as an arrow and looking strangely tall—his head thrown back and his strange eyes flashing lightning. "Look at me!" he flung up at Ben Weatherstaff. "Just look at me—you! Just look at me!"

"He's as straight as I am!" cried Dickon. "He has all his toes and is as sane as any lad i' Yorkshire!"

What Ben Weatherstaff did Mary thought queer beyond measure. He choked and gulped and suddenly tears ran down his weather-wrinkled cheeks as he struck his old hands together.

"Eh!" he burst forth, "th' lies folk tells! Tha'rt as thin as a lath an' as white as a wraith, but there's not a trace of the Forsaken in thee. Tha'lt make a mon yet. God bless thee!"

Dickon held Colin's arm strongly but the boy had not begun to falter. He stood straighter and straighter and looked Ben Weatherstaff in the face.

"I'm your master," he said, "when my father is away. And you are to obey me. This is my garden. Don't dare to say a word about it! You get down from that ladder and go out to the Long Walk and Miss Mary will meet you and bring you here. I want to talk to you. We did not want you, but now you will have to be in the secret. Be quick!"

Ben Weatherstaff's crabbed old face was still wet with that one queer rush of tears. It seemed as if he could not take his eyes from thin sane Colin standing on his feet with his head thrown back.

"Eh! lad," he almost whispered. "Eh! my lad!" And then remembering himself he suddenly touched his hat gardener fashion and said, "Yes, sir! Yes, sir!" and obediently disappeared as he descended the ladder.

Chapter 22: When the Sun Went Down

When his head was out of sight Colin turned to Mary.

"Go and meet him," he said; and Mary flew across the grass to the door under the ivy.

Dickon was watching him with sharp eyes. There were scarlet spots on his cheeks and his eyes were wide, but he showed no signs of illness or transforming. Had Mary not told him that his blood carried the infection, Dickon would not think it true now.

"I can stand," Colin said, and his head was still held up and he said it quite grandly.

"I told thee tha' could as soon as tha' stopped bein' afraid," answered Dickon. "An' tha's stopped."

"Yes, I've stopped," said Colin.

Then suddenly he remembered something Mary had said.

"Are you making Magic?" he asked sharply. "Not dark Aghori magic but a white sort of Magic?

Dickon's curly mouth spread in a cheerful grin.

"Tha's doin' Magic thysel'," he said. "It's same Magic as made these 'ere work out o' th' earth," and he touched with his thick boot a clump of crocuses in the grass. Colin looked down at them.

"Aye," he said slowly, "there couldna' be bigger Magic than that there—there couldna' be."

He drew himself up straighter than ever.

"I'm going to walk to that tree," he said, pointing to one a few feet away from him. "I'm going to be standing when Weatherstaff comes here. I can rest against the tree if I like. When I want to sit down I will sit down, but not before. Bring a rug from the chair."

He walked to the tree and though Dickon held his arm he was wonderfully steady. When he stood against the tree trunk it was not too plain that he supported himself against it, and he still held himself so straight that he looked tall.

When Ben Weatherstaff came through the door in the wall he saw him standing there and a loud, "Caw Caw" came straight at him in a flash of black feathers.

"Soot!" Dickon called out and the Rook alighted on his shoulder. Dickon looked at the bird and whispered as if having a conversation. Ben did not notice this, he stared at Colin and he heard Mary muttering something under her breath.

"What art tha' sayin'?" he asked rather testily because he did not want his attention distracted from the long thin boy figure who could possibly lunge at any moment and infect him.

But she did not tell him. What she was saying was this:

"You can do it! You can do it! I told you you could! You can do it! You can do it! You can!" She was saying it to Colin because she wanted to make Magic and keep him on his feet looking like that. She could not bear that he should give in before Ben Weatherstaff. He did not give in. She was uplifted by a sudden feeling that he looked quite beautiful in spite of his thinness. He fixed his eyes on Ben Weatherstaff in his funny imperious way.

"Look at me!" he commanded. "Look at me all over! Am I a rotting corpse? Have I chewed up all my toes?" Colin stuck his foot out slightly and wiggled his toes.

Ben Weatherstaff had not quite got over his emotion, but he had recovered a little and answered almost in his usual way.

"Not tha'," he said. "Nowt o' th' sort. What's tha' been doin' with thysel'—hidin' out o' sight an' lettin' folk think tha' was Accursed an' half-witted?"

"Half-witted!" said Colin angrily. "Who thought that?"

"Lots o' fools," said Ben. "Th' world's full o' jackasses brayin' an' they never bray nowt but lies. What did tha' shut thysel' up for?"

"Everyone thought I was going to die and become one the Forsaken," said Colin shortly. "I'm not!"

And he said it with such decision Ben Weatherstaff looked him over, up and down, down and up.

"Tha' die!" he said with dry exultation. "Nowt o' th' sort! Tha's got too much pluck in thee. When I seed thee put tha' legs on th' ground in such a hurry I knowed tha' was all right. Sit thee down on th' rug a bit young Mester an' give me thy orders."

There was a queer mixture of crabbed tenderness and shrewd understanding in his manner. Mary had poured out speech as rapidly as she could as they had come down the Long Walk. The chief thing to be remembered, she had told him, was that Colin was getting well—getting well. The garden was doing it. No one must let him remember about decaying and turning into a cannibal.

The Rajah condescended to seat himself on a rug under the tree.

Soot took off and cawed loudly again circling over them. Dickon had a concerned look on his face.

"What work do you do in the gardens, Weatherstaff?" Colin inquired.

"Anythin' I'm told to do," answered old Ben. "I'm kep' on by favor—because she liked me."

"She?" said Colin.

"Tha' mother," answered Ben Weatherstaff.

"My mother?" said Colin, and he looked about him quietly. "This was her garden, wasn't it?"

"Aye, it was that!" and Ben Weatherstaff looked about him too. "She were main fond of it."

"It is my garden now. I am fond of it. I shall come here every day," announced Colin. "But it is to be a secret. My orders are that no one is to know that we come here. Dickon and my cousin have worked and made it come alive. I shall send for you sometimes to help—but you must come when no one can see you."

Ben Weatherstaff's face twisted itself in a dry old smile.

"I've come here before when no one saw me," he said.

"What!" exclaimed Colin. "When?"

"Th' last time I was here," rubbing his chin and looking round, "was about two year' ago."

"But no one has been in it for ten years!" cried Colin. "There was no door!"

"I'm no one," said old Ben dryly. "An' I didn't come through th' door. I come over th' wall. Th' rheumatics held me back th' last two year'."

"Tha' come an' did a bit o' prunin'!" said Dickon. He had relaxed his face as he spoke but Mary noticed that he held the handle of knife. She gave him a quizzical look but he ignored her kept on. "I couldn't make out how it had been done."

"She was so fond of it—she was!" said Ben Weatherstaff slowly. "An' she was such a pretty young thing. She says to me once, 'Ben,' says she laughin', 'if ever I'm ill or if I go away you must take care of my roses.' When she did go away th' orders was no one was ever to come nigh. But I come," with grumpy obstinacy. "Over th' wall I come—until th' rheumatics stopped me—an' I did a bit o' work once a year. She'd gave her order first."

"It wouldn't have been as wick as it is if tha' hadn't done it," said Dickon. "I did wonder."

"I'm glad you did it, Weatherstaff," said Colin. "You'll know how to keep the secret."

"Aye, I'll know, sir," answered Ben. "An, it'll be easier for a man wi' rheumatics to come in at th' door."

"I am surprised you were able to climb that ladder today," Dickon said slowly. "What with you getting' hurt and all."

Ben Weatherstaff said, "Nah, it was only a little mouse nibble. Offered him my cheese and he went for me hand instead. Should'a know'd better than ta feed a wild 'un."

"A mouse bit you?" Mary asked very concerned. She looked at Dickon and he wordless told her to act calmly. Mary felt that with a single look Dickon could communicate a whole letter. She musn't give it away that the man might be infected and had less than a day to live.

Ben Weatherstaff looked up at Dickon. "How did you know? I mean why did you think that I was hurt?"

"I men' your back aches from the rheumatics. Least you won' have any need for that there big ladder any more.

"No, I guess not," he replied.

On the grass near the tree Mary had dropped her trowel. Colin stretched out his hand and took it up. An odd expression came into his face and he began to scratch at the earth. His thin hand was weak enough but presently as they watched him—Mary with quite breathless interest—he drove the end of the trowel into the soil and turned some over.

"You can do it! You can do it!" said Mary to herself. "I tell you, you can!"

Dickon's round eyes were full of eager curiousness but he said not a word. Ben Weatherstaff looked on with interested face.

Colin persevered. After he had turned a few trowelfuls of soil he spoke exultantly to Dickon in his best Yorkshire.

"Tha' said as tha'd have me walkin' about here same as other folk—an' tha' said tha'd have me diggin'. I thowt tha' was just leein' to please me. This is only th' first day an' I've walked—an' here I am diggin'."

Ben Weatherstaff's mouth fell open again when he heard him, but he ended by chuckling.

"Eh!" he said, "that sounds as if tha'd got wits enow. Tha'rt a Yorkshire lad for sure. An' tha'rt diggin', too. How'd tha' like to plant a bit o' somethin'? I can get thee a rose in a pot."

"Go and get it!" said Colin, digging excitedly. "Quick! Quick!"

It was done quickly enough indeed. Ben Weatherstaff went his way forgetting rheumatics. Dickon took his spade and dug the hole deeper and wider than a new digger with thin white hands could make it. Mary slipped out to follow Ben Weatherstaff. Soot followed but remained silent. Mary waited until Ben was quite a bit ahead then watched him closely. He had only been infected for a few hours or so but despite the fine weather, Mary saw him wipe sweat from his brow. Soot watched him too, ruffling his feathers and clicking his beak at him.

Mary wondered what she should do. By this time tomorrow he would be either dead or one of the Forsaken. Should she tell someone? Ben Weatherstaff was not the kind of person who would except that he had been infected and be rationale about stayin' away from folks. He would deny it to the end. She looked at Soot and he looked at her. For a moment she felt that she possessed the Magic of Dickon for she felt that Soot knew just what she was thinking and he nodded in agreement. They would have to take care of Ben Weatherstaff, and they would have to do it tomorrow and quietly.

Mary returned and Dickon had deepened the hole then Colin went on turning the soft earth over and over. He looked up at the sky, flushed and glowing with the strangely new exercise, slight as it was.

"I want to do it before the sun goes quite—quite down," he said.

Mary thought that perhaps the sun held back a few minutes just on purpose.

THEY WOULD HAVE TO TAKE CARE OF BEN
WEATHERSTAFF, AND THEY WOULD HAVE TO DO
IT TOMORROW AND QUIETLY.

Ben Weatherstaff brought the rose in its pot from the greenhouse. He hobbled over the grass as fast as he could. He mopped the sweat from his forehead with his handkerchief and already appeared slightly pale. He knelt down by the hole and broke the pot from the mould.

"Here, lad," he said, handing the plant to Colin. "Set it in the earth thysel' same as th' king does when he goes to a new place."

The thin white hands shook a little and Colin's flush grew deeper as he set the rose in the mould and held it while old Ben made firm the earth. It was filled in and pressed down and made steady. Mary was leaning forward and thought, 'how sad and fitting that his last gardening should be here planting a rose for his Mistress's son'. Soot continued to circle over Ben Weatherstaff but now that a plan was in place, he didn't need to make any warning calls. Nut and Shell chattered about it from a cherry-tree.

"It's planted!" said Colin at last. "And the sun is only slipping over the edge. Help me up, Dickon. I want to be standing when it goes. That's part of the Magic."

And Dickon helped him, and the Magic—or whatever it was—so gave him strength that when the sun did slip over the edge and end the strange lovely afternoon for them there, the half- accursed boy who never walked actually stood on his two feet—laughing.

Chapter 23: Dark Magic/ White Magic

Dr. Craven had been waiting some time at the house when they returned to it. He had indeed begun to wonder if it might not be wise to send someone out to explore the garden paths. Colin was so precious to Master Craven's research that if anything happened to him the Doctor would be in serious danger of losing his position. He needed Colin to die naturally or turn fully into an Accursed. When Colin was brought back to his room the poor man looked him over seriously.

"You should not have stayed so long," he said. "You must not overexert yourself."

"I am not tired at all," said Colin. "It has made me well. Tomorrow I am going out in the morning as well as in the afternoon."

Dr. Craven did not like the thought of Colin being made well. "I am not sure that I can allow it," he answered. "I am afraid it would not be wise. If anything were to befall you, your father would be very displeased."

"It would not be wise to try to stop me," said Colin quite seriously. "I am going. And do not speak to me of my father again.

It is *you* he will be displeased with if his research subject is ill-used. So you will do as I say or you will never know peace."

Even Mary had found out that one of Colin's chief peculiarities was that he did not know in the least what a rude little demon he was with his way of ordering people about. He had lived in his own sort of personal Hell all his life and as he had been the Lord of it he had made his own pains and horrors and manners and had had no one to compare himself with. Mary had indeed been rather like him herself and since she had been at Misselthwaite had gradually discovered that her pains were self-inflicted never having understood what is was to love or be loved and her own manners had not been of the kind which is usual or popular. Having made this discovery she naturally thought it of enough interest to communicate to Colin. So she sat and looked at him curiously for a few minutes after Dr. Craven had gone. She wanted to make him ask her why she was doing it and of course he did.

"What are you looking at me for?" he said.

"I'm thinking that I am rather sorry for Dr. Craven."

"So am I," said Colin calmly, but not without an air of some satisfaction. "He won't get Misselthwaite at all now I'm not going to become Accursed and have to be beheaded."

"I'm sorry for him because of that, of course," said Mary, "but I was thinking just then that it must have been very horrid to have had to be polite for ten years to a boy who was always threatening him and being rude. I would never have done it."

"Am I rude?" Colin inquired undisturbedly.

"If you had been his own boy and he had been a slapping sort of man," said Mary, "he would have slapped you."

"But he daren't," said Colin. "I'd spit in his eye and then he'd be dead."

"No, he daren't," answered Mistress Mary, thinking the thing out quite without prejudice. "Nobody ever dared to do anything you didn't like—because they had to keep you alive, and your fits gave you fevers, and fever might make you turn. They had to try and keep you calm because who knows what they would've done if your fever and fits did cause you to become one of *them*."

"But," announced Colin stubbornly, "I am not going to be one of *them*. I won't let people think I'm one. I stood on my feet this afternoon. I showed Ben Weatherstaff my toes."

"It is the dreadful blending of always having your own way while being chained and starved that has made you so queer," Mary went on, thinking aloud.

Colin turned his head, frowning. "Am I queer?" he demanded.

"Yes," answered Mary, "very. But you needn't be cross," she added impartially, "because so am I queer—and so is Ben Weatherstaff, though not for long I fear." Mary said this bit quietly to herself. "But I am not as queer as I was before I began to like people and before I found the garden."

"I don't want to be queer," said Colin. "I am not going to be," and he frowned again with determination. "What does it mean, anyway?"

"It means you treat people strangely and think about things strangely and don't care how anyone else feels or thinks. I was like that, but when the robin showed me the key and Dickon taught me to..." Mary did not want to bring up how she learned to kill the

Accursed. "When Dickon taught me to see how to make things grow I became less queer."

Colin was a very proud boy. He lay thinking for a while and then Mary saw his beautiful smile begin and gradually change his whole face.

"I shall stop being queer," he said, "if I go every day to the garden. There is Magic in there—you know, Mary. I am sure there is."

"So am I," said Mary. "Good Magic."

"Even if it isn't good Magic," Colin said. "Even if it is the same black Aghori Magic that made the Forsaken, I don't care because it gives me strength. Something is there—something!"

"It's Magic," said Mary, "but not black. It's as white as snow."

Mary continued to think about White Magic giving her power over the Accursed as she planned how she would dispatch of poor Ben Weatherstaff. Right now he might even be home, feeling ill but not knowing what would happen. Maybe he would not come to the garden tomorrow. But if he did come he would be feverish and shaky and pale and finally his eyes would be washed over with a cloud of black ooze and he would lose his mind and soul to the devil. It would have to be at that instant that Mary would have to kill him. She couldn't let him wander and get caught. Medlock would lock everyone inside if she knew her gardeners were afflicted. They might also blame the infection on Colin and chain him up tighter than ever.

Mary hardly slept for her mind wouldn't stop thinking. She thought about everything from what she would wear and how she would throw her knives, to where she would lead Ben Weatherstaff and make sure Colin didn't know a thing about it.

Mary was dressed before the sun even peeked over the Moor. If she hurried she would be able to watch the sun rise in the Secret Garden. The instant the oak doors to the manor closed behind her, she brought the throwing knives out of her pocket. She still had some time before Ben Weatherstaff would turn, but she wanted to talk with Dickon first and get the story straight for Colin.

Just before she turned the corner in the kitchen gardens heading towards the ivy wall, Ben Weatherstaff appeared suddenly from the path to the back gate. He looked terrible, worse than even Mary had imagined he would. His ashen face was sunk leaving purplish depressions under his eyes and in his cheeks. His skin appeared to hang off him he was so ragged. His clothes were covered in dirt and Mary realized that he was wearing the same clothes as the day before. Maybe he knew he was afflicted and never returned home. Maybe he had wandered the gardens all night. Whatever Ben Weatherstaff had suffered Mary knew it she would have to end it.

Ben Weatherstaff did not look surprised to see her, he didn't seem to have the energy to be surprised. He only put his finger to his lips and then pointed back down the path. He held a shovel in his right hand and the Robin flew down from his silent perch on the wall and landed on the handle. Ben nodded at the Robin who gave him a soft chirp and then flew low down the path. Mary approached slowly and together they followed the Robin. Ben Weatherstaff whispered hoarsely to Mary.

"I done a wicked thin', Miss Mary. An' I hope as you'll forgive an ol' fool one day."

Mary was very surprised by this and didn't know what to think. Ahead, the Robin was twittering nervously, fluttering his wings and fluffing out his red breast. He hopped about excitedly and Mary knew he wanted her to follow.

"Promise me, you'll take care of the roses." Ben Weatherstaff spoke so quietly Mary had to move a little closer than she wanted to in order to hear him. "She was main fond o' them—she was," Ben Weatherstaff said. "She liked them things as was allus pointin' up to th' blue sky, she used to tell. Not as she was one o' them as looked down on th' earth—not her. She just loved it but she said as th' blue sky allus looked so joyful."

He paused as the Robin turned down the path that led to the large Iron Gate, behind which Mary had met Dickon. He held his shovel in front of him.

"I wen' out the gate las' nigh'. I was goin' to go out on the Moor and git as far from here as I could, but I 'ememer that I lef' the gate wide open and curse it all, had to come back. They got in, Miss. They is in this here garden for certain, they is. That Robin knows where they be hidin'. I got to kill um and then you have to lock me out."

"Lock you out?" Mary asked.

"I'm done fer, Miss. I'm Accursed and doomed to wander the Moor forever, but I mus' protect the gardens firs'." Mary was heartbroken by his confession and his noble heart. She never would have thought it possible in the surly stubborn old man. Just then the Robin flew at them in a flurry and just before he would have collided with Mary, he flew up and over the wall towards the Secret Garden.

Ben Weatherstaff and Mistress Mary tightened their grips on their weapons. They moved slowly and softly and then Mary heard the sound of gravel crunching underneath heavy feet. Ben raised his shovel and waited. A man walked onto the path. His hair was gone save for a few stringy strands and tip of his nose was rubbed away. His threadbare clothes were faded from the sun, covered in dried soil and hung off his emaciated body. The man saw them and reached out his arms pitifully and moved towards them as fast and his bony legs would carry him. As he approached, Mary could see that his fingers were worn off at the tips and she thought this must be one who clawed his way out of the grave.

Ben Weatherstaff patiently waited and when the Accursed was within a few feet he swung his shovel smashing the man in the head. It knocked the man over and but did not stop him. Ben was weak and feverish and his strength had left him. He dropped the shovel and collapsed. Mary quickly threw her blades at the Accursed man hitting him square in the temple. She pulled them back tearing his flesh and his brains spilled out onto the garden path.

Without warning, Mary's hair was grabbed from behind. An Accursed had come over a garden wall and snarled excitedly pulling Mary's head back exposing her throat. Mary quickly swung her arm around throwing all her weight toward's the Accursed and plunged her curved knife into the side of its head, just as she had seen Dickon do when she first saw him. Falling to the ground with it, Mary scrambled to untangle the creature's fingers from her hair as yet another of the Forsaken closed in upon her.

"Bloody Rotters!" She cried and wildly threw her blade at the heavy man coming towards her. The blade sliced across his face but he did not even pause. Mary stood having freed herself from the crumbling fingers and did not have time to pull her blade from the man's head.

The large man reached for her but she managed to swiftly spin away from his fat fingered grip and run to the other side of the path. He came pounding towards her and she discovered she stood among a cluster of large garden stones, laid there probably to build a wall. Mary lifted a heavy stone and threw it, though it did not go far. As the massive man stomped closer, she lifted another one not sure what she would do when the corpulent Accursed tripped on the first stone. He fell with a great thud at her feet and Mary wasted no time. She raised the stone and plunged it down onto his head cracking the skull. She hit him several more times to be sure she had disabled the brain than finally dropped the stone as dark ooze seeped down onto the path.

The sun had now risen over the horizon casting an orange glow around the garden walls. Mary did not move and only listened for more footsteps in the gravel. Ben Weatherstaff gave several raspy coughs and Mary ran to him.

His choked breaths made his speech broken, but he said, "The Devil's pullin' me under. I goes now ta Hell o' me own makin'. And th' mun' take care of th' roses. She was main fond o' them—she was..."

Mary watched as Ben Weatherstaff coughed violently until he suddenly stopped. He stood, straighter than Mary had ever seen him stand. He wide eyes stared blankly forward and for second Mary thought he might still be himself. Then he doubled over spewing the black ooze and when he looked up his eyes were black as pitch. In the whole night of imagining how to kill Ben Weatherstaff, Mary had not imagined standing alone without her knives ready. One was laying somewhere on the garden path and the other was imbedded in the head of the Accursed woman.

Suddenly she was the same little girl playing in her garden staring into the face of an Aghori cursed cannibal, defenseless and naïve. Then she remembered Dickon and Martha and their Mother and all twelve children living in one little house and surviving by never giving up and always fighting.

Soot flew overhead and gave a great Caw Caw! Ben Weatherstaff took two raspy breaths and than licked his dry wrinkly old lips. He lunged for Mary but she spun out of the way and grabbed his shovel from the ground. She held it high over her head and as he turned to come at her again she brought the sharp edge of Ben Weatherstaff's shovel down upon his head slicing him through the eyes.

She dropped the shovel handle as he collapsed in a heap and Soot came to land upon her shoulder clicking in approval. Dickon came running around the path and stopped and stared as if his eyes were playing tricks. There stood Mary with Soot on her shoulder and four dead Accursed at her feet.

He explained to Mary that it was the Robin that told him there was danger. "After he was done flutterin' n' fussin' 'bout I was able to understand that you was out in the garden somewhere in trouble. Soot foun' you first and I heard his call. But it seems as though you ain't needin' my help."

Mary laughed as she retrieved her throwing blades. "I could use your help clearin' this path. If anyone finds this mess, Medlock'll keep us out o' the garden, for sure!

After he dragged the corpses outside the iron gate and locked it up tight Dickon said to Mary, "You really are somethin' unexpected, Miss Bloody Mary. Eh! Like a true Purifier tha' art. Maybe you are right and there is White Magic here. You brought it with you.

They always called it Magic and indeed it seemed like it in the months that followed—the wonderful months—the radiant months—the amazing ones. Oh! the things which happened in that garden! If you have never had a garden you cannot understand, and if you have had a garden you will know that it would take a whole book to describe all that came to pass there. At first it seemed that green things would never cease pushing their way through the earth, in the grass, in the beds, even in the crevices of the walls. Then the green things began to show buds and the buds began to unfurl and show color, every shade of blue, every shade of purple, every tint and hue of crimson. In its happy days flowers had been tucked away into every inch and hole and corner. Iris and white lilies rose out of the grass in sheaves, and the green alcoves filled themselves with amazing armies of the blue and white flower lances of tall delphiniums or columbines or campanulas.

The seeds Dickon and Mary had planted grew as if fairies had tended them. Mary's own special garden under the large tree was growing beautifully. She cleared the area around the Death Cap mushrooms that had grown in abundance in one area and planted the Hellebore seeds that Dickon had bought in the market. One morning he held something behind his back and surprised Mary with two exquisite flowering Asphodel plants that he dug up from the cemetery behind the now abandoned church in the village. The white flowers were bursting off the thick green stems with a tower of buds waiting to blink open into the sunlight. Mary had planted them among the Death Caps and Hellebore and now they were a riot of white petals among the deep purples and pale yellows of the Hellebore flowers. They danced in the breeze by the score, gaily defying flowers which had lived in the garden for years and which it might be confessed seemed rather to wonder how such new and noxious neighbors had got there. The jewels of the garden-under-the-tree were the little green stars cradling perfectly round shiny black berries. Atropa Belladonna, deadly nightshade. It had taken Dickon two weeks and a full month's savings of Mary's shillings to acquire the seeds from an herbalist, but they grew quickly and how they glistened in early morning dew, dripping water down onto the Death Caps below them. Dickon said it was the loveliest and deadliest place he had ever seen.

"Your garden is like yerself, Miss Bloody Mary," Dickon said one morning, "lovely and deadly."

And the roses—the roses! Rising out of the grass, tangled round the sun-dial, wreathing the tree trunks and hanging from their branches, climbing up the walls and spreading over them with long garlands falling in cascades—they came alive day by day, hour by hour. Fair fresh leaves, and buds—and buds—tiny at first but swelling and working Magic until they burst and uncurled into cups of scent delicately spilling themselves over their brims and filling the garden air.

Colin saw it all, watching each change as it took place. Every morning he was brought out and every hour of each day when it didn't rain he spent in the garden. Even gray days pleased him. He would lie on the grass "watching things growing," he said. If you watched long enough, he declared, you could see buds unsheath themselves. Also you could make the acquaintance of strange busy insect things running about on various unknown but evidently serious errands, sometimes carrying tiny scraps of straw or feather or food, or climbing blades of grass as if they were trees from whose tops one could look out to explore the country. A mole throwing up its mound at the end of its burrow and making its way out at last with the long-nailed paws which looked so like elfish hands, had absorbed him one whole morning. Ants' ways, beetles' ways, bees' ways, frogs' ways, birds' ways, plants' ways, gave him a new world to explore and when Dickon revealed them all and added foxes' ways, otters' ways, ferrets' ways, squirrels' ways, and trout' and water-rats' and badgers' ways, there was no end to the things to talk about and think over.

And this was not the half of the Magic. The fact that he had really once stood on his feet had set Colin thinking tremendously and when Mary told him of the spell she had worked he was excited and approved of it greatly. He talked of it constantly.

"Of course there must be lots of Magic in the world," he said wisely one day, "but people don't know what it is like or how to make it. Perhaps the beginning is just to say things are going to happen until you make them happen. I am going to try an experiment."

The next morning when they went to the secret garden the Rajah stood on his feet under a tree looking very grand but also very beautifully smiling.

"Good morning, Dickon," he said. "I want you and Miss Mary to stand together and listen to me because I am going to tell you something very important."

Dickon and Mary listened intently.

"I am going to try a scientific experiment," explained the Rajah. "When I grow up I am going to make great scientific discoveries and I am going to begin now with this experiment. It will involve Magic. All my life I have been a subject. An experiment to find the restoration of the Accursed- though I am only half so. I do not wish to be an experiment, I never have. I sometimes wished that everyone would become afflicted so that no one would want to conduct examinations on my blood again, but I have determined that the discovery of a restorative draught could never come from my blood or my father should have discovered it in the last ten years. No, the affliction began with magic and shall only end with magic."

It was the first time Mary had heard of great scientific discoveries, but even at this stage she had begun to realize that, queer as he was, Colin had read about a great many singular things and was somehow a very convincing sort of boy. When he held up his head and fixed his strange eyes on you it seemed as if you believed him almost in spite of yourself though he was only ten years old—going on eleven. At this moment he was especially convincing because he suddenly felt the fascination of actually making a sort of speech like a grown-up person.

"The great scientific discoveries I am going to make," he went on, "will be about Magic. Magic is a great thing and scarcely any one knows anything about it except a few people in old books—

and Mary a little, because she was born in India where there are
Aghori. I believe Dickon knows some Magic, but perhaps he
doesn't know he knows it. He charms animals and people. I would
never have let him come to see me if he had not been an animal
charmer—which is a boy charmer, too, because a boy is an animal.
I am sure there is Magic in everything, only we have not sense
enough to get hold of it and make it do things for us—like
electricity and horses and steam."

This sounded so imposing that Mary and Dickon both had to
sit down.

"When Mary found this garden it looked quite dead," the
orator proceeded. "Then something began pushing things up out
of the soil and making things out of nothing. One day things
weren't there and another they were. I had never watched things
before and it made me feel very curious. Scientific people are
always curious and I am going to be scientific. I keep saying to
myself, 'What is it? What is it?' It's something. It can't be nothing!
I don't know its name so I call it Magic. It makes things come alive
that were dead. The Magic here has brought the dead garden back
to life. The dark Aghori magic brought dead people back to life.
Magic makes things rise up that couldn't before. I have never seen
the sun rise but you two have and from what you tell me I am sure
that is Magic too. Something pushes it up and draws it. Magic is
always pushing and drawing and making things out of nothing.
Everything is made out of Magic, leaves and trees, flowers and
birds, badgers and foxes and squirrels and people. So it must be all
around us. In this garden—in all the places. The Magic in India
was abused and used for demonic purposes, so the Magic fought

back and cursed them and all of us for their sins. The Magic in this garden has made me stand up and know I am going to live to be a man. I believe it is the same Magic. I am going to make the scientific experiment of trying to get some and put it in myself. I will make it push and draw me and make me strong and then I will make it destroy all the Accursed. I don't know how to do it but I think that if you keep thinking about it and calling it perhaps it will come. When I was going to try to stand that first time Mary kept saying to herself as fast as she could, 'You can do it! You can do it!' and I did. I had to try myself at the same time, of course, but her Magic helped me—and so did Dickon's. Every morning and evening and as often in the daytime as I can remember I am going to say, 'Magic is in me! Magic is making me strong! I am going to be the world's salvation for I will destroy them all!' And you must all do it, too. That is my experiment. Will you help?"

Dickon and Mary applauded and nodded vigorously.

"If you keep doing it every day as regularly as Purifier soldiers go through horde attack drills we shall see what will happen and find out if the experiment succeeds. You learn things by saying them over and over and thinking about them until they stay in your mind forever and I think it will be the same with Magic. If you keep calling it to come to you and help you it will get to be part of you and it will stay and do things."

"I once heard an officer in India tell my mother that there were fakirs who said words over and over thousands of times," said Mary. "They could control magic and walk on fire and sleep on beds of nails. They could charm snakes to dance for them."

Dickon had remained silent listening to the lecture, his round eyes shining with curious delight. Nut and Shell were on his shoulders and he held a long-eared white rabbit in his arm and stroked and stroked it softly while it laid its ears along its back and enjoyed itself.

"Do you think the experiment will work?" Colin asked him, wondering what he was thinking. He so often wondered what Dickon was thinking when he saw him looking at him or at one of his "creatures" with his happy wide smile.

He smiled now and his smile was wider than usual.

"Aye," he answered, "that I do. But I don' think it is the same Magic o' the fakirs o' 'goris. Tha' is all wickedness and conceit. None o' that here. The Magic here'll work same as th' seeds do when th' sun shines on 'em. It'll work for sure. Shall us begin it now?"

Colin was delighted and so was Mary. He understood what Dickon was saying but he truly felt that all Magic was the same and that if he could harness its power for good he would be able to stop the Accursed. He, Colin, would finish the work his Father began.

Fired by recollections of fakirs and devotees in illustrations Colin suggested that they should all sit cross-legged under the tree which made a canopy.

"It will be like sitting in a sort of temple," said Colin. "I'm rather tired and I want to sit down."

"Eh!" said Dickon, "tha' mustn't begin by sayin' tha'rt tired. Tha' might spoil th' Magic."

Colin turned and looked at him—into his innocent round eyes.

"That's true," he said slowly. "I must only think of the Magic." It all seemed most majestic and mysterious when they sat down in their circle. Mistress Mary felt solemnly enraptured. Dickon held his rabbit in his arm, and perhaps he made some charmer's signal no one heard, for when he sat down, cross-legged like the rest, the crow, the fox, the squirrels and the lamb slowly drew near and made part of the circle, settling each into a place of rest as if of their own desire.

"The 'creatures' have come," said Colin gravely. "They want to help us."

Colin really looked quite beautiful, Mary thought. He held his head high as if he felt like a sort of priest and his strange eyes had a wonderful look in them. The light shone on him through the tree canopy.

"I will chant," he said. And he began, looking like a strange boy spirit. "The sun is shining. That is the Magic. The flowers are growing—the roots are stirring. That is the Magic. Being alive is the Magic—being strong is the Magic. The Magic is in me—the Magic is in me. The Magic that will end the Accursed dominion. It's in every one of us. Magic! Magic! Come and help!"

He said it a great many times—not a thousand times but quite a goodly number. Mary listened entranced. She felt as if it were at once queer and beautiful and she wanted him to go on and on. She began to feel soothed into a sort of dream which was quite agreeable. The humming of the bees in the blossoms mingled with the chanting voice and drowsily melted into a doze. Dickon sat cross-legged with his rabbit asleep on his arm and a hand resting on the lamb's back. Soot had pushed away a squirrel and huddled close to him on his shoulder, the gray film dropped over his eyes. Mary thought she could hear the slow rhythmic beating of her own heart, but realized it was coming from outside of herself, somewhere close in the garden. Somewhere very close... At last Colin stopped. Mary was brought out of her state and she ceased to hear the humming bees or the rhythmic beating.

"Now I am going to walk round the garden," he announced.

Everyone, including the animals, stood up and the procession was formed. It really did look like a procession. Colin was at its head with Dickon on one side and Mary on the other. The "creatures" trailed after them, the lamb and the fox cub keeping close to Dickon, the white rabbit hopping along or stopping to nibble and Soot following with the solemnity of a person who felt himself in charge.

It was a procession which moved slowly but with dignity. Every few yards it stopped to rest. Colin leaned on Dickon's arm, but now and then Colin took his hand from its support and walked a few steps alone. His head was held up all the time and he looked very grand.

"The Magic is in me!" he kept saying. "The Magic is making me strong! I can feel it! I can feel it!"

It seemed very certain that something was upholding and uplifting him. He sat on the seats in the alcoves and leaned on Dickon, but he would not give up until he had gone all round the garden. When he returned to the canopy tree his cheeks were flushed and he looked triumphant.

"I did it! The Magic worked!" he cried. "That is my first scientific discovery."

"What will Dr. Craven say?" broke out Mary.

"He won't say anything," Colin answered, "because he will not be told. This is to be the biggest secret of all. No one is to know anything about it until I have grown so strong that I can walk and run like any other boy. I shall come here every day in my chair and I shall be taken back in it. I won't have people whispering and asking questions and I won't let my father hear about it until the experiment has quite succeeded. Then sometime when he comes back to Misselthwaite I shall just walk into his study and say 'Here I am; I am like any other boy. I am quite well and I shall live to be a man. I have found the cure to the Accursed affliction. It has been done by a scientific experiment.'"

"He will think he is in a dream," cried Mary. "He won't believe his eyes."

Colin flushed triumphantly. He had made himself believe that he was going to get well, which was really more than half the battle, if he had been aware of it. And the thought which stimulated him more than any other was this imagining what his father would look like when he saw that he had a son who was as alive and strong as other fathers' sons. One of his darkest miseries in the unhealthy morbid past days had been his hatred of being a sickly weak half-dead boy whose father was going to one day murder him.

"He'll be obliged to believe them," he said. "One of the things I am going to do, after the Magic works to make me strong, strong as Dickon and before I begin to make scientific discoveries, is to kill as many Accursed as I can."

Chapter 24: Let Them Rot

The secret garden was not the only one Dickon worked in. Round the cottage on the moor there was a high wall of rough stones. The wall surrounded the thatched cottage and had only one heavy door with an iron lock that Dickon himself had fashioned. Early in the morning and late in the fading twilight and on all the days Colin and Mary did not see him, Dickon worked there adding more stones that he had collected on his walk and planting or tending potatoes and cabbages, turnips and carrots and herbs for his mother. In the company of his "creatures" he did wonders there and was never tired of doing them, it seemed. While he dug or weeded he whistled or sang bits of Yorkshire moor songs or talked to Soot or Captain or the brothers and sisters he had taught to help him.

"We'd never 'ave survived this long or get on as comfortable as we do," Mrs. Sowerby said, "if it wasn't for Dickon's wall and garden. The Forsaken 'ave tried but never been able t' break through. An' anything'll grow for him. His 'taters and cabbages is twice th' size of any one else's an' they've got a flavor with 'em as nobody's has."

When she found a moment to spare she liked to go out and talk to him. After supper there was still a long clear twilight where one could see far across the moor while keeping watch and that was her quiet time. She could sit upon the sentry stones Dickon had piled to see over the wall and look on and hear stories of the day. She loved this time. There were not only vegetables in this garden. Dickon had instructed the other children to gather sticks and stones on the moor and whittle the sticks to sharp points and fashion sling shots for the stones. This stock pile served them well allowing the family to destroy the Forsaken from the comfort of ones seat without having to venture outside the walls. The high wall was one of the prettiest things in Yorkshire because Dickon had tucked moorland foxglove and ferns and rock-cress and hedgerow flowers into every crevice until only here and there glimpses of the stones were to be seen and no light would show through the other side.

"All a chap's got to do to keep th' Forsaken away," he would say, "is to cover every crevice that would show light an' don't make too much noise during twilight when the sound travels o'er the moor as if a great wave were rollin' through the sea. If'n a Tormented does come near we mustn' waver about who they used t' be. Nor should we fault them for who they are now. They want to eat same as we do. But we mus' take them out of their miserable tortured condition. If I were to let one live I should feel as if I'd been a bad lad and somehow treated them heartless."

It was in these twilight hours that Mrs. Sowerby heard of all that happened at Misselthwaite Manor. At first she was only told that "Mester Colin" had taken a fancy to going out into the grounds with Miss Mary and that it was doing him good. But it was not long before it was agreed between the two children that Dickon's mother might "come into the secret." Somehow it was not doubted that she was "safe for sure."

So one beautiful still evening Dickon told the whole story, with all the thrilling details of the buried key and the robin and the gray haze which had seemed like deadness and the secret Mistress Mary had planned never to reveal. The saving of Miss Mary by Dickon and how it had been told to him, the doubted half-accursed Mester Colin and the final drama of his introduction to the hidden domain, combined with the incident of Ben Weatherstaff becoming afflicted and fighting the Forsaken in his last moments and Miss Mary taking down all the Accursed, delivering Ben Weatherstaff from torment. Ending with Mester Colin's sudden indignant strength and his plans to rid the world of the Accursed affliction through scientific studies of magic made Mrs. Sowerby's nice-looking face quite change color several times.

"My word!" she said. "It was a good thing that little lass came to th' Manor. It's been th' makin' o' her an' th' savin, o' him. Standin' on his feet! An' us all thinkin' he was a poor half-witted lad ready to turn into a Forsaken at any time."

Just then Mrs. Sowerby noticed some forms appearing out on the Moor. She narrowed her eyes and had Dickon come look. He gathered up some stones and prepared the slingshots. Mrs. Sowerby grinned as he handed her one. Waiting for the Accursed to draw closer she asked a great many questions and her blue eyes were full of deep thinking.

"What do they make of it at th' Manor—him being so well an' not complainin' an' never eatin' meat when all he got before was raw?" she inquired. "They don't know what to make of it," answered Dickon. "Every day as comes round his face looks different. It's fillin' out and doesn't look so sharp an' th' waxy color is goin'. But he has to do his bit o' complainin'," with a highly entertained grin.

"What for, i' Mercy's name?" asked Mrs. Sowerby.

Dickon chuckled. "He does it to keep them from guessin' what's happened. If the doctor knew he'd found out he could stand on his feet he'd likely chain 'im up double so he wouldn' be able to attack in the middle of the night and he'd likely write and tell Mester Craven. Mester Colin's savin' th' secret to tell himself. He's goin' to practice his Magic on his legs every day till his father comes back an' then he's goin' to march into his room an' show him he's as unafflicted as other lads. He doesn' even know for sure if'n he can infect other people. But him an' Miss Mary thinks it's th' best plan to do a bit o' groanin' an' snarlin' now an' then to throw folk off th' scent."

Mrs. Sowerby was laughing a low comfortable laugh long before he had finished his last sentence. Dickon sat next to his mother on the stone seat and closed one eye pulling back the slingshot and taking aim. Made by his own hand, the wooden fork held steady in his grip. The rubber, taken from a tube in an abandoned home, stretched to the point of rupture while the small stone waited in the leather sheath. Dickon released his hold on the leather and his stone rocketed through the graying night air. It hit its mark directly between the eyes of the Accursed. It fell and he loaded another stone.

The creature began to rise again but Mrs. Sowerby hit it in the temple with perfect accuracy.

"Eh!" she continued, "that pair's enjoyin' their-selves I'll warrant. They'll get a good bit o' actin' out of it an' there's nothin' children likes as much as play actin'. Let's hear what they do, Dickon lad." He shot one more stone at the still Accursed just to be sure then turned to tell her. His eyes were twinkling with fun.

"Mester Colin is carried down to his chair every time he goes out," he explained. "An' he flies out at John, th' footman, biting at him through the iron mask. Once he is strapped down in the chair he makes himself as helpless lookin' as he can an' never lifts his head until we're out o' sight o' th' house. An' he grunts an' frets a good bit when he's bein' locked into his chair. Him an' Miss Mary's both got to enjoyin' it an' when he groans an' complains she'll say, 'Poor Colin! Does it hurt you so much to be shackled and chained? Are you so tormented as that, poor Colin?'—but th' trouble is that sometimes they can scarce keep from burstin' out laughin'. When we get safe into the garden they laugh till they've no breath left to laugh with. An' they have to stuff their faces into Mester Colin's cushions to keep the gardeners from hearin', if any of 'em's about."

Several more Accursed drew within striking distance. Dickon and Mrs. Sowerby let loose with stones crushing the skulls of the lot of them. A darkness out of the Moor suggested more were approaching.

"Th' more they laugh th' better for 'em!" said Mrs. Sowerby, still laughing herself. "Good healthy child laughin's better than blood drainings or leeches any day o' th' year. That pair'll plump up for sure."

"They are plumpin' up," said Dickon. "They're that hungry they don't know how to get enough to eat without makin' talk. Mester Colin threw fits until they stopped bringing him raw meat. Said he didn't want animals and jokin'ly said he only ever wanted people flesh. Well that got the cooks in a dither I'm sure so they started sendin' what he asked for, same as what Mary ate. He says if he keeps sendin' for more food they won't believe he's an invalid at all. Even though he turns his meat away he still eats everything else. Miss Mary says she'll let him eat her share, but he says that if she goes hungry she'll get thin an' they mun both get fat at once."

Mrs. Sowerby laughed so heartily at the revelation of this difficulty that she quite rocked backward and forward in her blue cloak, and Dickon had to remind her to be quiet in the twilight hours. The dark mass in the distance became individual shapes and Dickon jumped down from the seat to gather up more stones and the sharpened sticks as well.

"I'll tell thee what, lad," Mrs. Sowerby said softly as she placed the stones by her side, "I've thought of a way to help 'em. When tha' goes to 'em in th' mornin's tha' shall take a pail o' good new milk an' I'll bake 'em a crusty cottage loaf or some buns wi' currants in 'em, same as you children like. Nothin's so good as fresh milk an' bread. Then they could take off th' edge o' their hunger while they were in their garden an' th, fine food they get indoors 'ud polish off th' corners."

At least a dozen of the Accursed moved quickly over the Moor towards the echoes of Mrs. Sowerby's laughter. Together, she and Dickon began firing stones.

"Eh! mother!" said Dickon admiringly, "what a wonder tha' art! Tha' always sees a way out o' things. They was quite in a pother yesterday. They didn't see how they was to manage without orderin' up more food—they felt that empty inside."

Half the Accursed were dead before Dickon was able to see their faces. He loaded his slingshot now with the sharpened sticks, resting the pointed end in the Y frame. As the Accursed advanced, Dickon let loose the rudimentary spear and it pierced the skull of the closest. It stood for a moment staring blankly ahead then fell flat on his face.

"Excellent shot. My turn now." Mrs. Sowerby held two sticks in her sling shot and aimed at a pair of seemingly new Accursed. Their clothes were not as torn as the others and their skin had yet to become rotten and squalid. She released the short arrows together and they split apart, each racing with holy purpose. They struck the Accursed, running them through the skull. Both Accursed jolted backwards to the ground and never moved again. She turn to Dickon and continued.

"They're two young 'uns growin' fast, an' health's comin' back to both of 'em. Children like that feels like young wolves an' food's flesh an' blood to 'em."

Mrs. Sowerby and Dickon defeated the horde before any reached within twenty meters of the cottage.

"That was uncommon." Mrs. Sowerby said as Dickon moved the sticks and stones back into place in the garden. "A group that size this far out should've been seen by the villagers before reachin' us. Better keep a watch out tonight, and several nights. We'll clean up the mess in the mornin'. Tell your brothers and sisters their duties."

Dickon nodded and turned to go but stopped as his Mother picked up again.

"And warn Miss Mary and Mester Colin. If'n he does fancy fightin' he may want a weapon that doesn't take much strength." Then she smiled Dickon's own curving smile. "Eh! but they're enjoyin' theirselves for sure," she said.

She was quite right, the comfortable wonderful mother creature—and she had never been more so than when she said their "play actin'" would be their joy. Colin and Mary found it one of their most thrilling sources of entertainment. The idea of protecting themselves from suspicion had been unconsciously suggested to them first by the puzzled nurse and then by Dr. Craven himself.

"Your appetite is improving very much, Master Colin," the nurse had said one day. "You used to eat nothing, and so many things disagreed with you."

"Nothing disagrees with me now except nasty meat," replied Colin, and then seeing the nurse looking at him curiously he suddenly remembered that perhaps he ought not to appear too well just yet. "At least things don't so often disagree with me. It's the fresh air."

"Perhaps it is," said the nurse, still looking at him with a mystified expression. "But I must talk to Dr. Craven about it."

"How she stared at you!" said Mary when she went away. "As if she thought there must be something to find out."

"I won't have her finding out things," said Colin. "No one must begin to find out yet." When Uncle Dr. Craven came that morning he seemed puzzled also. He asked a number of questions, to Colin's great annoyance.

"You stay out in the garden a great deal," he suggested. "Where do you go?"

Colin put on his favorite air of dignified indifference to opinion and drooled a bit knowing the doctor feared being spat at.

"I will not let anyone know where I go," he answered. "I go to a place I like. Everyone has orders to keep out of the way. I won't be watched and stared at. Anyone who comes near me is in danger. You know that!"

"You seem to be out all day but I do not think it has done you harm—I do not think so. The nurse says that you eat much more than you have ever done before."

"Perhaps," said Colin, prompted by a sudden inspiration, "perhaps it is an unnatural appetite."

"I do not think so, as your food seems to agree with you," said Dr. Craven. "You are gaining flesh rapidly and your color is better."

"Perhaps—perhaps I am bloated and feverish," said Colin, assuming a discouraging air of gloom. "People who are infected and going to turn are often—different."

Dr. Craven shook his head. He was holding Colin's wrist and he pushed up his sleeve and felt his arm.

"You are not feverish," he said thoughtfully, "and such flesh as you have gained is healthy. If you can keep this up, my boy, we need not talk of dying and reanimation. Your father will be happy to hear of this remarkable improvement."

"I won't have him told!" Colin broke forth fiercely. "It will only disappoint him if I get worse again—and I may get worse this very night. I might have a raging fever. I feel as if I might be beginning to have one now. What if being weak is the only thing that has kept me from turning all these years? What if becoming strong means that my blood will blacken and my mind and soul will no longer be my own? I won't have letters written to my father—I won't—I won't! You are making me angry and you know that is bad for me. I feel hot already. I hate being written about and being talked over as much as I hate being stared at!"

"Hush-h! my boy," Dr. Craven soothed him from a safe distance. "Nothing shall be written without your permission. You are too sensitive about things. You must not undo the good which has been done."

He said no more about writing to Mr. Craven and when he saw the nurse he privately warned her that such a possibility must not be mentioned to the patient. He too was reluctant to write as it would look poorly on him if Colin were to relapse. He also secretly began to think of a plan if Colin really was getting better. He convinced Colin to give him a blood sample so it might be tested for any changes in the infection. Colin was curious himself, though he did not say so.

"The boy is extraordinarily better," he said to nurse. "His advance seems almost abnormal. But of course he is doing now of his own free will what we could not make him do before. Still, he excites himself very easily and nothing must be said to irritate him." Mary and Colin were much alarmed and talked together anxiously. From this time dated their plan of "play actin'."

"I may be obliged to have a tantrum," said Colin regretfully. "I don't want to have one and I'm not miserable enough now to work myself into a big one. Perhaps I couldn't have one at all. That lump doesn't come in my throat now and I keep thinking of nice things instead of horrible ones. But if they talk about writing to my father I shall have to do something."

He made up his mind to eat less, but unfortunately it was not possible to carry out this brilliant idea when he wakened each morning with an amazing appetite and the table near his sofa was set with a breakfast of home-made bread and fresh butter, snow-white eggs, raspberry jam and clotted cream. Mary always breakfasted with him and when they found themselves at the table—particularly if there were hot cheese-covered fluffy eggs sending forth tempting odors from under a hot silver cover—they would look into each other's eyes in desperation.

"I think we shall have to eat it all this morning, Mary," Colin always ended by saying. "We can send away some of the lunch and a great deal of the dinner."

But they never found they could send away anything and the highly polished condition of the empty plates returned to the pantry awakened much comment.

"I do wish," Colin would say also, "I do wish the slices of tomato were thicker, and one muffin each is not enough for any one."

"It's enough for a person who craves raw flesh and is going to die," answered Mary when first she heard this, "but it's not enough for a person who is going to live. I sometimes feel as if I could eat three when those nice fresh heather and gorse smells from the moor come pouring in at the open window."

The morning that Dickon—after they had been enjoying themselves in the garden for about two hours—went behind a big rosebush and brought forth two tin pails and revealed that one was full of rich new milk with cream on the top of it, and that the other held cottage-made currant buns folded in a clean blue and white napkin, buns so carefully tucked in that they were still hot, there was a riot of surprised joyfulness. What a wonderful thing for Mrs. Sowerby to think of! What a kind, clever woman she must be! How good the buns were! And what delicious fresh milk!

"Magic is in her just as it is in Dickon," said Colin. "It makes her think of ways to do things—nice things. She is a Magic person. Tell her we are grateful, Dickon—extremely grateful." He was given to using rather grown-up phrases at times. He enjoyed them. He liked this so much that he improved upon it.

"Tell her she has been most bounteous and our gratitude is extreme."

And then forgetting his grandeur he fell to and stuffed himself with buns and drank milk out of the pail in copious draughts in the manner of any hungry little boy who had been taking unusual exercise and breathing in moorland air and whose breakfast was more than two hours behind him.

This was the beginning of many agreeable incidents of the same kind. They actually awoke to the fact that as Mrs. Sowerby had fourteen people to provide food for she might not have enough to satisfy two extra appetites every day. So they asked her to let them send some of their shillings to buy things.

There was a bit of difficulty at first as Dickon returned the next day, late in the morning, with a surprising story. He had walked early to go to the village closest to the cottage and found it abandoned with only few dead in the Highstreet. Then he told of the dozen Forsaken that had come near the cottage two days prior and wondered if an even larger group were out on the Moor somewhere. But Dickon made it to the next town where he bought a small cart as well as provisions and a surprise for Colin.

Dickon made the stimulating discovery that in the wood in the park outside the garden where he had first rescued Mary there was a deep little hollow where you could build a sort of tiny oven with stones and roast potatoes and eggs in it. Roasted eggs were a previously unknown luxury and very hot potatoes with salt and fresh butter in them were fit for a woodland king—besides being deliciously satisfying. You could buy both potatoes and eggs and eat as many as you liked without feeling as if you were taking food out of the mouths of fourteen people.

After a satisfying breakfast, Dickon presented Colin with his surprise. "It's a real professional made slingshot, that is. Oak wood, tanned leather and the best elastic, vulcanized rubber."

Colin marveled at this new device as Dickon placed a small seed in the leather saddle, held tight to the Y-shaped wooden handle, pulled back hard on the leather stretching the rubber and letting go turning the small seed into a deadly projectile. On his first try Colin was only able to stretch the rubber far enough to send the seed a few feet. But he was determined to be as strong as

Dickon and learn to kill the Accursed. He was determined that Magic was going to help him.

Every beautiful morning the scientific experiment on Magic was worked by the mystic circle under the plum-tree which provided a canopy of thickening green leaves after its brief blossom-time was ended. After the ceremony Colin always took his walking exercise and practiced pulling back the elastic on the slingshot. Throughout the day he exercised his newly found power at intervals. Each day he grew stronger and could walk more steadily and cover more ground. Each day the slingshot became easier to hold steady and he could pull the leather pocket back farther. And each day his belief in the Magic grew stronger—as well it might. He tried one experiment after another as he felt himself gaining strength and it was Dickon who showed him the best things of all.

"Yesterday," he said one morning after an absence, "I went to Thwaite for mother an' near th' Blue Cow Inn I seed Bob Haworth. He's the strongest chap on th' moor. He's the champion Purifier an' he can out run the Accursed faster than any other chap an' throw th' hammer farther. He's gone all th' way to Scotland fightin' the Rotters some years. He's knowed me ever since I was a little 'un an' he's a friendly sort an' I axed him some questions. Th' gentry calls him the Beefy Purifier and I thought o' thee, Mester Colin, and I says, 'How did tha' make tha' muscles stick out that way, Bob? How is it tha' you can rip a Rotters head clear off wit yer bare hands? What is yer secret fer killin' all them Accursed? Did tha' do anythin' extra to make thysel' so strong?' An' he says 'Well, yes, lad, I did. A Purifier that came to Thwaite once showed me how to exercise my arms an' legs an' every muscle in my body while at the same time teaching 'em to move in ways that defend and attack.' An' I says, 'Could a delicate chap make himself stronger with 'em, Bob?' an' he laughed an' says, 'Art tha' th' delicate chap?' an' I says, 'No, but I knows a young gentleman that's gettin' well of a long illness an' I wish I knowed some o' them tricks to tell him about.' I didn't say no names an' he didn't ask none. He's friendly same as I said an' he stood up an' showed me good-natured like, an' I imitated what he did till I knowed it by heart."

Colin had been listening excitedly.

"Can you show me?" he cried. "Will you?"

"Aye, to be sure," Dickon answered, getting up. "But he says tha' mun do 'em gentle at first an' be careful not to tire thysel'. Rest in between times an' take deep breaths an' don't overdo."

"I'll be careful," said Colin. "Show me! Show me! Dickon, you are the most Magic boy in the world!"

Dickon stood up on the grass and slowly went through a carefully practical but simple series of exercises that moved in the arms and legs in an ancient oriental fighting style. Colin watched them with widening eyes. He could do a few while he was sitting down. Presently he did a few gently while he stood upon his already steadied feet. Mary began to do them also. Soot, who was watching the performance, became much disturbed and left his branch and hopped about restlessly because he could not do them too.

From that time the exercises were part of the day's duties as much as the Magic was. It became possible for both Colin and

Mary to do more of them each time they tried, and Dickon taught them how to be more deadly using their weapons. They spent all day gardening, chanting, exercising, and knocking chunks of moss and lichen from an old marble statue of a cherub with the throwing blades and slingshot. Such appetites were the results that but for the basket Dickon put down behind the bush each morning when he arrived they would have been lost. But the little oven in the hollow and Mrs. Sowerby's bounties were so satisfying that Mrs. Medlock and the nurse and Dr. Craven became mystified again. You can trifle with your breakfast and seem to disdain your dinner if you are full to the brim with roasted eggs and potatoes and richly frothed new milk and oatcakes and buns and heather honey and clotted cream.

"They are eating next to nothing," said the nurse. "They'll die of starvation if they can't be persuaded to take some nourishment. And yet see how they look."

"Look!" exclaimed Mrs. Medlock indignantly. "Eh! I'm moithered to death with them. They're a pair of young Satans. Bursting their jackets one day and the next turning up their noses at the best meals Cook can tempt them with. Not a mouthful of that lovely Vegetable Stew did they set a fork into yesterday—and the poor woman fair invented a pudding for them—and back it's sent. She almost cried. She's afraid she'll be blamed if they starve themselves into their graves."

Dr. Craven came and looked at Colin long and carefully, He wore an extremely worried expression when the nurse talked with him and showed him the almost untouched tray of breakfast she had saved for him to look at—but he was even more worried when he sat down by Colin's sofa and examined him. He had been called to London on business and had not seen the boy for nearly two weeks. When young things begin to gain health they gain it rapidly. The waxen tinge had left Colin's skin and a warm rose showed through it; his beautiful eyes were clear and the hollows under them and in his cheeks and temples had filled out. His once dark, heavy locks had begun to look as if they sprang healthily from his forehead and were soft and warm with life. His lips were fuller and of a normal color. In fact as an imitation of a boy who was a confirmed infected invalid he was a disgraceful sight. Dr. Craven held his chin in his hand and thought him over.

"I am sorry to hear that you do not eat," he said. "That will not do. You will lose all you have gained—and you have gained amazingly. You ate so well a short time ago."

"I told you it was an unnatural appetite," answered Colin.

Mary was sitting on her stool nearby and she suddenly made a very queer sound which she tried so violently to repress that she ended by almost choking.

"What is the matter?" said Dr. Craven, turning to look at her. A dark thought had entered his head.

Mary became quite severe in her manner.

"It was something between a sneeze and a cough," she replied with reproachful dignity, "and it got into my throat."

"But," she said afterward to Colin, "I couldn't stop myself. It just burst out because all at once I couldn't help remembering that last big potato you ate and the way your mouth stretched when you bit through that thick lovely crust with jam and clotted cream on it."

"Is there any way in which those children can get food secretly?" Dr. Craven inquired of Mrs. Medlock.

"There's no way unless they dig it out of the earth or pick it off the trees," Mrs. Medlock answered. "They stay out in the grounds all day and see no one but each other. And if they want anything different to eat from what's sent up to them they need only ask for it."

"Well," said Dr. Craven, "A thought has come to me which you will not like. He and Mary are very close and Mary seems to have no fear of him. He has been improving as well as Mary while they are gone all day and they do not eat here... Has anyone gone missing in that time?"

Mrs. Medlock gasped. "Yes. One of the gardeners, Ben Weatherstaff, has not been seen by anyone here in weeks. And one the kitchen maids and a footman disappeared months ago, same time as Master Colin started going out." She had to cover her mouth to keep from screaming with the new suspicion in her head.

"It may be that Colin is gaining the sustenance that we have always denied him. Human flesh. And Mary, what if he has infected her somehow and she is also only half Accursed. The boy is a new creature, and we have never discovered the reaction of Colin infecting someone.

"It is possible about the girl," said Mrs. Medlock in horror. "They are thick as thieves, an' she is always so close to him. She's begun to be downright pretty since she's filled out and lost her ugly little sour look. Her hair's grown thick and healthy looking and she's got a bright color. The glummest, ill-natured little thing she used to be and now her and Master Colin laugh and whisper together like a pair of conspirators. If she is now like him and they are out everyday with bodies to feed on... Perhaps they're growing fat on that."

"Perhaps they are," said Dr. Craven. "If you see any aggressive behavior in Miss Mary she will have to be chained up too. I would like a blood sample but so long as going without food agrees with them we need not disturb ourselves. They will be hungry again soon enough. Keep absolutely everyone away. Make sure the garden gates are locked. Feed them nothing. When they begin to ask for food again, we will know they have run out. Until then, let them rot."

Chapter 25: The Curtain and the Hidden Door

The secret garden bloomed and bloomed and every morning revealed new miracles. While death and decay deteriorated the world outside, inside the walls life flourished. In the robin's nest there were Eggs and the robin's mate sat upon them keeping them warm with her feathery little breast and careful wings. At first she was very nervous and the robin himself was indignantly watchful. Even Dickon did not go near the close-grown corner in those days, but waited until by the quiet working of some mysterious spell he seemed to have conveyed to the soul of the little pair that in the garden there was nothing which was not quite like themselves—nothing which did not understand the wonderfulness of what was happening to them—the immense, tender, terrible, heart-breaking beauty and solemnity of Eggs. If there had been one person in that garden who had not known through all his or her innermost being that if an Egg were taken away or hurt the whole world would whirl round and crash through space and come to an end—if there had been even one who did not feel it and act accordingly there could have been no happiness even in that golden springtime air. But they all knew it and felt it and the robin and his mate knew they knew it.

Mary felt that she was a Misselthrush and the garden was her nest. The flowers were her eggs and she would defend them. Watching how careful the robin protected her eggs, Mary realized she needed to do more to heighten the security of the garden. Working in the garden, she would constantly allow her eyes to flicker upwards and would listen closely for any new or unusual sounds. A new routine was developed that did not go unnoticed by Dickon or Colin where Mary would often check the door to be sure it was locked from the inside. She felt that if even one Accursed came inside it would destroy the sanctity of what had now become a holy place. A place where magic, white magic, worked miracles. She promised herself that if ever a Rotter got in she would make it chase her out so that she could slay it outside the garden. The alarming thought of the thick black blood oozing onto her flower beds made her want to to cry.

Quickly, Mary pushed those thoughts from her head. 'It will only disrupt the Magic if I allow myself to be terrified or to dread something that is sure to never occur.'

The nest in the corner was brooded over with a great peace and content by the Robin and his mate as they became more comfortable now that the strange boy who used to wear iron chains and walk with irregular, jarring movements was walking and running about and digging and weeding like the others. Fears for the Eggs became things of the past. Knowing that your Eggs were as safe as if they were locked in a bank vault and the fact that you could watch so many curious things going on made sitting a most entertaining occupation. On wet days the Eggs' mother sometimes felt even a little dull because the children did not come into the garden.

But even on wet days it could not be said that Mary and Colin were dull. One morning when the rain streamed down unceasingly Mary and Colin waited for breakfast and wondered how they would be able to restrain themselves from eating it all. But the food never came. They decided they would not ask because it would show that they were truly hungry and they might become suspicious. Colin was beginning to feel a little restive, as he was obliged to remain on his sofa because it was not safe to get up and walk about, then Mary had an inspiration.

"Now that I am like a real boy," Colin had said, "my legs and arms and all my body are so full of Magic that I can't keep them still. They want to be doing things all the time. If it were not for the infection living in my blood, I do not think I would be any different from any other boy alive. Do you know that when I waken in the morning, Mary, when it's quite early and the birds are just shouting outside and everything seems just shouting for joy—even the trees and things we can't really hear— as if there was no infection at all, I feel as if I must jump out of bed and shout myself. If I did it, just think what would happen!"

Mary giggled inordinately.

"The nurse would come running and Mrs. Medlock would come running and they would be sure you had gone crazy and they'd send for the doctor," she said.

Colin giggled himself. He could see how they would all look— how horrified by his breaking free of the chains and how amazed to see him standing upright.

Then a thought came to him. "Mary, we never spoke of it, but there were a couple of times before, when I was stuck up in this room that I felt... I felt like I was... I don't know, feeling aggressive, strong, as if I wanted to attack you but I didn't know I was doing it. As if the infection were taking over. I would feel that way sometimes towards the nurse or the doctor, but I was always chained. I have thought about it a lot and wondered why I don't feel it now. I am not chained. I could attack you. But I don't feel that strangeness anymore. I think it is because I have become stronger and learned to do other things. I think I can control it more. And I feel that I could turn that feeling towards the Accursed. They are the ones I should like to attack."

Mary nodded. She had wondered the same thing about Colin's outbursts. He was now free with her all the time. Alone with her, and had not tried to grab her again.

"I wish my father would come home," he said. "I want to tell him myself. I'm always thinking about it—but we couldn't go on like this much longer. I can't stand lying still and pretending, and besides I look too different. I wish it wasn't raining today."

It was then Mistress Mary had her inspiration.

"Colin," she began mysteriously, "do you know how many rooms there are in this house?"

"About a thousand, I suppose," he answered.

"There's about a hundred no one ever goes into," said Mary. "And one rainy day I went and looked into ever so many of them. No one ever knew, though Mrs. Medlock nearly found me out. I lost my way when I was coming back and I stopped at the end of your corridor. That was when I saw... that was the second time I heard you crying."

Colin started up on his sofa.

"A hundred rooms no one goes into," he said. "It sounds almost like a secret garden. Suppose we go and look at them. Wheel me in my chair and nobody would know where we went."

"That's what I was thinking," said Mary. "No one would dare to follow us. There are galleries where you could run. We could do our exercises. There is a little Indian room where there is a cabinet full of ivory elephants. There are all sorts of rooms."

"Ring the bell," said Colin.

When the nurse came she expected them to ask for breakfast. She was surprised when Colin gave his orders.

"I want my chair," he said. "Miss Mary and I are going to look at the part of the house which is not used. John can push me as far as the picture-gallery because there are some stairs. Then he must go away and leave us alone until I send for him again."

The nurse looked terrified of the prospect that Colin, the afflicted, would be freely moving about the house. But then she remembered that he would be locked up in his chair and unable to do anything without Mary or anyone else's help.

Rainy days lost their terrors that morning. When the footman had wheeled the chair into the picture-gallery and left the two together in obedience to orders, Colin and Mary looked at each other delighted. As soon as Mary had made sure that John was really on his way back to his own quarters below stairs, Colin got out of his chair.

"I am going to run from one end of the gallery to the other," he said, "and then I am going to jump and then we will do the beefy Purifier's exercises."

And they did all these things and many others. They looked at the portraits and found the plain little girl dressed in green brocade and holding the parrot on her finger.

"All these," said Colin, "must be my relations. They lived a long time ago. That parrot one, I believe, is one of my great, great, great, great aunts. She looks rather like you, Mary—not as you look now but as you looked when you came here. Now you are a great deal fatter and better looking."

"So are you," said Mary, and they both laughed.

They went to the Indian room and amused themselves with the ivory elephants. They found the rose-colored brocade boudoir and the hole in the cushion where the baby mice still lay rotting with their brains gnawed out. Colin grinned as Mary told him how she killed her first Accursed mouse and left its smashed body under the pillow. They saw more rooms and made more discoveries than Mary had made on her first pilgrimage. They found new corridors and corners and flights of steps and new old pictures they liked and weird old things they did not know the use of. It was a curiously entertaining morning and the feeling of wandering about in the same house with other people but at the same time feeling as if one were miles away from them was a fascinating thing.

"To think this house was full of people before the Scourge," Colin said. "It makes me wonder what happened to them all and why would they leave the safety of this fortress."

"Probably the same reason we want to go out. It stops being a protector when it feels like a prison."

Colin grinned. "It shall be our protector again. I'm glad we came," Colin said. "I never knew I lived in such a big queer old place. I like it. We will ramble about every rainy day. We shall always be finding new queer corners and things. We shall know this house better than anyone, better even than Medlock. But we should start smuggling some food. We must save some the potatoes and buns and bring them back here so we don't starve on rainy days."

They continued walking through rooms until they came to a new hallway.

"This is strange." Mary commented.

"What is strange?" Colin skipped down the hallway simply because he could.

"This hall has no doors except that one at the end. And the floor looks as though it is regularly utilized. See? There is not as much dust here."

"Let us continue with caution then." Colin replied. "We cannot be seen."

Mary and Colin moved slowly down the hallway listening for footsteps or voices. Colin had made it to the far door but Mary had stopped in the center of the hall listening.

"Mary?" Colin walked back to her.

"Listen. Do you hear that? It sounds like..."

"Chains." Colin had heard that sound every moment as long as he could remember. They listened hard and Colin put his ear against the wall. A low faint sound resonated through the wood.

"Mary, I hear something. But only you will be able to recognize it. Listen here."

Mary leaned up against the wall and placed her ear to the wood. She did not hear anything at first but then a faint moaning appeared and seemed to grow louder until it seemed to be right in her ear. Mary jolted backwards and the fear in her eyes confirmed Colin's suspicion.

"There must be a secret room here," he said running his fingers over the wall. "And a secret door, like the garden."

"I do not care to find that door, Colin. Let's go back."

"No," Colin stopped, his fingers finding a small latch in the wall. "This is my home and I shall know everything going on in it. I shall not have secrets kept!" He pulled the latch and the panel of wall slid open revealing a dark room. Mary had her throwing blades in her hands. Colin loaded his slingshot.

"Come, Mary, there is a light." Colin led the way, his curiosity taking precedence over fear. He was burning to see one. To actually know what the demons looked like and compare himself. They moved into the dark long room with nothing more than a desk and a chair at the far end. The room smelled terrible and Mary put her sleeve to her mouth. Colin moved along a dark wall and motioned Mary towards the lone lantern burning across the room. She picked it up and walked closer to Colin. As the lantern illuminated the room Mary froze staring at Colin with eyes wide and did not blink. Her hands shook and the lantern quivered. Colin stood still staring at Mary questioningly.

Behind Colin, a wall of bars had been erected and just inside those bars stood two large Accursed men with rotting yellow skin, stringy hair, sunken cheeks and black blood filled eyes. They had turned towards the light and saw them. Colin faced the light as well and seeing Mary's face he knew he was in terrible danger. He turned around just as the Accursed thrust their groping fingers through the bars and their bony hands clawed past Colin's shoulders towards Mary. Colin stepped back just out of their reach, but they were not reaching for him. They were ignoring him. He looked at them closely and their eyes were fixed upon Mary, as if he wasn't even there.

"Colin, we must go. Please get away from them!" Mary held up a throwing blade and Colin held up his hand.

"No, I must conduct an experiment. The Magic led us here and it is trying to tell me something." Colin walked forward.

Mary shrieked and ran towards him, but the Rajah put his hand up to stop her. The Accursed, still focused on Mary, snapped and snarled and groped and pressed their faces into the bars, but they did not acknowledge Colin's presence at all. He looked back at Mary triumphantly. "You see, Mary. I am one of them. That is why they don't kill me. I am just another Forsaken to them." His eyes grew large. "I am immune."

As Mary held the lantern higher she could see that the Accursed were chained by the ankles and wrists to bolts in the wall and attached to ropes so they could be pulled away from the bars. The skin around their wrists had torn completely away leaving only tendon and bone remaining. The locked door to the iron cage had a large keyhole.

"Please, Colin, get away from them. We must go before someone hears them and comes." Mary did not like the nasty sunken faces and greenish bony fingers and gaping mouths with flicking tongues all intent upon her.

Colin did come away but he did not head for the door. "Quick, bring the lantern. We must look around first."

Mary joined Colin and together they looked through the room. They found a ledger with notes in the top drawer of the desk.

"This belongs to to your Uncle Craven!" Mary said.

"And my father knows of this? Why would he keep Accursed here?" The first few pages of the ledger explained that the Accursed were to be experimented on using Colin's blood to attempt a curative draught. They had been injected directly with Colin's blood and subsequent purifications and concentrations of it to no effect. The ledger documented dozens of Accursed of different ages, races, gender, and even length of time being Accursed. Colin flipped through the pages of the ledger to the last pages and found the date matched the last time the Dr. had taken his blood.

"Dr. Craven keeps them here for my father! They have been trying to find a cure but they fail because they are denying the true nature of the Scourge. Magic created these hellspawn and only Magic of the strongest kind will defeat them.

They put everything back and left the room. Mary could not help looking back as Colin closed the door on the desperate frenzied creatures. She wanted to kill them but knew it would only cause trouble once they were discovered. After closing the secret door, they went through the door at the far end of the hall. This led to other halls and after a minute Mary stopped.

"What is it?" Colin asked.

"I know where we are. Come, look!" Mary led Colin through one more corridor and turning the corner they ended up right in front of his chambers.

"The Accursed are kept a stone's throw away from me!" Colin cried.

"Hush!" Mary was sharp and then she told him of the first night she had been seeking Colin she had seen an Accursed on a chain and Mrs. Medlock had shooed her away quickly.

"Why have you never told me of this before?" Colin whispered harshly as they doubled back through the corridors.

"I thought perhaps it was a dream. Mrs. Medlock told me I had seen nothing. Of course, I heard you and you weren't nothing." They sprinted down the hallway past the secret door and made it all the way back to Colin's wheelchair. Mary locked him in his shackles and wheeled him through the main corridor back to his room.

After walking what seemed like miles through the house they had found among other things such good appetites that when they returned to Colin's room they expected an enormous luncheon. But again no food had been laid out for them except two glasses of water.

Mary decided she was too hungry to stay silent and when she asked the nurse about lunch she explained what she had been told to say if they asked for food. That because they refused to eat anything for so long the cook up and left leaving no food in the house. Colin looked at Mary and asked her quietly if he should have a tantrum until they go out and get lunch.

"No," said Mary. "Something else is going on. Do you think the servants are going without food? I think not. We are not the only ones doing experiments now. Let us say nothing. We must starve until tomorrow and we shall bring back food and hide it."

The nurse returned down-stairs she slapped her hands down on the kitchen table so that she rattled the highly polished dishes and plates in front of Mrs. Loomis, the cook.

"This is not right!" she said. "This is a house of mystery, and those two children are the greatest mysteries in it. They eat like they are insatiable, then stop eating, now they ask for food and we do not give it to them!"

"If they keep this up every day," said the strong young footman John, "they'll starve and there'd be small wonder that he weighs half as much to-day as he did a week ago. He'll be able to slip right out o'is shackles and I should have to give up my place in time, for fear of him causin' me an injury."

That afternoon Mary noticed that something new had happened in Colin's room. She said nothing but she sat and looked fixedly at the picture over the mantel. The curtain had been drawn aside.

"I know what you want me to tell you," said Colin, after she had stared a few minutes. "I always know when you want me to tell you something. You are wondering why the curtain is drawn back. I am going to keep it like that."

"Why?" asked Mary.

"Because it doesn't make me angry any more to see her laughing. I wakened when it was bright moonlight two nights ago and felt as if the Magic was filling the room. The room was quite light and there was a patch of moonlight on the curtain and somehow that made me pull the cord. She looked right down at me as if she were laughing because she knew my secret. It made me like to look at her. I want to see her laughing like that all the time. I think she must have been a sort of Magic person perhaps."

"You are so like her now," said Mary, "that sometimes I think perhaps you are her ghost made into a boy."

That idea seemed to impress Colin. He thought it over and then answered her slowly.

"If I were her ghost—my father would be fond of me."

"Do you want him to be fond of you?" inquired Mary.

"I used to hate it because he was not fond of me. If he grew fond of me I think I should tell him about the Magic. I would tell him that I was working on the cure and that I would rid the world of the Scourge. It might make him more cheerful."

Colin looked up at his mother's portrait and Mary knew he was thinking about how she died. He still did not know the full story of how she had been sitting on the tree branch in the garden when the Accursed interrupted the peaceful splendor pulling her off the tree and biting her.

"She smiles because she knows my secret. A secret that I have only just discovered. The Accursed do not want me and that gives me power over them. The cure is not only within me. The cure *is* me! I shall become full of Magic and be the greatest Purifier of them all and rid this world of the Scourge forever!"

Chapter 26: It's Mother!

Their belief in the Magic was an abiding thing. After the morning's incantations Colin sometimes gave them Magic lectures.

"I like to do it," he explained to Mary, "because when I grow up and make great scientific discoveries I shall be obliged to lecture about them and so this is practice. I can only give short lectures now because I am very young."

But when Colin held forth under his tree Mary fixed her eyes on him and kept them there. She looked him over with critical affection. It was not so much the lecture which interested her as the legs which looked straighter and stronger each day, the boyish head which held itself up so well, the once sharp chin and hollow cheeks which had filled and rounded out and the gray eyes which had begun to hold a light as if the morning sun were peeking through the mist. Sometimes when Colin felt her earnest gaze he wondered what she was reflecting on and this morning when she had seemed quite entranced he questioned her.

"What are you thinking about, Mary?" he asked.

"I was thinkin'" answered Mary in her Yorkshire, "as I'd warrant tha's gone up three or four pound this week. I was lookin' at tha' calves an' tha' shoulders. Even yer eyes look brighter."

"It's the Magic and—and Mrs. Sowerby's buns and milk and things," said Colin puffing out his chest. "You see the scientific experiment has succeeded."

"Speaking of milk and food, where is Dickon? I am so hungry I might eat some of the roses!"

"I could hardly sleep for my stomach grumbing so loudly."

That morning Dickon was too late to hear the lecture. When he came he was ruddy with running and his funny face looked more bothered than usual.

"What is it? Are you well?" Mary asked.

"Aye, Miss." He sat and rested a moment. "Only I had a testin' night las' eve an' you would'n believe the troubles out on the moor. 'The Scourge is renewed', I heard someone say, and the numbers of Accursed is growin'. They say the rats carry the affliction now and spread it by biting people in the night. The Accursed is moving through the parishes an' walls don' seem to keep 'um at bay as they climb on top o' e'other crushing all them as below. I never seen such a wave come through an' I had t' hide all night like a fox in a hole. You mun warn Mrs. Medlock that the hoards are near at her gate."

"So you didn't bring any food then?" Colin asked desperately. Mary's stomach growled terribly just then.

"There ain't nowhere left t' buy eggs an' potatoes. Couldn' risk going all the way ta the cottage. Poor Mother must 'av wondered where I was, but I've spent many a night before sleepin' under the stars on the moor."

"What are we to do?" Mary cried. "We haven't eaten since the day before yesterday!" She looked around the garden and thought eating the roses was not such a crazy idea.

"Wha' about the kitchen gardens?" Dickon said. "There's food there alright. I'll go and see what I can find."

Dickon returned shortly with some vegetables including carrots, a handful of peapods, and three apples from the orchard. Mary and Colin ate them all within a minute and though still hungry, they could now think of other things.

As they had a good deal of weeding to do after the rains they fell to work. They always had plenty to do after a warm deep sinking rain. The moisture which was good for the flowers was also good for the weeds which thrust up tiny blades of grass and points of leaves which must be pulled up before their roots took too firm hold. Colin was as good at weeding as any one in these days and he could lecture while he was doing it. "The Magic works best when you work yourself," he said this morning. "You can feel it in your bones and muscles. I am going to read books about bones and muscles, but I am going to write a book about Magic. Magic and the purging of the Scourge. I am making it up now. I keep finding out things. Just wait until I tell you what I discovered yesterday, Dickon. The Magic has given me powers, powers over the Forsaken."

It was not very long after he had said this that he laid down his trowel and stood up on his feet. He had been silent for several minutes and they had seen that he was thinking out a lecture, as he often did. When he dropped his trowel and stood upright it seemed to Mary and Dickon as if a sudden strong thought had made him do it. He stretched himself out to his tallest height and he threw out his arms exultantly. Color glowed in his face and his strange eyes widened with joyfulness. All at once he had realized something to the full.

"Mary! Dickon!" he cried. "Just look at me!"

They stopped their weeding and looked at him.

"Do you remember that first morning you brought me in here?" he demanded.

Dickon was looking at him very hard. Being an animal charmer he could see more things than most people could and many of them were things he never talked about. He saw some of them now in this boy. "Aye, that we do," he answered.

Mary looked hard too, but she said nothing.

"Just this minute," said Colin, "all at once I remembered it myself—when I looked at my hand digging with the trowel—and I had to stand up on my feet to see if it was real. And it is real! I'm well—I'm well!"

"Aye, that th' art!" said Dickon.

"I'm well! I'm well!" said Colin again, and his face went quite red all over.

He had known it before in a way, he had hoped it and felt it and thought about it, but just at that minute something had rushed all through him—a sort of rapturous belief and realization and it had been so strong that he could not help calling out.

"I shall not turn into one of the Accursed. I shall not rot away and wander the ages as a mindless cannibal. I shall NOT suffer to live forever and ever and ever!" he cried grandly. "I shall grow up and I shall find out thousands and thousands of things. I shall find out about people and creatures and everything that grows—like Dickon—and I shall never stop making Magic. I'm well! I'm well! I feel—I feel as if I could make the whole world feel well and no one would ever suffer the affliction again! Dickon, I must tell you what I discovered yesterday, about the infection in my blood. It..."

Colin was looking across the garden at something attracting his attention and his expression had become a startled one.

"Who is coming in here?" he said quickly. "Who is it?"

The door in the ivied wall had been pushed gently open and a woman had entered. Dickon had left the door unlocked when he brought in the vegetables and she had come in silently and had stood still listening and looking at them. With the ivy behind her, the sunlight drifting through the trees dappling her long blue cloak, and with her face hidden by the deep hood she was rather like a softly colored illustration in one of Colin's books. Under the hood she had large blue eyes which seemed to take everything in—all of them and the "creatures" and every flower that was in bloom. Unexpectedly as she had appeared, not one of them felt that she was an intruder at all. Dickon's eyes lighted like lamps.

"It's mother—that's who it is!" he cried and went across the grass at a run.

Colin began to move toward her, too, and Mary went with him. They saw that she carried a basket and hoping it contained vast amounts of biscuits with butter and cream they both felt their pulses beat faster.

"It's mother!" Dickon said again. "I knowed tha' wanted to see her an' I told her where th' door was hid."

As Dickon approached he slowed and came to a stop long before he could embrace her. His blue eyes filled with worry. "Wha's th' matter, Mother? Are you ill?"

"My Darling, I am so sorry." She sounded on the verge of tears and slowly pulled back her hood. Her face was sunken and yellow. Sweat pooled in the creases of her feverish brow and she licked her parched lips with a dry tongue.

Dickon stumbled backwards as though he had been dealt a deadly a blow to the chest. Mary had so wanted to feel a warm hug but now stood still as stone. Only Colin was not rendered speechless by her present condition. He walked right up to her and held out his hand with a sort of flushed royal shyness but his eyes quite devoured her face.

"Even when I was ill I wanted to see you," he said, "you and Dickon and the secret garden. I'd never wanted to see anyone or anything before."

The sight of his uplifted face brought about a sudden change in her own. She flushed and the corners of her mouth shook and a mist seemed to sweep over her eyes.

"Eh! dear lad!" she broke out tremulously. "Eh! dear lad!" as if she had not known she were going to say it. She did not say, "Mester Colin," but just "dear lad" quite suddenly. She might have said it to Dickon in the same way and Colin liked it.

"Are you surprised because I am so well?" he asked. She put her yellow hand on his shoulder and smiled the mist out of her sunken eyes. "Aye, that I am!" she said; "but tha'rt so like thy mother tha' made my heart jump."

"Do you think," said Colin a little awkwardly, "that will make my father like me?"

"Aye, for sure, dear lad," she answered and she gave his shoulder a soft quick pat. "He mun come home—he mun come home."

Susan Sowerby coughed an uncomfortable deep throaty cough.

She held both hands out to Mistress Mary who stepped closer. She had experience now with people who turned and she realized that Mrs. Sowerby was not quite ready to let go of life just yet. Mrs. Sowerby looked her little face over in a motherly fashion.

"An' thee, too!" she said. "Tha'rt grown near as hearty as our 'Lisabeth Ellen. I'll warrant tha'rt like thy mother too. Our Martha told me as Mrs. Medlock heard she was a pretty woman. Tha'lt be like a blush rose when tha' grows up, my little lass, bless thee."

She did not mention that when Martha came home on her "day out" and described the plain sallow child she had said that she had no confidence whatever in what Mrs. Medlock had heard. "It doesn't stand to reason that a pretty woman could be th' mother o' such a fou' little lass," she had added obstinately.

Mary had not had time to pay much attention to her changing face. She had only known that she looked "different" and seemed to have a great deal more hair and that it was growing very fast. But remembering her pleasure in looking at the Mem Sahib in the past she was glad to hear that she might some day look like her.

Dickon had not yet recovered and remained sitting in the grass in a daze. His sky blue eyes had darkened to the color of a stormy sea.

Susan Sowerby put down the basket and went round their garden slowly with Colin at her side pretending there was nothing strange at all in her appearance or behavior. She only stopped a few times to hack out a most violent cough while being told the whole story of the garden and shown every bush and tree which had come alive. Mary maintained a short distance from Mrs. Sowerby, though Colin kept looking up at her once comfortable rosy face that was now sunken and a pale greenish-yellow color.

Soot followed her and once or twice cawed at her and flew upon her shoulder pecking at her neck and flapping his large black feathery wings in her face as if trying to get her to move out of the garden. When they told her about the robin and the first flight of the young ones she laughed a motherly little mellow laugh in her throat.

"I suppose learnin' 'em to fly is like learnin' children to walk, but I'm feared I should be all in a worrit if mine had wings instead o' legs," she said.

It was because she seemed such a wonderful woman in her nice moorland cottage way and pitiful due to her current state of infection that she was told about the Magic.

"Do you believe in Magic?" asked Colin. "I do hope you do."

"That I do, lad," she answered. "I never knowed it by that name but what does th' name matter? I warrant they call it a different name i' France an' a different one i' India. Some o' it is on th' side o' life and some is on th' side o' death. Keepin' the balance. Sometimes th' world gits out o' th' balance and sommit has to set it right. Th' same thing as set th' seeds swellin' an' th' sun shinin' made thee a well lad an' it's th' Good Thing. It isn't like us poor fools as think it matters if us is called out of our names. Th' Big Good Thing doesn't stop to worrit, bless thee. It goes on makin' worlds by th' million—worlds like us. Never thee stop believin' in th' Big Good Thing an' knowin' th' world's full of it—an' call it what tha' likes."

"Mother." Dickon finally stood and approached. His round face was furrowed with worry. "Tell me what happened last night at the cottage. Tell me how much time..."

"Come and sit and I shall tell you everything, my darling."

Mary and Colin took this opportunity to open the basket which held a regular feast. They all sat down under their tree and Susan Sowerby watched them devour their food as she licked her cracked lips and wiped the sweat from her yellow forehead. Dickon watched his mother and waited patiently for her to begin. After coughing violently for a moment she told them the story in broad Yorkshire.

"Las' nigh' we all of us had a lovely meal, 'cept Martha and Dickon who weren't there, and began singing songs together near dusk. Just the ten includin' the little ones. A cry suddenly come from the watcher on the wall that Accursed was headin' our way. We doused the fires an' the candles an' became deathly quiet but they knew we was there and they were at the walls in a minute. I took a peek over the wall an' couldn' believe me eyes. They were hundreds of 'um out there. I never seen so many all at once. We fired every stone we had but they started climbin' and scrapin' their way up. We 'ad to chop them down as they came but they 'ad surrounded th' cottage and were comin' up from every direction. They was climbin' on top o' the dead ones and they was in a fierce desperation hissing and near shriekin' to get us! They began tumblin' in over the walls and we had to fall back into the cottage. The youngon's was mad with terror and I knew the Rotters would be tearing down the wooden door soon. I had to get them out somehow but th' only way out was th' front and a hundred rotters waited outside."

Dickon looked terrified. His mouth hung open as if in a silent scream. Colin and Mary continued to munch on the buttery biscuits and cold chicken and sweet bread covered in strawberry preserves. As she listened, Mary, who had little imagination, wondered how a house full of children could have defended themselves against such a number. Colin appeared to be deep in thought and had his eyes fixed on Mrs. Sowerby as she spoke.

After a long pause of Mrs. Sowerby hacking and shaking to the point that Mary began to feel apprehensive about how much longer she had, the story began again but did not relieve the disquiet and discomfort caused in the first half.

"Trapped we was. The door hinges were crackin' as the hoard outside crushed themselves upon it. And th' children began t' lose their heads screamin' and beatin' the floor. I knew somethin' drastic would have t' be done or none o' us would escape. A sacrifice would 'ave t' be made."

She paused and Dickon had stood bolt upright and paced across the garden path.

"I took th' ol' ladder stored under th' potato an' flour bags an' punched a hole in the ceilin' with my axe. I pulled everyone up onto th' roof one by one just as the front door gave an' they piled into the cottage. We ran over the thatch to the back. The mess o' rotters was not so big here but it was still scores of 'em and no way through. I knew they would 'ave to be distracted..."

"WHO?" Dicken yelled. "Who did you throw off the roof, Mother? Who did you sacrifice?!"

Susan Sowerby slowly turned to look at her son and smiled at him, with eyes full of a mothers love. "Myself dear. Myself."

She pulled the string on her cloak and let it fall to her feet. Dark stains of blood coated her cotton dress and a chunk of flesh hung from her bare shoulder. The back of her dress had been torn away and deep gouges were scraped down her back. A chunk of hair had been ripped out leaving behind a red and raw wound on the side of her head.

Dickon dropped to his knees and buried his face in his hands. Mary knew that she would have to be the one kill her. She reached into her pockets and fingered the throwing daggers.

Susan Sowerby's head twitched violently. But she still had a story to tell.

"I told 'em t' run as fast as they could an' find a hidin' spot out on the moor until daylight, then they were to come 'ere, to Misselthwaite, where I knowed they would be safe. I jumped down first and distracted them while all me lit'l 'uns got away."

Mrs. Sowerby twitched violently again. Mary became worried that her flower beds were in danger of having black ooze spewed all over them. She would have to get Mrs. Sowerby out of the garden as soon as possible.

"I fough' 'em a long time, until I could no longer see my children as they disappeared onto the Moor. Then I began to run, even as they clutched and bit my legs. I hacked them down with my axe. Tha' will see, Dickon, when you return to the cottage. I left a great trail o' them wrecked on the ground behind me. Tha' mun find your brothers and sisters and keep 'em safe. Tha' mun return home one day. Th' cottage now belongs to you, my dear boy."

Dickon looked in awe at his brave mother and could not find any words. His full blue eyes, normally like the summer sky were now dark as the deep blue ocean. He said goodbye with those eyes.

Mary decided this was the time to move Susan Sowerby out of the garden. She picked up the blue cloak and placed it back around her wounded shoulders. She softly pushed Mrs. Sowerby's weak form forward and tried to change the subject as they walked.

"Thank you for the food, Mrs. Sowerby. We were mighty hungry. Where did you get it?"

"I stole it."

Mary gasped.

"From Misselthwaite's kitchens. I couldn' 'ave asked. If anyone 'ad seen me I would've been done for. But I knew tha' would be 'ere and I knew tha' would be migh'y 'ungry."

Mary suddenly realized that with Susan Sowerby gone there would be no food coming at all if Medlock and the Doctor had truly agreed to keep food from them. She told this to Mrs. Sowerby while walking her closer to the garden door. Colin followed right behind.

"What should we do?"

"Bless us all, I can see tha' has a good bit o' thievin' to do," said Susan Sowerby. "But tha' won't have to keep it up much longer. Mester Craven'll come home."

"Do you think he will?" asked Colin stepping forward. "Why?"

Susan Sowerby bent over suddenly, like a twig breaking. She coughed so violently her back spasmed. She recovered and in a raspy voice replied.

"To see how tha' has healed. I suppose it 'ud nigh break thy heart if he found out before tha' told him in tha' own way," she said. "Tha's laid awake nights plannin' it."

"I couldn't bear any one else to tell him," said Colin. "I think about different ways every day, I think now I just want to run into his room."

"That'd be a fine start for him," said Susan Sowerby. "I would've liked to see his face, lad. I would that! He mun come back—that he mun."

Mary opened the door to the Secret Garden and and saw that Mrs. Sowerby had left her bloodied axe just outside the door. She stepped forward to depart but Colin stood in her way seeming to deliberately block her.

"Colin! What are you doing? Let Mrs. Sowerby leave the garden!"

Preventing her from moving the few last steps to the door, Colin stood quite close to Susan and fixed his eyes on her with a kind of bewildered adoration and manic fascination. He suddenly caught hold of the fold of her blue cloak and held it fast.

"You are just what I—what I wanted," he said quietly. "I wish you were my mother—as well as Dickon's! I am sorry that you must go, and we will take care of you. You will be in heaven very soon."

All at once Susan Sowerby bent down and drew him with her cold arms close against her bosom—as if he had been Dickon's brother.

"Eh! dear lad!" she said. "Thy own mother's in this 'ere very garden, I do believe. She couldna' keep out of it. Thy father mun come back to thee—he mun!"

The quick blackness swept over her eyes. Her grip on Colin tightened and he held still listening to her slow raspy breath and weakening heartbeat. Her head jerked up suddenly and black blood flowed from her mouth down her neck and onto her large cloak.

Mary cried, "Colin, move!"

"No!" Colin ordered. "Wait. I must see."

Susan Sowerby licked her cracked black stained lips and looked down at Colin with bulging dead eyes. Her hands held his shoulders in a tight grip and her mouth gaped and oozed and hissed.

She paused, then let her grip on Colin go pushing him aside as she lunged for Mary! Dodging quickly, Mary led Susan Sowerby out of the garden into the dead-end orchard. Running through the trees, Mary turned and threw her dagger. Mrs. Sowerby jerked to the side suddenly and the dagger missed. Mary exclaimed using language she learned from Ben Weatherstaff and kept running.

Colin was on his feet in a second and he picked up Mrs. Sowerby's axe. He was amazing by his own strength in lifting the axe and remembered all the hours spent pulling back the slingshot and pushing himself up from the ground during his exercises. He raced after them and found Mary cornered in the dead-end orchard armed with only one small knife. He sprinted up behind Susan Sowerby and grabbed her by the hair pulling backwards. She ignored him as if he wasn't even there. She seemed confused and swiped wildly towards Mary. Colin clumsily chopped his axe into Mrs. Sowerby's neck causing black ooze to bubble out from her throat. She spun violently around gripping Colin by the shoulders but her eyes wandered aimlessly as if searching for her attacker. Colin just stood there staring at the Accursed as the dark emulsion seeped from her throat down onto her dress. Looking into her lifeless eyes, Colin's fascination left him and was replaced with pity. Pity for the wonderful woman she used to be, now suffering as a walking corpse.

Mary approached slowly, in awe of Colin's seeming power to control the Accursed. Mrs. Sowerby suddenly snapped her head around focusing her eyes on Mary. Colin pushed her away from him and swung his axe slicing her knees open. She buckled and kneeled at his feet. He swallowed hard and swung the axe strong and sure this time, right down the center of Mrs. Sowerby's head. She fell to the ground in a heap. Colin looked down at the still body. He felt excited for his first kill, feeling adrenaline course through his body in a way he had never felt. He felt strong and for the first time he felt special. He was immune to the Accursed. They treated him like one of their own. He could walk among them safely and kill them all without fear of attack. He truly was the Cure. Mary came to him and put her hand on his shoulder.

"Colin," Mary said softly. "Do you know what you are? You are the Savior. You will be the greatest Purifier in all the world."

"We need to burn her," Dickon said. He had watched everything from the entrance to the Orchard.

Mary took Mrs. Sowerby's cloak and covered the body. Colin gathered dry leaves from around the orchard and Dickon started the fire with pieces of flint stone.

Soon the fire raged around the body and black smoke rose into the air.

"Someone is sure to see this and come looking," Mary said. "We had best get back to the house before anyone comes."

Dickon nodded his head in agreement and wiped the tears from his face as he watched his mother burn. They quickly gathered their things from the Secret Garden and made sure the door was well hidden. Dickon came with them wanting to join his sister Martha and find out if any of his other siblings had come. As they approached the Manor, Mary heard a strange and familiar sound.

"Stop! Do you hear that?" Everyone became silent and listened without breathing. It was the low hum of the moaning of the Forsaken. Not one or two. This hum resonated throughout the garden, echoing off the stone walls through the narrow corridors. This was a hoard. Mary pulled out her throwing blades, Dickon brandished his slingshot and had his knife ready at his waist, and Colin raised his newly acquired axe. They turned the corner out of the gardens by the stone fountain to look on the lawn leading to the manor. Dozens upon dozens of Accursed stood between them and the Manor. Most of them were right up on the Manor walls pushing in at doors and windows. More and more came streaming onto the lawn from the path along the giant stone wall encircling the estate.

"How did they get in?" Mary asked as Colin said, "Where did they all come from?"

"I'll find out." Dickon said softly. He whispered to Soot who flew high into the air. Dickon put his finger to his lips and quiet as a mouse he disappeared back into the garden. Mary and Colin waited. Suddenly the sound of breaking glass and screams passed over the lawn from Misselthwaite and gun shots pierced the air causing wandering Accursed to turn their attention on the Manor.

Mary was so focused on searching where from the manor the gunshots originated that she did not notice the approaching Accursed until it turned the corner right in front her. She jumped back just as two more stumbled upon their hiding place. Colin swung his axe and buried it into the chest of the first Accursed. The creature stood confused as he struggled to pull it out. Mary ran in a circle around the fountain chased by the other two. She jumped up onto the edge of the fountain and plunged both blades into the temples of the Accursed who was inches from clawing her in the back. She was able to pull one out and fell backwards into the water. Colin tore the axe from the creature's chest and swung again, this time cleaving into the top of its skull. It fell and Colin had to place his foot on the Accursed's face to pull the axe back out. The third climbed clumsily but quickly into the fountain. It splashed towards Mary who was trying to regain her footing. The bottom of the fountain was slippery with algae and her feet slid out from under her. Facing the Accursed, she kicked at it as it grabbed for her legs. She threw her blade but it dug deep into its cheek just below its left eye. The Accursed kept coming. What used to be a poor village maid grabbed Mary's leg hard and her nails dug deep into Mary's stockings. It's mouth opened wide and just as it began to bite down on Mary's ankle an axe sliced clear through its neck. Mary kicked hard away from the dead Accursed and looked up at Colin in awe as he pulled the axe up and grabbed the head by the hair and tossed it out of the fountain.

He looked down at Mary and his triumphant grin dropped. His eyes widened. "Mary!"

Mary looked down at the water to see a small stream of blood coming from her torn stockings. The Accursed's nails caked in the dried blood of the dead had broken through Mary's skin. The infection was spreading through her.

"Don't tell Dickon," she said softly. "I still have time to fight."

Colin fell to his knees in the water and embraced her. "There must be a way... there must be something..."

But Mary pushed him off. "Come on! We've got to move!" The commotion had attracted the attention of nearby Forsaken and they were approaching at an increasing rate. Mary and Colin ran down the garden path the way Dickon had gone. Mary heard the familiar cawing of Soot and saw him just above. Dickon suddenly rounded the corner.

"Run!" He cried.

Mary and Colin ran down a new path towards the large stone border wall with a fresh group of the Accursed chasing after Dickon.

"The hoard broke through the back garden gate," Dickon yelled. "More're comin' every minute! We mun get into the Manor."

"Misselthwaite has been breached!" Colin yelled back.

Dickon ran ahead with renewed determination. "We mun find my brothers 'n sisters! My mother's sacrifice will not be in vain!"

He ran ahead along the wall towards the side servants entrance. As they approached the door flung open and maids and footmen, cooks and servers ran out panicked.

"Go back in ya fools!" Dickon cried as he pushed through them. No one seemed to notice Colin with his axe running as strong as any healthy boy. The servants scattered in a panic some running directly into the massive hoard outside the manor, others running around towards the front. Several unlucky footmen were surprised by the Accursed that had been chasing Dickon along the wall. As they were devoured, Dickon had time to open the door and after Mary and Colin were inside he slammed it shut and locked it.

Dickon shouted, "Martha!"

"Shh! Dickon, you'll bring all the Forsaken upon us!" Mary whispered harshly. "These corridors are thin and the doors lead to many passages. They could be anywhere!"

"Let me go ahead." Colin said. "I am safe here. I am the cure and I will begin with the Purification of my home."

Colin went ahead. The first person they came upon was the cook, the woman who had mistakenly listened to orders to serve Colin raw foods and nearly starve him his whole life. She cradled her left arm which had been bitten and torn.

"Who is this coming? Please help me? End my life before I become one the Tormented!"

Colin looked upon her shamefully and in his full rajah voice he scolded the woman.

"How dare you give up? You have many hours yet to live and now you have nothing to fear. Get up! Take up that knife! Go and kill as many Accursed as you can. If you fight valiantly I will dispatch you well before you become one of them. If you do not, I will have you chained in the basement, as you once chained me!"

The cook looked in awe at Colin, the half dead boy, who now appeared fully alive. She stood and held her large carving knife in her right hand.

"Now follow behind us and watch our backs!" Colin once again led the way followed by Mary, Dickon and the cook. Mary directed Colin through the dark corridors towards the center hallway. They reached the door leading to the main stairwell. They could hear shuffling feet on the other side.

"Stay inside." Colin said.

"No," Mary replied. "I do not fear them, I will go with you!"

"Open th' door and let's see wha' is hap'nen!" Dickon held his knife tightly and Colin slowly cracked open the door. A pile of Accursed were all gathered over a few bodies, gorging themselves on the remains. Several others were milling around on the staircase as if they were not sure whether to go up or down. Dickon looked closely at the pile of bodies trying to see who they were.

Mary said, "I bet Martha took them all upstairs, Dickon."

"Let me go first!" Colin insisted. "I know I can do this!" Colin bravely walked out alone into the grand hall.

The cook gasped, "What is the young master doing?"

Colin walked right up to the first Accursed and sliced its head clean off. The others did not even turn to look. One by one Colin walked up to the black-eyed, sallow skinned, rotting cannibals and smashed his axe into their brains.

Colin began to have fun and spun the axe playfully before bringing it down onto the back of the neck of one crouched over its raw meal. He danced around slicing the necks of the Accursed who did not seem to notice the slaughter of their meal companions. Colin walked up the stairs leaving a pile behind him and began cutting down the wanderers. Dickon ran out and looked at the bodies of those who were being consumed. He sighed with relief that they were not his brothers and sisters but did recognize some the staff. He proceeded to stab each one in the temple with his knife. Colin returned having cleared the stairs. "What are you doing?"

"Remember, victims arise quickly after they are killed. The wounded take a day to turn but the dead can awaken within an hour or less."

This was new information to Colin and he realized there were probably many things he did not know about them. Dickon also stabbed the heads that Colin had severed.

"You must destroy the brain. The heads can still bite even if the body is detached."

Colin looked down to see that one of the heads still moved, its eyes glaring up at Dickon. Colin smashed the head with the butt of the axe. Mary and the cook joined them and as they began to climb the stairs the doors from the lower hall burst open and dozens more Accursed streamed in.

They ran and Colin stayed at the back hewing down any that ventured after them. Up the stairs, the long series of doors stood closed. Mary led the way towards her own room. She tried opening the door and it was locked.

"Martha!" Mary knocked on the door and whispered harshly. "Its Mary and Dickon! Let us in!"

Martha's voice came through the door. "Is anyone infected?"

Mary knew she could hide her own wound but the cook was clearly in bad shape. She had to get her to open the door. More and more were coming up the stairs and Colin would not be able to dispatch them all before they reached them.

"No, we are here to save you! Now open the door!" Several Accursed pushed past Colin and the cook and Dickon began fighting them. The cook yelled as an accursed grabbed her injured arm and dug its nails into it. She stabbed the Accursed in the head and kicked it down the stairs.

"What's going on, Mary? Is everything alright?"

"Yes! Just open the door and let us in. We will get all of you out of here!" Mary tried to control her fear as the noise had attracted the hoard to race up the stairs.

"I heard screaming, is someone hurt?"

"Martha, just open the door now!" Mary ordered in her most contrary way.

The door lock clicked and Mary burst the door open. "Come on!" She yelled.

Martha screamed as she saw dozens of crazed Accursed racing down the hallway after Dickon, Colin and the cook. Once they were inside, Mary slammed the door in the face of a snarling rotter.

They banged on the door with frightening strength.

Dickon hugged his sister and then saw with delight all his brothers and sisters. They embraced him and then Martha turned to Mary shaking with fear and anger.

"Save us? You 'ave led them all right t' our door! And she is infected!" She pointed at the cook.

"She is still alive and is fighting to help us," Mary said. "Besides, you stand in the presence of the savior, the cure to the Affliction!"

Martha suddenly recognized Colin and fell to her knees in shock. She looked at this strong young man, standing straight and tall and any healthy boy of the Moor, clothes splattered with blood, wielding an axe.

"Tha' axe!" Martha said. "Tha's ours!"

"Mother had tha' axe!" One of the children said.

"Yes," Colin stated. "This is your mother's axe. She came to the garden to see Dickon and Mary and me with her last few minutes. She saved you all and her sacrifice will not be forgotten. I use her axe now to again save her children. For you are all as dear to me as if you were my own brothers and sisters. I will save you. I will destroy them all."

They looked at Colin in awe as the banging on the door became stronger.

"Martha, where is Medlock? My uncle, Dr. Craven?"

"I donna know where Dr. Craven is, but last I seen Mrs. Medlock she was fightn' a whole lot o' th' Rotters in the sitting room. I rushed th' children up 'ere and we been waitin' since. Now we're trapped wit' all those Rottas ou' there."

"Actually, there is another way out," Mary said. She showed them the passage through the fireplace that she found the night she had followed the moaning sounds to Colin.

"I will go first." Colin said "Once the area is clear I will return for you."

"I am coming with you!" Mary demanded.

"Then so am I," declared Dickon.

"No. Please. You must let me do this. I need to do this alone. I will come back." Colin slipped through the flue.

"Has anyone thou' 'bout where it is we're goin' once we leave this room?" Martha asked?

Mary thought. They couldn't just find another room to hide in, there was no food. They could perhaps go to the kitchens but the pantries were not large enough to hold everyone.

"The garden," Mary blurted out. Dickon turned to her wide eyed. "The garden is the safest place. There is water and we can get food from the kitchens before we go. At least enough for a day or two." Mary knew she would not be eating any of it.

Dickon nodded his head. "Yes, we'll take you all t' the Garden. Mary's Secret Garden. She has brought it back t' life!"

The children all knew the story of the shut up garden that no one was to ever go into. They gasped when they heard Dickon tell them of how Mary found it and how she told him the secret.

A loud crack brought all the attention back to the wooden door. The Accursed pushed it hard, crushing each other trying to get through. The voices of the children had driven them mad with hunger. The door creaked and cracked again, the small metal lock breaking loose through the wood. Mary, Dickon and the cook stood in front of the children, their weapons ready.

Mary took a breath in as the door burst open. Several Accursed fell forward, crushed by the weight of the throng behind them. One Accursed moved into the doorway and snarled at Mary, his black eyes wide. Then an axe swung across the doorway slicing its head from ear to ear. Colin appeared in the doorway, panting. He had a triumphant smile on his blood spattered face.

"The path is safe, though you will have some climbing to do." Colin said.

Mary looked out the doorway and her jaw dropped. The hallway was filled with bodies all the way to the staircase.

"Colin!" Mary gasped. "You did all this yourself?"

"It's easy when they don't fight back," he shrugged and gave Mary a winning smile.

Colin and Dickon led the way across the bodies and down the stairs. They only had to dispatch a few Accursed on the way to the kitchens.

'Where are all the other Accursed?' Mary wondered. Certainly there had been more outside. The door to the kitchens was locked. Colin knocked hard and demanded he be let in using his greatest rajah voice. Then he stood at the back of the group keeping watch for any approaching Accursed.

They could hear hushed voices on the other side, then the door creaked open. Mrs. Medlock peeked through the opening to see Mary, Dickon, Martha and a gang of Sowerby children.

"Come in! For heavens sake! Don't mess about!" She whispered harshly. They quickly filed through the doorway and lastly Colin walked in and turned to face them. Mrs. Medlock was with a couple of gardeners, the nurse, and Dr. Craven, all who jumped back in fear from Colin. Covered in blood and carrying an axe, the invalid boy who could now walk upright looked like one of the Forsaken. The nurse screamed and the doctor lowered his shotgun, his finger on the trigger. Mary jumped at the doctor pushing his shotgun to the side just as it fired! Everyone gasped and froze as they turned to see the cook, who had been standing next to Colin, now bleeding out through the stomach. She fell to the ground and Dickon kicked the shotgun from the doctor.

The blast of the shotgun had turned the head of every Accursed that was wandering about the manor and just outside. They began moving quickly towards the kitchens.

Colin leaned down to the cook and said, "You fought bravely until the end, and I will not let you turn. Close your eyes."

The cook closed her eyes and Colin stood up. To the shock and amazement of Mrs. Medlock, the nurse and the doctor Colin raised the axe up high over his head, twirled it for momentum and swung it down straight through the woman's skull. Then he turned to Dr. Craven.

"Uncle! Look at me! See what I am. See what you kept chained down and starved for years! You wasted all your time trying to find a cure from my blood when the cure was actually me! You failed doctor. And now look what you have brought on us!"

Mrs. Medlock had pulled back the curtain of the window to see dozens of Accursed all racing into the Manor. Martha slammed the kitchen door and then screamed. "The lock! Bloody hell, it 'as been shot out!" The shot gun blast had gone straight through the cook and blasted out the wood frame of the door.

The children quickly pulled over the large chopping table to block the door and piled the chairs on it.

Dickon told Martha, "Gather as much food as ya can carry, quick! We'll find another way out."

Mrs. Medlock pulled out her large obsidian daggers from their sheaths, her face hardened with her signature harsh look. "There is no other way out."

The Sowerby children came out of the pantry with several bags of food each. A loud bang on the door meant the Accursed had found them. Their black eyes searched through the crack in the door. The nurse panicked and ran into the pantry.

"The door locks!" the nurse cried. "It is the only way! Come in quickly and lock the door!"

Dr. Craven, whose weapon was in the hands of Dickon, rushed to join her. "Medlock, come on!"

She replied sternly, "No! You'll be trapped in there with no way out for God knows how long! We're going out the windows!"

Medlock grabbed a giant cooking pot and smashed the windows with it. The drop to the lawn was six feet below and thorny bramble bushes had been planted there for protection.

The children had no hesitation and threw the food down first. Dickon jumped down as far out as he could and took out several of the Accursed that had not run into the house. All his brothers and sisters followed with Martha being last. Mary jumped next leaving Colin and Mrs. Medlock.

"Go Medlock! I will keep them at bay."

The Accursed had now pushed the door open enough to squeeze through and were ducking to crawl under the table. Colin took the heads off the first two that made it.

"Nurse! Uncle! Get out of there!"

But the doctor slammed the door shut. Mrs. Medlock ran to the door and locked it from the outside. "I hope I shall be able to come back for you!"

Then she took her turn to jump out the window. She landed to see fourteen children holding off the Accursed using sling shots and knives. She gasped as Mary expertly threw her blades into the foreheads of two approaching Accursed. Dickon held the shotgun but did not use it. He used his large knife protecting his youngest sister. Mrs. Medlock tried to stand but realized her large bustle was caught in the brambles. She pulled hard tearing her dress and freed herself just in time to stand and kick back a nasty snarling flesh eater. She held the obsidian hilts of her large blades tightly and crossed her arms as the creature lunged forward again. She sliced across the creatures neck stepping to the side and plunged the blade into the back of its head. She ran to join the others.

"Where is Colin?!" Mary cried and she led them running towards the garden.

"There!" Dickon pointed. Colin ran out through the smashed back doors and crossed the field through the hoard without being chased. Mrs. Medlock marveled at his running.

"It's a miracle!" she exclaimed.

"To the Garden!" Mary shouted. She and Dickon ran ahead to clear the garden pathways and Colin stayed behind to dispatch any who followed. It seemed that many more Accursed had entered through the garden gate and they rushed toward the children as they wound their way through the gardens. Finally Mary made it to the ivy wall.

"We are trapped!" Medlock shook her head. "That orchard is a dead end!"

But Mary pulled back the ivy, turned the key and beckoned them all inside the Secret Garden.

Colin entered last and turned the key from the inside. Everyone was hushed. Not only because they were hiding from the Accursed but because they were in awe of the beauty that surrounded them. Mrs. Medlock dropped her knives and fell to her knees under the fountains of falling roses draped over the boughs of climbing flower vines. Dickon put down the shotgun and sat and hugged all his animals that came out to him. Soot landed on his shoulder and Nut and Shell skittered around him.

"Silence is th' key," Dickon whispered. "Them wil 'ventu'ly move on."

Night fell and every sound of feet scraping and tormented moaning from outside the walls sent shivers down Mary's spine.

The light of the waxing moon shined down upon them but the darkness in the shadows became unnerving. They had all washed up as much as possible using some of the collected rain water in the garden pots. They organized the food and set out a small dinner for each of them. Mary didn't touch hers. She had already begun to feel nauseous and knew that by late afternoon tomorrow she would be dead. Dickon noticed that she offered her dinner to Colin and watched her closely.

The night was very long and the Sowerby children sat huddled together. For hours Colin walked along the garden edges listening for Accursed. Mary breathed in slowly and shuttered. She could feel her lungs becoming tight and heat in her ears. Dickon followed her as she moved away from the group to sit in the shadows under the large tree in her Bloody Mary garden of nightshade and hellabore and asphodel. She had picked some of the nightshade and made a small bouquet.

"Mary," Dickon said quietly as he sat next to her. "I know why you' come here."

Mary swallowed and tried very hard not to cry. She leaned over and laid her head on Dickon's shoulder.

"I can already feel it, Dickon. It's like something crawling in my stomach. My blood feels hot, my throat is dry, I am feverish and sweaty. I don't want to turn, and I don't want any of you to have to kill me. I planted this garden around the red caps to remind myself of who I used to be. Bloody Mary, quite contrary. I'm not contrary anymore. And I not only like people now but I love too. I love you, Dickon, and Colin too and I know you will save everyone. But it's too late for me. So I will eat from my garden and lay my head upon my knife point. Then I will become a part of my garden and lie here forever."

Dickon held Mary and kissed her hair. He didn't know what to do for her.

"I'll promise ye, Mary. I won' let you become one o' them. I'll take care of you, Mary. That's a promise."

Colin walked over and saw them together. He understood that she had told Dickon. He sat on the other side of Mary and put his arm around her too.

"You still have strength in you, Mary." Colin whispered. "Don't give up yet. There must be a way... I won't except it..."

They sat in silence holding each other. The air was so still that Mary could hear her own heart beating in her ears. Then she heard that sound again. The sound she had heard when she first began working on the garden. She listened closely and slowly looked around. Coming up from underneath her special garden where the red cap mushrooms grew, came a low scratching sound, only it sounded faster now... frenzied...

Suddenly there was a loud blast! Soot cawed and flew into the air as all the animals scattered. Dickon jumped up and ran to find his youngest brother holding the shotgun, shaking and still pointing it up towards the wall.

"There were a Rotter up there! A' th' top o' th' wall!"

Dickon pulled the gun away from his brother. "And now every Accursed in Misselthwaite will be coming this way!"

Colin looked up to where the boy had pointed. "That is where Ben Weatherstaff first looked over the wall at me. He had climbed a ladder. Do you think the ladder is still there?"

Dickon shrugged. "We'll need to be on watch now. Use slingshots! No guns. We've got to keep it quiet!"

But the blast from the shot gun had echoed through the garden walls and rang through Misselthwaite Manor. At the sound of the blast every Accursed on the property fiercely turned its head and began moving toward the Secret Garden.

Another Accused appeared over the wall, its dark silhouette visible in the moon light. Colin pelted it with his slingshot. The stone hit the creature's face but did not phase it. Mary worried that the creature would fall in and foul her flowerbeds with its black ooze. The children quickly began searching for stones and sharp pieces of wood that they could fire. They shot stones until the Accursed fell backwards. They waited for a few breathless seconds and then another popped its head over the wall.

"We have to find a way to push down that ladder!" Colin said between shots. As they fought back the climbers, they did not realize the hoard outside was clawing through the ivy, finding the walls and moving along them in all directions.

The Robin was keeping a close watch on the wooden door, flitting nervously back and forth across the garden. Only the Robin noticed the locked door wiggle as an Accursed pushed against it.

Mary stood underneath the large dead tree looking up nervously at Dickon as he climbed to the top. Nearly level with the top of the wall he jumped from the branch and grabbed the wall edge. He pulled himself up and looked over.

"What do you see?" Mary asked. Dickon did not answer, he only shook his head. He stood up and walked along the top of the wall.

The Sowerby children continued to send projectiles upwards knocking the Accursed off the top of the ladder one at a time. As soon as one was dispatched another replaced it. Dickon carefully made his way towards the ladder firing down upon the Accursed below with his sling shot. He took out his large knife as he reached the ladder and stabbed the ascending Accursed in the top of its soft decaying head. It hung on the ladder blocking the half-dozen others below. Dickon quickly sat on the wall and reached down with his foot trying to kick the ladder down.

"Be careful, Dickon!" Martha called out.

The Robin twittered as loud as he could zipping back and forth across the wooden door. The Accursed had scratched and pushed and pressed on the door, renewing their efforts as voices could be heard from within. Under the pressure, the aged wood around the metal lock began to give way.

Mary finally heard the Robin and came closer to look in the darkness. The Robin was in a near panic now, swooping across the door whistling at his highest pitch.

"Robin," Mary wondered. "What is the matter? The door is locked." Then Mary watched as the door creaked forward and the wooden frame cracked. Several torn yellow fingernails slowly creeped through the crack in the door followed by a rotting, flesh-torn, boney hand.

"Colin!" Mary called. She knew if this door gave way her beautiful Secret Garden would have hundreds of insatiable dead racing to consume them trampling all her flowers.

Colin, who had been watching Dickon struggle with the ladder, heard Mary's cry but before he could run to her side another sound filled his ears. A sickening sound. A raspy moaning sound *within* the protected walls of the garden. He ran towards it.

"I cannot reach the ladder without climbing down!" Dickon yelled. The Accursed had pulled away the one blocking the ladder and now two came up together clutching at Dickon's legs. He stood back up on the wall working out how to kill them.

Mary called for Colin again but it was Mrs. Medlock who came. She saw the hand and the cracking door frame then took in a deep breath.

"Well, Miss Mary," she unsheathed her obsidian blades, "It is time to discover the truth about yourself. Are you the helpless contrary little thing I picked up all those months ago or have you learned to love something greater than yourself. Will you cower and shrivel or will you face death head on?"

Mary tightened her grip on the throwing blades. "I have learned to love. And I *am* Death." The door frame gave way and the door flew wide open.

Colin ran towards the terrible moaning sound. He wondering how an Accursed could have gotten in? He reached the great tree and stopped suddenly, frozen in horror. Pulling itself out of the ground at the base of the tree, buried underneath the garden for ten years, was the black eyed, decomposing, snarling form of Mrs. Craven, Colin's mother.

Chapter 27: In the Garden

In each century since the beginning of the world horrible tragedies have afflicted the Earth. In the last century more horrible things happened than in any century before. In this new century still more horrible things have happened than any other time in the history of man. But man has always come back to fight and find new ways to overcome. Even the smallest, weakest person may find astounding discoveries that will be brought to light. At first people refuse to believe that a terrible new thing has occurred, then they begin to hope it will go away, then they see it is crashing through their front door- and all the world wonders why no one has done anything about it yet. One of the terrible new things people began to find out in the last century was that thoughts— just mere thoughts—are as powerful as disease of the blood —as good for one as vaccination or as bad for one as infection. To let a sad thought or a bad one get into your mind is as dangerous as being bitten by the Accursed. If you let it stay there after it has got in, you may never get over it as long as you live.

So long as Mistress Mary's mind was full of disagreeable thoughts about her dislikes and sour opinions of people and her determination not to be pleased by or interested in anything, she was a yellow-faced, sickly, bored and wretched child. Circumstances, despite the near extinction of humanity, were very kind to her, though she was not at all aware of it. They began to push her about for her own good. The Scourge destroying her family and home had been beneficial for her and moving to an isolated manor with a tortured half-Accursed boy as wretched as she had been changed the way she thought about herself. When her mind gradually filled itself with robins, and moorland cottages crowded with children, throwing blades, queer crabbed old gardeners and common little Yorkshire housemaids, with springtime and with secret gardens coming alive day by day, and also with a dagger wielding moor boy who saved her, and his "creatures," there was no room left for the disagreeable thoughts which affected her liver and her digestion and made her yellow and tired.

So long as Colin was chained up in his room and thought only of his fears of becoming a rotting mindless cannibal, his weakness due to muscle atrophy and lack of nutrition and reflected hourly on his eyes filling with blackened blood and spending forever as living death, he was a hysterical half-crazy little hypochondriac who knew nothing of the sunshine and the spring and also did not know that he could get well and could stand upon his feet if he tried to do it. He did not know the virus flowing through his blood gave him immunity and strength against the infected. When new beautiful thoughts began to push out the old hideous ones, life began to come back to him, his blood ran healthily through his veins and strength poured into him like a flood. His strength brought a confidence that helped him understand the potential of his gifts, though not fully. His risky experiments were quite practical and simple and proved that bravery, not fear, was the key to all healing. Much more surprising things can happen to anyone who, when a disagreeable or discouraged thought comes into his mind, just has the sense to remember in time and push it out by putting in an agreeable determinedly courageous one. Two things cannot be in one place.

"Where, you tend a rose, my lad, A thistle cannot grow."

While the secret garden was coming alive and two children were coming alive with it, there was a man wandering about certain far-away beautiful places in the Norwegian fiords and the valleys and mountains of Switzerland and he was a man who for ten years had kept his mind filled with dark and heart-broken thinking. He was a tall man with a drawn face and crooked shoulders and the name he always entered on hotel registers was, "Archibald Craven, Misselthwaite Manor, Yorkshire, England."

He was a scientist traveling the world searching for an answer to the Scourge. He had looked for areas of the world free of infection and he had searched for the origin of it in vain. In his mobile lab he tested the blood of different peoples hoping to find a change in the infection like he had found in Colin. He tested Colin's blood, which contained a dormant infection, against healthy cells, but the dormant strain turned active when mixed with healthy blood. He daren't try it on a live person for fear he would turn them into an Accursed. When his blood was mixed with the black blood of the Accursed both strains ignored each other with no change in the Accursed. Experiments on the Accursed continued at Misselthwaite to no avail.

Traveling abroad had given him an excuse to stay away from Misselthwaite and its memories for he had lost hope before he even began his quest. He had not been courageous; he had never tried to put any other thoughts in the place of the dark ones. After ten years of failure in finding a cure and ten years of watching the world fall into ruin, a terrible sorrow had fallen upon Archibald Craven and he had let his soul fill itself with blackness and had refused obstinately to allow any rift of light to pierce through. He had forgotten and deserted his home and his duties. When he traveled about, darkness so brooded over him that the sight of him was a wrong done to other people because it was as if he poisoned the air about him with gloom destroying any vestiges of hope remaining in them. Most strangers thought he must be either half mad or a man with some hidden crime on his soul. And they were right. He fruitlessly searched for a cure when he had lost hope and he avoided going home where he had left his brother to experiment on his afflicted son. He didn't want to know Colin or see him as a person for fear he would realize the atrocity he had committed in neglecting and torturing him. He had traveled far and wide since the day he saw Mistress Mary in his study and told her she might have her "bit of earth." He had been in what used to be the most beautiful places in Europe, though he had remained nowhere more than a few days. Despite his intent to find a cure, he had chosen the quietest and remotest spots far from the origin of the Scourge. He had wandered by blue lakes, the Accursed reflected in the still water, and he had fought them; his pistols always loaded and his aim superior. He had lain on mountain-sides with sheets of deep blue gentians blooming all about him and flower breaths filling all the air and he had fought them, questioning his own reasons for staying alive. Tiny villages high in the remote nearly uninhabitable places of the North had fallen victim to the infected, many Accursed now trapped in hard packed snow, others wandering aimlessly reaching out with frozen finger tips that cracked off at the slightest touch. He had been on the tops of mountains whose heads were in the clouds and had looked down on other mountains when the sun rose and touched them with such light as made it seem as if the world were just being born.

But the light had never seemed to touch himself until one day when he realized that for the first time in ten years a strange thing had happened. He was in a wonderful valley in the Austrian Tyrol, and he had been walking alone through such beauty as might have lifted any man's soul out of shadow. He had walked a long way without any signs of the infliction and it had not lifted his. But at last he had felt tired and had thrown himself down to rest on a carpet of moss by a stream. It was a clear little stream which ran quite merrily along on its narrow way through the luscious damp greenness. Sometimes it made a sound rather like very low laughter as it bubbled over and round stones. He saw birds come and dip their heads to drink in it and then flick their wings and fly away. It seemed like a thing alive and yet its tiny voice made the stillness seem deeper. The valley was very, very still. As he sat gazing into the clear running of the water, Archibald Craven gradually felt his mind and body both grow quiet, as quiet as the valley itself. He wondered if he were going to sleep, but he was not. He sat and gazed at the sunlit water and his eyes began to see things growing at its edge. There was one lovely mass of blue forget-me-nots growing so close to the stream that its leaves were wet and at these he found himself looking at a ring of uncharacteristic fungi and moss that circled around two black stones. Craven slowly crawled closer to look when the black stones flickered towards him revealing a face at the edge of the water. An Accursed had decomposed into the land, traces of its body were outlined by flowers growing over its body. Its mouth had been buried and fallen away but the open eyes still twitched here and there at his approach. He imagined that little burrowing worms might dig their way into its brains finally ending the movement of the black hungry eyes. He began to think that the earth would eventually swallow up all the infected transforming them into lovely moss and flower beds. Perhaps the true cure would be time.

He did not know that just that simple thought was slowly filling his mind—filling and filling it until other things were softly pushed aside. Hope. It was as if a sweet clear spring had begun to rise in a stagnant pool and had risen and risen until at last it swept the dark water away. Hope for an end to the Scourge, like he had once felt long ago. He did not know how long he sat there or what was happening to him, but at last he moved as if he were awakening and he got up slowly and stood on the moss carpet over the Accursed, drawing a long, deep, soft breath and wondering at himself. Something seemed to have been unbound and released in him, very quietly.

"What is it?" he said, almost in a whisper, and he passed his hand over his forehead. "I almost feel as if—I were alive!"

He left the flashing eyes behind and the singular calmness remained with him the rest of the evening and he slept a new reposeful sleep; but it was not with him very long. By the next night, after having to fight off a group of infected, he had opened the doors wide to his dark thoughts and they had come trooping and rushing back. He left the valley and went on his wandering way again. But, strange as it seemed to him, there were minutes— sometimes half-hours—when, without his knowing why, the black burden seemed to lift itself again and he knew he was a living man and not a dead one. Slowly—slowly—for no reason that he knew of—he was "coming alive" with the garden.

He began to think of Misselthwaite and wonder if he should not go home. Now and then he wondered vaguely about his boy and asked himself what he should feel when he went and stood by the carved four-posted bed again and looked down at the sharply chiseled ivory-white face while it slept, not betraying the infection living within, the black lashes rimmed so startlingly the close-shut eyes. He shrank from it.

One marvel of a day he had walked so far that when he returned to his villa the moon was high and full and all the world was purple shadow and silver. He walked down to a little bowered terrace at the water's edge and sat upon a seat and breathed in all the heavenly scents of the night. He felt the strange calmness stealing over him and it grew deeper and deeper until he fell asleep.

He did not know when he fell asleep and when he began to dream; his dream was so real that he did not feel as if he were dreaming. He remembered afterward how intensely wide awake and alert he had thought he was. He thought that as he sat and breathed in the scent of the late roses and listened to the lapping of the water at his feet he heard a voice calling. It was sweet and clear and happy and far away. It seemed very far, but he heard it as distinctly as if it had been at his very side.

"Archie! Archie! Archie!" it said, and then again, sweeter and clearer than before, "Archie! Archie!"

"Lilias! Lilias!" he answered. "Lilias! Where are you?"

"In the garden," it came back like a sound from a golden flute. "In the garden!"

His wife sat upon the low hanging branch of the large oak tree in the garden. Her white dress shining in contrast to the hanging boughs of red roses. She smiled sweetly, calm and secure in her love for her husband and their unborn child. Her gray eyes turned down slowly as she ran her hand over her large belly. She looked up and her smile turned to horror. Craven watched himself in the dream, unable to stop the vision he had so long attempted to suppress. A man with bleeding black eyes ran through the garden and tore Lilias from the tree branch throwing her violently to the ground. Her screams pierced the peaceful air and Craven pulled the man back only to see its black mouth full of shiny red. He slammed his cane into the creature cracking its skull and the creature fell and was still. He lifted Lilias from the ground, forgetting his back was bent, forgetting he was weak and carried her back to the manor even as she bled from the large wound in her neck.

From outside her room, Craven nearly tore his own hair out listening to her screams. The nurse came out only once to tell him the baby was coming. Hours later, the nurse returned holding a small bundle, tears streaming from her eyes. He pushed past into the room to find his wife lying in blood soaked sheets. Her neck wrapped in white gauze, her gray eyes staring blankly into nothingness. He took her body to the garden, laying her in a soft bed of clover. Night came, and he waited. Her white dress was now grey in the moonlight splotched with black stains. He knew it was only a matter of minutes, only a few minutes to see her peaceful face and grey eyes before...

Her fingers twitched. Her eyes closed slowly.

Craven held his shotgun in his shaking hands. He wasn't ready. Her eyes opened and black blood oozed out of them. He couldn't let her go. She moved to her feet and stood still, her arms draped at her sides, black eyes unblinking. She opened her mouth and spewed black ooze onto the garden floor. Craven lost his nerve and ran out of the garden. He locked the door.

"Where is the child?" He called out into the dark manor. "Is it dead?"

His brother, Dr. Craven answered. "No, he is not dead. But he is not alive. The infection spread to him in the womb, and yet..."

Archibald walked into the nursery that had been such a joy for his wife to prepare. Now every piece of furniture, every bit of decor was abhorrent to him. He leaned over the crib to see a swaddled baby, tiny, pale and calmly looking up with dark gray eyes.

"This is not my son. When it turns, kill it." Archibald Craven walked out and refused to see the child. For the next month he hid himself away in his study until Mrs. Medlock came to the door.

"Sir, excuse me, Sir, but I must report to you that the gardeners, Sir, are very distressed about... please Sir, go to your lady's garden. You must do something."

Mr. Craven unlocked the garden door and walked inside. He brought a shovel intending to bury his wife. She was not where he left her. He walked through the garden with no sign of her, then there she was, standing under the oak tree. She turned and reached out to him, her hair was stringy hanging limply over her boney shoulders. Her yellowed nails were cracked where she had dragged them along the stone walls. Her face was sunken, and her teeth yellow. Snarling, she lunged at him and he swung his shovel across her head knocking her to the ground. She didn't get up.

He quickly dug a grave and placed the body in a large wooden tool box. He buried his wife that day, locked the door behind him and buried the key. He vowed that no one would ever go in again.

But in this dream he did go in again. The garden door was open and spring had renewed the beauty of this place. At the oak tree, a vision appeared of Lilias waiting as a beautiful woman speaking softly.

It was such a real voice and it seemed so natural that he should hear it.

"In the garden!" He wanted to step closer, to embrace her, only he stopped as her eyes darkened, her mouth dripped blackness and her face sank in. Before his eyes, she deteriorated into a rotting corpse and, snarling, she lunged forward.

And then the dream ended. When he did awake at last it was brilliant morning and a servant was standing staring at him. He was an Italian servant and was accustomed, as all the servants of the villa were, to accepting without question any strange thing his foreign master might do. No one ever knew when he would go out or come in or where he would choose to sleep or if he would roam about the village taking blood samples or work in his lab all night. The man held a salver with some letters on it and he waited quietly until Mr. Craven took them. When he had gone away Mr. Craven sat a few moments holding them in his hand and looking at the lake. His strange calm was still upon him and something more—a new dread, as if the cruel thing which had been done had not happened as he thought—as if something had changed. He was remembering the dream—the real—real dream.

"In the garden!" he said, wondering at himself. "In the garden! But the door is locked and the key is buried deep. *She* is buried deep."

When he glanced at the letters a few minutes later he saw that the one lying at the top of the rest was an English letter and came from Yorkshire. It was directed in a plain woman's hand but it was not a hand he knew. He opened it, scarcely thinking of the writer, but the first words attracted his attention at once.

"Dear Sir:

I am Susan Sowerby that made bold to pull you out of the over turned carriage once on the moor. I will make bold again. Please, sir, I would come home if I was you. I think you would be glad to come with all the changes happening out on the moor and your family and—if you will excuse me, sir—I think your lady would ask you to come if she was here.

Your obedient servant,

Susan Sowerby."

Mr. Craven read the letter twice before he put it back in its envelope. He kept thinking about the dream.

"I will go back to Misselthwaite," he said. "Yes, I'll go at once."

And he went through the garden to the villa and ordered Pitcher to prepare for his return to England.

In a few days he was in Yorkshire again, and on his long railroad journey he found himself thinking of his boy as he had never thought in all the ten years past. During those years he had only wished to forget him. Now, though he did not intend to think about him, memories of him constantly drifted into his mind. He remembered the black days when he had raved like a madman because the child was alive and the mother was dead. He had refused to see it after that first day, and when he had gone to see it again at last it had been such a weak wretched thing that everyone had been sure it would die or become an Accursed any day. But to the surprise of those who took care of it the days passed and it lived and then everyone believed it would be a demonic cannibalistic creature. Dr. Craven was the first to suggest Colin's blood may be special in that it showed infection under the microscope yet the boy maintained his cognizance. Thus began the experiments on the blood. First in the lab then on the Accursed themselves. Mr. Craven brought back infected blood samples from across Europe, Africa, and Asia to be tested using Colin's blood, but no effect could be found other than the two infectious entities ignoring each other and when Colin's blood was mixed with healthy blood it became infected.

He had not meant to be a bad father, but he had not felt like a father at all. He had supplied doctors and nurses and luxuries to keep Colin alive, knowing the importance of his blood but he had shrunk from the mere thought of the half-Accursed boy and had buried himself in his own misery. The first time after a year's absence he returned to Misselthwaite and the small miserable looking thing languidly and indifferently lifted to his face the great gray eyes with black lashes round them, so like and yet so horribly unlike the happy eyes he had adored, he could not bear the sight of them and turned away pale as death. After that he scarcely ever saw him except when he was asleep, and all he knew of him was that he was a confirmed invalid, who had to be chained at all times with a vicious, hysterical, half-insane temper and intense desire to bite the nurses. He could only be kept from furies dangerous to himself and others by being given his own way in every detail.

All this was not an uplifting thing to recall, but as the train whirled him past deserted towns and Accursed infested plains the man who was "coming alive" began to think in a new way and he thought long and steadily and deeply.

"Perhaps I have been mistaken for ten years," he said to himself. "I have been away too long and have been searching for the cure in the wrong way. Perhaps if I had concentrated more on the boy than the blood. Ten years is a long time. It may be too late to do anything—quite too late. What have I been thinking of!"

He wondered if Susan Sowerby had taken courage and written to him only because the motherly creature had realized that the boy was much worse—was fatally ill. If he had not been under the spell of the curious calmness which had taken possession of him he would have been more wretched than ever. But the calm had brought a sort of courage and hope with it. Instead of giving way to thoughts of the worst he actually found he was trying to believe in better things.

"Could it be possible that she sees that I may be able to do him good and control him? Could the cure to the infection be discovered in another way?" he thought. "I will go and see her on my way to Misselthwaite."

But when on his way across the moor he discovered the devastation of his country, all the towns along the road had been lost and destroyed. Darkness fell on the Moor, the gray sky turned purple than black with only the pale moonlight revealing the road in the vast dark sea and Mr. Craven had no place to stop for the night. He instructed the carriage driver to move slowly and dowse all lights. Yet everything was eerily quiet, with no Accursed to be found. He stopped the carriage at the Sowerbys, expecting to see seven or eight children playing about only to find a ruined and empty cottage filled the bodies of slain Accursed. He followed the path of the hewn down bodies and realized they led towards Misselthwaite.

The drive across the blood strewn moor was a taxing thing as he tracked dozens of shuffling footfalls along the road. Yet it did seem to give him a sense of homecoming- which he had been sure he could never feel again. And that sense of belonging to a place that needed his protection increased at drawing nearer to the great old house which had held those of his blood for six hundred years. How he had driven away from it the last time, shuddering to think of its closed rooms and the half-dead boy lying in the four-posted bed with the brocaded hangings and iron chains. How real that dream had been of that terrible vision of his wife not laying dead as she should—how close and clear the voice which called to him, "In the garden—In the garden!"

"I will try to find the key," he said. "I will try to open the door. I must—though I don't know why- I must see the grave."

When he arrived at the Manor late into the night no servants received him. Pitcher pulled out a shotgun and unlocked the large wooden front door. Upon entering the great hall Mr. Craven lifted his lantern and his eyes fell upon a pile of bodies, some half-devoured servants and others decapitated Accursed. The mess of bodies continued up the staircase.

"Medlock!" He called out. There was no answer as his voice echoed through the empty manor. He walked through the servants hall, a way he had not walked in many years, and searched for any survivors among the path of dead servants and Accursed. Reaching the kitchens he was intrigued by the state of the blown out door and piled furniture.

"What have we missed, Pitcher? We come only a day late it seems."

A sudden knock came from the pantry door and Pitcher lowered his shotgun. Mr. Craven nodded to Pitcher to be ready and he unlocked the door. The nurse and Dr. Craven burst out somewhat excited and curious and flustered.

"Tell me all that as happened, brother." Mr. Craven demanded. "How has it come to be that Misselthwaite has fallen?"

The doctor explained how a sudden hoard of Accursed broke through the iron gate into the gardens and made their way to the back of the manor before anyone took note of them.

"The Sowerby children tried to warn us, sir. For they had all arrived telling tales of their lost cottage and how their mother saved them all."

Mr. Craven's thoughts turned to his son and he realized that it was Colin's nurse and doctor hiding out, lone survivors among his servants.

"What of Master Colin, Nurse?" he inquired. "Did you both leave him chained and defenseless as the Accursed attacked?

"No, sir," the nurse answered frightfully, "he's—he's not chained anymore. He's different, in a manner of speaking."

The doctor said, "He is completely altered!"

Mr. Craven's heart fell believing they meant that Colin had finally fully turned into a mindless Tormented One.

"How did this occur?" Mr. Craven asked softly.

The nurse really was flushed.

"Well, you see, sir," she tried to explain, "neither Dr. Craven, nor Mrs. Medlock, nor me could exactly make him out. To tell the truth, sir, Master Colin's appetite, sir, was past understanding—and his ways—"

"Had he become more—more like the infected?" her master asked, knitting his brows anxiously.

"That's it, sir. He grew very peculiar—when you compare him with what he used to be. He used to eat nothing and then suddenly he began to eat something enormous—and then he stopped again all at once and the meals were sent back just as they used to be. You never knew, sir, perhaps, that out of doors he never would let himself be taken. The things we've gone through to get him to go out in his chair would leave a body trembling like a leaf. He'd throw himself into such a state that Dr. Craven said he couldn't be responsible for forcing him. Well, sir, just without warning—not long after one of his worst tantrums he suddenly insisted on being taken out every day by Miss Mary and Susan Sowerby's boy Dickon that could push his chair. He took a fancy to both Miss Mary and Dickon, and Dickon brought his tame animals, and, if you'll credit it, sir, out of doors he will stay from morning until night."

"How did he look? Darkened eyes, sallow skin?" was the next question.

"If he had took his food natural, sir, you'd think he was putting on flesh—but we were afraid it may be a sort of bloat. We think he may have killed a housemaid, Sir. and had been feeding on her outside. And Mistress Mary, Sir. We think he may have infected her too, for she is like him; never eating but getting fatter. All the time outside with no one watching them. Dr. Craven never was as puzzled in his life."

Dr. Craven said nothing, he only turned pale in color.

Mr. Craven had grown very angry at this news. He had never experimented with Colin's blood in having him infect an uninfected person before. He did not know the effect it would have. To imagine his boy and Mistress Mary as small, mindless undead was more than he could bear.

"Where is Master Colin now?" He demanded.

"In the garden, sir. They all ran out into the garden."

Mr. Craven scarcely heard her last words.

"In the garden," he said and repeated it again and again. "In the garden!"

He had to make an effort to bring himself back to the place he was standing in and when he felt he was on earth again he turned and left the kitchen and walked out the smashed back door. He would find them. He would clear his land of the Forsaken and end the misery of the last ten years. If Colin had finally turned it was his duty to end the experiments and end the suffering he had caused. Pitcher followed close behind and held out a lantern as they moved quietly through the gardens. He took his way, as Mary had done, through the shrubbery and among the laurels and the fountain beds. The fountain was playing now but the water was black with the blood of the Accursed that laid there slain. He crossed the lawn and approached the kitchen gardens yet did not walk quickly, but slowly, and his eyes were on the path. He felt as if he were being drawn back to the place he had so long forsaken, and he did not know why. As he drew near to it his step became still more slow. He could hear the moaning and shuffling of a large number of Accursed ahead. Then he heard the voices of children screaming. Mr. Craven pulled two pistols from his holster and then turned into the Long Walk by the ivied walls followed by Pitcher. He stopped and stood still, looking about him, and almost the moment after he had paused he started asking himself if he were walking in a nightmare.

The Accursed filled the path, all shoving and clawing towards the ivy wall. Mr. Craven was bewildered. The ivy had hung thick over the door, the key was buried under the shrubs, no human being had passed that portal for ten lonely years—and yet inside the garden there were sounds and the Accursed were fighting their way in. They were the sounds of running scuffling feet, slashing and pounding, exclamations and smothered cries.

One of the Forsaken happened to turn and see Mr. Craven and Pitcher. It hissed in excitement and thrust forward into the lantern light, clawing for them. Unloading his pistols, Mr. Craven send bullets coursing through the skulls of every Accursed within reach of the light. As he reloaded, Pitcher fired his shotgun into the fray. Fighting his way towards the door, Mr. Craven heard the voice of Mrs. Medlock.

"Mary! Draw back! Draw back!"

Was he losing his reason hearing voices he should not hear from inside the garden? Together, Pitcher and Mr. Craven shot their way up to the open garden door leaving scores of Accursed in their wake and pushing inside to discover a surprising and impossible scene.

Mistress Mary, once contrary, sallow, weak and numb, now kicked an Accursed backwards plunging her blade into its temple while simultaneously pulling back a blade she had thrown into the mouth of another, tearing its flesh up through its ears. Both creatures fell together and Mary spun around tossing both her blades into the scalp of a lunging cannibal. She ran behind it, pulling the blades through its head. Mrs. Medlock enthusiastically battled the dead slaying one after the other, driving her obsidian handled knives into their heads as they charged her.

Mary nearly fell over in shock when she saw the pale faced, black suited man with the crooked back, the uncle she so feared and had only met once. She didn't say anything. She didn't have time to as a hand grabbed her from behind pulling her backwards.

She threw herself down, spinning to get out of the painful grip and then jumped up onto a garden bench. She sank her curved blade into its brain just as she heard Dickon yell from the top of the wall.

Mary, Mrs. Medlock, Mr. Craven and Pitcher all ran to the other side of the garden to join the Sowerby children who were fighting off the Accursed inside the walls and those coming up the walls. Dickon still had not been able to kick the ladder down and he had retreated back on the wall as the ascending Accursed overwhelmed him. They climbed up and then threw themselves over the wall into the garden landing with sickening crunches only to rise and, stumbling, attack the children. Pitcher and Mr. Craven opened fire at the tumbling Accursed and Pitcher moved too close to the wall. One of the falling dead landed directly on top of him and wasted no time in tearing out his throat. Mr. Craven shot it down too late and frowning he sent a bullet through his loyal servant's head.

Dickon looked down at Mary and their eyes locked for a moment. He nodded at her and then smiled his crooked smile. Mary watched in horror as he ran forward along the wall kicking down the Accursed and then jumping down onto the ladder below. She screamed along with the Sowerby children as Dickon disappeared from view. They heard a crash as the ladder fell and no more Accursed came over the wall again. The Sowerby's rushed out of the garden to go find Dickon and Mrs. Medlock followed them.

And then the moment came, the uncontrollable moment when all sounds of fighting and gunshots ceased and when all enemies seemed to be vanquished on the still of the battlefield, one warrior was missing.

Mary looked around realizing Colin was not there. She heard a cry of sadness and she ran, followed by Mr. Craven to the large oak tree. There stood Colin, silhouetted by the moonlight filtering through the leaves, holding his axe out facing one of the Forsaken. She wore what was once a white dress, her stringy hair hanging past her shoulders and her neck wrapped with deteriorating gauze. Mrs. Craven. It only took a moment to realize she had been buried underneath the oak tree and had finally clawed her way up through the wooden casket. She was preserved enough to see the resemblance in her face to Colin, who hesitated, a tear streaming down his face. She had been standing listlessly before Colin, but at the sight of Mary her eyes widened and she opened her black mouth and hissed. Boney thin arms reached out and Colin hesitated no longer. Raising the axe above his head, he spun around for momentum and cleanly sliced her head in two. He caught his mother's body as it fell and he lifted her up, carried her to the grave she had crawled out of and lowered her back in gently.

At that moment, the sun lifted from behind the wall, bathing the garden in a soft orange light. Colin picked up his axe and walked down from the tree, only now seeing his father, whom he hardly knew, but knew at once.

Mr. Craven stared unable to comprehend that his son was standing before him, a strong, tall boy, fearless and powerful.

Colin was glowing with life and the fighting had sent splendid color leaping to his face. He threw the thick hair black from his forehead and lifted a pair of strange gray eyes rimmed with black lashes like a fringe—eyes full of dark memories and great hope. It was the eyes which made Mr. Craven gasp for breath. "Who— What? Who!" he stammered.

This was not what Colin had expected—this was not what he had planned. He had never thought of such a meeting. And yet to have his father here to see how he could fight, to see him do what he could not do ten years ago, to end his mother's suffering— perhaps it was even better. He drew himself up to his very tallest. Mary believed that he managed to make himself look taller than he had ever looked before—inches taller.

"Father," he said, "I'm Colin. You can't believe it. I scarcely can myself. I'm Colin."

Like the nurse and the doctor, he did not understand what his father meant when he said hurriedly:

"In the garden! In the garden!"

"Yes," hurried on Colin. "It was the garden that did it—and Mary and Dickon and the creatures—and the Magic. I'm well, I can slay Accursed and they cannot harm me. I'm going to be a Purifier. I am the cure!"

He said it all so like a healthy boy—his face flushed, his words tumbling over each other in his eagerness—that Mr. Craven's soul shook with unbelieving joy.

Colin put out his hand and laid it on his father's arm.

"Aren't you glad, Father?" he ended. "Aren't you glad? I'm going to end the Scourge! I am going to be the cure!"

Mr. Craven put his hands on both the boy's shoulders and held him still. He knew he dared not even try to speak for a moment.

"Let us begin with clearing out the Scourge from the garden, my boy," he said at last. "And you can tell me all about it."

Together, Mary, Colin and Mr. Craven went running through the gardens in search of the others and dispatching all the Accursed they found. Colin raced ahead to show his father how the infected ignored him and he was especially exuberant in his kills to show how strong he had become. Soon they ran into Dickon, Martha, Mrs. Medlock, and the other ten Sowerby children.

Dickon said cheerfully, "The Gardens 'r clear! I chained up the iron gate. It still needs mendin' but it'll keep 'um out fer now."

They all returned to the Secret Garden and began clearing the bodies. They marveled at the late roses that climbed and hung and clustered and at how the sunshine deepened the hue of the yellowing trees making one feel that one stood in an embowered temple of gold. Mr. Craven stood silent just as the children had done when they came into its grayness. He looked round and round.

"I thought it would be dead," he said.

"Mary thought so at first," said Colin. "But it came alive."

Then they sat down under their tree—all but Colin, who wanted to stand while he told the story.

It was the strangest thing he had ever heard, Archibald Craven thought, as it was poured forth in headlong boy fashion. Mystery and Magic and wild creatures, the weird midnight meeting, Mary gaining her color while learning to fight—the coming of the spring—the finding of the Accursed caged inside the manor, Colin discovering his powers by fearlessly facing a murderous Mrs. Sowerby. The odd companionship, the play acting, the great secret so carefully kept. The listener laughed until tears came into his eyes and sometimes discovering tears came into his eyes when he was not laughing. The Lecturer, the Scientific Discoverer, the Purifier was a lovable, healthy, powerful young human thing.

Mary stood out of the way.

"Mary, my child, are you feeling well?" Mr. Craven asked.

Mary nodded but found she did not have the energy to speak. Colin moved quickly to her side just as she fell faintly into his arms.

"What is wrong? What is happening?" Mr. Craven cried.

"She is infected." Dickon revealed. "And she doesn't have long."

The others gasped only now noticing the blood soaked wrapping around her ankle.

Colin fell to his knees holding Mary. "I will not let you turn! You will not! Understand me?" he shouted in his most powerful Rajah voice. "What good is being the cure if I can't save you?" Then he softened and closed his eyes. Bringing Mary closer to him he chanted, "The Magic is in me, the cure is me. The cure is *in* me, the cure is *me!*"

Colin kissed Mary on her forehead then leaned down and kissed her lips gently. The warmth of her skin suddenly filled him with the same intense desire he had felt before. He could her her heart beating and smell the blood beneath her skin. He breathed in slowly. He paused, an idea suddenly filling him with hope. To the shock of everyone, he suddenly bit her on the lip hard causing her to bleed. Dickon grabbed him by the hair and pulled him away from her. Colin fought back, shoving Dickon away as Mary lay motionless on the ground.

"'ave you gone mad? What're you doin'?" Dickon cried.

"A scientific experiment." Colin replied.

He kneeled down again facing Mary. Everyone waited anxiously, knowing she might awaken at any moment, blackness oozing from her soulless eyes. Her body twitched and Dickon pulled out his knife.

Colin threw his arms wide. "No! Don't touch her!"

"I promised her, Colin. I can' let her wake up Accursed." Dickon had tears in his eyes as he clenched his blade.

"Just wait. I have to see. She won't turn, she can't! Mary," Colin whispered. "Come back to me. Come back."

Mary awakened. She moaned and brought her hands to her face. Slowly, she sat up and opened her eyes. They were gray, as always, and full of life!

Mrs. Medlock threw up her hands and gave a little shriek while all twelve Sowerby children gasped with their eyes almost starting out of their heads.

Dickon knelt down and embraced Mary. Even the Robin twittered down bobbing and ruffling in excitement. Lord Craven, the Master of Misselthwaite, shook his head in wonder.

"Ten years and I never thought to inject Colin's blood into an infected person who had not yet turned! I had been going about it all wrong. When the dormant strain interacts with the active strain before it turns the blood, the active infection becomes dormant as well! Mary is now like Colin, a carrier of the dormant infection."

Colin stood in awe at what he had discovered. He had cured her by infecting her. Many questions filled his mind: would Mary now be immune to the Accursed as well, could his father use his blood to cure people or would he have to bite everyone who becomes infected? Was it possible that this moment was the beginning of the end of the deadly Scourge?

Mary stood and embraced Colin. "You saved me!"

Colin held Mary tightly. "No, Mary, you saved me. You and the Garden."

Mr. Craven took the children by their hands and together with Mrs. Medlock and the Sowerbys they made their way across the lawn back towards Misselthwaite. As they approached, Dr. Craven and the nurse came down the steps to greet them.

Martha spoke, "Does the nurse seem rather wobbly t' anyone else?"

Dickon narrowed his eyes, "The Doctor also does not appear steady," Soot flew off his shoulder blaring out a warning cry as the doctor let out a hiss and began running in their direction. All at once, a dozen Accursed poured out of Misselthwaite.

The Sowerbys pulled out their weapons while Mary had already begun spinning her blades. Archibald Craven cocked both his pistols and looked as they had never seen him, full of hope. And by his side with his head up in the air, his grip on his axe and his eyes full of vengeful anticipation walked as strongly and steadily as any boy in Yorkshire—the Purifier Master Colin.